Why, she wondered, was he here alone?

And especially at this time of year, when families gathered together, drawn by love, memories and layers of tradition.

Stephanie herself couldn't wait to get home.

But this man didn't believe in Christmas. She frowned as she remembered Damian's words. "Go away," he'd growled. "I don't do Christmas."

She hugged her arms around herself and leaned toward the sofa. Why? she wanted to ask the sleeping man lying there.

Why don't you do Christmas?

Grace Green was born in Scotland and is a former teacher. In 1967 she and her marine engineer husband John emigrated to Canada, where they raised their four children. Empty-nesters now, they are happily settled in west Vancouver in a house overlooking the ocean. Grace enjoys walking the sea wall, gardening, getting together with other writers...and watching her characters come to life, because she knows that, once they do, they will take over and write her stories for her.

Grace has written for the Harlequin Presents® series, but now concentrates on Harlequin Romance®—bringing you deeply emotional stories with vibrant characters.

Books by Grace Green

A Miracle
for Christmas
Grace Green

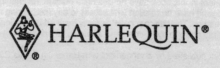

HARLEQUIN®

TORONTO • NEW YORK • LONDON
AMSTERDAM • PARIS • SYDNEY • HAMBURG
STOCKHOLM • ATHENS • TOKYO • MILAN • MADRID
PRAGUE • WARSAW • BUDAPEST • AUCKLAND

For my granddaughter, Robyn

ISBN 0-373-17404-7

A MIRACLE FOR CHRISTMAS

First North American Publication 1998.

Copyright © 1997 by Grace Green.

This edition published by arrangement with Harlequin Books S.A.

® and TM are trademarks of the publisher. Trademarks indicated with
® are registered in the United States Patent and Trademark Office, the
Canadian Trade Marks Office and in other countries.

Printed in U.S.A.

CHAPTER ONE

DAMIAN MCALLISTER hissed out an oath as he glared at the toy store situated directly across the street from his office. That damned sign in the window! Its neon message had been winking at him since November and was driving him crazy:

Merry Xmas To U And Yours

I can't stand it. He fisted a hand hard against the top of his mahogany desk. *I can't stand it one more minute.*

He lurched to his feet.

'Mrs. Sutton!' he bellowed.

Marjorie Sutton, the McAllister Architectural Group's senior secretary, put down the chocolate doughnut she'd been on the point of dunking into her morning coffee. Casting it a regretful sigh, she heaved her snugly corseted body out of her chair and walked through to the adjoining office.

Her boss's blue eyes, she noted, had a wild expression, and his black hair looked as if he'd been trying to tear it out, strand by glossy strand. Yet she wished—as she did on a disturbingly regular basis considering she was quite happily married—that either she were thirty years younger or that the president of the M.A.G. wasn't such a dreamboat.

'Yes, sir?' Her tone was light.

His answering scowl was dark. 'Cancel all my appointments till the New Year. I've decided to take off for my place in Vermont earlier than planned.' As he spoke, he kept his back rigidly to the window, though he could have sworn he saw the reflection of the toy store's Christmas lights and gratingly upbeat message flickering on the wall facing him.

'Are you feeling all right, Mr. McAllister? You look white. As if you'd...seen a ghost.'

The ghost of Christmases past. 'I seem to be coming down with something...probably that flu that's going the rounds.' Dismissively he slackened the knot of his silk tie, and flicked open the top button of his gray shirt. 'Now—'

'What about the big party Friday night?'

'Party?'

'The Anthony Gould cocktail party. Your invitation came in the mail last month. You accepted, remember?'

Last month. When he'd convinced himself that this year would be different. This year he wouldn't be a coward. This year he wouldn't run from Christmas. 'I remember. Gould's going to be showing off his new fiancée.' He cleared his throat...and winced. His tonsils felt as if he'd raked a cheese grater over them. He opened his desk drawer, rummaged till he found a cough drop and thrust it into his mouth. 'Cancel,' he mumbled around the cherry-flavored lozenge. 'The last thing I feel like doing at this moment is watching Boston's finest parade his latest trophy—'

'Mr. McAllister!'

He heard the chiding in her tone, but there was no evidence of remorse in his eyes...eyes that had begun to water as he felt a sneeze gather. 'Phone.' He accepted the man-size tissue his secretary obligingly whipped from the box sitting by his fax machine. 'Get me off the hook?'

'Right. So—' she paused while his sneeze reverberated through the office and fluttered a blueprint that lay on his drawing board '—will that be all, sir?'

Grabbing his suit jacket from the back of his chair, he shrugged it on, and crossed to hold the door open. 'I'll leave everything in your capable hands.'

Mrs. Sutton walked past him but instead of taking her seat at her desk, stood by it…as if waiting for something.

He gritted his teeth. Season's greetings, perhaps?

He opened his mouth, tried to say the words—Merry Christmas—but they stuck. He muttered something unintelligible. She could decipher his mumblings however she wished, he decided with a feeling of desperation.

And fled.

When he drove out of the underground parking lot a few minutes later, he kept his eyes averted from the Warmest Fuzzies Toy Store…and what a pie-in-the-sky name *that* was! But even with his attention focused glazedly on the traffic ahead, he couldn't block out the neon pattern of reds and greens winking from the store window…or the sound of the music blasting from a purple Corvette in the next lane…

Garth Brooks, informing him—and possibly everyone else in Boston—that 'Love Came Down at Christmas.'

Stephanie Redford bit her lip uneasily as she searched the black-tie, black-dress crowd. Where was Tony? She had to talk with him right away. What the Whitneys had said—it was surely all a silly mistake—

Her taffeta blouse rustled as somebody trailed a light fingertip down her spine. She spun around, spilling a few drops of champagne from her glass...and there was Tony, his wavy blond hair gleaming under the crystal chandelier.

His pale eyes were warm with approval.

'Darling.' He ran a possessive hand up her arm in an intimate caress. 'You're a huge success. I'm so proud of you. Now you must come and be introduced to the Cabots. They're eager to meet the future Mrs. Anthony Gould—'

'Tony, the Whitneys just told me that you—'

'Lower your voice, darling.' A shadow of displeasure flickered over her fiancé's patrician features. 'Paula Whitney's looking this way.' Grasping her arm, with smoothly murmured apologies he wove a path through the crowd and out into the deserted hallway. This was the first party he'd put on at his penthouse condo since he'd had it redecorated, and Stephanie knew he wanted nothing to mar the occasion.

'Now, darling—' his lips were curved in a smile that didn't quite reach his eyes '—what exactly is the problem?'

Stephanie placed her champagne glass on the Louis XVI table by her side and took in a deep breath.

'The Whitneys,' she said, 'have just told me they're delighted we've accepted their invitation to spend Christmas week with them at Aspen.'

'You've never been to the Whitneys' ski lodge, darling. It's old-world bijou—you'll love it—'

'Tony, we agreed weeks ago that we'd drive to Rockfield and spend the holidays with my folks. The

Redford clan always get together for Christmas—it's a family tradition.'

Tony took her left hand and held it, palm down, by her fingertips. He let his gaze linger for a long thoughtful moment on her lustrous sapphire ring before he responded.

'Stephanie, I'm going to be marrying you soon. You'll be a Gould, and we'll be making our own traditions. You'll be moving in a different circle. My circle. My friends all like you, darling—the Laskers, the Gibsons, the Loebs...'

Stephanie drew her fingers free. Although Tony's condo was electronically kept at a very comfortable temperature, the air seemed suddenly chilly. 'You promised, Tony. My parents are looking forward to meeting you—'

'Darling.' Tony's eyes had a coaxing glint. 'I believed the Whitneys were planning to go abroad this year, and they were...but their arrangements fell through, so they've organized this ski party and it's going to be a blast—'

'I don't want to go to Aspen.' Stephanie met his gaze steadily. 'I want to go home.'

The tension that had been sputtering between them exploded with an intensity that rocked her. Tony obviously felt it, too. His eyes became wary, a nerve ticked in his neck, directly above his bow tie...

And then, with an unexpectedness that totally threw her, he grinned. Cocking a teasing brow, he drew her into his arms. 'Darling,' he said ruefully, 'are we having our first fight?' Without giving her a chance to reply, he pulled her hard against him and kissed her.

After a brief moment of resistance, Stephanie exhaled a sigh and yielded. She did love him so, and the comfort and pressure of his body, along with the expert thoroughness of his kiss, swiftly dissipated her tension. Tony loved her, just as she loved him, and he'd sworn, when he proposed to her, that he'd devote his life to making her happy. He wouldn't let her down. Not on this. It was too important.

She pulled back, and looked up at him with a tender smile. 'We'll go, then,' she said softly, 'to Rockfield?'

He released her abruptly. 'Stephanie.' Irritation emanated from his every pore. 'Have you not been listening to what I've been saying? We're going to Aspen. You know how important the Whitneys are to me. They were my first clients when I set up my law practice, and they are still my biggest clients—'

'You're missing the point.' Stephanie threaded a shaky hand through the heavy mass of chocolate brown hair that tumbled around her shoulders. 'A promise is a promise. You just have to tell the Whitneys we'd already made plans. They seem like nice people…they'll understand.'

'I'm going to Aspen, Stephanie, let me make that quite clear. You have a choice. You can spend Christmas in Vermont with your family, or you can spend it in Colorado with me.'

Stephanie stared at him disbelievingly. 'A choice… or an ultimatum?'

Her fiancé lifted his shoulders in a deliberate shrug. 'If that's how you want to look at it.'

What other way could she look at it? Tony believed he was giving her a choice, but he was wrong. She had promised her parents she'd be home for the holidays.

Her fingers trembled as she slipped off her engagement ring. She held it out, in the palm of her hand,

and the sapphire had never looked more beautiful. Tony stared at it, didn't take it. He was obviously taken aback. It was probably the first time in his life, Stephanie reflected as she struggled to control her welling unhappiness, that anyone had ever said no to Anthony Howard Gould III.

Gold tinkled against wood as she dropped the ring on the side table. 'I'll go and gather up my things, then.'

'You're making a mistake, Stephanie. Don't do this to me.' For the first time, there was urgency in Tony's voice. 'What am I to tell the Whitneys? What am I to—'

Stephanie brushed past him, and made for his bedroom. She was thankful she was managing to control her tears; they would wait, she prayed, till she could get to her van.

Her blue canvas bag was lying half open on the burgundy duvet draped over Tony's bed. In it she could see a fold of her black lace negligee…the filmy, outrageously expensive negligee she'd been planning to wear later tonight, when she and Tony, for the very first time—

Fiercely she rasped the bag's zipper closed.

She shrugged on her calf-length red coat, tucked her evening purse into one of the pockets, slung the canvas bag's strap over her shoulder and hurried out to the hallway again. Once there she paused, and then, hesitantly, looked back. Her heart gave a painful lurch when she saw that Tony was standing where she had left him. His face was as devoid of color as the snow blanketing the world outside. For a moment, she wavered—but just for a moment. She tightened her lips and pulled her coat around her, as if it were a shield.

If Tony didn't believe in keeping promises, they had no future together.

Tonight, he had revealed a side of himself she hadn't known existed. A side she didn't like. It must always have been there, though…only she had been too blinded by love to see it; blinded by love and—yes, she admitted with raw honesty—bedazzled by the wonder and sheer exhilaration of being courted by one of Boston's most eligible bachelors. She should have known better, she thought with an unfamiliar feeling of bitterness, than to get mixed up with someone from the so-called 'upper crust.' She shook her head grimly. That was one mistake she would never make again.

Her high-heeled shoes made no sound on the plush carpet as she crossed the hall toward the private elevator; the only sound she could hear was the leaden *thud-thud-thud* of her heartbeat against her breastbone.

She stepped into the elevator, and didn't look around till the door began to close. Then it took only a glance to tell her that Tony was no longer standing in the hallway. It was once again deserted.

He hadn't even waited till she was gone, she realized sorrowfully, before going back to join the party.

'Tony Gould is a jerk.' Janey Martin flopped down on Stephanie's bed and watched as her flatmate rammed gaily wrapped stuffed animals into an enormous orange plastic bag. 'Aspen indeed! I just hope he breaks a leg skiing.'

Stephanie chose not to respond to her friend's uncharitable remarks. Instead she muttered a triumphant

'Gotcha!' as she finally succeeded in tucking in the neck of a two-foot-high giraffe.

'He's not only a jerk—' Janey's speckled gray eyes had a derisive expression '—he must be out of his mind! Where does he think he's going to find someone like you again? Not in this life. And I'm not just talking about your looks, though Lord knows you're gorgeous enough to be a movie star! You're also one of the nicest people around.'

Stephanie secured the bulging bag with a twist tie, dragged it across the carpet and added it to the three others slumped by the door. Only then did she turn to Janey and say firmly, 'I don't want to talk about him anymore.'

'Okay…but he was going to drive you to Rockfield in his Jag, and now you're stuck with taking your old van, and you know it's not all that reliable. It's been stalling and—'

'I'll have my dad look at it when I get home.'

'You should have someone look at it here, before you leave.'

'Can't afford garage bills right now—'

'You almost wiped out your bank account with that Louis Féraud cocktail blouse.' Janey sighed. 'You were out of your league, sweetie pie—'

'Janey…' Stephanie's tone had an edge of warning.

Janey scowled. 'It's just that I'm worried you might get stuck on a back road somewhere, and that's no fun in these winter conditions. Why don't you go home by bus?'

'Can you see me carting all these bags onto a bus?'

'Leave the toys. The kids won't mind.'

'My nieces and nephews won't mind if they don't get a sample of my Warmest Fuzzies for Christmas?

Janey, my stuffed animals are a highlight of their holidays!' Stephanie dusted her palms on the seat of her cream slacks. 'Now if you'll quit scolding and help me carry everything out to the van, I'd like to get on my way.' She crossed to the dresser mirror, and sneaking the opportunity to blink away threatening tears, adjusted her white-trimmed red toque to a saucy angle that was at direct odds with her aching misery.

When she turned, it was with a bright smile.

'Right,' she said, 'I'm ready.' She scooped up her red coat from the end of the bed, and slipped it on.

Janey's russet hair, waist-long and uncompromisingly straight, swung out like it were a sheet of flame as she got to her feet. 'Have you called your parents? Do they know you're coming home a day earlier than planned?'

'No—oh, darn, how did you get down there!' Stephanie bent to pick up a teddy bear from under the wicker rocking chair. He was her favourite creation this current season; soft and cuddly, in plush nutmeg brown, he had glass-bead eyes and an endearingly lifelike expression. She undid the thong fastening her duffel bag, and pushed the toy down atop her clothes. There wasn't quite room, and as she started tightening the thong again, the bear's head bounced out and he looked up indignantly, as if to say, *Hey, I need air!* Her lips curved in an amused smile as she gathered the thong firmly around his neck—

'Steph…your parents?'

'I haven't told them. If they knew I was traveling on my own, they'd worry. We can talk once I get there.'

'And the Warmest Fuzzies Toy Store?'

'Joyce's going to look after the store, and her

daughter Gina's going to help out. Apparently Gina's expecting a baby in June, and she and her boyfriend are saving to get married, so the extra cash will come in handy.'

'You seem to have everything under control.' Janey took charge of two of the orange bags and led the way out to the corridor. 'How long will you be on the road?' she asked over her shoulder as Stephanie had a last look around.

'Four or five hours.' Trailing the remaining bags behind her, Stephanie followed her friend along the lobby of the triple decker building. 'Since it's the day before Christmas Eve, the traffic will in all likelihood be busy, but there's been no new snow for the last few days so the roads should be okay...

'With luck, I should reach Rockfield before dark.'

The day was bright when Stephanie left Boston, but by the time she reached Montpelier, where she stopped at an Esso station to fill her gas tank, the sky had changed ominously from its previous milky blue to a bruised charcoal gray.

'Darkness is settin' in early today.' The straw-haired attendant squinted heavenward as he returned her Visa card. 'And a bad storm forecast for tonight. Goin' far?'

'Rockfield.'

'Rockfield, huh? Watch out for them narrow mountain roads once you leave the highway. They can be right tricky this time of year.'

She gave him a wry smile as she agreed with him. And as he jogged away to attend a waiting truck, Stephanie promised herself she would indeed be very careful as she tackled those 'right tricky' mountain roads.

But when she turned the key in the ignition and a foreboding silence greeted her, she had to ask herself if she would be driving those roads that day at all. And after six increasingly frantic attempts to start the engine, she surrendered to the inevitable. Getting out, she clutched her coat around herself and made for the service bay, her nostrils prickling as they were exposed to the frosty air.

A mechanic came out and inspected the van's innards. 'Yup,' he said, 'we can fix 'er, but we won't get to 'er till tonight. You can pick 'er up after we close at nine.'

Nine! Good Lord, how was she going to fill in the time till then!

The mechanic directed her to a nearby mall, where she browsed aimlessly for a couple of hours, had a burger and then lingered for a long while over several cups of coffee, before taking in a movie. When she came out of the mall at quarter to nine, a gusty wind was whipping along the dark street—an icy cold wind, with the smell of fresh snow in it. Chin tucked into her coat collar, she hurried along to the gas station.

The van was ready and the repair cost a bundle. But as she headed out to Route 89, she decided that by the time her Visa bill came in, she should be able to meet it.

At least she had her van...and it was now reliable.

The blizzard struck after she'd left the highway.

She was on a side road, and emerging from the shelter of a covered bridge, when it hit with sudden savage force. Snow billowed down over the windshield, blinding her for a few unnerving seconds till she got the wipers going.

Oh, Lord, she thought, slowing as she peered into the porridge-thick mass and concentrated on keeping to her own side of the road, what have I let myself in for? If only Tony were here—

Scrub that thought! Anthony Howard Gould III was a fake—all style, and no substance. She needed him like she needed a hole in her head!

She had been driving for the best part of an hour when she realized to her dismay that somewhere along the way—disoriented by the storm—she had taken a wrong turning.

She knew that by this time she should have been climbing up the gentle mountain slope leading to Rockfield, not, as she was doing now, going downhill, leading to…?

With a feeling of growing horror, she noted that the gradient here was fast becoming dangerously steep. She braked, but the van gathered speed, continued to gather speed. Damn! She pressed her foot down on the pedal more firmly, praying the van would slow its pace. It didn't.

She panicked. Rammed her foot to the boards.

The van slewed into a sideways skid.

With her fingers clawed around the steering wheel, she peered desperately into the dark and swirling storm.

And didn't even see the snowbank till she was in it.

CHAPTER TWO

DAMIAN MCALLISTER groaned, and with a feeling of utter despair, buried his stubbled face deep into his pillow.

'Go away.' His muffled entreaty came out hoarsely. 'For God's sake…go away and leave me alone…'

The hammering and the bell-ringing—loud, persistent, demanding—continued unabated…perhaps even with renewed vigor…and the bell shrill enough to waken the dead. Which was exactly what he wished he was…

At first he'd thought the sounds existed only in his head, another torture inflicted on him by the flu that had grabbed him by the throat the day he left Boston and had brought him to his knees, literally, when he reached his destination and staggered from his car to the front door.

And now that door, he surmised with another, deeper groan, was going to crash in at any moment. Whatever his visitor wanted, it was patently obvious he had no intention of leaving till he got it.

Better get up and get it over with.

It took him a few minutes to crawl out of bed, find a pair of jeans, drag them on, zip them up, with curses erupting all the while. Keeping himself vertical by grabbing one piece of furniture after the next, he stumbled to the bedroom door. Descending the stairs might present more of a challenge, he acknowledged grimly. But he made it, though by the time he got to

the last step, he was more than ready to call it a day.
Or a night? He'd left all the lights on when he arrived
on Tuesday, and now he could see blackness pressing
in through the ground-floor windows.

He lurched across the hall and fell against the front
door, hitting it with his shoulder. As he dragged back
the dead bolt, the bell shrilled again, paining his ear-
drums.

'Hang on,' he croaked. 'Don't be so damned impatient.'

He flung open the door.

And two things happened at once.

Firstly, an arctic wind blasted his naked chest with
a brutality that sucked the air from his lungs.

And secondly, he saw that his visitor was not a
man.

He stared disbelievingly at the woman gazing back
at him with eyes that were as wide and startled as his
own. Her clothes were partially snow-encrusted, but
in the light from the overhead lamp, even with the
snowflakes whirling around her, he could see her coat
was bright red; her boots were black; her rakishly
tilted toque was red with white trim...

And the small sack slung over her shoulder was
leather. Creamy white leather. Butter soft. Crammed
full. And in it...dear God, over her shoulder, from the
top of the sack, peered a...teddy bear?

The stranger said, in a husky voice, breathless and
more than a bit shaky, 'Oh, thank heavens!' She
swung the sack down and rested it on the stoop. 'I
was beginning to think there was no one home!'

Santa Claus...

Female version.

Ho, ho, ho!

But shouldn't she have come down the chimney?

Damian shuddered. His legs wobbled and he grabbed the edge of the door to keep himself upright. He felt every inch of his bare flesh shrink from the icy air.

'Go away,' he croaked. 'You've come to the wrong place. *I don't do Christmas.*'

The creature swayed toward him as he started to close the door. Her eyes were pleading. And as she cried 'Wait!' he noticed something else. Those eyes—as green as pine and exquisitely fringed with silky brown lashes—were dark with exhaustion…and red-rimmed, as if she'd been crying.

He hesitated. A voice of caution whispered in some sane but distant part of his brain—

'May I please come in and use your phone?' she begged. 'You see I've had an accident. My van's stuck in a snowbank at the end of your drive—'

'Are you hurt?'

'Bumped. Winded. Shocked. But thankfully not hurt. I just need to call for a tow truck for my van. Then I'll be out of your way…honestly…as soon as I possibly can.'

Van? Shouldn't it have been…reindeer? Damian tried to hold onto the voice of caution but in the face of the stranger's desperate pleading, it faded away.

With a sigh of surrender, he swept a hand sideways.

She kicked the snow off her boots and walked past him, bringing in with her a flurry of snowflakes, and the faint scent of French perfume.

He slammed the door, and with a tilting gait, followed her into the living room.

'Your phone?' she asked.

'Over there.' He cleared his raspy throat, gestured

vaguely toward the massive oak coffee table, shivered and wrapped his muscled arms around his chest. 'Help yourself.'

She put the sack down; it hovered, and fell over. The bear looked up unblinkingly as the stranger whisked off her toque and shook out a tumbled mass of glorious curls that were the same rich silky brown as Belgian chocolates. Her brow was sweet, her nose pert, her chin dimpled. She unbuttoned the coat and glancing at him, she murmured, 'If you don't mind, I'll take this off otherwise I'll feel the cold terribly when I go out again.' She crossed to the fireplace, shook the snow into the empty hearth and draped the garment over a wing chair adjacent to the fire. She was wearing a ribbed red sweater, he noted vaguely, and—tucked into her boots—a pair of neatly fitting cream slacks that revealed a very attractive—

'Where am I?' She looked around at him, and he saw that her lips were curved in a wry smile. 'When I tell the tow truck people to come, I'll have to tell them where.'

The fever was burning him up. The chills were making him shiver. Her words were echoing in his head in a diminishing spiral. Suddenly all he could think of was getting back to bed, burying himself under the covers.

'Tell them it's the McAllister place on the Tarlity side road,' he growled. 'Look, I've got this damned flu and I'm not in any state to entertain. Make yourself at home till the truck comes—phone book's under the table. Call Grantham Towing—Bob's the only game in town, but he's reliable.' Groggily he tipped two fingers to his brow in a salute, and wheeling around in a quick move that made his head swim, he made his way unsteadily to the stairs.

When he was halfway up, he heard the riffle of pages and guessed she was hunting the phone book for the number. By the time he reached the landing, she was talking to someone.

He swung the bedroom door shut behind him, and it closed with a loud click. Reeling across the room, he plunged into bed, fumbled for the duvet and pulled it up over his marble-cold shoulders.

But even as he told himself he'd never sleep nor ever in this life get warmed up again, he went out like a light.

'I'm sorry, miss. We can't possibly make it tonight.'

'Are you absolutely sure? Thing is, Mr. Grantham, I'm stranded at the back of beyond with a complete stranger.' Stephanie lowered her voice and went on, in little more than a whisper, as she glanced furtively at the stairs. 'For all I know, the man might be a serial killer—'

A hearty laugh came across the line, making her jump. 'You said you were calling from the McAllister place?'

'That's right.'

'Hell, I've known McAllister for years. The man's a loner but he's no more a serial killer than I am—'

'But—'

'Take my word for it. Gotta go—the switchboard's lit up like a Christmas tree! I'll send somebody out tomorrow for sure…depending, of course, on the weather.'

And with that, the owner of Grantham Towing hung up.

At her end, Stephanie dropped the telephone onto the cradle. Well, she challenged herself, what am I to do now!

There was only one answer to that. She would have to ask the growly McAllister man if she could spend the night. No, not ask. She would have to *tell* him she was going to have to spend the night.

Tugging off her boots, she made for the stairs with reluctant steps, shivering though the house was quite warm.

Certainly Mr. Grantham of Grantham Towing had vouched for her host, but after all, she had no proof that the man upstairs was McAllister. The tall stranger wearing nothing but a scowl and a pair of tight blue jeans—her shiver intensified—could, of course, be McAllister. Or—and she felt her heartbeat take a flying leap into space—he could be an ax murderer who had already slain McAllister and was at this moment lying in wait upstairs for his next victim.

When she reached the upstairs landing, she saw four doors. Three were open. Feeling like Goldilocks, she tiptoed around the landing and peeked in the open doors. The rooms were unoccupied. She moved to the fourth door.

Turning the handle quietly, she pushed, inch by silent inch. In the dim light filtering in from the landing, she could make out a king-size bed, with a puffy plaid duvet. Under the duvet she saw the sprawled shape of a man, whose black hair formed a dark shadow against a white pillow.

'Mr. McAllister—' she addressed him in a hiss, from just inside the door '—are you awake?'

There was no answer.

Biting her lip, she took six tentative steps forward,

and heard a rhythmic snoring, half-muffled by the pillow. She took another six steps, and was now close enough to touch him. Which she did. A light pressure, with the tips of her fingers, on what looked to be his rump. 'Mr. McAll—'

The figure jerked spasmodically, erupted in a groan and croaked, 'Go away!' and burrowed deeper under the duvet.

'I have to stay the night.' Stephanie said the words clearly, but the hammering of her heart made them vibrate. 'I just thought I ought to let you know. Is it all right?'

She thought he hadn't heard her. She waited for a long moment. Then, as she was about to turn away uncertainly, his right arm came flailing out. The thumb, she saw in the glimpse she got before his arm dropped limply over the edge of the bed, was turned up.

'Thank you,' she whispered, and crept away, closing the door softly behind her.

Going into the nearest bedroom, she dragged the duvet off the bed, and along with a pillow, took it downstairs to the living area.

A quick reconnaissance of the main floor in search of a bathroom revealed a modern kitchen; a dining room adjacent to the living area; an invitingly cosy TV room; and—she was just about to give up hope when she found it—a powder room.

It took her only a few minutes to get washed and ready to turn in. Then, clad in her red T-shirt nightie, with her hair in a ponytail, she turned off all the lights save the one on the table by the sofa she'd chosen for her bed.

Before she cuddled down under the duvet, she

reached out to switch off the lamp—and paused nervously as she noticed how the lone light cast eerie shadows around the room...over the Oriental rugs, over the tall bookcases, over the plump cushions on the low-slung seating...and over a massive oil painting whose spooky atmosphere gave her the creeps. Gothic, she thought with a shiver, very Gothic!

And as she fell into a fitful sleep, her last conscious thought...more of an apprehensive prayer, actually, than a thought...was that if the man upstairs was not McAllister but an ax murderer, his weapon would be sharp and her end mercifully quick.

What a helluva night it had been!

Damian McAllister rolled over onto his back, and stared bleary-eyed at the ceiling. Hallucinations were one thing—he'd had them a few times before when a bad flu had driven his temperature to abnormally high levels—but hallucinations like those he'd experienced over the past few hours were something else. They'd seemed as real to him as the mattress under his back.

Of course he was used to having nightmares around Christmas time—he'd been tormented by them since he was a kid...though they had, of course, become much worse during the past five years, since—

He swiped a shaky hand over his eyes.

Don't think about that.

With an effort, he dragged his thoughts from the past.

Sweeping the duvet aside, he swung himself off the bed, and on legs that threatened with every step to give way under him, made his way across to the en-suite bathroom.

Once there, he planted his palms on the counter and stared starkly at his reflection in the mirror.

'Ye gods!' The man staring back at him looked like a criminal from an America's Most Wanted poster. Black hair sticking up every which way, jaw scruffily bearded, eyes shot with blood—the red striations on the whites forming a lurid contrast to the steel blue irises.

He needed a shower and a shave...desperately needed a shower and a shave...but he was pretty sure he'd keel over if he tried to stand upright in the shower stall. First he had to get something in his stomach. And a cup of coffee would hit the spot.

He closed his eyes. Coffee. He wanted it so damned badly he could swear he smelled the fragrance in the air, aromatic and devilishly tantalizing...

'...and the storm that hit northeastern Vermont late yesterday, shows no signs of letting up...'

Damn! Stephanie frowned as she snapped off the Sony ghetto blaster she'd clicked on when she'd come through to the kitchen ten minutes earlier. Pouring herself a mug of coffee from the six-cup pot, she crossed to the patio doors facing what was possibly the back of the house. She stared out, though she might as well have saved herself the bother, she thought bleakly. There was nothing to be seen but white. And Grantham Towing, she surmised as she took the first sip of her coffee, would be as likely to send someone down the treacherously steep Tarlity side road in this blizzard as they would send one of their trucks to the moon.

So here she was, stuck in a remote lodge with a—

'Well, hello and good morning.'

Stephanie swiveled, convulsively swallowing the coffee she'd been swirling around her tongue, and stared wide-eyed at the man standing in the doorway.

McAllister.

If indeed he was McAllister...

He was tilted forward, and he had a hand pressed flat on either jamb, at shoulder level. He was wearing what seemed to be the same pair of jeans he'd had on the night before; certainly he was wearing the same scowl. And he looked for all the world like one of America's Most Wanted...but at least he wasn't carrying an ax. Not that he would have needed a weapon to overpower her, Stephanie reflected as her gaze skimmed over the sleek muscles cording his arms, his dark-haired chest, his powerful thighs—

She flicked her gaze up and noticed with dismay that his eyes—slightly bloodshot but keen—were fixed with interest on her own thighs, revealed beneath the hem of her short nightie. She'd awakened so early she'd decided she'd be safe enough to have a mug of coffee before showering and getting her clothes on. A mistake.

'I hate to be a nuisance,' she said, 'but you did indicate last night that I could stay over.'

'You're real.' His mouth quirked up at the edges.

'Real?'

'I thought you were Mrs. Claus.'

She raised an incredulous eyebrow.

He dropped his arms and slumped sideways against the doorjamb, the brown of his tanned skin accentuated by the crisp white of the door's painted trim. 'The red coat, the red-and-white hat...the sack of toys...'

'Oh.' Stephanie chuckled. 'My duffel bag. No, it's just got a few clothes and my toilet things...not toys. The teddy bear—well, I stuffed him on top at the last minute.'

Her host scratched a hand over his chest, and yawned, showing a glimpse of perfect white teeth. 'I thought, this morning, that I'd been hallucinating last night, but I wasn't. Your reindeer—' he corrected himself '—your van...it's in a snowbank?'

'I lost control coming down the hill, ending up slewing off to one side and got stuck at the bottom of your driveway. I can't tell you how relieved I was when I saw this place—all the lights on, and every sign of being inhabited. But I admit I began to panic when—'

'When I took so long to answer the bell.' He pushed himself lazily from the doorjamb. 'I seem to recall telling you to make yourself at home.' His gaze drifted to the mug in her hand. 'I see you took me at my word.'

Stephanie indicated a second mug on the table. 'I was going to pour you some shortly and bring it to your room.'

'Had I but known...' Amusement lurked in his voice.

Was the man flirting with her? Good Lord, that was all she needed! In a prim tone, she said, 'Cream and sugar?'

'Just cream. Thanks.'

He was halfway to the nearest chair, when he started to wobble.

Stephanie frowned. 'Are you all right? You look—'

He started to keel over.

In a flash she was at his side, grasping his arm,

trying to steady him. Might as well have been a tug nudging a listing freighter! she thought as she felt his powerful body sag against her slender frame…yet her support seemed to do the trick. He steadied and threw an arm around her shoulders. The arm was lifeless, and so heavy she thought she might crumple under its weight. She didn't.

'Should have stayed in bed,' he muttered.

'Let's get you back upstairs then.' Her breath came out in a series of strained grunts. 'Here, turn around.'

The maneuvre was a complicated one and they somehow got all tangled up, she trying to guide him one way, he starting to turn the other. He lost his balance, and she was unable to keep him from toppling backward, and still under the weight of his arm, she found herself reeling with him. They ended up together, over by the door, their progress halted abruptly when they clattered against the wall. His back was to it, his arm was around her as if a trap.

And her palms were pressed against his chest.

She could feel the erratic hammering of his heart under her fingertips; could feel the texture of his hair-roughened skin, slick with sweat. She thought she felt his eyes on her. It was an uncomfortable sensation.

She jerked her head up. His head was angled back against the wall, but he was slanting his gaze down toward her, through lashes that were almost closed. Gorgeous lashes. Thick, as black as soot, and turning up ever so slightly at the ends—

'My,' he drawled, 'you *are* a pretty one!'

She could barely see his eyes; his eyelids were drooping even as he spoke. He was, she realized, on the verge of flaking out.

'And you,' she retorted as she hauled his arm even more securely around her shoulders, 'are not!'

His chuckle had a cracked sound. 'And that's the truth—'

'Let's get you through to the other room and onto a sofa—'

'Up to bed...'

'No, you'll never make it. For heaven's sake, just do as you're told.'

'Yes, ma'am.'

They staggered together through to the living area, where Stephanie steered him over to the long sofa where she'd spent the night. Seconds before he toppled sideways onto it, she whisked off the duvet she'd left there earlier. His head landed on the pillow; and even before it did, his eyes were closed.

'Cover me,' he said in a fast-fading voice. 'I'm freezing...'

Stephanie was only too glad to throw the duvet over him. She had never seen such a magnificent male body, and it seemed almost voyeurish to stare, though she did...for just a moment...before she covered him. Caveman type, she decided, with his overly long hair, unshaven face, rugged features, powerful physique; a type that had never appealed to her...but he seemed harmless enough.

'Your coffee,' she said; 'would you like me to...'

But she saw he was already out of it.

Exhausted from the effort she'd put into getting him where he was, she threw herself down into the nearest chair and looked at him broodingly.

Why, she wondered, was he here alone? And especially at this time of year, when families gathered together, drawn by love, memories and layers of tradition.

She herself couldn't wait to get home.

But this man didn't believe in Christmas. She frowned as she remembered the words he'd spoken to her the night before. *Go away,* he'd growled. *I don't do Christmas.*

She hugged her arms around herself, and leaned forward in her seat, toward the sofa. *Why?* she wanted to ask the man lying there. *Why don't you do Christmas?*

Even in sleep he looked forbidding. It was the scowl, of course. It was deeply etched, and looked as if it might be a permanent fixture on that hard male face. Her gaze became drawn inexorably to his mouth. The lips...though they were slightly parted she could detect a firmness there, that spoke of control...but along with that firmness was a sensuality, that spoke of something else.

She sighed.

He stirred, and murmured something that sound like 'Ashley...' and then settled back into sleep.

He didn't waken again till early afternoon.

Damian remembered telling her that morning that she was pretty. He had been wrong. Now, half-awake and unnoticed, he scrutinized her as she sat curled up on the sofa across from his, engrossed in a magazine. She had changed into an emerald green sweater and navy stretch pants, and her hair was tied back with an emerald green velvet ribbon. His lidded gaze took in the delicacy of her bone structure, the sweet curve of her lips, the copper highlights in her hair. She was more than pretty, he reflected; she was beautiful. The subtle kind of beauty that could sneak up on a man if he wasn't careful, and steal his heart. If he believed in Christmas, he would also believe in miracles, and he would believe she'd been sent to him, meant for him...

A Christmas miracle.

But if he believed in anything it was that Christmas, and miracles, were for other men. Never for him.

He cleared his throat. 'You're still here?'

She looked up, closed the magazine and laid it on the cushion beside her. 'Mmm.' Her full pink lips hovered between a grimace and a pout. 'How are you feeling?'

'On the mend.'

'Good.'

He stretched, and clasped his hands behind his head. 'What day is it?'

'The twenty-fourth.'

His grin was wry. 'Already? So...where were you making for last night, when you ended up in my snowbank?'

'Home for Christmas.' She was wearing dangling silver earrings; earrings with a dark green stone that picked up the color of her eyes. As she lifted her shoulders in a shrug, the earrings swung and briefly touched her pale neck, the silver glinting in the light. 'I'm not expected till today—I was going to surprise them by coming early.'

'Them? Your family?'

'Mmm. They all live in Rockfield. Two grandmothers, two parents, several aunts and uncles, four brothers and their wives and an assortment of nieces and nephews ranging from a newborn baby with colic, to a teenage boy with acne and raging hormones.'

Family. Boy, did this woman ever have a family. Envy pierced him. 'And you've brought only one teddy bear?'

Her laugh had the clear tinkle of water gurgling over white pebbles in a brook. 'Of course not. I've loads more presents in the van.' For a moment, as she spoke, her eyes had sparkled, but as he watched, the sparkle faded. With a barely concealed sigh, she got up from the sofa, crossed to the window and hugged her arms around herself. She was looking out, but there could be little to see but the falling snow. She stood still for a long while. Silence filled the room, except for the occasional howl of the wind outside, the frequent blatter of snowflakes against the window.

She wiped the fingertips of her right hand over the mist her breath had made on the pane. He saw her shift restlessly; flick back her ponytail.

'You're anxious to get going,' he said.

She turned. Her expression was strained. 'I phoned Grantham Towing again while you were asleep and they won't be sending anyone out till the storm's over and the side road's been ploughed. I may be stuck here for another night.'

He shoved back the duvet and got up. He swayed a little, but as she moved toward him, he steadied himself. 'I'm okay,' he reassured her. 'Just dizzy there for a sec.' He crossed over to where she was standing and held out his hand. 'Damian McAllister.'

'Stephanie Redford.' He noticed that her fingertips still retained the damp from the windowpane, but her skin was soft. Now she was close, and he was conscious again of her perfume. Faint and elusive, yet intensely disturbing, it made him think of moss and roses...and slow sensual kisses.

He swallowed, released her hand and rubbed the heel of his thumb over his stubbled jaw. Dangerous, he told himself, to let himself think that way.

'I'm going up to have a shower,' he said.

'I'll fix us something to eat.'

'Cupboard's pretty bare.'

She smiled faintly. 'Not totally.'

His head was getting a bit dizzy again. 'Good.'

As he ascended the stairs, he realized he was whistling contemplatively under his breath, and with a frown, put a stop to it. Irritably he admitted he'd been wondering what it would feel like to untie the green velvet ribbon, spread out that glorious brown hair and let the lustrous strands spill through his fingers.

And even more irritably, he admitted he'd been wondering what it would feel like to sink down with this woman on a bed of green moss, with the scent of pink roses all around, and claim her pouting lips in a passionate kiss.

He glowered. His instincts warned him that Stephanie Redford was not the type to take such kisses lightly. She was beautiful and desirable—but she was also 'nice'; his deepest instincts told him that, as they also told him that here was a woman who believed in love and marriage...and all the trimmings.

Christmas, for example. It was clear she believed in Christmas.

He did not.

He muttered an oath as he pushed open his bedroom door. He would have to make sure he never kissed her, because his deepest instincts told him something else. They told him that if he ever did kiss her, she'd be impossible to forget.

CHAPTER THREE

TEARS rolled down Stephanie's cheeks, and with a choking sob, she clumsily wiped them away with her sweater sleeve as she hurried across the kitchen to click off the radio.

She should have known better than to switch it on; should have known that the airwaves would be joyous with the music of Christmas.

'Stille Nacht! Heilige Nacht!

Alles schläft; einsam wacht...'

Even though the choir had been a German one, and the language unfamiliar, the sweet purity of the children's voices as they sang 'Silent Night' had moved her unbearably.

She loved Christmas and had always been emotional at this time, but her feelings were especially near the surface this year because of her broken engagement—

'Smells good.'

Stephanie froze. McAllister. Hoping she had dashed away all signs of her tears, she forced a bright smile and turned around...to find not the man she expected, but a complete stranger standing in the doorway. No—she blinked incredulously—not a stranger. It *was* McAllister...

And this was the man she'd classed as a caveman? She put a hand on the countertop to steady herself. Now that his beard was gone, his face was revealed in all its angular male perfection—she could see the hard slash of strong cheekbones, the firm set of a determined jaw, the deep lines etched either side of his mouth. His hair was as shiny as tar, his eyes clear and the same steel blue as the exquisite alpaca sweater he wore so casually over a pair of old jeans.

In his previous scruffy state she'd labeled him one of America's Most Wanted. And now? Oh, certainly he would be one of America's Most Wanted...wanted by every woman in the country who had a drop of red blood in her veins!

Breathlessly, as if her heart had tilted against her lungs for support and was squeezing out all the oxygen, she said, 'Oh, there you are. I found some sausages in the freezer section, and eggs and milk in the fridge. The Best Before date on the bread was yesterday, but it seemed okay.' The toast popped up. She turned away and busied herself buttering it. 'How do you like your eggs?'

'Sunny-side up, please. Here, I'll pour the coffee.'

He had to pass her to get to the coffeepot, and as he brushed by, she caught the spicy scent of his shaving cream. Tantalizingly male. And disturbingly intimate...

She took a deep breath, and scooped up a spatula.

By the time he had filled two mugs with the steaming coffee, the toast was on the table, and she'd flipped a couple of fried eggs and several nicely browned sausages onto a warmed plate for him, and one egg and a couple of sausages onto another for herself. She set the plates on the place mats, and he pulled out a chair for her.

'Thanks,' she murmured, and as he took his seat she passed him the cream jug. 'You take cream, don't you, and no sugar?'

He did a double-take. 'Are you psychic?'

He was sitting directly across from the window and the light from the snow outside seemed reflected in his eyes, making the blue so electrically dazzling she almost blinked. 'No,' she laughed lightly. 'I offered you coffee when you came downstairs this morning. You don't remember?'

'Oh...now...vaguely.' He stirred cream into his coffee and took a thirsty gulp. 'Mmm,' he said. 'Good and strong.'

For the next few minutes, they ate without talking. And as Stephanie occasionally peeked at him from under her lashes, it occurred to her that an outsider looking in might think them comfortably married. But they weren't married; and she at least didn't feel at all comfortable. Not since the rather frightening caveman had turned into the most elegantly attractive man she'd ever—

'So—' stretching back in his chair, he looked at her over the rim of his coffee mug '—tell me something about yourself. What do you do for a living?'

She saw that he had finished his meal, as she had, except for one small triangle of toast. She nibbled it, and looked at him teasingly. 'Guess.'

'Give me a clue.' He put down his mug.

'You've already had one.'

'I have?' He scratched his head. 'Let me see. Ah, you're a short-order cook.'

'Try again.'

He stared at her as if trying to read the answer in her face. 'You smash vans for the Rent-a-Wreck company?'

She gave a gurgling laugh and tilting her chair, reached across to the countertop for the nutmeg teddy bear, which she'd set there earlier. 'This is what I do.' She tossed it to him. 'I design stuffed animals—I have them manufactured to my specifications by a Montpelier firm.'

He caught the bear, and held it. Held it gingerly, she thought with some amusement, the way a man— unused to children—might hold a baby for the first time. He looked down at it and, oddly, his features seemed to tighten. Then abruptly he flipped the bear back onto the counter.

'Then what?' His tone was neutral. 'You sell them?'

'I have my own store. My own business.' She corrected herself. 'The premises are rented.'

'Where? Montpelier?'

'Boston.' She saw his eyes widen, as if she'd caught him by surprise. 'I've been there three years. The first couple were tough, but business is quite brisk now.' She smiled. 'If you're ever in Boston, you must pop by. My place is called the Warmest Fuzzies Toy Store.'

Stephanie knew it was a whimsical name—which was why she had chosen it—and usually, when people heard it for the first time, they smiled. McAllister didn't smile. For a long moment, he stared at her, his eyes suddenly as glassy as the bear's, and then his black brows lowered in a scowl, a dark scowl, as if she'd said a four-letter word.

She put down her mug. 'What's the matter?'

He shoved back his chair and got up. 'Nothing.' His voice had become as churlish as his scowl. 'If you're finished eating,' he added tersely, 'refill your mug and take it through to the other room—I'll tidy up here.'

What on earth had she said or done to change his mood? Had he thought—heaven forbid—that her invitation to pop by her store had been…a come-on?

Oh, Lord…

Cheeks pink, she got to her feet. She shifted her plate to the sink, refilled her mug and made for the door. McAllister leaned against the counter, arms folded impassively over his chest, waiting for her to leave.

She carried on by him into the living area, walking so quickly her coffee almost lipped over the edge of her mug.

As she crossed to the picture window, she heard a great clattering from the kitchen…an angry clattering…as if he was giving vent to whatever frustration he was feeling, by directing it toward the dirty plates and the frying pan.

But if he was annoyed with her because he thought she'd been making a move on him, perhaps, she reflected defiantly, she should have reminded him of the moves he had made on her. When she'd told him in all innocence that she'd been planning to bring his coffee up to his bedroom, hadn't he said, in a suggestively inviting tone, 'Had I but known…'? And then, when they'd bumped together against the wall, hadn't he looked down at her from under his long sooty lashes and said, in a smoldering voice, 'My, you *are* a pretty one!'

Huffily Stephanie turned from the window and crossed to the nearest bookcase. After a few moments' deliberation, she chose the hardback copy of *Untimely Graves,* a thriller she'd been meaning to read for the past several years. She carried it with her to a nearby sofa. Curling up in a corner, she tucked her feet under, and then paused, staring into space, with her fingers curved around the closed book.

Damian McAllister obviously didn't want her company.

So...from now on, she would make it just as obvious she didn't want his!

With that thought firmly in mind, she opened the book.

And saw, inscribed on the inside front page in graceful copperplate, written with a fine-nibbed black pen:

To darling Damian, with all my love, Ashley.

'Miss Redford—'

Stephanie almost jumped out of her skin. She was well into the fourth chapter of *Untimely Graves,* and McAllister's voice had slashed into her sharply just as the murderer was creeping up on his second unsuspecting victim. She wrenched her head around, her pulse racing, and saw her host standing behind her, just a few feet away.

He was swinging an ax in his hand.

Her stomach turned over.

She held the book pressed to her chest for protection and felt her heart thud violently against it. 'What...?'

'I'm going out back to chop some wood for the fire.'

Her grip on the book slackened. Slightly. 'Shouldn't you...be...taking it easy today?'

'I need to get some air.'

The blade of the ax glinted in the light from the overhead lamp. Stephanie swallowed.

'Off you go then,' she said, and if he wondered why her reply came out threadily, she didn't care. She was cursed with an overactive imagination, that was all.

With a brusque nod, he turned and departed along the narrow lobby leading to the back of the house. A few seconds later, she heard a door slam shut.

Her breath hissed out with the sound of a deflating balloon, and she gave a shaky giggle. What an idiot she was! She was quite safe here with McAllister. It was only that the creepiness of the novel had put her in a nervous mood, and his coming up behind her had caught her off guard.

Putting down the book, she got up and stretched. She, too, felt like getting a breath of fresh air…and had he invited her to go out with him, she would probably have gone. But he hadn't. He'd wanted to be alone.

She walked absently to the window…looked out on a land blanketed in white…and gasped. Good Lord, the snow had stopped! The sun was shining from a cloudless sky and streaming through the icicles that daggered down from the eaves above, transforming them into brilliantly colored prisms. Dazzled, she gazed beyond, and saw a wide sweep of valley adorned by frozen forest, river and lake. A winter wonderland, she thought with awe; Vermont at its very best.

Smiling, she whirled around and made for the phone.

She dialed the Grantham Towing number, and when Bob Grantham came on the line, she said quickly, 'Mr. Grantham, this is Stephanie Redford again, calling from the McAllister place. I see the snow has let up and I was wondering—'

'They're ploughing the Tarlity roads this afternoon, miss. I'll have somebody out your way by early evening.'

Thank heaven, Stephanie thought, as she hung up the phone after asking a couple more questions. She couldn't wait to get home...

Yet...despite McAllister's gruff demeanor, she couldn't help worrying about him. Certainly he wouldn't welcome her interest, or her concern...but she knew she'd be thinking about him over Christmas. Wondering how he was faring. Wondering what he'd be doing, here on his own.

Who was Ashley—the woman whose name he had murmured in his fever, the woman who had given him the thriller...along with all her love?

Was she still in his life? If so, why wasn't she here with him? And if she wasn't still in his life, why did he dream about her, and whisper her name in his sleep?

It was a mystery, Stephanie thought regretfully...and would probably remain a mystery.

But it piqued her curiosity mightily.

McAllister didn't come in again till the sun had gone down and darkness was falling.

She heard the back door slam, heard the purposeful tread of his booted feet in the lobby as he approached.

Face ruddy, and bringing a blast of cold air with him, along with a pile of chopped wood, he gave her only a glance as he made for the hearth. Bending over, he rolled up some newspaper, set kindlers on it and put a match to the paper. Once it had flared up, he added several logs. Within minutes, flames were leaping up the chimney's wide throat.

Only then did he take off his parka, fling it down on a chair and swipe his palms down the side of his jeans.

'So,' he said in a cool tone, sniffing the aroma coming from the kitchen, 'you've been busy? What's cooking?'

She shrugged carelessly. 'It's only a macaroni and ham casserole. It's time you went grocery shopping, Mr. McAllister. If you don't die of pneumonia, you may well die of starvation.'

He grunted. 'Fancy a drink?'

'A drink?' She quirked an eyebrow. 'As in...?'

'As in Scotch, wine, you name it?'

She wanted to snub him, but the prospect of a glass of wine was just too tempting. After all, it was Christmas Eve, and so far there had been little cheer for her in this festive season. Especially not in this house; there wasn't even a sprig of holly indoors, to celebrate the holidays.

'White wine,' she said, 'would be nice.'

'Coming up.'

He went into the kitchen and came back a couple of minutes later. After handing her a glass three-quarter filled with wine, he held up his glass of Scotch, the ice cube tinkling musically against the fine-cut crystal.

'Good health.'

'Good health,' she murmured. And without thinking, added, 'Merry Christmas.'

He didn't respond to that, other than with what sounded like an unpleasant '*Hrmmph!*' as he turned his back and crossed to the window. From where

Stephanie was sitting, she could see his reflection in the darkened glass. What a grump he was, she thought, as she made out his now-familiar scowl. What an absolute grump.

'You'll be pleased to know,' she said sweetly, 'that I'll be out of your way soon. I phoned Grantham Towing when I saw the snow had stopped, and they're going to be sending out a truck early this evening.'

He wheeled round. 'And what do you intend to do if your van is out of commission? It's possible you may have damaged the transmission, or—'

'Mr. Grantham said if there's any problem, I'll get a drive back to Tarlity with the driver of the tow truck, and I can go on from there by taxi or bus or whatever.'

He frowned. 'Did you make any other calls?'

'No,' Stephanie snapped, 'and don't worry, I'll pay you for the three I made to Grantham Towing. Really, I—'

'Miss Redford,' his voice had a weary edge, 'I don't give a damn about the money. I was just concerned that since you've been stranded here, there might be someone—other than family—who might be concerned about you if they knew you hadn't reached your destination.'

'Oh.' Suddenly she felt very small. 'Sorry.'

'Well?' he barked. 'Is there?'

'Is there...what?'

'Anyone else in your life!'

He meant a man, of course. Though why that should have made him sound so mad was beyond her. At any rate, she wasn't about to tell him about Tony— Tony, who'd be in Aspen now, partying with the

Whitneys...and with their beautiful daughter Tiffany, who'd been crazy about him for years.

'No.' Stephanie kept her voice light. 'There's nobody in my life. At this moment.' And she certainly didn't want to discuss the matter further. 'So,' she went on, running a fingertip around the rim of her glass as she looked up at him, 'tell me, Mr. McAllister, what do you do for a living?'

He had taken up a stance at one side of the fire, and was leaning now against the mantelpiece. At her question, his eyes became shuttered.

'I draw.' She thought he sounded oddly evasive. Then his gaze flicked to the large oil painting that had given her the creeps the night before. 'And paint. Which is why I built this place. The scenery here is—well, you don't need me to tell you about the beauty of Vermont.'

Putting her glass down on the coffee table, Stephanie got to her feet, and rounding the sofa, walked over to look at the painting from several feet away. 'You did this?'

'Yes.'

'You're exceptionally talented,' she said quietly after a long moment. She turned, to find he was still over by the hearth, but he was watching her. Waiting.

'That's not much of a critique,' he said in an off-handed manner that didn't fool her.

She hesitated, before turning to look at the oil again. 'The effect is stunning, compellingly vivid and dramatic, and the reflections in the lake so cleverly done...'

'But...?'

He had heard the doubt in her voice. Damn! She squared her shoulders. 'I'm afraid, though, that I shouldn't like to have this particular work in my home. I should find it too…unsettling.'

'Unsettling?' His cool voice prodded her.

'Mmm. And disturbing. The darkness of the valleys, the blackness of the clouds, the vague sense of threat from the vulture hovering over the wounded deer—'

'It's not a vulture, Miss Redford—it's an eagle.'

'Oh, I know it's an eagle,' she said impatiently. 'But I like eagles and the effect here is more… sinister.' She grimaced and made a small sound of distress. 'I'm sorry.' She walked back across the room and dropped into the sofa again. 'That's obviously not what you wanted to hear, but I have to be honest. You see, I like to surround myself with pictures that give me pleasure. There's enough ugliness in the world without choosing to bring it into one's home.' She went on hesitantly, 'Had I seen this in a gallery, I'd have thought the artist must have been very unhappy at the time he—'

'My God, can't you just look at the picture and see what's there, without delving for something underneath?' He sounded furious; he crashed his glass down on the mantelpiece so abruptly it was a wonder the crystal didn't shatter. 'Everyone's a psychologist! Did I look at your damned teddy bear and say, "You're exceptionally talented, and this little bear is a beautiful shade of brown…but I wouldn't want him in my house because it would be a reminder that every home is not a happy home and every child does not get a teddy bear for Christmas?"'

Aghast, Stephanie stared at him, and felt the blood drain from her face. How she hated being shouted at; it hurt her as much as a slap. 'Excuse me.' With a painful lump swelling in her throat, and her eyes stinging, she rose from the sofa and started toward the lobby, hoping she'd get to the powder room before she dissolved into tears. But she'd gone barely ten feet when with long strides, he caught up with her.

His hand on her shoulder was firm. He hauled her around to face him. And saw she was crying.

'Oh, for God's sake...' With a rough groan, he pulled her against him, burying her face in the beautiful blue alpaca sweater. 'Don't be so damned sensitive! I only—'

'*Sensitive?*' Outraged, Stephanie pulled her head back, though her body was still captured by the arms clamped firmly around her. 'You wouldn't know ''sensitive'' if it sat up and punched you in the nose, Mr. McAllister!' Her eyes sparked fire, her breasts quivered with each furious breath. 'If you did, you wouldn't be in this position now—'

'There's nothing wrong with this position.' His tone had changed, his voice had become husky. With the pad of one thumb, he caressed away a tear that had trembled over and was trickling down her cheek. 'In fact, it's a position that I find extremely...interesting.'

Interesting? Stephanie almost moaned. What he found merely interesting, she found positively electrifying. With his beautiful steel blue eyes regarding her lazily from under his thick sooty lashes, with his hard-muscled arms holding her so intimately against his magnificent lean torso, she had gone from wild outrage to total meltdown in less time than it took her heart to stagger from one beat to the next. She pushed his arms away and stood back from him.

'I think—' her voice came out breathlessly '—you're out of line, Mr. McAllister.'

His slanting grin held no hint of apology.

'Yeah,' he said, 'I guess I was.'

'There's no guessing necessary,' she snapped.

'No, ma'am.'

Head in the air, Stephanie took off for the powder room marveling that her wobbly legs could carry her.

And that was a narrow escape!

McAllister rolled his eyes as he moved through to the kitchen. One kiss...so close...and yet he knew that was all it would take. One kiss...and he'd be lost.

Holding her in his arms had been like holding a dream. She was everything a man could want. And he wanted her. Boy, did he want her! She was sweet, feminine, beautiful, and smelled so damned good he'd ached to strip off her clothes and kiss every pulse point on her body where she'd dabbed that tantalizing perfume. Even now though she'd gone the scent of her hung in the air, driving him crazy...

Just as that Christmas sign in her store window had driven him crazy for the last month! Good Lord, whoever said it was a small world hadn't known the half of it. This woman was into toys and kids, into Christmas and everything connected with Christmas, and he wanted no part of her.

Wrong. He wanted every part of her.

He raked a hand through his hair with a gesture of supreme frustration, and made for the kitchen, his thoughts in a turmoil.

Snatching a towel from the rack, he slammed down the oven door, lifted out the casserole and placed it on a cork mat on the counter. It looked delicious, and cooked to perfection, the grated cheese topping all crusty and golden brown. Half an hour ago, while he'd been chopping wood, he'd been starving. For food. Now he was starving for something else, and food was the last thing on his mind.

Concentrate, he warned himself. Concentrate on this casserole. Much safer.

He heard her come into the kitchen. She was wearing only socks on her feet, but he still heard the soft padding sound. Without turning around, he said, 'This looks great.'

'Thanks. It's an old standby of mine.'

'Would you like another glass of wine?'

'No, thanks...this is enough.'

Finally he turned and saw that in one hand she was holding the drink he'd poured for her earlier. In the other, his own glass of Scotch. She put it on the table, and the movement released a faint hint of her perfume.

He cursed silently.

She stood there. Took a small sip from her glass. 'I never have more than one drink, if I'm to be driving.'

Driving. Of course, she would be driving soon. Whenever Grantham Towing turned up, she'd be off.

'Right.' He slid his gaze from her steady look, and took out a spoon. 'Sit down,' he said, 'I'll dish up.'

There was a tension between them that hadn't been there before. Sparking. Disturbing. Dangerous.

He put the plates on the table, and took his seat across from her. Offered her the salt and pepper.

She shook her head. 'No, thanks. But you'll probably need salt. I didn't put much in.'

'No,' he said, 'I'm sure it'll be fine.'

It was more than fine. It was delicious. Surprisingly his appetite came back…his appetite for food, that was. His aching to kiss her had never gone away.

He looked up, and found that she hadn't started eating. She was sitting with her hands in her lap, watching him. Her eyes—as green as the forest in spring—were fixed on him unblinkingly.

'Who is Ashley?' she asked.

CHAPTER FOUR

STEPHANIE felt her breath catch. Where had that question come from? When she'd sat down she'd had no intention of asking it. And now, as she saw the dull color rise in McAllister's face, she realized she'd made a big mistake. Nervously she waited for his response.

'Who the hell,' he said with soft menace, 'told you about Ashley?'

Stephanie decided not to confess she'd overheard him whisper the name in his sleep. Instead she said lightly, 'The book I was reading had her name inscribed in it.'

'She was my wife.' His expression was grim and closed. 'She died five years ago.'

'Oh, I'm sor—'

'Sorry?' he exploded. 'How can you be sorry about somebody you never met!' His grip on his fork had tightened till the bones of his knuckles shone like ivory. 'We were married. She's now dead. End of story.' He glared at Stephanie, and then after inhaling a deep breath in an obvious attempt to regain control of himself, devoted his attention to his food.

Stephanie felt shaky and a bit sick. How she wished she had never seen the book, or the name Ashley!

She usually enjoyed macaroni and cheese; now she found herself picking at it. Finally she pushed her plate away, accidentally knocking the pepper mill. It fell over with a clatter.

He glowered at her.

Her fingers trembled as she set the mill upright. 'If you'll excuse me,' she said, 'I'll go and pack my things. The man from Grantham Towing should be here soon.'

She got up...and noticed that he got to his feet, too, briefly. At least he had some kind of manners, she thought, but for the most part he was a boor. Bob Grantham had characterized him as a loner, and if it were true, it was probably not even by choice. Who would want to be around a man prone to such drastic and irrational mood swings!

But by the time she had finished packing her duffel bag, she had cooled down, and actually felt a surge of compassion for him. He had lost his wife—a wife he'd loved; that much was obvious from the tender way he'd whispered her name in his sleep. Perhaps he'd been a different person when she was alive. Perhaps it had been her death that had made him the way he was now.

She sighed. Why did she always have to worry about other people? In this instance, particularly, it was a pure waste of time. Once she left here, she would never see Damian McAllister again!

She had barely contemplated the thought when the doorbell rang. Could it be the driver from Grantham Towing? Hesitantly she looked around, to see that her host was coming out of the kitchen.

'I'll get it,' he said tersely.

She watched him open the front door, and saw a man on the outside step, a beefy six-footer in heavy winter gear. She could hear the rumble of the stranger's deep voice but couldn't make out what he was saying. Beyond him, far down the driveway at the junction with the road, she could see flashing lights. The tow truck...

She hurried over to the door.

'You got my van out okay?' she asked eagerly.

'He's not from Grantham's,' McAllister growled.

'We have a problem here, ma'am,' the stranger said. 'Your van was so far into the snow I didn't see it till it was too late. The plow totaled it. Sorry about that, but you really shoulda had a warning flasher on it.'

Stephanie suddenly felt her legs begin to wobble. She was aware that McAllister was frowning down at her, and even as she opened her mouth to try to speak, he grasped her arm and despite her protests marched her back to the living room and sat her down in the wing chair by the fire.

'Stay there,' he commanded. 'I'll deal with this.' He scooped up his parka from where he'd left it earlier. 'Sit!' he thundered, as Stephanie started to push herself up from the chair. 'I told you—I'll look after things.'

Stephanie sank back weakly. He went out and banged the door behind him. The sound vibrated through the room, setting the fire irons shaking.

Totaled. The man's voice echoed in her head. *Her van was totaled.*

What was she going to do? Panic set her thoughts ascramble. How would she get home?

Shakily she got to her feet, and crossed into the kitchen. She poured herself a glass of water, and drank it while she stared unseeingly in front of her. This Christmas was *not* shaping up to be one of her best.

She was still standing there when McAllister came

back in. She heard the front door open, and shut, followed by an impatient, 'Where the hell are you?'

She hurried out of the kitchen. 'Here.'

McAllister's cheeks were flushed with the cold, his hair rumpled with the wind. His eyes were blank of emotion.

'Grab your things,' he said. 'I'll drive you home.'

She stared. 'You'll drive me home? No.' She shook her head. 'There's no need—'

'You want to walk?' His voice had a scathing edge.

'Of course not! But now that the road's clear, someone can come for me. I'll phone my mom and dad…they'll—'

'Are you kidding? The last thing I want is a horde of Redfords on my doorstep. Now get your things—' his tone was exaggeratedly patient '—and let's get on our way.'

'You are the rudest man I have ever met.'

'Then you can't have met many men in the course of your sweet young life. I'll go out and get my truck warmed up.' He swiveled away and strode toward the door.

'What about Grantham Towing?' she called after him.

'I used the cell phone on the snowplow to contact them. Everything's organized.' He opened the door, and called back over his shoulder, 'Be out front in three minutes.' Then he was gone.

The man wasn't only rude, Stephanie decided, he was also arrogant and detestable. But she had to admit it was good of him to drive her home…no matter how selfish his reasons!

It took her only a couple of minutes to get her coat and toque on, and she was just about to pop the teddy bear into her duffel bag, when she changed her mind. Snatching it up, along with the duvet and the pillow she'd used the night before, she ran across the open area and up the stairs. After putting the duvet and pillow back where she'd found them, she scooted through to McAllister's bedroom.

Crossing to his bed, she saw that her host slept with only one pillow. She plumped it up, and sat the teddy bear on it. She wished she had time to write a Thank-you note, but just then she heard a brisk *honk!* from outside.

Heart thudding, she fled from the room. When would he find her gift? she wondered as she clattered down the stairs at top speed. And what would he do with it when he saw it? Would he toss the bear aside as indifferently as he'd done that morning?

She grimaced. The sad thing was, she'd never know.

McAllister's vehicle was a late-model four-wheel-drive truck. That was about as much as Stephanie was allowed to see before he bundled her up into the front seat.

'Right?' he asked curtly, putting the vehicle in gear as she snapped her belt buckle shut.

'Yes. Thank you.'

He had the heater on, but the warmth did nothing to dispel her tension, which increased as the truck crunched slowly down the driveway. When they approached the road, she could see her van in the headlights, and her heart gave an unpleasant twist. The vehicle was fit only for the junkyard. Closing her eyes, she clenched her hands in her lap. The truck slowed, and paused, before making the left turn and starting up the hill—the hill she'd slid down so ignominiously less than twenty-four hours before.

'Oh!' Eyes flying open, she wrenched her body around in her seat. 'We'll have to go back. My presents—'

'I've got them. They're in the back of the truck. One of the bags was slightly ripped, but if there's nothing inside but stuffed animals, there should be little damage.'

'Thank you so much. That was very thoughtful of you.'

'I took your papers from the glove compartment, too.' He gestured toward a plastic bag on the seat between them.

'I do appreciate all you've done for me.'

He grunted, and as he changed gear, he shifted slightly, putting his shoulder to her, as if to cut off further conversation.

When they reached the top of the steep hill, she asked, tentatively, 'Do you know your way to Rockfield?'

'Yup.'

There was silence, for about five miles.

'I'm sorry,' she said quietly, 'to have been such a bother to you. You obviously aren't fond of company—'

'What makes you say that?'

'Well, your house is off the beaten track...and you live alone...'

'I'm not always alone,' he said. 'But at Christmas, I *choose* to be alone.'

'It seems odd to me,' she said softly. 'Christmas is such a special time—'

'Do you mind,' he interrupted her, 'if I listen to the

news?' He flicked on the radio, and they were just in time to hear the beginning of the top-of-the-hour newscast.

And that put her in her place, Stephanie reflected wryly.

When the newscast was over, he flicked off the radio, but she had gotten the message. He wanted to be left in peace, and even if he begged her to speak to him now, she would rather bite her tongue off than say one more word.

They drove for more than an hour before they reached the outskirts of Rockfield. During that time, apart from her earlier attempt at conversation, neither of them had spoken. It was McAllister who finally broke the extended silence.

'I need you to direct me now,' he said.

When Stephanie heard the weariness in his voice, any lingering resentment she might have been clinging to, gave way to a feeling of guilt. The man was recovering from a rotten bout of flu, and really shouldn't be out of doors at all. The least she could do was be polite. And gracious.

'It's at the end of town,' she said. 'Do you see that school on the next corner? Turn left there, and go on for five blocks, and turn right at the Waverley General Store.'

In no time at all they were pulling up in front of the white frame house where Stephanie had been born, and she excitedly drank in the welcome and familiar Christmas scene. On the house's high-pitched roof was an illuminated reindeer, pulling Santa's sleigh; on the door hung a wreath; and in the uncurtained bay window stood a six-foot spruce, with winking lights and a shining silver angel. She could see people sitting around—and her heart gave a pleasurable little skip of anticipation when she spotted her mother.

'Those boys in the front yard—' she gestured toward four youngsters building a snowman that was silver-glazed by the moon '—are some of my nephews.' She pushed open her door and called out, 'Hey, Garry—could you come and give us a hand with these bags?'

When the boys recognized Stephanie, they whooped, and shuffled over eagerly, their faces as red as holly berries. She jumped down to hug them, and as she did, McAllister tossed the four plastic bags down onto the snow. The boys grabbed one each and scrambled off with them.

Stephanie turned...to find McAllister standing at the side of the truck...looking at the house. The expression on his face made her heart turn over; she'd never seen such a look of bleak unhappiness. What was he seeing, she wondered, to cause that look? Just her family, sitting around in the living room.

'You must come in,' she said, 'and meet everybody.'

'No, I need to get going.' He turned away.

'Please?' She crossed to him, and touching his arm, looked up into his face. Her expression was tender. 'My parents would like to meet the man who rescued me.'

She could see him hesitate. But even as he did, she heard a voice calling her from the open front door.

'Steph—' it was Jeff, her oldest brother '—come on, we have a surprise for you!'

Stephanie frowned, her hand still on Damian's arm.

'Go ahead,' he said. 'I'll follow on in a minute. I'll just lock up the truck.'

'You promise?'

'Sure.'

He saw her eyes light up, brighter than the stars in the sky above, and she beamed at him. 'Oh,' she whispered gleefully, 'it's so wonderful to be home. Home for Christmas! It's the very best time of the year—I love it, I just love it!' And with a joyful laugh, she was off, tromping fast through the snow in her high black boots, the hem of her red coat swinging around her long legs.

'Hey,' he called after her, 'you forgot your duffel bag.'

But she didn't hear him.

A voice came from behind him. A gruff voice, young and diffident. 'It's okay. I'll get it for her.'

He turned, and in the truck's headlights, saw a teenage boy approach, a lanky figure clad in a parka and jeans, with brown hair tied back in a ponytail. He was a nice-looking lad…even taking into account a bad case of acne.

'You must be Stephanie's oldest nephew,' Damian said.

'Yeah.' He hoisted up the duffel bag and swung it easily over his shoulder. 'And you're…?'

'Just someone who gave her a drive when she needed one.'

'Okay.' The boy gave him a shrewd once-over, before turning his attention to the truck. He gave it an even more thorough inspection. 'Cool,' he said. 'Really rad.' He jerked his head toward a black Jaguar XJ parked across the street, half-hidden by the drooping branches of a snow-laden tree. 'If I had a choice,

I'd take your truck over that any day. It's a smooth enough ride, but—' He broke off with a scornful shrug. 'I always thought Steph had good taste but her boyfriend's like his car…smooth as an eel's back.'

Damian drew in a deep lungful of cold clear air scented with evergreens. When he exhaled, his breath made ragged white smoke in the headlights. 'Boyfriend?'

'More than a boyfriend. He's her fiancé, actually. They're getting married in September.' The boy kicked at the snow, bad-temperedly. 'He's a jerk, you know? Comes out with these little put-downs, and then laughs them off like he was joking?'

'Well.' Damian turned his head and looked at the house again. He could see Stephanie now, in the midst of her family…but she wasn't standing alone. A man was with her. Tall. Blond. Wide-shouldered. They had their backs to the window, but Damian could see that the man had an arm around her. Firmly. Possessively. Intimately. 'I'm off.' His voice sounded as if someone was tightening a thin wire around his throat.

The boy scowled. 'I thought I heard you tell Steph you'd follow her in.'

Yes, he had promised he would. In one wild and crazy moment, he had promised he would do just that. He had looked into her eyes as she stood with her hand on his arm, and in the pine green depths he had seen caring, and…he had foolishly thought…the hint of something more. It was almost as if a covenant had passed between them. Just as petals unfolding from a tiny bud gave unspoken assurance that if tenderly nurtured, blossoms would follow, he had seen in her eyes a similar covenant. Or so he had thought. He had been mistaken. At that very moment when he'd dared to hope that a miracle could, after all, be his if he were only bold enough to reach for it, bold enough to take that risk, it had dissolved into nothing.

A mirage, not a miracle, after all.

He realized the boy was waiting for an answer.

'No,' he said. 'I've changed my mind.'

'What'll I tell her?'

He opened the truck door, and his boots clattered tinnily on the floor as he jumped up into the cab. 'Nothing,' he said, starting the engine. 'It's okay.' He noticed the plastic package on the seat, with the papers he'd taken from the van. 'Here.' He tossed it out the window. 'Catch.'

As he drove off, the boy called after him, 'Merry Christmas, then…right?'

'Yeah.' Damian had never felt less merry in his life. 'Right.'

Stephanie sat in the passenger seat of the Jaguar and stared at the sapphire ring on her engagement finger.

'Happy, darling?' Tony's voice was low, intimate.

She turned to look at him. They were parked across the street from the Redford house, the car engine idling. After they'd spent an hour with her family and she'd caught up on all the news, Tony had suggested they go for a short drive.

'You understand,' he'd said to her parents with a disarming smile. 'We haven't seen each other since Friday!'

Her mother—apparently charmed by him—had said, 'Don't keep her too long, young man. We haven't seen her since September!' Everyone had laughed.

Except Jason, her favorite nephew. He'd sat in a

corner scowling at her...as he had done ever since he'd come inside and tossed her duffel bag down. The angry look he'd given her as he'd covertly jerked his head toward the window had made her blink. She'd glanced out...and had been in time to see the taillights of McAllister's truck disappearing along the street. So, he'd decided not to come in after all. She'd felt a vague sense of regret, of things half-finished...but what on earth had put Jason into such a disgruntled mood!

'*Steph?*' Tony slid an arm along the top of her seat.

She pulled back. 'You told me,' she said stiffly, 'that you were going to Aspen.'

'I know. But when I started packing for the trip, it hit me suddenly that I couldn't bear to spend Christmas apart from you!' He pulled her into his arms. 'Oh, my darling, please forgive me for having been so foolish.'

And with that, he claimed her lips in a lingering kiss.

In the past, Stephanie had always given herself up wholeheartedly to his kisses, but now a memory drifted into her thoughts and stole her attention—a memory of being held in McAllister's arms, a memory of his huskily murmured 'There's nothing wrong with this position.' Something tingled deep inside her as she recalled the tender way he'd brushed her tear from her cheek with the pad of his thumb.

'Now—' Tony released her '—let's take the drive—just a quick one. Well, it would be quick, wouldn't it.' His laugh was patronizing. 'This isn't exactly a metropolis!'

He moved the Jaguar forward. 'I was pleased I was able to slip your ring on again before anyone noticed you weren't wearing it. It's been burning a hole in my pocket! Steph.' He glanced at her. 'About this New Year's Eve engagement party your mother has planned—did you know about it?'

At mention of the party, Stephanie felt the same panicky sensation she'd felt when Tony had slipped the ring back on her finger; a sensation that she was losing control of her life, that she was being swept out to sea on a tidal wave. 'No, it came as a complete surprise.'

'But a wonderful one!' Tony sounded smug. 'They've really accepted me, haven't they? Did you know that until she heard of our engagement, your mother hadn't had a good night's sleep since you left home and moved to the city?'

'I'd no idea Mom worried about me!' Dismayed, Stephanie stared at him. 'She's always seemed so up-beat—'

'A front. But I've assured her that in my care, you'll be absolutely safe...and living in the lap of luxury. By the way, I didn't notice your old van. Where did you park?'

Stephanie's mind was still on her mother. 'I skidded on the way here,' she said in a distracted tone, 'and ended up in a snowbank, had to have it towed. I got a drive.'

'So the accident held you up, otherwise you'd have been here before me. I arrived around five.'

Stephanie realized he'd assumed she'd left Boston that day. She opened her mouth to set him right—and closed it again. He'd grill her endlessly if he found out she'd spent the night with a stranger, but there was no need for him to know. No need, in fact, for anyone to know. McAllister himself would never talk about it; it would be easier to extract a set of impacted wisdom teeth than to get private information out of that man. Besides, she and McAllister lived in two different worlds. Her secret was safe.

'Yes,' she murmured. 'The accident did...hold me up.'

'Steph, I *am* sorry I gave you that Christmas ultimatum. It was a huge mistake, and I plan on making it up to you. My love for you is the most important thing in my life.'

A month ago, Stephanie would happily have echoed his declaration; now, the words remained strangled in her throat. Certainly Tony had tried to rectify his mistake, but had his gesture come too late? At his party she'd seen a side of him she'd never seen before and it had changed her feelings for him. She'd have to sort those feelings out.

But not now. And not here.

For her mother's sake, she would maintain the status quo...only, however, for the duration of the holidays.

Once she got back to Boston, she would face her problem squarely, and decide whether or not to call off the wedding.

By the time McAllister got home he was exhausted, and so light-headed that when he staggered from his truck to the door, anyone watching might have thought he'd been drinking.

He had overdone it, of course. What the hell had he been trying to prove, chopping wood when he was still as weak as water! But he'd had to get away from her.

When he'd come downstairs after his shower, he'd

heard Christmas music coming from the kitchen. And
when he'd seen her, and realized she'd been crying—
the nostalgic music must have gotten to her—he'd felt
his heart give a strange twist. At the same time, he'd
been almost overcome by a passionate urge to haul
her into his arms and kiss those tears away...but he'd
somehow restrained himself. It was going to be hard
enough to forget her without indulging in any kind of
sexual involvement. But the picture of her in his
kitchen, looking so at home there as she cooked their
breakfast, was something that would stay with him
forever. Her ghost would haunt his house.

A house that now seemed empty without her.

He kicked the front door shut behind him and
walked into the living room. His gaze drifted to the
sofa, where she'd sat reading...again, looking as if
she belonged there.

Which she didn't. And never would.

She was already spoken for.

And that was a fact. Stephanie Redford was someone else's miracle. Not his. Never his.

He made his way slowly up to his bedroom. Without putting on the light, he stripped and slumped
down onto the mattress. He inhaled deeply...and
shuddered. The scent of her was everywhere, even in
his bed. But it couldn't be. She'd never been in his
bed. He must be imagining things. He pulled back the
duvet, and rolled under it.

His head struck something lumpy. Frowning, he
reached up, and discovered a soft plush object. What
the...?

The scent of her was now all around him, choking
him. And the object in his hand? He didn't need to
put on the light to identify it; it was the nutmeg teddy

bear she'd tossed to him so casually that morning across the breakfast table. She'd left it for him. A Christmas present.

With a guttural curse, he flung it away from him. He heard it hit something on the dresser, heard the sound of shattering glass. He twisted around and smashed his face into the pillow, in a futile effort to drown out the rush of bitter memories.

Memories of childhood Christmases, when the heart of one small boy had still held a shred of hope—hope that once, just once, he would waken on Christmas morning and find a present at the foot of his bed.

CHAPTER FIVE

'OUR apartment always seems so bare at the beginning of January.' Janey wrinkled her nose as she glanced around the living room. 'With the tree and the decorations all gone.'

'Mmm.' Stephanie wandered over to the window. The night was dark and cold. Snow had fallen lazily all day, but had tapered off just as she got home from the toy store.

At the end of the block, she could see several vehicles lined up at a red light. 'I'll be off in a minute,' she murmured. 'I think that's Tony's Jag at the intersection.'

Janey crossed to stand by her. 'Yes, it is.'

The lights changed and Stephanie stifled a sigh as she watched the Jaguar slide forward.

'Steph—' Janey sounded worried '—what's wrong? Since you came back from Rockfield, you've been so...distracted.'

Stephanie grimaced. 'I'm sorry, Janey, I didn't realize it showed. It's just that Tony's working all hours on a complicated case and we never have time to talk. We haven't had two minutes alone together since the holidays!'

'But he's taking you out for dinner tonight.'

'We've been invited to the opening of Harry Loeb's new restaurant, the Trocadero Six, but even so it's going to be a business dinner—Tony has invited someone from the M.A.G. to join us.'

'The M.A.G.?'

'A group of architects. Boston's finest, apparently. Tony has hired their top gun to design his new house.'

'*His* new house? Surely you mean... *your* new house? You're both going to live in it, aren't you?' Janey teased.

Stephanie shrugged. 'I tend to think of it as Tony's,' she said evasively. 'He bought the lot years before we met, and has very definite ideas on the kind of home he wants.'

'But after dinner tonight—' Janey cut back to their earlier conversation '—you'll have him all to yourself?'

The intercom buzzer sounded, and Stephanie's nerves jumped. 'I hope so,' she said.

'Well, that'll be nice.'

No, Stephanie reflected as she scooped up her purse, it wouldn't be nice. Hurting someone was never nice. And what she was going to say to Tony tonight would hurt him deeply.

The foyer at the Trocadero Six was wall-to-wall people. For this opening evening, it had been set up as a reception area, with a crescent-shape bar adjacent to a table laden with piping hot hors d'oeuvres. The tantalizing aroma of spicy food and rich sauces permeated the air, mingling with the scent of wine, expensive perfumes and dewy-fresh roses.

After Tony had checked their coats, they made their way to the bar. With an arm around her, he raised his voice so he could be heard over the din. 'Champagne, Steph?'

A group jostled past, throwing her against him. She

tried to draw back, but he caught her in a light embrace.

Startled, she looked up into his eyes—to find them hazed with passion. 'Darling,' he murmured, 'you look ravishing with your hair in that upswept style. I want you to come back to my place tonight, and stay over—'

Oh, Lord. 'No, Tony. But we do have to talk—'

She broke off. Somebody had come up behind her and was standing so close it made the fine hair at her nape rise on end and sent a shiver goose-bumping over her skin. She'd never before been so aware of an unseen presence.

'Gould—' a voice came from the presence '—good evening.'

Stephanie froze. She recognized that voice. No, she hastened to reassure herself, she'd just thought she recognized it. She must be wrong!

'Ah...good evening, McAllister,' Tony said.

Her heart lurched violently. She ordered it to be calm. This must be another McAllister. After all, what would the McAllister she knew—that dark and brooding recluse—be doing in a place like this?

Still, her heartbeat stuttered and staggered as if it were a road drill on the fritz as Tony turned her around.

Oh, it was her McAllister all right...and if she was surprised to see him here, it was nothing as to the shock he obviously got at seeing her: he flinched, as though she'd slapped him, and in one incredulous stark-eyed glance, took in her sophisticated hairstyle, black taffeta blouse and long velvet skirt. She stared back at him just as incredulously and felt as if she'd been caught up in a whirlwind.

Luckily Tony had chosen that moment to snag a waiter passing by with drinks, and in doing so had missed the impact of their mutual recognition. When he gave Stephanie her champagne flute, she clutched it as if it were a lifeline.

'Let's get out of here,' he shouted to McAllister over the hubbub, 'where we can talk.' With his arm still around her, he led the way through the crowd.

Stephanie could feel McAllister's eyes burning a hole in her back; she could have sworn she smelled singeing taffeta. She inhaled deeply in an effort to regulate her heartbeat. It'll be over in a few minutes, she promised herself. And if it's not, if Tony doesn't break away, then I'll tell him I'm feeling a bit faint, and suggest we go into the dining room so I can sit down. That should do it.

She realized, thankfully, that Tony was headed toward a spot close to the dining-room doors. He drew to a halt beside a fountain and a graceful arrangement of greenery. The noise of the crowd was muffled by the frondy plants, and by the splash of the cascading water.

'It's a zoo over there,' Tony said. 'Can't even hear ourselves speak. Now, for introductions. Stephanie...'

She had no option but to turn and face McAllister once more. And as she looked at him, the whirlwind caught her again. This time, she felt as if it had tossed her high in the air, and left her in freefall. In ancient jeans and a casual sweater, the Vermont artist had been a hunk. In a dark dinner suit, with a crisp white shirt, silver cuff links, and impeccably knotted striped tie, he was dynamite.

'Darling.' Tony's voice seemed to be coming from

another planet. 'This is Damian McAllister. McAllister, my fiancée, Stephanie Redford.'

Oh, Lord. Stephanie felt a sudden stab of dismay. If McAllister announced they'd already met, Tony would want to know where and when.

'Mr. McAllister,' she said quickly, extending her hand, 'it's a pleasure to meet you.'

She saw the almost imperceptible rise of his brows. But then smoothly he took her hand in his. 'Miss Redford, the pleasure is all mine. But do call me Damian.'

'And you must call me Stephanie!'

'Gould,' he drawled, never taking his eyes from her for one second, 'you're one helluva lucky man.'

'Oh, I know it! Stephanie is a treasure.'

A treasure. She could see by the cynical glint in McAllister's eyes that he might at this moment be thinking her many things, but a treasure was not one of them. How unfortunate that he should be here...tonight of all nights!

If only the architect from the M.A.G. would turn up, she reflected tautly, then Tony would tell McAllister they had a table booked for dinner, and they'd be rid of him!

'Well,' Tony said, 'we may as well go in and sit down.'

With a bright smile, Stephanie waited for him to take their leave of McAllister. To her consternation he did no such thing. Instead he guided her through the open doorway into the dining room...with the other man close on their heels. What was going on? Had McAllister also booked a table for dinner? Yes, of course, that must be it.

The maître d' approached, flourishing a clutch of cobalt leather-bound menus. He addressed Tony.

'You have a reservation, sir?'

'Gould. Table for three.'

'Come this way, please.'

It was with a sense of rising irritation that Stephanie realized McAllister was tagging along behind them as she and Tony followed the maître d' to their table. The waiter pulled back her chair and she sat down, hardly noticing when he whisked a napkin across her lap because not only did Tony take a seat, but McAllister sat down, too. At her left. And so close she could smell that familiar spicy scent of his after-shave. It made her remember...

Perspiration pricked her upper lip. Vaguely she was aware that the dining room was beginning to fill up; intensely she was aware that McAllister's eyes were on her. Nervously she toyed with a wisp of hair by her ear.

'What a magnificent sapphire!'

She started, jerked her head around to look at him and found that his gaze was fixed on her upraised hand. Quickly she let it fall but he caught it at table level.

'May I?' He turned her hand over to inspect the ring.

His hands were warm, and Stephanie could feel the blood pulsing in his veins. Could he feel the rush of blood in hers? Did the intimate contact, flesh to flesh, disturb him, as it disturbed her? If so, his gaze showed no sign of it. Flicking a glance at Tony, who was watching with an indulgent smile, he said, 'A lovely ring for a lovely lady.'

He turned his attention to Stephanie again. 'Belated

best wishes on your engagement. I was hoping to meet you at the party your fiancée held for you, but unfortunately I couldn't make it.'

'You had a bad case of flu, I heard.' Tony leaned back in his seat. 'Your secretary told mine you'd taken off for your place in Vermont. Must have been damned lonely, all on your own, over the holidays.'

McAllister had been in no hurry to release her hand. His grasp would have appeared casual to Tony; it was anything but. From under her lashes, Stephanie threw him a resentful look as she succeeded in prying her fingers free.

'I never find it lonely when I go there,' he said lazily, 'but this Christmas was specially interesting. I rescued a maiden in distress—she was beautiful, exciting...and best of all, unattached. At least—' he directed a conspiratorial smile toward Tony, a man-to-man smile that implied *You know what I mean, old buddy!* '—at least, she said she was. And who was I to call her a liar!'

Stephanie swigged back the last of her champagne though the urge to fling both the glass and its contents in his face was almost overwhelming. She wondered if he could feel the fury emanating from her. How dare he call her a liar!

But of course she had told him there was no man in her life. The memory was crystal clear in her mind. And to his credit, he had no way of knowing she had been free...at that time. Still...she'd love to take him down a peg or two.

The opportunity presented itself a second later as Tony was approached by the sommelier and became involved in conversation with him.

She turned around and looked straight into a pair

of dazzling steel blue eyes. 'Mr. McAllister,' she began, her voice as sweet as pecan pie, only to have him interrupt her.

'Damian.' His expression was mocking. 'Please.'

She curled her lip and went on in a patronizing queen-to-serf tone, 'It's been lovely meeting you, Mr. McAllister, but don't let us keep you. I know you must be anxious to get to your own table, and I'm sure the maître d' will be delighted to escort you there.'

He stared at her blankly...and then she saw a look of unholy delight come into his eyes. A low rumble of laughter came from deep in his chest, and tilting back his chair, he looked at her from under his sooty lashes, his expression so smug she could have slapped him.

'What's so damned funny?' she hissed.

The sommelier glided away and, unaware of any tension, Tony said benignly, 'Now, let's take a look at the menu.'

'Gould.' McAllister's eyes had a sardonic glint. 'Your fiancée is laboring under the impression that I'm a gate-crasher. Would you be so good as to set her straight?'

'A gate-crasher? Good Lord, Steph, how could you imagine such a thing! I assumed you'd realized—'

'Realized what?' Stephanie blinked confusedly.

'Damian is the president of the M.A.G., darling...the McAllister Architectural Group. He's an architect. The one who's going to design our new home.'

'An architect?' To her own ears Stephanie sounded as if she were an exceedingly dull-witted parrot.

'Mmm. And when I'm too busy to meet with him

you will, of course, take my place and pass on all the plans you and I have discussed in such detail over the past months. Luckily the M.A.G. offices are directly across the street from your store, so your get-togethers will be easy to arrange.'

It was almost eleven before Stephanie got home.

As Tony walked her from the parked Jag to her building, she said in a strained voice, 'I'm sorry I was such a wet blanket this evening. I've had a blinding headache.'

'Darling, I'm disappointed you didn't feel like coming back to the condo, but I understand. I did notice, soon after McAllister joined us, that you'd become deathly pale.'

She opened her purse and took out her key. She hadn't invented the migraine; it was drilling her brain, blurring her vision, making her sick. All she wanted was to lie down in a dark room, but there was something she had to do first.

She knew it wasn't the right moment but was there ever a right moment to break an engagement?

'Tony.' Her voice shook. 'There's something I need to say to you—'

'About the house? Darling, if there's anything you—'

'No, it's not about the house.' Her skin felt clammy, her legs wobbly. 'It's about our feelings for each other.'

'Steph, I know I've neglected you shamefully since the holidays, but let's leave talking about it till I get back.'

'Get back?' Stephanie stared at him confusedly.

'I have to fly out to the East Coast early tomorrow. I'm afraid I'll be gone for two or three weeks.'

'Tony.' Stephanie felt faint. 'What I have to say can't wait for two or—'

'Of course it can!' Over her protests, he took her key, opened the door, put the key into her purse and guided her inside. 'We'll have a long talk when I get b—'

'Tony, *please* listen to me. This can't w—'

He cupped her head, and trapped her mouth in a deep-delving kiss that almost smothered her.

'Now you get off to bed,' he said firmly. 'And get well. I'm depending on you to fill McAllister in on all our plans. Any problems, you can reach me through my office.'

And as she struggled to catch her breath, he left, and her pleas for him to wait echoed, unanswered, in the foyer.

Frustration intensified the poleaxing pain in her head as she sagged against the foyer wall.

She'd blown it.

She was still engaged.

And would now have to remain so till Tony got back. A woman could hardly disengage herself from a man without his being the first to know. It wouldn't be fair.

She sighed. So...she'd have to play out a charade. But only for a couple of weeks; she could handle that.

Especially knowing her decision to call off the wedding was the right one. After intensive soul-searching, she'd realized Tony could never repair the damage his ruthless ultimatum had done to their re-lationship. She was no longer in love with him...if what she'd felt for him had been love in the first place, and she was beginning to doubt that.

Still, she felt a pang of guilt. He was going to lose face when his friends and colleagues found out he'd been jilted. She felt badly about that; really badly. But there was nothing she could do about it.

He was going to be very upset, too, when he came back, if his housing project wasn't under way.

Now *that* was a matter she *could* do something about.

She pushed herself from the foyer wall and started wearily toward the elevator. It wouldn't kill her, she acknowledged with a feeling of bleak resignation, to meet with McAllister a couple of times, and pass on Tony's plans.

Surely it was the least she could do.

Under the circumstances.

She was working in the store window the next day, dismantling the Happy New Year To I And All sign that had been blinking there since the Merry Xmas To U And Yours had come down, when she had the feeling someone was watching her.

When she'd come in to work earlier, the first thing she'd done was to ascertain where the M.A.G. offices were. According to the gilt lettering on the windows, the firm took up the entire second floor of the building directly across the four-lane street.

Now, as she turned, she found her eyes caught by a movement in one of those windows. And despite the glint of sun on glass, she saw the outline of a tall figure. A man. But even as she recognized him, he moved away.

McAllister.

Her stomach did a backward flip. Swiftly she finished dismantling her sign and then hopped back down onto the floor of the store, where her assistant was unpacking Valentine's Day trappings from a huge box.

Joyce Pym was almost six feet tall, with cropped brown hair, an affable nature and boundless energy. She had been an employee at the Warmest Fuzzies for over a year, and she and Stephanie had developed a friendly working relationship.

'Joyce,' Stephanie said in a deliberately offhand manner, 'that building across the street...'

'Which one?' With a glossy red heart in her hand, Joyce paused and looked up questioningly from her task.

'The...architects' building.'

'Oh, the M.A.G. What about it?'

'Is their parking area around the back?'

'No, underground. My friend Marjorie Sutton works there. She has a parking spot in the basement.'

'I didn't know you had a friend working there.'

Joyce grinned. 'Sure, and she talks about little else! She works for the senior man—apparently he's God's gift to women. The McAllister, she calls him and Lord a'mighty, you'd never think her fifty-five and happily married, the way she goes on and on about him.'

Stephanie turned her back and started packing away the New Year lights. 'McAllister,' she said carelessly, 'I believe he's the architect Tony has hired. Damian McAllister.'

'That's him.' Joyce sighed. 'He lost his wife five winters ago, poor man. They'd only been married a few months, and to make matters worse, the poor mite was pregnant. According to Joyce, The McAllister went off the deep end and has never surfaced since.

Ashley, I believe her name was. Ashley Cabot. Her family had pots of money. But there you are.' She shook her head sadly. 'Money doesn't always guarantee happiness, does it!'

He called her the next day, just before noon.

'McAllister,' he said when she answered the phone. 'When can we meet?'

Never, she wanted to say. But didn't. 'My schedule is probably more flexible than yours. You set a time.'

'How about now?'

'Now?'

'You just told me to set a time—'

'No need to snap my head off. Just a sec.' She put the phone down, and walked to the back room where her assistant was unpacking a delivery of velvet swans. 'Joyce, can you keep an eye on the counter? I have to go out for a while.'

'Sure.'

When she picked up the receiver again, she could hear what sounded like fingertips irritably tapping a desktop. 'Mr. McAllister—'

'Damian.'

She gritted her teeth. 'Now is fine. Where shall I—'

'I'll pick you up outside your store in five minutes.' He hung up.

Stephanie tried to control a surge of temper.

Joyce wandered through. 'So,' she said, 'where are you off to, this nice sunny day? Playing hooky?'

'The McAllister and I are going to have a meeting to discuss house plans,' she said lightly. 'He's going to pick me up out front in a few minutes.'

She went through to the back to pay a visit to the washroom, and get her jacket. When she returned, she found Joyce waiting for her, her face pink with excitement.

'He's out there! And oh, Lordy...what a dreamboat!'

'Now you know why your friend keeps raving about him,' Stephanie said lightly. 'I guess you both have a weakness for dark brooding types!' She scooped up her bag and made for the door. Through the plate glass, she could see an older model silver-and-navy Mercedes idling by the curb. McAllister was sitting with his arms over the steering wheel, staring ahead, his expression distant.

'Bye, Joyce. I've no idea when I'll be back. If not by five-thirty, just lock up and go home.'

As she walked to the car, he got out, rounded the hood and opened the passenger door.

He was wearing a flannel shirt, narrow-fitting blue jeans and a beautiful tweed jacket with a steel blue fleck that picked up the color of his eyes. His expression, when he dipped a glance her way, was a shade cool.

As she moved past him to slide into her seat, the musky scent of his body and hair launched a silent attack on her senses. She cleared her throat. 'Where are we going?'

He made her wait till he had got in beside her and set the vehicle in motion before he answered.

'I'm taking you out to have a look at the site.'

'Oh.'

'Your fiancé said you haven't seen it yet.'

'No.'

'I should have thought—'

He broke off, and Stephanie turned to look at him. His jaw was shadowed; she guessed the skin would feel slightly rough to the touch. A nerve quivered somewhere deep inside her, as faint as the flutter of a butterfly's wing. The sensation was as unsettling as it was pleasurable; she clenched her stomach muscles in an effort to put a stop to it. 'Thought...what?'

'Nothing.'

'No...what?'

He threw her a sideways glance. 'If I were building a house for the woman I was going to marry—' his hands tightened on the wheel '—I'd want to take her to see the lot myself—at least the very first time, rather than have an architect fill in.'

'If you feel this is not your responsibility,' Stephanie said stiffly, 'then please drive me back to the store.'

'You misunderstand. Even if you had already checked it out with Gould, I'd still want to spend some time there with you. I need to show you where I intend to place the house, and so on. My point was—'

'Point taken.' Stephanie pushed her legs out in front of her, and stared moodily at the toes of her leather boots. 'Tony's been too busy to drive me out. His workload—'

'You don't need to make any excuses for your fiancé. I'm well aware of how Tony Gould operates.'

Now there was a statement that could be taken several ways, yet the tone in which it was spoken was noncritical. Why then did she feel as if he was implying something sinister? She sensed an underlying hostility, not only to Tony, but to her, too. Bad enough meeting him under false pretences, as she felt she was, but being with him was going to be totally unpalatable unless his attitude changed.

'There's something I'd like to clear up,' she said. 'The other night, you called me a liar. I admit I told you, in Vermont, that there was no man in my life. I just want to explain why I said—'

He jerked his head around and his expression froze her explanation before she could get it out.

'When your fiancé introduced us—' his tone was curt '— you made it clear you wanted me to forget we'd ever met before—'

'Yes, but that was because—'

'I don't give a damn what your reasons were! You say I need to know? Like hell I do! It was your choice, not mine, to keep our little interlude secret. I had nothing to hide. So let me tell you…I've put it right out of my mind. Just don't ever refer to it again. It never happened. Understand?'

Oh, she understood all right! Damian McAllister was cold and hard and overbearing; he had not one ounce of sensitivity in his whole body!

But even as she glared at his jutting profile, she couldn't help but see the lines etched around his eyes and bracketing his mouth, couldn't help remembering what Joyce had told her just a short time before: Not only had McAllister lost his wife, but he'd lost his unborn baby, too.

She had, of course, noticed those lines around his eyes and mouth before, but because she'd known little of his history, it hadn't occurred to her that they might have been etched there by pain, or by suffering.

Compassion swelled inside her and she felt the faintest smarting of tears. The man was not cold, or hard.

He was just a man with a broken heart.

CHAPTER SIX

THE building lot Tony had purchased was on a wide, maple-lined street. Several new houses were already occupied, and Stephanie thought each one was more palatial than the next.

A bitter wind was blowing, and as they got out of the car, she shivered. Zipping up her anorak, she dug her hands into her pockets.

'Well,' McAllister said abruptly, 'what do you think?'

'It's a beautiful spot. Look at those old trees at the back—they must be nice and shady in summer.'

They crossed the sidewalk and started across the lot, their feet making crunching sounds in the crisp-topped snow.

'The back of the house faces south, and will have the sun all day,' McAllister said.

'Then the kitchen should be at the rear, shouldn't it? With patio doors leading to the garden. And it'll have to be a huge modern kitchen, because Tony plans to do a lot of entertaining.' She heard the stilt-edness of her voice and it made her want to grit her teeth. How she hated this charade she was playing. And how she hated the awkwardness between herself and McAllister. She couldn't tell him she was no longer going to marry Tony but there was *something* she could do that might relax the unpleasant tension between them. She stopped walking.

Frowning, he stopped, too.

'What's up?' His tone was terse.

She took in a deep breath and spoke in a rush, so he wouldn't have time to stop her. 'I broke my engagement to Tony just before I left for Vermont at Christmas. I didn't lie to you. I *was* fancy free when I stayed at your place.'

The wind had brought a glisten to his eyes, had flipped his hair back from his brow. He stared at her, the moments ticking away silently between them as he assimilated what she'd said. She counted up to fifteen before he responded.

'Then—' his voice had a husky edge '—I apologize for calling you a liar.'

'Apology accepted.'

He stared at her some more, and she was just about to ask what he was thinking, when he said, 'I'm curious about something.'

'What?'

'You're different from the kind of woman we're all used to seeing on Tony Gould's arm—'

'And what kind would that be?'

'Rich, sophisticated, brittle.' He grinned. 'Snobbish.'

'Is there a compliment hidden in there somewhere?'

His eyes smiled at that. 'And though rarely a week goes by that his name doesn't appear on the society pages, I don't recall ever seeing your name there…before your engagement, that is. You obviously didn't move in the same circles, so where the hell did your paths cross?'

'Tony owns the block across the street from your office. About a year ago, he was thinking of selling, and he brought a prospective buyer into my store to have a look around. That's how we met.'

'And it was love at first sight?'

'For Tony, apparently.'

'And for you?'

She shrugged. 'For me, it took a little longer.'

'And you're getting married in September?'

September had been Tony's choice, not hers, but she had given in...to please him. 'How did you know that?'

'Your nephew mentioned it.'

'Jason?'

'We talked a bit, after I dropped you off.'

'He's my godson.'

'And he thinks the world of you.'

'The feeling's mutual.'

'But he doesn't care for your husband-to-be.'

'Jason told you that?'

'Not in so many words.'

'Am I right in thinking you don't like Tony very much?' she asked bluntly.

'Surely all that's important is that the woman he's going to marry likes him' was the unruffled reply.

'Yes.' She firmed her lips to contain the ironic smile that threatened to twist them. 'That is all that's important.'

'Yet...you and he fought.'

'As Shakespeare said, "The course of true love..."'

'"...never did run smooth." Still, it couldn't have been more than a tiny ripple that ruffled the smoothness in your case.'

'What makes you so sure?'

'You made up so easily.'

'How do you know we made up easily?'

'When I looked into your parents' living room before I left Rockfield, I saw Gould had already taken possession.'

'Oh.' That threw her...but not for long. 'I thought it was a big enough ripple at the time.'

'Over...what?'

She frowned, stared at him and felt like telling him to mind his own business...and would have been fully justified in doing so. But to her own surprise, she didn't.

'Tony and I had a difference of opinion about where we were going to spend Christmas. We'd promised my family we'd spend the holidays at Rockfield with them, but at Tony's party, the Whitneys invited us to go to Aspen...and Tony accepted. I was upset that he'd broken his promise—so I gave him back his ring.'

'But he turned up at Rockfield after all, because...'

'Because when he was packing for the ski trip, he realized that where he wanted to be was with me.'

McAllister didn't respond for a couple of minutes, and then, in a tone that bewildered her by its harshness, he said, 'So...what did Gould tell the Whitneys?'

'The truth, of course...that he'd already made other plans, and he'd have to turn down their invitation. He said they understood.'

'Your fiancé is quite something, isn't he!'

There was no mistaking the sarcasm in his voice. It grated on Stephanie, despite her own changed feelings for Tony, and she said tautly, 'Don't you think you're being hypocritical, taking this job, if you don't like Tony?'

'Business is business. And this is business, isn't it?'

She flinched inside, his caustic tone a hurtful attack

that put an end to the cease-fire she'd hoped was on the horizon.

'Yes,' she said, 'business is exactly what it is.'

Her body crackled with hostility as she resumed walking. 'So let's get on with it!'

He drove her back to the store an hour later, and as he watched her stalk regally over the sidewalk and open her door, he cursed under his breath.

How could he have done that? How could he have taken his disgust with Tony Gould out on her? But it had made him see red, when she'd told him Gould had followed her to Rockfield because he couldn't bear to spend Christmas without her. Bull! The man knew damned well that the Whitneys' place in Aspen had burned to the ground two days before Christmas. Paula Whitney herself had told McAllister that. When she'd called the M.A.G. to ask him if he'd design their new lodge, she'd happened to mention that Gould had actually gotten as far as the airport boarding lounge, on his way to Colorado, before she managed to track him down with the news that the skiing holiday was canceled.

What did a woman like Stephanie Redford see in that jerk! It was beyond him. But it wasn't his place to set her right; if she couldn't see it for herself, she'd just have to suffer the consequences. But he'd almost blurted out the truth. Dammit, why hadn't he? Because she would have hated him, that was why. Didn't people always hate the messenger who brought bad news?

He wished now that he'd never accepted this job. It was going to be hell, seeing her all the time. It was going to be *worse* than hell, looking into those pine green eyes, inhaling the sweet sensual fragrance of her, and all the time imagining her in bed with Tony Gould.

It was enough to drive a man to drink.

Stephanie was standing on the sidewalk at ten-thirty the following morning, admiring her new B Mine, Sweet Valentine sign, when Joyce called her in to the phone.

To her surprise, the caller was McAllister. He'd told her yesterday that he'd be in touch within a couple of days; she just hadn't expected him to phone so soon.

'Can you spare an hour or two this morning?' he asked.

'I'm afraid we're really busy right now...'

'How about this evening then, after your store closes?'

'Sure. Where do you want to meet?' She kept her tone as cool as his.

'Here. Take the elevator up—my office is just along from it.'

'See you at five-thirty, then.'

That evening, after an exhausting day, Stephanie didn't get away till well after five-thirty. By the time she'd hurried along to the intersection, crossed the wide street and raced along to the M.A.G. building, she was out of breath.

By the time the elevator had whisked her to the second floor, she felt faint. And when McAllister opened his door to her knock, she swayed.

'Hey—' his dark brows lowered in a scowl '—what's the matter?' He swept her inside, and deposited her in a roomy swivel chair in front of his desk.

Thankful to get off her feet, Stephanie sank back with a sigh. She'd never been in an architect's office before, and this one was brightly lit, spacious and tidy. Next to the mahogany desk was a drawing board with a high stool in front of it and an angled fluorescent lamp above. And along one wall was a stretch of wide windows that had a view—as she knew only too well—of the Warmest Fuzzies Toy Store.

She realized McAllister was holding out a glass of water. She took it, drank some, and gave back the glass.

'Thanks,' she said.

He set the glass on the desk. 'How are you feeling?'

'I'm all right. Just dizzy, for a moment.'

'When did you last eat?'

'You know,' she managed a faint smile, 'I don't think I've had anything solid since breakfast. All hell broke loose this morning, and never let up. I did have a coffee at lunch time...'

'Idiot! Look, why don't we go out and have a bite to eat? There's a great pizza joint just a few blocks away. We can just as well talk there as here.'

She hesitated, but when her stomach emitted a warning growl, she grimaced. 'I can't argue with that, can I!'

He grinned. ''Fraid not!' Crossing the room, he scooped up his jacket and swung it on.

'Okay,' he said, 'let's go—oh, damn. I was expecting someone to return a call.' He thought for a moment, and then said, 'Tell you what...I'll try calling again. Maybe they're home now.'

Moving back to the desk, he picked up his phone

and pressed a speed dial button. Hitching his hip onto the edge of the desk, he glanced over at Stephanie, and put his hand over the mouthpiece. 'I don't expect there'll be—oh.' He nodded to her, and took his hand from the mouthpiece. 'Hi, it's Damian. I got your message. Tomorrow's okay for dinner, but I'll be a little late.' Stephanie heard a feminine voice at the other end, and then McAllister said, 'I'll pick you up at eight-thirty.' Again, the woman started to speak, but he broke in. 'I can't talk now, Tiffany. I'm on the way out the door with a client. I'll see you tomorrow.'

Surely there were hundreds of Tiffanys in Boston, but Stephanie could think of only one: socialite Tiffany Whitney. Beautiful and sophisticated, the thirty-year-old blonde was from one of Boston's oldest and most respected families. She and Tony had been an item at one time, but though that had been several years before Stephanie met him, Tiffany had made it clear to Stephanie the first time they'd met that she'd love to get her opal-tipped claws into him again. Now, it seemed, she was hitting the social circuit with someone else.

And that someone else was Damian McAllister.

Suddenly Stephanie felt chilled.

Though why that should be, she really didn't care to ask herself.

'I can see by your drooling expression that we've come to the right place! So...what's it to be?'

Stephanie met McAllister's eyes over the checkered tablecloth at Poppa's Perfect Pizzas, and felt the by-now familiar but none the less disturbing stab of attraction. 'I, er, don't like anchovies. Do you?'

'Yeah, but I can live without them. Can you live without pineapple?'

Stephanie screwed up her face, and appeared to consider it. 'Well, I guess...'

'Any other no-nos?'

She shook her head.

'Right,' he said, 'it's a trade.' Handing over the menus, he said to the waiter, 'We'll have one large Poppa's Special, hold the anchovies and pineapple.' He glanced at Stephanie. 'What would you like to drink?'

'Coffee, please.'

He said to the waiter, 'And two coffees. Thanks.'

He tilted back his chair and looked at her lazily.

Feeling uncomfortable, she turned her head, and stared out into the darkened parking lot. When she turned back again, it was to find he was still watching her. Why did he seem to have the upper hand, even though they weren't even talking? she wondered. Was he actually enjoying her discomfiture? He certainly seemed to be. Well, perhaps she could make him feel a little uncomfortable, for a change.

She waited till the waiter had served their coffee, then she said, fixing him with a steady gaze, 'You were very quick to condemn me when you thought I'd lied to you in Vermont...yet when I asked you at that time what you did for a living, you said...and I quote...''I draw.''' Her tone was liberally laced with accusation as she went on, 'It must have been clear to you that I assumed you were an artist living there year-round. Why the half-truth?'

She had expected him to look guilty. Instead, to her irritation, he grinned. 'I don't think you want to know the answer to that.'

'Try me,' she snapped.

'You won't like it.'

'Let me by the judge.'

He shrugged. 'When you told me about your store, I realized we were almost neighbours and that you, of course, didn't know it. I didn't want to get involved in any emotional entanglement, and I thought that if I gave in to temptation and took you to bed, there was a danger that once back in Boston, you might—'

'*What?* If you gave in to temptation and took me to bed? I can't believe what I'm hearing! Let me tell you, Mr. God's-gift-to-women McAllister, that sleeping with you was the furthest thing from my mind—and to imply that if you had managed to seduce me, I would then make a nuisance of myself once we got back here, is an absolutely foul thing to say!' She leaned across the table and glared at him. 'I would never get involved with a man who doesn't believe in all the things I believe in...and that includes Christmas!'

'Hey, hold on there!' He put his hands up to stop her and because she'd run out of steam, she stopped. But her cheeks didn't lose their hot color, nor did her fists unclench, nor did her heartbeat slow down. If she'd had a custard pie in her hand, she'd have slapped it right in his face. 'I warned you,' he went on mildly, 'that you wouldn't like it, but you insisted—'

'Excuse me.' The waiter pushed aside the vase of plastic daffodils centered on the table, and placed an enormous, delicious-smelling pizza between them. 'My name is Alfonse, I'm your waiter this evening. Enjoy.'

She hated when waiters did that: My name is

Alfonse. Who the heck needed to know their waiter's name! Seething with ill will, Stephanie narrowed her eyes, and glared at the pizza. It looked absolutely scrumptious, the deep crust just the way she liked it, the pepperoni and vegetables sizzling in a tantalizingly gooey bed of cheese. She wanted to throw it. She wanted to eat it.

'Go ahead.' McAllister's voice was as smooth as silk-velvet but she could tell, by the underlying laughter, that he had read her mind. 'Your choice. There's a third one, of course. You could just stomp out of here in a towering rage, and leave me to scoff the whole thing myself.'

Her stomach growled. Her mouth watered. She picked up the spatula, and helped herself to the largest slice in the pan. Eyes fixed on the plate, she handed him the spatula, snatching her hand back in disgust when his fingers brushed deliberately against her own.

'Enjoy,' he said, echoing the words of the waiter.

'Hmph!' she muttered, through a mouthful of pizza.

CHAPTER SEVEN

SNOW was drifting down in feathery flakes when they came out of Poppa's. It must have been falling for some time, Stephanie mused; at least an inch of new snow lay over the parking lot. She had become so engrossed in the discussion she and McAllister had had about housing design—after her temper had subsided!—that she had been oblivious to the change in the weather. And she'd even forgotten, once in a while, to feel guilty about pulling the wool over his steel blue eyes, as she'd listened to him talk about solariums, indoor pools, skylights, solar heat, atriums...his topics had been endless, and endlessly fascinating.

Now as snowflakes drifted onto her warm cheeks, she shivered, and flicked up the collar of her jacket.

'I guess your car's parked at the store,' he said. 'I'll drive you back there.'

'I don't have a car at present—'

'You didn't replace your van?'

'Not yet. I've been using the bus...so we can part company here. There's a bus stop just around the corner.'

'I'll drive you.' He grasped her elbow and ushered her toward his car.

She tried to tug her arm free but his grip was secure. 'It's not necessary,' she protested. 'I can easily—'

'I'm not leaving you standing around in the dark.'

He unlocked the passenger door and after a brief mental struggle, she surrendered to the temptation of a drive home. With a murmured 'Thanks,' she slipped by him and sat down. He shut her door, before rounding the car and taking his own seat. Once he had fastened his belt, he started the engine.

'So—' with deft fingers he turned the wheel and drove out onto the street '—Gould's place?' He glanced at her.

She stared at him. 'I beg your pardon?'

'That's where you want me to take you,' he said impatiently. 'You do live with him, don't you?'

'That's quite an assumption to make!'

'You're engaged to the man.' He shrugged his wide shoulders. 'It's not much of a stretch to conclude you're sleeping with him.'

This was not a discussion she wanted to have with Damian McAllister—and even if she hadn't been planning to break her engagement, there was no way she would have admitted to him that she had never slept with Tony. It was none of his business…and couldn't she just see those black eyebrows shoot up if she told him she was still a virgin?

'One can sleep with a man without having to live with him,' she said pertly. 'But for the record, I share an apartment with a friend. A woman friend.'

She gave him her address, and then averted her head, making it plain that the conversation, as far as she was concerned, was at an end.

He made no attempt to start it up again, and there was silence between them till he had brought the car to a halt, fifteen minutes later, outside her apartment building. When he put a hand out to open his door, she said quickly,

'Don't bother to get out. I can—'

'No problem.'

With snow drifting down onto his hair and his jacket shoulders he rounded the car and opened her door.

Together they walked up the path to the front door. On the stoop, with her fingers hovering on the catch of her purse, she looked up at him.

'Thank you for dinner,' she said, 'and for the drive. When should we get together again?' She tried for a businesslike tone, which was difficult, with his eyes fixed on her in a way that made her feel as if she was being held underwater.

'When would you like us to get together again?' With a fingertip, he brushed away a snowflake that had landed on the tip of her nose.

She jerked back as if she'd been stung. 'That's up to you, isn't it?' Her voice held an edge of anger, but the anger was directed at herself, at her reaction to him, though he would have no way of knowing that.

'How about Saturday? That'll give me time to work on some of the things we talked about tonight, make some rough sketches for you to look at. Call my secretary—she'll set up a time. Afternoon okay for you?'

'Should be.' She opened her purse, and bent her head over as she hunted for her keys. Her hair tumbled forward, getting in her way, but before she could raise a hand to sweep it aside, McAllister reached out and drew back the mass of curls. The warm pads of his fingertips brushed her neck, and she froze. She heard him catch his breath, felt his fingers linger on her skin. Adrenaline whirled through her like a windstorm, almost knocking her off her feet.

With a muffled protest, she pushed his hand away from her neck, and fell back against the door.

His gaze trapped hers. 'You feel it, too, don't you,' he said, and it was a statement, not a question.

'What do you expect me to say?' Her response came out weakly.

'I expect you to admit that there's something going on between us—'

'There's nothing going on between us,' she said, knowing it was a lie. How she wished she'd worn her hair twisted back, instead of hanging loose; then this whole episode wouldn't have happened. Would it? Or would he have found some other reason to...touch her?

'But there could be, couldn't there? If you weren't engaged—'

'You mean an affair? It would have to be that, wouldn't it, because I know you're not in the market for anything more serious. No, Mr. McAllister, I would not be interested in having an affair with you—'

'Steph! Hi, there!'

Startled, Stephanie jerked her head around, and saw Janey hiking along toward them in the snow, her long red hair and her emerald parka white with flakes. Her impish face was alight with a grin, a grin that widened as her open gaze skimmed appreciatively over McAllister.

'Hi, Janey.' Stephanie hoped her friend wouldn't sense the tension sparking in the air. She glanced at the white, gold-embossed cardboard box Janey was carrying, and couldn't help a smile. 'You've been to the CakeTin, I see.'

She heard McAllister clear his throat; the man was

not about to be ignored. Besides, where were her manners?

'Janey,' she said, 'this is Damian McAllister—he's the architect I told you about. Mr. McAllister—' she saw him raise a mocking brow at her formality '—this is Janey Martin.' Why did she find it so hard to call him Damian? Even in her thoughts, he was McAllister. Why? Was she afraid of the intimacy implied by the use of his first name?

Janey pumped McAllister's hand energetically and subjected his face to a penetrating scrutiny. She must have liked what she saw, Stephanie reflected, because she said to him, 'I've just bought a calorie-laden white chocolate mousse with dark chocolate shavings and fresh strawberries. Care to come up and have some coffee and dessert?'

'Janey.' Stephanie gave her friend a look that should have made her squirm, but obviously didn't. 'Mr. McAllister must be in a hurry to get home—'

'No.' He slanted a killer smile at Janey. 'I'm in no hurry. Besides, I have this awful weakness for chocolate mousse…not to mention redheads,' he added with a chuckle that was greeted by a delighted hoot from Janey.

A weakness for redheads indeed! Resentment surged through Stephanie in a hot crimson tide. The man was a womanizer of the first order. A minute ago, he'd made it plain he'd like to have an affair with her; now in the blink of an eye, he'd switched his attention to Janey!

She fumed all the way up in the elevator, and once they reached the apartment, she excused herself curtly and went through to her bedroom. The man was Janey's guest; *she* could entertain him! Flinging off her jacket, she whirled it onto the bed, and stalked into the bathroom.

She glared at her reflection in the mirror, and then savagely dragged her hair back from her face and secured it with a rubber band. But as she stared defiantly at her anger-bright eyes, she realized that the moment McAllister saw her starkly rearranged hairstyle, he'd guess the reason for the change; and he'd realize just how upset she'd been when he'd slipped his fingers through the glossy strands.

With an irate mutter, she snatched off the rubber band again, and swept her bristle brush through her hair till it crackled. There, she thought fiercely, try to touch that now and see what happens!

With a bit of luck, he'd be electrocuted!

It took several long minutes before she had cooled down. Only when she felt in control of herself once more did she return to the living room.

Janey and McAllister were standing together by the coffee table—and they were laughing. Uproariously. Over *what*?

Janey spotted her first. 'Oh, there you are!' The words came out on a gurgling giggle. 'Coffee'll be ready in a minute. Let's get started on our dessert.'

Three plates were on the coffee table, each with a generous helping of mousse. McAllister remained standing till Stephanie and Janey were seated with their plates, and then, even as Stephanie braced herself, expecting him to sit beside her on the sofa, he perched instead on the arm of Janey's overstuffed chair.

Janey scooped a dainty forkful of mousse into her mouth, and a moment later said, dreamily, 'Blissful!' She looked up at McAllister as she spoke, and

Stephanie had to wonder if she was referring to the dessert...or to how it felt to be sitting in such close proximity to this hunk who professed to be so crazy about redheads.

'Damian and I,' Janey went on, glancing across at Stephanie, 'have discovered we have exactly the same taste in movies. He has seen *Four Weddings and a Funeral* even more times than I have—'

'And another thing!' McAllister waved his fork to emphasize his words—in a decidedly unmannerly fashion, Stephanie decided sourly. 'Janey and I have discovered that we both listen to the same group on our headphones...The Proclaimers...when we're jogging.'

'And get this, Steph!' Janey's eyes fairly sparkled. 'Damian and I have actually been going to the same bookstore for years and we both adore the Mystery section—'

'And Janey's favorite writer is P.D. James—'

'Damian's is, too!' Janey finished triumphantly. 'Isn't it just too much?'

The mousse in Stephanie's mouth tasted like mud. Good grief, Janey, she wanted to scream, these are all my favorite things—I was the one who dragged you to that movie so you could see Hugh Grant. I was the one who introduced you to The Proclaimers' music. I was the one who gave you your first P.D. James novel! If anyone can claim to share those interests with McAllister, I'm that one!

'Fascinating.' She swallowed the mouthful of mud. 'Oh, by the way, I noticed Hugh Grant's latest movie is premiering at the plaza on Friday night—since you're both such fans, why don't you take it in together?'

If she'd thought to put McAllister on the spot, she was mistaken. He took her up on the suggestion immediately.

'Friday night?' He glanced down at Janey, his gaze keen. 'Can you make it?'

'Sure I can—'

'Don't you have a standing date to go out with *Fred* on Friday nights?' The words were out before Stephanie could stop them.

'*Pfft*, Fred!' Janey gave an airy wave of her hand. 'He's history. So, Damian...the early show?'

'What the heck.' McAllister grinned. 'Let's go out for dinner first and go to the late show. I'll take you to a terrific pizza place. Steph and I ate there tonight, and she can recommend it...right, Steph?'

For a minute, Stephanie could do nothing but stare. It had all happened so fast—

'Steph?' Janey's voice seemed to be coming from far away.

'Mmm?' Stephanie came to her senses. 'Oh, the pizza place. Sure, I can recommend it.' She tried to move her mouth in a smile, but her lips were bound and determined not to cooperate. In the end, she did somehow manage to quirk the edges up, but only ever so slightly, ever so briefly. She should have been happy for Janey, that she was going out on a date with this very gorgeous man. She wasn't. She felt depressed. Even miserable. But why should that be? It wasn't as if she wanted McAllister for herself— good Lord, not only was the man a confirmed bachelor, but he didn't even celebrate Christmas!

Perhaps, she reflected, what rankled was that he hadn't had the good manners to include her in the invitation.

Not that she would have accepted. No, certainly not. But for all his faults—and they were legion!—she had never known him to be guilty of bad manners.

This inconsistency in his behavior puzzled her.

Puzzled her deeply.

When McAllister left, Janey was bubbling with excitement, and eager to talk about her upcoming date. But Stephanie—albeit feeling as low as the lowest worm as she did—pleaded a headache and went straight to bed.

In the morning, Janey had already left for work by the time Stephanie got up.

The redhead had been running the Rubber Ducky Day Care for the past five years, and the center opened at seven every weekday. This morning, Stephanie was glad Janey wasn't around. Guiltily glad. She still hadn't gotten used to the idea of her friend and McAllister going out together...and yet she refused to let her mind come to grips with why she should find the situation so unsettling.

On Friday, when Stephanie got home from work, Janey was already dressed to go out. She was standing at the fake fireplace in the living room, admiring her reflection in the mirror above the mantelpiece. At Stephanie's bright, 'Hi, I'm home!' she turned, a beaming smile on her face.

'Steph, I've been waiting for you!' She spun around gaily to show off her outfit. 'What do you think? I went shopping in my lunch hour, and I just couldn't resist!'

'You look stunning,' Stephanie said—and meant it. The clinging terra cotta sweater and matching stretch pants showed off Janey's curvy little figure to perfection. 'New boots, too?' She nodded toward the elegant cream boots into which Janey had tucked the pants.

'The works! But hey—' Janey's eyes sparkled '—it's an investment, right?' She threw her hand up in the air and spun around again several times. 'Who knows where this night might lead!' Breathlessly she collapsed into her overstuffed armchair. 'It could be the start of something big! So—' she grinned up at Stephanie '—what are you up to tonight?'

'Tony's back.' Her voice sounded flat; she tried to put a lilt in it as she went on, 'We're meeting for dinner.'

'Great!' Janey jumped to her feet. 'Oh, and I've splurged on something else! A bottle of Wild Ecstasy—guaranteed to turn a man into a sex slave in three minutes flat. On my salary I can't really afford it, but what the heck, *carpe diem* and all that. Oh, Lord...I forgot to put on my earrings...and Damian's on his way up...it's a wonder you didn't bump into him in the lobby. Get the door when he knocks?' she called over her shoulder.

Feeling punch-drunk, Stephanie threw her purse down onto the sofa. Janey had spent her day with dozens of rambunctious preschoolers; where did she get her energy from? Her own day at the store hadn't been overly busy, yet she felt as drained as an empty bathtub.

Though it was expected, the brisk *rat-tatat* on the door made her jump. She exhaled a frustrated breath and stalked to the door, where she peeked through the peephole to check that the person out there was indeed Janey's date...and was glad she had. The secret inspection gave her a moment to catch her breath before facing him, because the sight of McAllister in a black leather jacket and a black turtleneck sweater had made her throat threaten to close.

Furious with herself, she snatched the door open. 'Come in.' Her tone was frosty.

He raised his eyebrows. 'Having a bad hair day?'

She slammed the door and flounced past him into the living room. 'Sit down,' she snapped, waving toward the sofa. 'Janey's almost ready. Now if you'll excuse me, I've just got in from work and—'

'Hang on a sec.'

Scowling, she turned around. 'What?'

'I never did thank you for the teddy bear.' He raked back his rain-damp hair in an absent gesture. 'I found it that night, when I got back from Rockfield. Why did you—'

'It was just an impulse.'

His eyes narrowed. 'One you now regret?'

'I can't answer that, can I...because I don't know if the gift was welcome. For all I know, you may have a cupboardful of bears already, saved from your childhood.'

His eyelids flickered. 'No,' he said, 'I have kept nothing that reminds me of my childhood.'

An odd tension had quivered into place between them, one she hadn't felt before. *Why?* she wanted to ask. *Why have you kept nothing?* Most people kept at least one or two mementos from their younger years. But she sensed that if she asked the question, his expression would become shuttered, and she would get no answer. So instead, she said, 'If you don't want it, feel free to give it away to—'

'My pillow smelled of your perfume. When I woke up the next morning, before I opened my eyes, while

I was still drowsy, I thought you must be lying beside me.'

Stephanie felt as if he'd pulled the rug from right under her feet. She put a hand on the back of the chair beside her, to steady herself. An image of herself, and this man, lying in his bed, rocked something inside her in a way she'd never experienced before. 'Why are you talking like this to me?' The words came out huskily.

He walked over to her. She knew she should step back, but she was powerless to move.

'Have you any idea how it felt, when I realized I was still dreaming?' There was anger in his tone, as there was in his eyes. He grasped her shoulders, pulled her toward him, their faces so close she could feel the warmth of his minty-fresh breath on her lips. 'And when I remembered that you were already spoken for?'

She wrenched herself free, her face pale. 'What you ought to be remembering is that you're here to pick up Janey, not me.' Her voice was as wobbly as her legs. 'You're some kind of a jerk, McAllister, making a hit on your date's flatmate. I just hope Janey knows what she's getting into.'

She fled from the room, misery welling inside her. She'd reached her own bedroom and had just hurried inside when she heard her friend call from the hallway.

'See you later, Steph!'

'Later,' she echoed faintly, and shut the door fast behind her.

She leaned back against the wooden panels, her breathing low and ragged. She heard Janey laugh, heard McAllister's low voice, heard them laugh together.

And then they were gone.

'Darling.' Tony's eyes were serious as they met Stephanie's over the restaurant table. 'I missed you terribly. And it brought home to me how screwed up my priorities had become. From now on, we'll be spending *much* more time together.'

Stephanie struggled to control her escalating panic. They'd finished dinner, and she hadn't yet found the right moment to tell Tony the wedding was off.

'I'm pleased,' he said, 'that you and McAllister have had a couple of meetings already. From what you've told me, the two of you have covered quite a bit of ground.'

'Yes.'

'You find him compatible?'

'Oh…sure. We had our second meeting over a pizza, and he drove me home afterward. Actually—' she forced a light laugh '—he and Janey met and hit it off—they've gone out on a date this evening. Dinner and the movies.'

Tony's expression was doubtful. 'I shouldn't have thought her his style—your friend's very different from McAllister's late wife. Ashley Cabot was a thoroughbred—all nerves and fire…one very classy lady indeed. I hope Janey won't get stars in her eyes and let them blind her. The man is not in the marriage market.'

The marriage market. What a perfect opening. Tony, she would say, I'd like to talk to you about that. Marriage, that is. Our marriage. She braced her-

self, feeling suddenly calm and ready, and waited for
him to finish what he was saying.

'...and a confirmed bachelor. He takes women out
but makes it clear from the beginning that he's not
interested in settling down. A prime example is Tiff
Whitney—'

'Tony Gould, are you taking my name in vain?'

Stephanie snapped up her head as she heard the
husky voice, and felt a stab of frustration when she
saw Tiffany Whitney, exquisite in bias-cut satin, looking down at them.

The blonde's timing couldn't have been worse.

'Tiff!' Tony got to his feet.

'Yes, sweetie, no other. Hi, Stephanie.' Without
waiting for a response, the blonde addressed Tony
again.

'I haven't seen you for ages.' She pouted. 'Where
did you disappear to over Christmas?'

Tony looked strangely agitated. 'I, er, drove up to
Vermont and spent the holidays with Steph and her
parents.'

'That must have been nice for you,' Tiffany said to
Stephanie. 'If it hadn't been for the fire, you'd have
been up in Vermont all by yourself—'

'Tiff,' Tony broke in urgently, 'I've been out of
town, and Steph and I have quite a bit to discuss tonight, about our new house, so if you don't mind...'

But Tiffany was in no hurry to move on. 'Damian's
your architect, isn't he?' she said to him. '*Great*
choice. We've hired him, too, to design our new lodge
at Aspen.'

'You're building a second lodge?' Stephanie said
politely.

'To replace the one that burned down just before

Christmas.' Tiffany's tone held a hint of impatience. 'Lord, that could have been such a tragedy if the fire had happened a couple of days later! As you know, we'd invited twelve guests for the week—and—' she turned to Tony '—I heard you'd actually gotten as far as the airport before Mom managed to contact you and tell you the ski party was off.'

Stephanie stared at Tony through eyes that were stark with disbelief. 'The lodge burned down?' Her voice shook. 'The party was canceled? But you said—'

'Steph.' Tony stood up abruptly. 'Calm down, darling.' He pulled her to her feet. 'Tiff, this has come as a shock to Steph...I didn't tell her about the fire, knowing how upset she'd be and that she'd react in exactly this way. Would you please excuse us? I'm going to take her home.'

Tony's fingers bit into her arms as if they were steel claws, but Stephanie was barely aware of them. He wanted to get her out of there before she made a scene. She was not about to make a scene. In order to make a scene, one had to care. She felt nothing at all. Only a cold, dead emptiness.

And the bitter realization that breaking her engagement was now going to be the easiest thing in the world.

CHAPTER EIGHT

STEPHANIE had just opened the store on Monday morning when the phone rang. Joyce picked it up.

'If it's for me,' Stephanie whispered quickly, 'just take a message.'

Joyce nodded. 'Warmest Fuzzies,' she said into the mouthpiece. 'Joyce speaking.' She paused for a moment, and then said, 'She can't come to the phone right now, Mr. McAllister. May I take a message? Right, I'll tell her.'

She put down the phone. 'He wants you to call and set up an appointment—for early in the week, if possible.'

'Thanks.' The doorbell pinged and an elderly woman came in. 'Will you take care of the customer, Joyce? I'll go through and put on the coffee.'

What was she going to do about McAllister? she wondered as she poured water into the coffeemaker. Wasn't it up to *Tony* to contact him, and inform him she would no longer be involved in the planning of the house? Tony would, of course, continue with his scheme to build; it had always been his project, not hers. The fact that she would not be moving into the finished house with him was his own fault.

She shuddered as she remembered the ugly scene that had taken place outside her apartment building when she'd told him she wasn't going to marry him—'

'Stephanie?' Joyce's voice came from the doorway. 'Whatever's wrong?'

'Oh—' Stephanie grimaced '—nothing. Well, not quite nothing.' She spread out her ringless left hand, and when Joyce stared, uncomprehendingly, she told her about the broken engagement.

She'd already told Janey. And she'd phoned her parents, who had taken the news surprisingly well. And when she'd talked with Jason later, he'd whispered that her mom was actually pleased, because though she'd liked Tony well enough, she'd felt in her heart that he wasn't the right man for Steph— which had made Stephanie feel a whole lot better.

Joyce *cluck-clucked* a bit and gave Stephanie a warm hug, and after murmuring something about 'hundreds of better fish on the beach,' she took herself off to the toilet.

Stephanie went through to the front, to find the shop deserted. She picked up the phone, and dialed the M.A.G.

She had expected a secretary to answer; to her dismay, she heard a familiar voice say, 'McAllister.'

'It's Stephanie Redford.' Her fingers were suddenly slick around the receiver. 'I got your message. Look, I won't be seeing you this week—you should talk to Tony about—'

'Can't you take an hour or two off? Are you so busy—'

'Yes…I mean, no.' Lord, this was difficult. 'Call Tony. He's back now, and he'll explain. I won't be taking any part in the discussions from now on. You'll be dealing only with Tony—'

'Is this because I took Janey out? For God's sake, I didn't think you had it in you to be so petty! Besides, as I recall, you were the one to suggest I take her to the movies. At any rate, I don't have time to play games. If you and your fiancé want your house to be ready for September, you're going to have to move some!'

'I said, call Tony.' Stephanie's voice was cold. 'From now on, all your consultations will be with him. I shall have no part in it because—'

'Because you're annoyed with me. Listen, you can't let your emotions get in the way in the business world.' His tone had become as cold as her own. 'So you were jealous because I took your friend out— tough beans! Just don't let your feelings of spite screw up our working relationship—'

'Phone Tony,' she said steadily.

'To hell with that! You're in no hurry to get the house finished? Fine. I have other clients—clients who, thank God, appreciate the fact that time is money. Call me once you've gotten over your little tantrum.'

'I—'

'Call me when you're ready to act like an adult. Till then, don't bother me!' And he slammed down the phone.

Stephanie didn't, of course, call him…and she had no way of knowing in the next few weeks whether or not Tony had contacted him.

With a determined effort, she blotted out all thoughts of both men, which wasn't too difficult at work, as she was kept busy, but in the evenings it was harder.

Janey never mentioned McAllister, and Stephanie had no idea if the two were dating…and would have bitten off her tongue rather than ask. Janey did seem to be going out more often than usual, though, and one Saturday, when she came floating in around midnight with a dreamy look in her eyes, Stephanie clicked off the TV show she'd been watching, and asked the question she'd sworn would never pass her lips.

'Are you seeing Damian McAllister?'

Janey's dreamy look faded. She took off her jacket, and dropped it onto a chair. Crossing to the fireplace, she stood with her back to it, and fixed her gaze on her friend.

'No,' she said quietly, 'I'm not. Our movie date was a one-shot deal.'

Stephanie felt her cheeks turn warm. 'I'm sorry. I know I put him on the spot. It was very rude.'

With a weary gesture, Janey shoved back her hair. 'You didn't put him on the spot. We would have gone out on a date even if you hadn't suggested we take in that movie.'

Stephanie swallowed. 'So…you were instantly attracted to each other.' Why did she find that notion so painful? 'Then why haven't you gone out again?'

'Steph, let me get something off my chest.' Janey sat down on the chair opposite Stephanie, and leaned forward, her expression serious. 'That night, when I came back from the CakeTin and came up on you and Damian at the front door…well, let's just say that the electricity between the two of you could have lit up the whole of Boston—'

'Janey, I don't want to listen to—'

'And when we came up here, and you took off into your room—apparently upset because Damian had accepted my invitation…he and I talked. And it became obvious within seconds that we both thought Tony Gould was the wrong man for you. And we both hated to see you make a mistake by marrying him.' Her chin tilted stubbornly. 'We decided to do something about it. Before it was too late.'

Stephanie stared disbelievingly. The date had been arranged for the sole purpose of making her *jealous?* Humiliation quickly flared into anger. 'So even had I not pushed him into asking you out, you'd have gone out anyway? Well, *that* takes a weight off my mind.' Her tone was icy cold, and heavy with sarcasm. 'And here I was agonizing over having been merely *rude,* when all the time the pair of you were deceitful and sly and treacherous and—'

'We had the best of intentions, Steph—'

Stephanie surged to her feet, her eyes burning with tears. 'And that's supposed to make it all right...that my best friend betrays me?'

Janey brushed aside the insults. 'Damian likes you, Steph.' Her tone was sorrowful. 'I mean...*really* likes you.'

'Oh, he may *want* me—' tight-lipped, and fighting her tears, Stephanie stalked to the window '—but that's all.' She pulled back the curtain, and peered down grimly through her blurred gaze.

'It's more than that—'

She whirled around. 'I've just come out of one disastrous relationship, Janey. I'm not ready for another—specially with someone like him.'

'Someone like him? What does that mean?'

'I want to get married.' Her anger had dissipated, as quickly as it had arisen, leaving her feeling shaky and helpless. 'I want the little house, the picket fence, the 2.4 kids...the whole ball of wax. I'll not settle for less. Damian McAllister's been married once, and he's made it clear he's not planning to go to the altar again. Even supposing I were interested in him, which I'm not saying I am, I'd never go out with him. What would be the point?'

'But if he fell in love with you, surely he'd—'

'Janey.' Her voice had steadied. 'The man doesn't even celebrate Christmas! It would take nothing short of a miracle to change him into the kind of man I want. Besides, my judgment's off. Look how wrong I was about Tony. No, I plan to wait a while before I throw myself back into the marriage market—perhaps, given time, my judgment will improve to the point where I can trust it again.' She took in a deep breath. 'So—' she forced a smile '—tell me who is responsible for the dreamy look that was in your eyes when you came in.'

Janey must have seen that their discussion about McAllister was over. And though her eyes had been troubled, they soon began to brighten as she told Stephanie about the new man in her life, someone she'd met through the parents of one of her day-care children.

Stephanie rejoiced in her friend's uncomplicated happiness, but even as she listened to her, she found herself wondering if McAllister had found out yet that she and Tony were no longer an item.

If he had, he would know she was free. And surely he must know by now? But if indeed he did, he had made no effort to contact her.

She had just told Janey she wouldn't date the man even if he called; then why did she feel so piqued by the fact that he hadn't!

*   *   *

'I've been searching the mystery section for James West's *Untimely Graves*,' Stephanie told the gum-chewing clerk behind the bookstore counter, 'but you don't seem to have a copy on the shelves.'

'Let me check.' The clerk looked bored as she pressed a few buttons on her computer keyboard and stared for a moment at the monitor before looking up again. 'Sorry, *Untimely Graves* is one of his earlier books and it's now out of print. I doubt you'll find a copy anywhere.'

She flicked her gaze past Stephanie, and preened herself visibly as she addressed the next customer. 'Good morning, sir.' Her smile was ingratiating.

Wrapped up in her disappointment, Stephanie turned away, only to find herself trapped by the man behind her...who showed no signs of budging.

She lifted her head, a cool 'Excuse me' on her lips, but the words died unuttered.

The man was McAllister.

He was wearing a teal bomber jacket with jeans and a beautiful taupe sweater, and energy and good health positively radiated from him. His tanned skin glowed, his clear eyes sparkled...and his dark hair was wind-blown, just begging to be smoothed. Stephanie's fingers ached to oblige. She curled her hands into fists at her side.

'You're looking for *Untimely Graves?*' he said. 'I'll lend you my copy.'

Her senses reeled from his tantalizingly familiar male scent. 'What are you doing here?' The question came out breathlessly.

He raised his brows. 'Surely you recall Janey's telling you this was my bookstore of choice?'

'Yes...but—'

'So...I come here often. I read a lot. Now, about the book—'

'I read the first few chapters at your place, and I hate starting a good book and not being able to finish it—'

'But you're having a hard time tracking it down. I'll phone the woman who caretakes my place in Vermont, have her root my copy out and courier it to you.'

'Thank you.' Stephanie's tone was as stiff as her body had become. 'But you know what Shakespeare said. "Neither a borrower, nor a lender be."'

'Ah, but Pythagoras said, "Friends share all things," and I think if we worked on it, we could qualify as fr—'

'Besides,' she blurted out, 'I don't think you really want to part with that particular book, even temporarily. It seemed to...mean a lot to you.'

A shadow darkened his expression for a moment, but it passed so quickly she decided it must have been a trick of the light. When he spoke, his voice was steady.

'You're a book lover,' he said. 'I'd trust you to—'

'Next *please!*' the clerk said sharply.

'—look after it.' McAllister dropped a hardback copy of Dick Francis's latest bestseller on the counter.

'It's okay,' she said. 'If I can't find a copy to buy, I'll check it out of the library. It's just that I have all West's other books, and I'd like to add *Untimely Graves* to my collection. But thanks anyway, for the offer.'

'Hang on a sec till I pay for this.' He reached into his hip pocket for his wallet. 'And I'll buy you a coffee.'

He took a Visa card from his wallet, and moved past Stephanie to hand it over the counter to the sales-clerk. While his back was turned, Stephanie slipped away.

The store was jammed with shoppers and browsers, and it took her a few moments to weave her way through the crowd. Once outside, she saw a bus about to leave from a stop in front of the store. She set off at a run, and managed to jump aboard, just before it set off.

Friends, he had said. If they worked at it, they could become friends. But she could never be just friends with him. And anything more was out of the question.

Ten minutes and one bus transfer later, she was sitting in a quiet corner of the Comfort Zone, her favourite Espresso bar. A copy of the Sunday paper was spread out on the small table, a mug of cappuccino wrapped in her hands.

She sipped from her mug, and started reading.

McAllister tucked his copy of the Sunday paper under his arm, paid for his cappuccino and started across the coffee bar towards his quarry.

She had draped her jacket over the back of her chair, and he could see she was wearing a navy-and-white striped shirt and dress pants. Her hair was loose, and a tumble of chocolate brown curls had fallen forward as she leaned over her paper. She pushed them back absently, revealing her brow, and the sweet curve of her cheek.

Her beauty did odd things to McAllister's heart.

As it always had done.

Which was why, ever since their last phone encounter, when he'd harshly told her to grow up, he'd stayed away from her. But when he'd caught sight of her unexpectedly in the bookstore, a rush of heady excitement had obliterated all sense of caution and self-preservation. *He wanted to spend time with her.* Was that so bad? Just to have a coffee with her? In a public place? No harm in that, surely?

So he'd invited her to join him…

But she'd taken off.

While waiting for his receipt, he'd glanced out the window and had seen her jump on a bus…and that was when he'd recalled what Janey had told him. Gould played squash every Sunday morning, and Stephanie had her own routine, a routine that never varied and always ended up at the Comfort Zone.

Like a lemming rushing headlong to a watery death, he'd set off in his Mercedes to search for the elusive coffee bar.

It had taken him almost twenty minutes to find it, and during those twenty minutes the thrill of the chase had pumped adrenaline through his body till he felt as high as a kite.

He came to a stop at her table. She was still engrossed in her paper. Her perfume drifted up to him. Green moss. Pink roses. Lingering kisses. Images swam through his brain. Images that were out of place, in this busy coffee bar, on a Sunday…or any other…morning.

'Well, now.' Lazily he tossed down his paper. 'Hello again!'

She jerked her head up. Her eyes were wide with surprise, her lips parted in dismay—those luscious lips, red and full and as tempting as sun-warmed summer strawberries. 'What are you doing here?' she gasped.

'You're repeating yourself, honey!' He put down his mug, slid off his jacket and slung it over the back of the vacant chair. 'May I?' And without giving her time to say 'No!' he drew out the seat and sat down.

He gulped down a mouthful of his cappuccino.

Licked the froth from his upper lip.

Extricated the Sports Section from his paper.

And throwing her an absent smile, started to read.

Stephanie stared at him, shock pounding her pulse.

It was surely no coincidence that he had turned up in this particular coffee bar. There were hundreds of coffee places in Boston. So...why had he ended up in this one? Oh, she knew the answer to that, only too well!

'You followed me!' Her tone was hard with accusation.

He looked up...and his expression was all injured innocence. 'Followed you? Hardly! I was still at the counter when I saw you jump on a bus! Hell, I'm not *Superman*.'

Not? Stephanie had to fight an urge to debate the point! He was the closest thing to Superman she had ever seen. 'So you're telling me this is pure coincidence?'

He smiled, his eyes teasing. 'Now you're putting words in my mouth!'

'Then if you didn't follow me, and your being here isn't just mere luck—'

'*Good* luck, right?'

'Now you're putting words in *my* mouth!' she retorted dryly.

'This is nice, isn't it? Spending Sunday morning together at your favorite coffee bar? I could easily be persuaded—' his eyes had a mischievous twinkle '—to make this part of my Sunday morning routine, too.'

So he knew this was her routine.

And the person who had told him must have been Janey.

The two had been in cahoots. She already knew that. She also knew they had gone out together only once. But how much had he learned about her, during that one date? Too darned much, she thought frustratedly.

'I really resent this intrusion,' she snapped. 'Being alone is the part of this particular routine that I appreciate the most. *Did Janey forget to mention that?*'

'No,' he said mildly, 'she mentioned it.'

'Then why—'

'A routine can become a rut.'

'A rut,' she retorted, 'can be good.'

'If it's shared with the right person,' he said. And grinned.

She melted.

And smiled back.

She couldn't help herself. He was just so damned charming, appealing, disarming…whatever. All three and more. 'Okay.' She shoved her paper aside. 'What do you want?'

'Dangerous question,' he said, his eyes laughing.

'Talking with you is like walking over a minefield.' She glared at him. 'Blindfold.'

He shrugged. 'You asked.' His lips were twitching.

'I'll rephrase the question. Why are you here?'

'I was curious to see the kind of place you liked to spend your Sunday mornings,' he said.

'Well, now you know.'

'Yes, now I know.'

His suddenly serious tone implied...what? Stephanie looked at him quizzically.

'It doesn't surprise me that you're not frequenting some trendy joint—'

'I'll have you know I frequent some *very* trendy joints!' She sounded indignant.

'Through the week, possibly. Or on Saturdays. But never on a Sunday.' He looked at her levelly. 'On Sundays you come here, because that's the day you miss your family most...and because this place is so cosily tucked away from the bustle of the city, and it has such a homey atmosphere.' With a wide sweep of his hand, he indicated the piles of newspapers strewn on a low table in the bay window; the two ginger cats lying dozing on the cushioned window seat; the Norman Rockwell prints on the walls; the posy of winter pansies on the table. 'Am I right?'

'You forgot the fire,' she said wryly, gesturing toward the brick hearth just two yards away, its alder logs crackling lustily up the chimney's sooty throat.

McAllister's husky laugh tore loose the armor plating her heart; and made her heart tremble.

'I rest my case,' he said.

'I wasn't going to argue it.' She cupped her mug in her hands, and tried to appear calm as she met his unwavering gaze. 'When I lived at home, we all went to the early-morning church service on a Sunday. After I moved here, I kept up the custom. But on my own. And afterward, when I came out of church, I always felt...depressed...'

'And lonely.'

'Mmm. I chanced on this place one day when I was wandering aimlessly...and liked the ambience.

It...seemed to fill a gap. I know a lot of the Sunday regulars now. It...almost...feels like home.' She felt a trifle teary. Clearing her throat, she said with an attempt at briskness, 'How about you? Do you have any family in town?'

His gaze had been fixed on her keenly, interestedly. Now his features tightened. 'No,' he said. He got to his feet. 'Your coffee must be cold. Here, give me your mug. I'll get you a refill.'

Stephanie felt her face become pale. He'd done it again—shut himself off from her. It was all right, it seemed, for him to pry into her life...which she didn't mind, because she had no secrets. But slamming the door on her when she tried to get to know him a bit better—it hurt.

She got to her feet, too.

'Thanks, but one cup's enough for me.' She swung up her jacket from the back of the chair. 'If you'll excuse me, I'm going home now and please don't follow me—or offer me a drive,' she added coldly as he attempted to do just that. 'I like to walk. It clears my head.'

She marched away from him, but even as she did, she felt a stab of remorse.

Was he, perhaps, as lonely as she?

But if he was, that was his problem, not hers.

So she kept on walking, and didn't look back.

Joyce's daughter was getting married on a Monday in mid-March, and Joyce invited her employer to the wedding.

Stephanie splurged on a new spring outfit for the occasion—a green silk dress and short matching jacket—but though she knew she looked fantastic in it, it did nothing to lift her depression. She'd been in the doldrums ever since breaking her engagement, and despite her best efforts, had found it impossible to regain her old bounce.

She'd decided she'd have to take a cab to the church, but when she mentioned this to Joyce a couple of days before the wedding, as they were getting ready to go home, Joyce told her Gina had arranged to have someone pick her up.

'She has?'

'Mmm. Her fiancé's mother's boss will call round for you—I haven't met him,' Joyce said in a vague tone, 'but apparently he's a very nice man. He's not married, and like you, he's not taking a partner.'

Was she being set up? A blind date? Stephanie tried to see some sign of that in Joyce's expression, but her eyes were clear, her smile guileless. Stephanie relaxed.

'That was thoughtful of Gina. When should I be ready?'

'He'll pick you up at four.'

They went out into the street, and as Joyce took off for her car, Stephanie saw, from the corner of her eye, a movement in one of the windows of the M.A.G. building. Unable to stop herself, she turned her head and looked up.

Two people were outlined in profile at one of the windows. One was McAllister. The other was Tiffany Whitney. They were standing quite close, and the blonde was looking up into McAllister's eyes. Stephanie felt her throat tighten as she sensed an intimacy between them.

At that very moment, as if he had felt her gaze on him, he turned his head and looked out. Their eyes met. Locked. Only for the briefest of moments...yet heat instantly flamed Stephanie's cheeks. As if pricked by a spur, she hurried away along the sidewalk.

Damn! Why had she allowed herself to look up!

Clutching the strap of her shoulder bag with both hands, she walked faster with each step, as if by putting as much distance between them as quickly as possible, she could blot out the image of McAllister and the sophisticated blonde.

But the picture seemed indelibly stamped on her retinas and didn't fade till long after she got home.

At precisely four o'clock on the afternoon of the wedding, Stephanie's buzzer went. When she picked up the phone, it was to hear a man's voice, badly distorted by static, say something that sounded like 'Transportation.'

'I'll be right down,' she answered.

And she hoped, with a trace of anxiety, that this man, whoever he was, hadn't been given the impression by Gina that she considered him to be her 'date' for the wedding.

When she stepped out of the elevator on the ground floor, she moved her lips in an automatic smile of greeting directed at the figure standing waiting for her. He was wearing a black tux, sparkling white shirt with ruffles down the front and a black bow tie. She felt her smile freeze as her gaze lifted to his face.

'What are you doing here?' she asked in a strangled voice.

McAllister raised his brows. 'I'm your driver. Didn't Joyce tell you I'd be the one picking you up?'

He'd never looked more devastating. Tall, dark and

handsome didn't even begin to do justice to his brand of looks. Her heartbeat kicked against her ribs and wouldn't quit. 'No. She said I'd be picked up by her daughter's boyfriend's mother's boss!'

He shrugged. 'That's me.'

Stephanie stared at him.

'My secretary's son is marrying your assistant's daughter. Marjorie Sutton—my secretary—and your assistant have been friends for years. Surely—'

'I know that part. About their being friends. But Joyce didn't think fit to explain to me exactly who Gina was marrying. What I can't understand is why Joyce didn't tell me you were the one picking me up. She knows we've met—she watched us drive off together the day you showed me the lot, for heaven's sake! Why—'

'I think—' irritation thinned McAllister's lips '—we have been set up. Without actually saying as much, Marjorie Sutton gave me the clear impression that you were well aware that I'd be the one picking you up. I'll kill that woman!'

'Is it going to be such a chore then, to drive me to the church?' Stephanie said in a haughty tone. 'Oh, don't think I'm not annoyed, too, but I think murder is a bit of an overreaction!'

'A chore?' Hard steel blue eyes skimmed over her. Her breath quickened as his gaze encompassed her curly brown hair, her full rosy lips, the green suit that skimmed flatteringly over her elegant feminine curves. The hard blue became smoky. 'No,' he said, 'it won't be a chore. But tell me...' He scooped up her hand and led her toward the door. 'Why isn't your fiancé driving you to the wedding?'

He didn't know. He still hadn't heard. So perhaps

that was why he hadn't contacted her—either before, or after, their accidental meeting at the bookstore. For a moment, her heart soared like a captive bird unexpectedly freed from its cage...then she remembered Tiffany Whitney, and the way the elegant blonde had been looking at McAllister a couple of days ago, and her heart plummeted.

'I don't have a fiancé.' She felt his hand slacken for a second, as if she'd taken him by surprise. 'I broke off the engagement several weeks ago. In fact—' she regarded him coolly '—had you not jumped to the erroneous conclusion that I was in a snit because you took Janey out, and had you not been in such an all-fired rush to decide I was having a jealous tantrum, I'd have explained way back *then* that I'd broken off the engagement.'

He had obviously recovered from his momentary surprise. She felt his grip tighten, felt the quickening throb of a pulse at the base of his thumb.

'So you've ditched Gould...again.' His tone was steady. 'And this time, it's...final?' He opened the door.

She stepped out into the sunshine. 'Absolutely.'

Somewhere, a songbird trilled a joyful aria. 'I assume,' he slid his hand up to circle her wrist, 'that Joyce knows about this?'

'Of course.'

'Then Marjorie Sutton also knows...though she has said nothing to me. Yes, they've set us up.' They walked down the path together; he didn't release his grip till they reached the car. He opened the passenger door, but as she made to slip past him and get inside, he put a hand on her forearm. 'Stephanie?'

She looked up at him. 'Mmm?'

He grinned, and her heart looped the loop. 'I have to say…despite the way we've been duped…I like the way this day is starting to shape up.'

She looked up at him. "Miriam"

He smiled, and her heart leaped the [...], "I have [...] regret, despite the way we've been treating, since the day is starting to brighten...

CHAPTER NINE

THE wedding ceremony was a moving one...but through it all, Stephanie was much more aware of McAllister sitting squeezed beside her in the narrow pew than she was of the groom or the bride or any of the words that were spoken.

Later, during the dinner, McAllister was an attentive partner, and charmed not only her, but everyone else at their table.

Stephanie couldn't help feeling a glow of pride that he was her escort, and despite her attempts to remain reserved, she found that happiness kept bubbling up inside her.

The bubble burst shortly after dinner.

She and McAllister had found themselves alone for the moment, at their table. And for the first time, he brought up the subject of her broken engagement.

'So,' he said, 'you finally gave Gould back the ring.'

'Yes.' It had been a shattering experience; one that had left her trembling. She didn't want to talk about it.

Or about Tony.

But McAllister apparently did.

'He never mentioned to me—or to anyone else, as far as I know—that the engagement was off. He just phoned my office one day and said he'd decided not to use my services. I assumed you were so mad at me for taking Janey out that you'd told him to find another architect.'

'I'd never have done anything like that!' Stephanie sputtered out indignantly.

'"Hell hath no fury…"' His eyes twinkled.

A leading comment…and one she'd be safer to ignore. 'Actually,' she tilted her chin primly, 'you were very rude to invite Janey out without including me in the invitation.'

'You're right…but sometimes the end justifies the means.'

'And the end was supposed to be…what?'

'To make you ask yourself if you could truly be in love with Gould, when all the time you were…lusting after me…'

Oh, yes, she did lust after him. Desperately! 'You really do have a high opinion of yourself!' She affected a tone of outrage.

'But you're not denying it, are you?' he queried. 'Just as I won't deny the feeling's mutual, and has been ever since we met. And whatever else might have been between you and Gould, that spark was missing—'

'So now you're claiming to have psychic powers?'

'No, just the simple power of observation. I saw the two of you together, that night we had dinner. And I'd have described your interaction as—let me be kind—bland.'

He was right, of course. Their relationship had been as dull as cold porridge. She hadn't realized it, though, till after she'd met McAllister. Her pulse gave a tremulous little flutter: the way *they* reacted to each other was anything but bland!

'Thank God,' he said, 'that you pulled the plug. I

guess you finally found out about the Whitneys' skiing party being canceled on account of their lodge burning down. I have to say that when I found out, that day we drove to the building lot, that Gould had told you he'd changed his mind about going to Aspen because he wanted to spend Christmas at Rockfield with you, I couldn't believe his gall—'

'You *knew?*' Stephanie felt her stomach cave in, as if he'd punched it. 'You knew…*then?*'

'Oh, yeah.' McAllister made a casual gesture. 'I knew. Paula Whitney got in touch with me at the end of December, because she and her husband wanted me to design their new lodge. She told me the whole story—about how you'd had to opt out of the Aspen trip because of a cousin's funeral, and about how Gould himself had actually gotten as far as the boarding lounge at the airport before she managed to reach him to tell him the party was off. Sure I knew…'

A cousin's funeral? Stephanie felt her mind reel. Another lie. The depths of Tony's deception made her sick.

And McAllister had been aware of it.

All this time.

She lurched to her feet and stared down at him. Her body was shaking, her cheeks drained of blood. She felt as if she was drowning in her own feelings of humiliation. 'You knew.' Her voice wobbled. 'And you didn't tell me. How you must have been laughing at me, thinking what a gullible idiot I was. And you told me that day in the bookstore that you thought we could be *friends*—'

He'd surged up from his seat, too, and put out a hand to her. 'Steph, I—'

She pushed his hand aside. '*Friends!* Let me tell

you something, Mr. McAllister, about friends. Friends don't lie, friends don't pretend, friends don't cover up.' Her eyes seemed suddenly full of sand; furiously she blinked to clear the gritty sensation away. 'You're the last person in the world I'd want as a—'

'I didn't tell you—' his features were set grimly '— because it wasn't my place. And I wasn't laughing at you, or thinking you were an idiot. If you think that's the kind of man I am, then you really *are* an idiot.'

'I don't *know* what kind of a man you are,' she spat back, 'because you cover that up, too!'

'Calm down, Steph. I know you've had a rough time lately, but...'

Calm down. That was exactly what Tony had said to her, after she'd found out the truth about him, and he'd wanted to avoid a scene. She hadn't cared then if she'd created a scene; but here, she did care. 'Oh, go away.' She choked the words out. 'Just go away and leave me alone.'

McAllister shoved his hands into his trouser pockets.

She saw compassion in his eyes, and part of her wanted to throw herself into his arms, and surrender to the comfort she knew he would give her.

But her pride wouldn't let her.

They stood with their eyes locked, neither giving an inch.

They had reached an impasse.

And he was the one who walked away.

But not before saying, in a quiet voice that twisted her heart,

'Okay, I'll go. But the next move is yours.'

McAllister kept his word.

He didn't come near her. Not even after the band

had struck up, and the dancing began.

Not that she sat wilting; she didn't. She had an overabundance of eager partners, and as she danced she concealed her unhappiness under a façade of laughter and gaiety. Anyone watching would have thought she was having a ball.

Somehow she managed to keep up the pretence all evening, though the strain was well-nigh unbearable.

Around twelve-thirty, she went to the ladies' room to splash cold water on her wrists, and when she returned to the table, she found it deserted. Taking a seat, she swept an under-the-lashes glance over the dance floor, and while she was doing so she was joined by Joyce.

Who had not only seen, but had correctly interpreted her furtive survey.

'He's over there,' she announced cheerfully. 'Dancing with Gina's sister Amy. He's really something isn't he, The McAllister? How many other women would have noticed that bashful little wallflower, far less taken the time or made the effort to draw her out.'

Stephanie forced a smile and a light tone. 'Yes, I saw him ask her up before I went to the washroom. She was hiding behind Marjorie and Bob, and you could see she was praying the floor would open up so she could sink through it.' But now despite the twelve-year-old's initial reluctance to join McAllister on the dance floor, she was obviously having a wonderful time—her ponytail flying as he whirled her around, her braces glinting as she giggled, her cheeks pink with exhilaration.

'He's a nice man,' Joyce said. 'Such a nice man.'

Before Stephanie could respond, Joyce's husband,

Angelo, and his brother Carlo joined them, and Joyce got caught up in their conversation.

And Stephanie found herself looking at McAllister again. Joyce was right. He was a nice man.

All at once, she felt tears smarting behind her eyes. He was a nice man...and she was an idiot. Why hadn't she calmed down when he'd asked her to? Why hadn't she tried to see things from his perspective? Everything he'd done had been done from the best of intentions, because he'd been concerned about her.

She took a tissue from her bag and dabbed away a tear as regret tore at her heart. She had spoiled what could have been a truly wonderful evening, with her pride and quick temper. She put her tissue away, and snapped her bag shut. Did she have the courage to go up to him? Apologize? Was it too late? Had he perhaps found someone else this evening, while she'd been busily riding her high horse?

She turned, and looked around at the floor. The dance was over. Gina's sister Amy was back sitting with her parents.

She felt a twinge of panic. Where was McAllister? Surely he hadn't left...?

Oh, Lord...she felt a sinking sensation of despair. But as it spiraled down to her toes, she felt someone tap her shoulder. From behind.

The fine hair at her nape stirred. And before she looked up, she knew with giddy certainty just who that someone was.

'Stephanie?' McAllister's hair had fallen over his brow as he danced; now he raked the heavy strands back. His eyes were grave. The band was playing

'Save the Last Dance for Me.' He held out his hand, and smiled, and Stephanie's heart turned over.

She got to her feet.

'I'm sorry,' she whispered.

'I know,' he said simply. And she knew it as all forgotten. Forgiven, and forgotten. They were, once more, in perfect accord.

He scooped up her hand, and clasped it firmly as he led the way to the dance floor. He swung her into dancing position, and she rested the fingertips of her left hand on his shoulder. He curled her other hand in his, tucked it snugly against his chest and pulled her close. Intimately close...

And she thought she'd never been happier in her life.

As McAllister savored the pleasure of having this woman at last in his arms, he acknowledged to himself that the pleasure was so intense it could almost have qualified as pain. But if it were pain, he decided, it was pain he could suffer with pleasure.

It had been sheer hell, staying away from her all evening. He had intended, though, to keep it that way. But when he'd seen her dab a tear from her eye, his hard stubbornness had melted as if it were a hailstone on a flame. Her damned pride was all that was keeping them apart. Her pride...and his own.

Her tears had swept his away.

And now her perfume, erotic in the most subtle of ways, was making him weak at the knees. The peaks of her breasts were pressing innocently against his chest, wreaking havoc with his precarious self-control. Her thighs, brushing his through the thin silk of her dress and the lightweight fabric of his trousers, were provoking thoughts that had no place on a crowded dance floor.

And stimulated a physical reaction that had no place anywhere but a bedroom.

He groaned.

She pulled back a little, and looked up at him. Her eyes—enormous, luminous—were dark with concern.

'Did I step on your toes?'

'No, nothing like that.'

'I thought I might have been responsible for that dreadful groan.'

'Why on earth would you think that?' Wry amusement twinkled in his eyes.

'My shoes have stiletto heels, and I thought perhaps I'd spiked you—'

'No, as I said—you didn't step on my toes.'

'Then what on earth caused you to groan like that, as if you were in—'

'Agony?'

'Are you in agony?'

His sigh was heartfelt. 'Mortal.'

'Is it something...physical?'

'It's a...problem...I have...but it's, er, personal.'

'Something you don't want to talk about?'

They reached a corner of the dance floor, and as he swung her around, he took advantage of the maneuver—rather cleverly, he thought!—to pull her even closer into his embrace.

She was still looking up at him—did her neck ache, at that unnaturally tilted angle? It was a beautiful neck—as pale as a swan's, and so graceful he knew that if he'd still been painting, he'd have wanted to paint it. To paint her. In all her glory—

'Ah.' Her eyes sparkled, teasing him. 'Now I know

what your problem is—I can tell, by the way you're staring at my neck that you're a vampire ravening for blood, and you just can't wait to drag me into a dark corner and siphon off some of mine!'

'Not guilty...of the vampire part, that is.' He lifted the hand clasped in his, and brushed a kiss across her delicate knuckles. 'But the dragging you off to a dark corner—' he cleared his throat '—had crossed my mind.'

He saw the faint rise of color in her cheeks, the faint flicker of her eyelashes—the response of an embarrassed maiden, he mused; and then immediately found himself wondering if she were still a maiden. Surely not. She and Gould had been engaged for months before they broke up. She was in all likelihood a very experienced lady.

'I think,' he murmured into her ear, 'it's time to leave. We'll go to my place, have a cup of coffee, a nightcap...'

Strands of her satiny hair tickled his lips, and he nuzzled into her neck, pressing a kiss on the sensitive skin below her ear. He felt her shiver. He slid his right hand around from her hip to the base of her spine, his fingertips splayed over the upper curve of her exquisite little bottom.

At the intimacy of his touch, a spasm rippled through her slender frame. The tremor was so faint as to be almost unnoticeable, but this evidence of her vulnerability touched something deep in his soul...awakening feelings he had never experienced before and rocking him to the core.

A moment ago, his intention had been to take this alluring creature to bed without delay; now he found his desire annihilated by an unexpected blossoming of tenderness. And in addition—of all things!—a wild burst of chivalry.

The sensation was head-spinning.

He'd realized from the beginning that if he were ever to kiss the lips of this beautiful enchantress he would be lost. What he had never guessed was that without even one kiss, she would have the power to ensnare his heart.

His heart, by heaven!

Panic was a knifepoint aimed straight at that most vital of organs. He shrank from it. He needed time. Time to think. Retreat was called for. A definite and immediate retreat, to give him an opportunity to strengthen himself against such an alarming turn of events.

'Yes.' Stephanie let her head drop; rested a cheek gently against his chest, over his shirt. 'I'd like to see your place. A nightcap sounds good, and...mmm...'

She sighed, and her warm breath drifted up to him. Wine-scented breath. He'd noticed her having a few glasses during the evening; not many, but he guessed she wasn't too used to liquor. There was a dreamy quality to her that hadn't been there earlier, during dinner. She pressed her cheek more closely to his chest, curled the fingertips of her left hand into his shoulder, flexing them, the way an adoring kitten might knead with its soft paws. He gritted his teeth as desire surged to the surface again and punched him in the gut—desire that was even more powerful, more intense than before, and mightily challenged his new-found feelings of tenderness, protectiveness and chivalry.

Grimly, he tightened his resolve and clenched his jaw.

'You sound sleepy.' He hardly recognized his voice; it had become as thick as clotted cream. 'Perhaps you'd like to take a rain check—you can see my place some other time.'

She moved her head in a negating movement; he felt the ridge of her cheekbone rub against his nipple. He sent up a prayer for strength. 'You're sure?'

She slipped her hand from his shoulder, and curved it tenderly around his nape. 'I'm sure.' She slipped her other hand free and twined it around his neck. 'Very sure.'

He'd really done it. How could he—without appearing the worst sort of cad—extricate himself from this position he'd put himself in? Vaguely he noticed that the lights had dipped and the hall had become shadowy dark. The band was playing the final bars of the nostalgic love song; the mood it had created so sentimental he felt himself wallowing in it like a moonstruck teenager. Miraculously he managed to restrain himself from dragging his pliant partner to the nearest corner and having his sweet way with her—but even as he congratulated himself on his self-control, she delved her fingers into his hair and snuggled even closer.

Calling on every ounce of fortitude he had available, he swooped her around as the band played its finale, and when the music faded away, he drew her hands from around his neck. Holding them lightly in his, he said, with what he hoped looked like a natural smile, 'My place, then.'

Stephanie wandered starry-eyed across the living room of McAllister's apartment, toward the huge wall of windows overlooking the city. The view was outstanding, but her mind was not upon it. All she could think of was McAllister himself, who was at present in the kitchen, making coffee.

She had expected he would offer her a nightcap, but he hadn't. Coffee, he'd said firmly, and she hadn't argued. After all, she'd already had a glass—or two—of wine during the evening. It had only added to the giddy excitement she'd been feeling.

She had thought that excitement would dissipate when they left the reception hall and stepped out into the brisk March night. Instead it had escalated, so that all she could feel now was a heart-pounding anticipation and the very odd feeling that she was walking on top of a glorious pink cloud.

She knew what she had let herself in for, by agreeing to come here; but she no longer had any control over herself, where McAllister was concerned. Any qualms she might have had had been annihilated by the desire that had welled up inside her as they'd danced, desire that now pulsed feverishly in her blood.

She shivered, and touched her fingertips to the cold pane of glass in front of her as she reached the window.

'Stephanie?'

She turned. Her host was walking in through the arched doorway, a teal blue ceramic mug of steaming coffee in each hand. He had taken off his jacket and his bow tie, and opened the top button of his shirt. She could see the shadow of black hair at his throat.

'Wonderful,' she breathed, moving toward him.

'The aroma of the coffee?' He arched a dark brow.

'That, too.'

She thought she saw him gulp. But before she could

be sure, he'd sidestepped her and crossed to the coffee table in front of the marble hearth, and deposited the mugs.

When he turned again, she was right behind him.

There was a determined glow in her eyes that set warning lights flashing even more frantically in his brain. 'How do you like your coffee?' he asked, backing away in the direction of the kitchen. 'Do you take cream or sugar?'

'Black,' she said.

'I...excuse me while I fetch some sugar...'

He fled. In the kitchen, he rummaged in the nearest cupboard. Sugar, he muttered, where the hell is the sugar. Not that he used it, but he'd desperately needed to get away from her, just till he—

'You don't take sugar.'

He whirled around. She was leaning against the doorjamb.

She wrinkled her delightful little nose at him. 'You just take cream.'

'You're right. I don't...regularly take sugar in my coffee...I mean. But sometimes at night, when I feel a bit...well, listless, for want of a better word, I take sugar to...you know...boost my energy.'

He was babbling and he knew it.

She floated across the floor toward him. Floating was the only way to describe how she approached. She'd taken off her shoes, and her nyloned feet were soundless on the tiles, her hips swaying in a way that made a mockery of his attempts to control his body's instant reaction to her tantalizingly sexy come-on. She stopped right in front of him, and reached up to snap the cupboard door shut.

'I don't think we need to worry about your energy

level,' she said softly, raising her hands to weave her hair from her face. She tilted her lips up to his, her eyelashes drooping over eyes that had lost their twinkle and become cloudy. Her expression was sultry, her mouth a passionate pout. Take me! She didn't say the words. She didn't have to.

He wanted her, more than he had ever wanted anything in his life. He wanted to haul her into his arms, and smother her with kisses. He wanted to sweep her off her feet, and carry her to his bed. He wanted to run his fingers through those brown silk curls, the way she had done, seconds ago.

He yawned—a wide yawn, a noisy yawn, an artificial but what he prayed was a convincing yawn—and twisted his features in an exaggeratedly sheepish grimace.

'Lord,' he muttered, rubbing a hand over his nape in a gesture that denoted embarrassment, 'I'm bushed. Steph, I'm going to have to cut our evening short. If I don't drive you home right now, I'll be falling asleep over the wheel.'

He made sure his eyes didn't quite meet hers, and as an added precaution kept his lids at half-mast in the hopes that the long lashes would shadow his irises, which he guessed would be hazy with the desire raging through him.

For a moment her face was blank. He knew he'd taken her by surprise. He could almost read her thoughts.

He was rejecting her.

Stephanie stared at McAllister dazedly, her lips fallen apart, her eyes wide open. She had thrown herself at him, in the belief that when he'd invited her back to his place, their goal was one and the same. To make love.

She had been wrong. She had misinterpreted the invitation. Mortification sent a surge of blood flooding up her neck to transform her cheeks to scarlet beacons.

She turned on her heel and stalked out of the kitchen. Her shoes were lurched drunkenly together by the sofa. Flicking them upright with her toes, she slipped them on. She scooped up her purse, and with her nose in the air, turned to McAllister, who had followed her through.

'Since you're so tired,' she said in a proud voice, 'I'll call a cab.'

He started to protest. She ignored him. There was a telephone on one of the end tables; she lifted it, and with her back presented squarely to him, dialed the number of a local cab company.

'What's the address here?' she asked with a disdainful glance over her shoulder.

'Look, I'll drive you home—'

The dispatcher came on at the other end of the line.

'The address, please,' Stephanie repeated stubbornly.

McAllister shrugged. And gave her the address.

After relaying it to the dispatcher, Stephanie hung up. With what she hoped looked like a great deal of aplomb, she moved to the coffee table, picked up one of the blue ceramic mugs and took a sip.

'You may not be the host with the most,' she said in a cool tone, 'but you do make a good cup of coffee.' She forced herself to look at him while she spoke...then wished she hadn't. He had that same anguished expression on his face as he'd had when they were dancing. He hadn't said what was wrong then; had glossed over it with an attempt at humor. Was he sick? Was that why he wanted her gone?

She frowned. Put down her mug.

'Is there something the matter?' she asked. 'I mean, other than just being tired. You look…you look as if you're in pain…?'

He looked very uncomfortable. And his smile was strained. 'It's nothing to worry about,' he said, shifting from one foot to the other. 'It's just a sort of—' he cleared his throat '— malaise…that overtakes me once in a while. I'll be all right after a good night's sleep.'

'Is there anything I can do to help?'

She saw his Adam's apple twitch. 'No.' Sweat sheened his brow, his upper lip. 'Not a damned thing.'

'Are you sure? I don't mind staying if there's anything at all I can do to—'

The buzzer went.

'Your cab.' McAllister took in a deep breath, crossed the room, lifted a hand as if to place it in the small of her back…and dropped it again. 'I'll see you down to the foyer,' he said gruffly.

Moments later, they were in the elevator. The ride down took only seconds, and then they were stepping out into the foyer. Outside, beyond the plate glass doors, Stephanie could see the driver. He was standing with his hands in his pockets, his cab in the road behind him, engine idling.

She looked up into McAllister's face. 'I'm really sorry you're not feeling up to par.'

'No cause to worry. I'll be fine.' His voice had a raspy edge. In the periphery of her vision, Stephanie saw the cabbie turn away, stroll toward his vehicle and open the back door.

McAllister walked her outside. They stood together for a moment on the sidewalk. The strains of a favorite country and western song drifted to her from the cab's radio...and McAllister's musky scent drifted to her, too, catching her totally off guard. It hurtled her, with rocket speed, back to her previous state of wild arousal. All she wanted at that moment was to rip off his clothes, and her own, and beg him to take her, then and there, on the sidewalk. And to hell with his low energy level—she had enough energy for both of them!

'Good night, then,' she said.

She turned away, but before she had taken even one step, she found herself hauled back by a pair of muscular arms. For a second their eyes met, his aflare with passion, hers wide with surprise. And then his mouth was on hers in a kiss so urgent and desperate she felt as if she was being ravished. Sweetly ravished...thoroughly ravished...and so very expertly ravished that every erotic nerve ending in her body jumped up and applauded. She yielded helplessly, and heard a moan come from her own throat, a moan that was part agony, part ecstasy.

There was nothing wrong with this man's energy level.

She felt the power in the caress of long fingers over her back; felt the pressure of hard thighs against her own; and felt the violent trembling of his strong body. But even as she drowned in the resurgence of her own frenzied desire, he made a ragged sound and released her.

'Go,' he ordered huskily. 'Go now. And for pity's

sake don't ever wear that perfume again. At least, not when you're near me.' He brushed a kiss over her brow, shook his head and as she stared at him in mindless confusion, he took her arm and walked her...almost pushed her...across to the cab.

'But I thought,' she whispered, 'you didn't want—'

'I want,' he growled. 'More than you could possibly imagine. Who the hell do you think is responsible for the agony I've been suffering the past couple of hours? But wanting...and surrendering to that want...are two different things. You, my sweet love, need more from a relationship than I'm prepared...or able...to give. And though I'm sorely tempted to take what you so generously offer, there's a price to pay for giving in to that kind of temptation. For me, that price is too high.'

He folded her into the back seat of the cab, and slammed the door shut. He paid the cabbie, and then touched his hand to his brow in a brief salute to her, as the vehicle pulled away from the curb.

Stephanie slumped back in her seat, feeling as if every bone in her body had turned to porridge. Blindly she stared ahead. He wanted her. She hadn't been wrong about that after all. But he wasn't into strings and commitment—and that was why he had rejected her.

Oh, damn! Tears smarted behind her eyes. Why did the man have to be so damned honorable! Easier by far had he been a scoundrel, because the kind of hunger from which he was suffering, was no more tormenting than her own.

It wasn't until after she was home, and had stood under the spray of an ice-cold shower for five minutes, that sanity returned and as it did, she finally realized the enormity of what she'd almost done. The sheer horror of it made her actually cry out. The noise woke Janey, who came and hammered on the bathroom door, yelling at the pitch of her voice, 'Are you okay?'

'Yes,' she shrieked back, 'I'm fine.'

And thank heaven for that! As she switched off the shower and wrapped a huge fluffy towel around herself, she shuddered...and knew the shudder wasn't only a reaction to the icy water. It was a reaction to the thought of how this evening might have ended. Had McAllister not been a gentleman, it could well have been another story, for carried away by the sheer happiness of the day—by the music, and the wine, and the charisma of her escort—she had come close to making the biggest mistake of her life.

Had she slept with him, it would have meant saying goodbye to all her dreams, because she knew that one night with Damian McAllister would never have been enough.

And what she wanted from him was so much more.

For the rest of the week, she didn't have time to fret over the traumatic incident. At least, not during the day. Joyce had taken time off to entertain some out-of-town wedding guests so Stephanie was alone in the store and a steady stream of customers kept her on the hop. But the evenings...oh, the evenings; they were something else. McAllister strode boldly into her thoughts, no matter how hard she tried to block him out. And when she went to bed, hoping that in sleep she'd be free of him, he gate-crashed her dreams with an arrogance that made her tremble.

But though he inhabited her dreams, he didn't come back into her life. She saw nothing of him during the month that followed, heard nothing of him till around the middle of April, when Joyce said one morning, in an offhand tone,

'The McAllister has gone to Aspen for Easter, with the Whitneys. Marjorie says Tiffany Whitney is looking very pleased with herself these days...'

Stephanie felt as if someone had poured a jug of acid over her heart. 'Really?' She pretended to be engrossed in the toys she was rearranging on a shelf.

'That poor man.' Joyce sighed. 'Somebody should do something about it.'

'About what?'

'Setting him straight, of course. That woman will never be able to have a genuine relationship with a man—she's in love with only one person—herself! She is exactly the opposite of the kind of woman The McAllister needs. According to Marjorie, her boss has quite lost his head and doesn't know what he's doing!'

Fortunately, at that moment the doorbell pinged, and saved Stephanie from having to make a response. But when she turned to greet the customer, and saw who that customer was, her relief turned swiftly to apprehension.

'Tony.' Carefully, she put down the gray felt rat she'd been holding. 'What...can I do for you?'

Joyce muttered, 'Excuse *me!*' and looking as if she'd just sucked a lemon, stomped off into the back room.

Tony came straight to the point.

'I'm planning to sell this building, Stephanie. I thought I should tell you now, rather than wait till your lease comes up for renewal at the end of the month.'

She gasped, but he barged right on.

'My buyer wants the whole block, and I should prefer to sell the whole block. However, since it would be disastrous for your business if you had to relocate—there's absolutely nothing available for rent in this area now—that part of my deal is something that's open to negotiation. What's the matter, Stephanie? You've become quite white.'

White? Every drop of blood seemed to have drained from her face. She had taken it for granted that her lease would be renewed at the end of the month; Tony had told her last year that he'd decided to keep the building permanently. What on earth had changed his mind?

'Let's have dinner,' he went on smoothly. 'If we put our heads together, I'm sure we can come up with a solution to your problem.' His nostrils sucked inward as he inhaled. 'Of course, if we were still engaged, I'd never have allowed such a situation to occur. You, er, follow my drift?'

Stephanie stared. He was giving her an ultimatum: marry me, or you lose your store. Grief, it was blackmail!

'No.' Concealing her rising fury, she raised her brows in guileless question. 'You'll have to spell it out for me.'

He closed the space between them angrily and grasped her shoulders. 'You know damned well what I'm saying!'

She tried in vain to wrench herself free. 'Then,' she choked out the words, 'you give me no choice but to leave—'

When his mouth—cold and wet—swooped down on hers, she was too stunned to react. But only for a moment. As adrenaline rushed through her, she gathered her strength and drove her knee into his groin. He doubled up, and staggered back with an agonized groan.

'You little bitch!' His entire body vibrated with rage. 'You've screwed yourself now, missy! You get yourself and your asinine toys out of here by the end of this month, or by heaven I'll take you to court!'

Joyce must have heard the shouting. She stormed through and hooked a bolstering arm around Stephanie.

'Get out!' Stephanie glared at her ex-fiancé through eyes blurred with tears of outrage. 'Or you're the one who'll end up in court, on a charge of assault!'

He left, slamming the door behind him so hard the walls shook and several stuffed toys tumbled off the shelves.

Joyce patted her back, as if she were a small child. 'You need to sit down for a bit, dear. Let's go through the back, and I'll make us a pot of tea. Hot and strong.'

She led Stephanie through to the back, and after seating her in a chair, put the kettle on to boil.

'You heard what he said?' Stephanie's voice was weary. 'We have to be out of here by the end of the month.'

Joyce came up behind her, and started massaging the knots in Stephanie's shoulders. 'We'll phone the *Globe* and put an ad in. We'll fine somewhere else.'

Stephanie closed her eyes. 'No,' she said dully. 'Thanks, Joyce, but no. No ad. I'm tired of the city, and oh Lord, I'm even more tired of city men. I'm going home.'

'Back to Rockfield?'

'Back to Rockfield.' Her smile was wan. 'It's funny—the reason I left home was I was looking for more excitement in my life. Rockfield had come to seem so...ordinary. Now I've had my fill of excitement, and ordinary has never looked so good. Can I persuade you to come with me, Joyce? We make a great team!'

Joyce chuckled. 'Thanks, but my family are all here in Boston. And you know, Gina wants to go back to work full-time once her baby's born, and she's asked me if I'd baby-sit weekdays. I've been meaning to broach the subject with you, but kept putting it off as I didn't want to let you down.'

'That's wonderful!' Stephanie said. 'You get to baby-sit, and I get to go home. All's well that ends well.'

But if she really meant that, she asked herself as Joyce infused the tea, why did she feel so miserable?

CHAPTER TEN

THE Tuesday following the Easter weekend, Stephanie dismantled the sunny yellow Easter display in her window. She was proud of herself, that she managed to do so without once checking to see if McAllister might be watching.

When she jumped down from the window platform onto the shop floor, ready to pack the display away, she saw Joyce dragging forward a huge box labeled Mother's Day.

She felt her throat muscles tighten.

'Put that away, Joyce.' Keeping her head averted in case Joyce saw the sudden shine of tears in her eyes, she wiggled a skinny Easter Rabbit into its plastic storage case. 'We won't be here on Mother's Day. You know that.'

'But we *are* going to be here for another week, and we always get such a fantastic response from your Mother's Day window.'

'It takes me hours to set it up, and I don't think it's worth the bother, not for just a few days. Actually we ought to get started on packing those toys stored on the back room shelves, and we'll make more speed if we don't have customers trekking in and out.' She avoided looking at Joyce as she dropped vinyl Easter eggs into a bag. 'Okay?'

'Yes, dear, whatever you wish. I'll just put this Mother's Day stuff back, and start clearing the shelves.'

'We'll need more boxes. I'll pop over to Pickways and get some.'

She finished packing away the Easter display, and then called through to Joyce, 'I'm going now. I'll be back in ten minutes.'

It was a lovely April morning, the gentle breeze sweet with the scent of hyacinths, the sky a soft pastel blue. Spring was in the air, and as she stepped outside, two young lovers passed by, arms around each other, laughing softly.

Stephanie's heart felt as if it were lead. While she walked to the corner and waited at the edge of the sidewalk for the lights to change so she could cross to Pickways, she found herself thinking bleakly about Tony. What a fool she'd been, to have been so mistaken about him. He was pathetic. Now Damian McAllister...there was a different kind of man. Oh, he had a hang-up or two, no doubt about that, but he was a man of honor, a man she could admire, a man she could—

'Stephanie.'

It was his voice. It came from right behind her. Or had she just imagined she heard him?

She turned, her nerves drumming.

It was McAllister all right, and the sight of him had her heart reeling groggily against her ribs, like a boxer spinning against the ropes after a totally unexpected slug. He was standing just two feet away from her, and he was breathing hard, as if he'd been walking fast. To catch up with her? 'Oh, hi there.' She sounded as breathless as he appeared to be. 'How are you?'

Silly question. He was gorgeous. Wider of shoulder

than she remembered, darker of eye, and…she felt a
hint of surprise…thinner.

'Just great.' His shirt was the same steel blue as his
irises; his suit jacket the same blue-black as his hair.
His gaze was searching, warm…*concerned?* 'But how
are you?' He frowned. 'You look…different.'

She hoped the breeze wouldn't stiffen; one strong
puff and she'd topple right over. This man made her
feel as if her limbs were barely capable of holding
her up. 'My hair, maybe?' Tremulously she shoved
back the mass of brown curls. 'It…needs cutting. I
just haven't had time.'

'No,' he said. 'It's not your hair. It's exactly as I
remembered it.' His face sobered. 'Wonderful.' As if
he couldn't help himself, he reached up and touched
the glossy curls resting on one shoulder. 'Like dreaming in silk.'

In the pit of her stomach, something tingled, something electrical, coiling, hot. 'Ah…there's the Walk
signal.'

'I'm in no hurry. You?'

No, she thought, I'm in no hurry, either. I could
stand here forever, just looking at you, wanting to be
in your arms, aching to feel your lips on mine.

'Yes.' Her voice was quiet. 'I…am in rather a
hurry.'

'Too bad. We could have gone for a coffee…or
something.'

Or something. Her nerves quivered as her mind
skimmed over the possibilities. 'That would have
been nice.'

He'd moved very close, edged toward her by pas-
sersby jostling to cross the street. His male scent

sought her, intoxicated her. She fought a feeling of faintness.

'I heard you'd gone to Aspen for Easter,' she said.

'I was staying with the Whitneys. I've just completed the first phase of their new place—'

'It's not habitable yet, surely?'

He shook his head. 'Mark and Paula have rented the lodge next door. They're spending a lot of time there—Mark likes to keep an eye on what the builder's doing. But there should be no problem. Jack Brock's an excellent man.'

'And...Tiffany was there, too?' The question flew out before she could stop it.

He grinned. 'There's no show without Punch.'

'So they say.' Stephanie was visited by a vivid Technicolor image of Ms. Whitney and McAllister waving gaily to each other as they skied down some death-defying slope—followed immediately by another of the two engaged in an acrobatically astonishing après-ski coupling on a sheepskin rug before a triumphantly blazing log fire. Bitchily, she superimposed an image of her own, one of an avalanche that left the lovers up to their necks in snow, their desire terminally chilled as their bodies turned blue. 'Well, I'm glad you had such a good time.'

'Tiffany had a good time.' His eyes were smoky with amusement. 'She met Enrico Cabido, the Italian billionaire playboy, her first day on the slopes, and they haven't spent one moment apart since.'

Her heartbeat skipped a little; so...he was no longer involved with the gorgeous blonde. Ruthlessly she ordered her heart to settle down; what difference would it make to her, whether or not the two were still seeing each other! 'You don't sound too upset that she deserted you?'

'Deserted?'

'You were...with her, weren't you? Haven't you been one of her regular escorts, recently?'

'You seem to be implying that we were...lovers.'

'Weren't you?'

'It was Tiff's father who gave me my start in this town, Stephanie, when I graduated from university so burdened with student loans that I wondered if I'd ever manage to pay them off. He not only asked me to design his new branch office in Cambridge, but he spread the word among his many contacts that I was an up-and-comer. I owe him a lot...and if that debt includes acting as an escort from time to time when his daughter needs one, I don't mind. Tiff knows the score.'

'The score?'

His gaze fell to her lips, and lingered. 'Marriage is not on my agenda, and even if it were...' His voice trailed away, but she sensed the words that had remained unspoken. Tiffany Whitney would not be a candidate. He was, however, too much of a gentleman to say it.

Which was one of the reasons she liked him so much. It was not only his bone-melting sexual magnetism that drew her inexorably to him, it was the very character of the man. And unlike Tiffany Whitney, she wanted the whole man, and was not willing to settle for less. So why was she standing here, subjecting herself to this exquisite torture?

She glanced at her watch and faked a look of dismay. 'Oh, dear, I've forgotten something. I have to go back to the store.' She made herself smile up into his face. 'It's been nice seeing you, but I really must fly.'

'It's all go, isn't it?' he remarked lightly.

'It is indeed,' she said, knowing he was totally unaware of how dead on his remark was. 'Go' was the operative word, and if he'd known how far she was about to go, and why, he would probably have been shocked.

'See you, then,' she said.

'Yeah, see you around.'

She turned away from him and walked briskly back along the street to the Warmest Fuzzies, trying to make her step as purposeful as she could. She certainly didn't want to give him the impression she was fleeing...though she was. Did he stand and watch her as she went? She didn't look around, yet she could have sworn she felt his eyes on her.

Joyce came through when she heard the bell.

'Oh,' she said, 'I thought it was a customer.' She raised her eyebrows. 'Didn't you get any boxes?'

'I've...decided to phone and have them delivered.'

Which was what she wished she had done in the first place. If she had, she wouldn't have bumped into McAllister, wouldn't have had her emotions all freshly churned up, wouldn't have all these wonderful new pictures of him in her mind, pictures that had no place there.

Thank goodness she'd be out of here in a week. Surely once she was back home, she'd be able to forget him?

'Mrs. Sutton!'

Marjorie Sutton jammed the lid back onto her container of peach yogurt and raised her corseted body from her seat. Patting her hair, she hurried to the adjoining office.

'Yes, Mr. McAllister?'

He was standing at the window, looking out. 'Come over here,' he said, gesturing without glancing around.

She crossed to stand by his side.

'Look down there,' he growled. 'And tell me... what's wrong with this picture.'

She looked. Everything seemed as usual to her—four lanes of traffic moving at a fair pace, sidewalks busy as they normally were in the lunch hour, lights functioning like clockwork at the intersection. 'Wrong, Mr. McAllister? I...don't know what you mean.'

'Down there!' He had a mechanical pencil in his hand, and he tapped it irritably against the windowpane. 'That store across the street—'

'The Warmest Fuzzies Toy Store? Where my friend Joyce works?'

'The window's empty.'

'Yes, the window's empty.' Though her tone was polite, it held a trace of anxiety; it wasn't like The McAllister to waste her time on trivialities. 'You're right. It is empty. Now, may I go? I'm just going to have my l—'

'Easter's past. May is almost upon us. Mother's Day is just around the corner. But the window's empty...' He sounded now as if he were talking to himself. 'Now that is damned strange.'

'Oh, I see! You're wondering why that pretty Miss Redford hasn't put her Mother's Day display in the window as she always has done in the past, right after Easter.'

'Correct, Mrs. Sutton.' Her boss's tone was edged with impatience. 'The minute St. Valentine's Day is over, the St. Patrick's display goes up. The minute St. Patrick's Day is over, the Easter display goes up. The minute Easter is over, the Mother's Day display goes up—and so on and so on and so on…right through Halloween and Thanksgiving till Christmas, at which point she drives me crazy with her eternally blinking Merry Xmas To U And Yours! Now why hasn't she put up the—'

'She's leaving, Mr. McAllister.'

A shocked silence followed her announcement. The room positively rocked with it. The McAllister stared at her, for a full ten seconds, absolutely motionless, his eyes stark and incredulous. Then with a ferocious scowl corrugating his forehead, he barked, 'Leaving?'

'Going back to Rockfield. And I tell you—' Marjorie lowered her voice to a whisper '—the Mother's Day sign didn't go up because Miss Redford's heart just isn't in it anymore. Joyce's worried sick about her.'

Shaking her head and murmuring unhappily, the secretary walked out of the office and back to her desk, where even the prospect of her favorite peach yogurt no longer held any appeal. Maybe later she'd feel like having it; but not now. She liked that pretty Miss Redford; it was a crying shame that she was so miserable. But there was nothing more she and Joyce could do about it. They'd tried, hadn't they, after she broke off her engagement to Tony Gould? They'd set her and The McAllister up at Gina's wedding, and thought he'd be smart enough to know when he'd had a miracle handed to him. But he hadn't. He'd blown it. And now he was starting to show a real interest. When it was too late. Much too late.

Men!

Two days before the end of the month, Stephanie was sitting behind her counter checking invoices when the door opened. Glancing up, she felt her heartbeat jar. McAllister. McAllister...in a toy store? That had to be a first!

And it must surely be a painful thing for him to do, to come into a place like this, with its poignant reminder of his own lost child. So what had driven him here?

She slipped off her stool, and walked around the edge of the counter, her nerves tight. 'Good morning,' she said.

'Good morning, Stephanie.'

He was wearing a navy polo shirt that clung to his chest, and faded blue jeans that delineated his long powerful legs. A dreamboat, Joyce had called him; oh Lord, he was that...and so much more.

He held out a gift-wrapped package. 'This is for you.'

'What...?'

'A going-away present.'

So...he had heard she was leaving—but of course he had not come to persuade her to stay. She felt his eyes on her as she slipped off the wrapping. When she saw the pristine hardback copy of *Untimely Graves,* she looked up slowly.

'Thank you.' She envisioned him trekking doggedly from store to store in pursuit of the elusive book, and had to swallow a sudden lump in her throat.

'I hope you haven't already finished reading it?'

She shook her head. 'I've been meaning to check it out of the library, but time's been running away from me recently. It'll be wonderful to have this copy for my own library.'

'Yeah, it's a keeper. So,' he watched as she put the book and wrapping paper on the counter, 'you're leaving. I must say I was very surprised to hear you were moving.'

'It wasn't by choice...at least, initially. My lease is up at the end of the month and Tony wouldn't renew it.' She smiled grimly. 'You said once that you were well aware of how he operated. This is the kind of thing you meant?'

'Good God, even for Gould this is an all-time low. What a petty piece of revenge!'

'More than revenge, actually. Attempted blackmail. He made it clear he'd renew the lease if I...went back to him.'

McAllister muttered something very coarse under his breath. Then he said tautly, 'Were you tempted?'

'Hardly! But in the long run he did me a favor. It forced me to make a decision, and I decided to go back to Rockfield. I realize now that that's where I belong. I'm a small-town girl, who just couldn't cut it in the city.'

'*Garbage!* You've proved beyond a doubt that you can make it in the city. Look, I have contacts here...give me a day or two and I guarantee I'll find you a place you'll love—if not in this area, then in one that's comparable.'

'Thanks, I do appreciate your offer, but I've made up my mind. Now,' abruptly she changed the subject, his kindness and his confidence in her a threat to her already precarious self-control. 'Let me thank you again for—'

'You can't let Gould chase you away.' The fierce expression in his eyes jellied her knees.

'My final decision had nothing to do with him—'

'That's arguable. But let's suppose that's the case. Even so, you're going to feel isolated in Rockfield, after Boston. Look, Steph,' he swept back his hair with an impatient gesture, 'let's talk this over. Have dinner with me tonight—'

'I'm sorry.' Her face was pale, her luminous pine green eyes enormous. She had never looked so beautiful—nor had she ever looked so fragile and vulnerable.

Remorse stabbed him. 'No.' His voice was gravelly. 'I'm the one who should be sorry.'

'For what?'

'For putting pressure on you—for trying to make you do something you don't want to do.'

'It's not that I don't want to have dinner with you—'

'I wasn't referring to the dinner.' His eyes darkened. 'I meant...I'm sorry for trying to persuade you to stay. It was selfish of me. I'll...miss having you around.'

'You shouldn't be saying things like that to me.' If anything, her face had become paler. 'Dinner...or staying...I can't do either. It's best I go. There's no point in becoming any more involved with you than I already am. Under the circumstances.'

'Circumstances?'

'You know what I mean. There's no point in prolonging this...' Her voice trailed away weakly.

'This what?' he persisted, and cursed himself again for putting her under more stress.

'This...whatever there is between us.'

'Relationship?'

'No.' Her cynical laugh was in itself a denial of his suggestion. 'We don't have a relationship. In order to have that, two people have to trust. They have to open up, to give of themselves, tell all their secrets—'

He retorted, with an edge of flippancy, 'I know a whole lot about you, Miss Redford!'

He knew by the expression in her eyes that she had noted his attempt at humor, but was not about to allow him that protective shield.

'Yes,' she said, 'you do, but I know next to nothing about you. Oh, I know you were once married—but you gave me the information under duress. I know, too, that your wife was pregnant when she died—' he flinched '—but that was something you didn't care to mention to me. I've talked to you about my home and my family but I know *nothing* about yours. You know I love Christmas...and I accept your right to hate it, but you haven't offered to tell me why you do. You've told me you'll never remarry, but your reasons remain known only to you. A relationship? I don't think so. What we have here is a one-way street—'

'Oh, sorry.' Joyce's voice came breathlessly from behind. 'I didn't realize you were with someone—'

Stephanie had forgotten all about her assistant, who had been doing some chores in the back room. She turned now, and said, 'It's okay, Joyce. Have you finished?'

'Yes, just finished. Hi, Mr. McAllister! Lovely day, isn't it? Steph, I'm going out for lunch. I'll be back in half an hour.' She swept across the store, and the bell pinged behind her as she left.

Stephanie exhaled wearily. 'Look, I have to be out of here the day after tomorrow, and I still have a lot to do—'

'You want a two-way street? I'll give you a two-way street.' McAllister's voice was harsh. 'You want to know about Ashley? I married her because she was—'

'Please don't, it's—'

'Pregnant.' He barreled right on. 'We'd been seeing each other for over a year, with no strings on either side. She was a fashion designer with a brilliant career ahead of her, and her focus was on that career, which was fine with me, as I wasn't looking for a wife. She'd been on the pill, but something went wrong— she blamed a flu that had made her violently sick. At any rate we were both appalled when we found out we were to have a child. But though marriage had never figured in our plans, we decided—for Felicia's sake—to tie the knot.'

Stephanie leaned back against the counter to support herself as she digested this unasked-for barrage of information. After a moment, she said, 'Felicia?'

'Ashley's mother. Felicia Cabot was in her seventies, and terribly frail after two heart attacks. She was...of the old school...and neither of us wanted to hurt her.'

'So you and Ashley weren't...in love?'

'We respected each other,' he said slowly, after a moment's thought to search out the best way to explain. 'We gave each other space. And we liked each other. Very much. But in love?' He shook his head. 'I certainly wasn't, and I'm not sure Ashley had it in her to give herself totally to any man. Her burning passion was her work, and she herself was like a dazzling flame—I used to wonder if she was afraid to slow down, in case the flame flickered, because if it did, she'd have had to accept that there were shadows, and Ashley was a golden girl. She didn't like shadows.'

'Were you close?'

'As close as two people can be, when one is afraid of shadows, and the other lives in the dark.'

He couldn't believe he had just said that. What did this woman do to him, that he could reveal something so intensely personal about himself? He felt a tearing pain in his heart as memories crowded in on him, memories of his childhood, as far back as he could remember, and perhaps even farther, to that time when darkness had fallen over his soul...an ugly darkness that had never lifted.

She started toward him, her eyes brimming with concern, and compassion...and questions. He moved away, crossed to the window, turned his back on her deliberately. He balled his hands in his pockets, his stance rigid.

She came no closer. 'Your oil painting,' she said softly, hesitantly, 'the one with the hovering eagle and the black valleys...when did you paint it?'

'Five years ago.' His voice was muffled.

Five years ago. Right after his wife and baby died. It was in the dullness of his tone; he had no need to say the words.

'When I was at your place in Vermont,' she murmured, 'you told me you'd built your house there because of the scenery, for your painting, but...I didn't see a studio...?'

He turned around. 'I don't paint anymore.' His tone was absolutely flat.

What a waste of talent, she ached to say…but she could tell it was something he didn't want to discuss.

There was an awkward pause. After a moment or two, he looked around restlessly. 'Can you close up for a while? Go round to the park, take a stroll?'

After a brief hesitation, she said, 'Okay, but it'll have to be a quick one. I really do have a ton of stuff to do.'

Barclay Lake Park was just a short walk from the store.

On this lovely April day, young mothers pushed babies in strollers; retired couples sat talking on benches; and men played shuffleboard in an open area by the tennis courts. The grass was wet underfoot after a spring shower, so McAllister led Stephanie to a path that circled the lake.

She sensed he wanted to talk to her, so she walked in silence, waiting. He didn't speak, till they were halfway around the lake. When he did, it was in a steady voice.

'That year,' he said, and he had no need to explain which year he was talking about, 'I went up to Vermont in mid-December. I'd just finished a big project and needed a break. Ashley was too busy to come with me, but she said she'd drive up on the twenty-fourth so we could spend Christmas Eve and Christmas Day together—'

'You were going to celebrate Christmas?' Stephanie stopped walking, and turned to look at him in surprise.

His skin looked too tightly stretched over his face.

'I was going to try,' he said. And taking her hand, gave it a tug and started her walking again. 'It was strange…my initial shock on learning I was to become a father had begun…very gradually…to give way to a heady feeling of anticipation. A new life was on the way. I was going to have a child! I found myself drifting off into thoughts of how it would be—'

His voice caught, and Stephanie said quickly, 'You don't have to go on if it's too—'

'Ashley phoned me, late on the evening of the twenty-third. She sounded tremendously excited…and happy. She told me the baby had begun to make fluttery movements, and she couldn't wait to see me, so I could put my hand on her belly and feel the movements, too. I knew then that her feelings about the pregnancy—like my own—had done a complete turnaround.'

Emotion had thickened his words, and he cleared his throat, before going on. 'We spoke for some time, we had one of the best talks we'd ever had, and before she hung up, I told her how much she had come to mean to me, and I wished her a safe trip the following day. The forecast was good and the roads were clear of fresh snow, so I wasn't concerned about her making the journey alone. Ashley was an excellent driver.

'On the way, she was involved in a freak accident. A couple of spaced-out teenagers had stolen a Cessna 172 from a local airport and they started buzzing the traffic on Route 89. They lost control and crashed into a transport rig. Eight vehicles were caught in the pileup. Ashley's white Porsche was the one directly behind the rig.'

'Oh, God.' At some point while he'd been talking,

he'd dropped her hand. Now Stephanie pressed it to her collarbone as she felt a choking sensation in her throat. 'I remember reading about it. Ten people were killed.'

'Ten adults...and an unborn baby. And when she heard the news of her daughter's death, Felicia Cabot collapsed. She died in hospital next day. Christmas morning.'

An aura as impenetrable as a barbed-wire fence surrounded him. Stephanie clenched her hands into fists to stop herself from reaching out to him. 'Your own family...did they help you through that rough time?'

'I had no family.' He had his back to the sun. His face was shadowed, but she could see his eyes clearly, and the expression in them chilled her. 'My mother died of cancer when I was three, my father was an alcoholic, a foul-tempered washed-up boxer whose only interest in life was booze—and he was dead by that time. Dead but not, by God, forgotten.' His lips moved in a travesty of a smile. 'You wanted me to open up—no, don't stop me. There's more. You wanted to know about my home? It was a grungy little house in Seattle, on the wrong side of the tracks. My very first memory is of my mother screaming as my father beat her up. After her death, he started in on me. My childhood—'

Stephanie gave a little sob, and he broke off, his jaw grimly set.

'Is that enough for you, Miss Redford? It's not exactly the kind of stuff one brings up with a woman if one wants to enter into a meaningful relationship, is it! Especially when that woman is part of a family so warm and close they would make even the Waltons look dysfunctional!'

Stephanie closed her eyes, unable to bear the pain she saw in his. She knew now why this man avoided Christmas; and knowing, how could she ever ask him to share her joy in that season of wonder, when all it had ever brought him had been misery and death.

She could have him, she knew, if she were willing to settle for less. Less than her dreams. But her dreams were so much a part of her, and Christmas so much a part of those dreams, she couldn't let them go. In any case, all he had ever offered her was an affair, and an affair was open-ended, like a plane ticket with no return date on it.

She couldn't live that way. She needed family, permanence, guarantees...

The agony she felt was like no agony she'd ever felt before.

'There's something I want you to know,' he said.

She opened her eyes, and felt the tears beading her lashes.

'I've never talked about this before,' he said. 'Not to anyone.'

'Surely Ashley knew you hated Christmas?'

'She knew that, yes...but she didn't know why.'

'You didn't tell her?'

'As I said, I've never told anyone. Until you.'

She drew a ragged breath. 'I wish—'

'What do you wish?'

'I wish things could have been different.' She wiped away a tear, a tear she didn't try to hide. 'I wish...we...could have been different.'

He framed her face in his hands, and drifted his gaze over her features, slowly, with painstaking care...as if memorizing them for eternity...before his gaze locked with hers again.

'If only wishing could make it so.' His voice was sandpaper rough. 'But I'm afraid it doesn't work that way. There's more to having a relationship than just opening up—I think you know that now. It's not that simple. It's the secrets we don't want to share, that make us the people we are. And sharing them doesn't change anything. It doesn't…unfortunately…change us.'

He pulled her close, held her close, for an endless bittersweet moment, before releasing her. 'Goodbye, Stephanie Redford. I wish you luck in your new life.'

He walked away, and he didn't look back. Not even once.

The cut he had made was a clean one, and she knew he was trying to be kind.

But his kindness was a two-edged sword. As it cut the cord between them, it also sliced her heart in two.

CHAPTER ELEVEN

THE weather changed on the last day of April. The temperature had dropped overnight, and when McAllister looked out his kitchen window in the morning, he saw a world that was gray. He decided its dismal mood matched his own.

He'd been late getting to bed, and then had had trouble falling asleep. When he'd finally drifted off, it had been to find himself smothering in dreams of silk. Brown glossy curls wound around his heart, cutting off his blood; soft silky lips provoked and tormented him, tantalizing him till he was a gibbering wraith. Waking up had been a relief.

Still he couldn't dismiss her from his thoughts...

The shine, the spark was gone from her now. She'd lost her zest for living. He'd have noticed it, even if Marjorie Sutton hadn't told him how worried Joyce was about her.

And did he have anything to do with that? Oh, God, yes, he knew he had. She didn't want an affair, which was all he had to offer. She wanted it all: marriage, house with white picket fence, children. And a husband with whom she and those children could celebrate Christmas.

He'd give almost anything, anything in the world to see those eyes shine again, as they had when he'd dropped her off at Rockfield on Christmas Eve. But the one thing she wanted was the one thing he was unable to give.

Feeling sudden stifled, he leaned across the sink

and threw open the window. The pure morning air immediately invaded the kitchen.

It held the unmistakable scent of snow.

When Stephanie got up, she found a note from Janey on the counter:

Flurries Are Forecast. Wear A Warm Jacket. Love J.

Thanks, Janey, she muttered, as she poured water into the coffeemaker. That's all I need on moving day—snow!

She slumped down onto one of the kitchen chairs, elbows on the table, chin resting on cupped hands, as she waited for the coffee to drip. She couldn't help thinking how she'd miss Janey. She was a real friend, always cheerful, always ready to lend a helping hand. Or give advice.

She smiled ruefully as she remembered how she'd ignored Janey's warning not to drive her van to Rockfield without having it checked out. And she recalled how excited she'd been on Christmas Eve, when McAllister had driven her home.

She was going home again tomorrow, but this time, she felt no thrill of excitement. Of course she would enjoy seeing her family once she got there...but for the life of her, she couldn't work up one single spark of enthusiasm.

With an unhappy sigh, she got up and crossed to the window. Throwing it open, she breathed in deeply to clear her head, cleanse her lungs.

There was a smell of snow in the air.

'The moving van's been at the Warmest Fuzzies all morning.' Marjorie Sutton paused by the filing cabinet in her boss's office. 'Joyce says they expect to finish loading by noon, then as soon as she and that pretty Miss Redford wash the floors they'll be gone, and—'

'The Bellevue files, Mrs. Sutton!' he snapped. 'Are we going to have them today or tomorrow?'

'Today, Mr. McAllister.' She was not in the least put out by the belligerence of The McAllister's tone. When she and Joyce had dined together last night, they'd agreed that since today was their very last chance to get Miss Redford and The McAllister together, the situation was desperate enough to require desperate measures.

Extricating the requested files, Marjorie clanged the metal door shut and walked sturdily across to The McAllister's desk. He was sitting behind it on his swivel chair, his hands planted aggressively on his thighs, a scowl darkening his face. His eyes burned with a strange fire.

Marjorie slapped the files down in front of him. 'It's not going to be the same around here, without Miss Redford. Of course, you'll be glad to see her gone. You never did like those signs blinking from her window. Very annoying you found them, didn't you—blinking all the time, the way they did—especially that Christmas message! Ah, well, she'll soon be out of here and you'll be happy. She'll be happier, too, once she gets back to Rockfield. Joyce tells me Miss Redford's just itchin' to get married and have kids and—' she crossed her fingers behind her back '—there's an old flame up there with pots of money, just waiting to snap her up the minute she gets home. According to Joyce—'

The McAllister shoved back his chair and lurched to his feet. 'That's enough, Mrs. Sutton! I don't know what's gotten into you today but you forget yourself. This is a place of business, not some...some... marriage broker's office!' His face had become a violent shade of crimson she'd never seen before except in a Hawaiian sunset.

'No, Mr. McAllister,' she said soothingly. 'I'm sorry, Mr. McAllister. It's certainly not that. Good heavens, don't we all know that you're not a suitable candidate for marriage, what with your dislike of Christmas, and all?'

Head in the air, she sailed out of the room, closing the door quietly behind her. Once in her office, she dropped her lofty demeanor and scurried to the phone. Pressing the speed-dial button that connected her to the Warmest Fuzzies, she perched on the edge of her desk, and moments later, with a cautious eye on the connecting door, whispered excitedly into the mouthpiece, 'Joyce, can you talk? Good. Now, remember what we discussed last night? She is? Oh, dear, you'll just have to think of some way to keep her there a little longer. No, I don't think it'll be very much longer.' She grinned, as she remembered the apoplectic color of The McAllister's face. 'He's taken the bait, I'm sure of it.' And mixing her metaphors blithely, she added, 'The ball's in your court now. Don't drop it!'

Stephanie shoved back an unruly clump of curls that had come trolloping forward over her shoulder as she worked, and skimmed a satisfied glance over the back room's shiny-clean floor. Resting her hands atop her mop handle, she said, 'Well, that's it, Joyce. We can call it a day.'

Joyce was over by the doorway, stuffing odds and

ends into a small garbage bag. Before she could answer, the phone rang at the front counter.

'I'll get it,' Joyce said quickly, 'while you empty your bucket.'

Stephanie crossed to the sink, squeezed out her mop and emptied the bucket. She tidied up the sink, and after washing her hands, she sauntered to the front.

Joyce was still on the phone.

Stephanie had assumed the caller was a customer. It had not occurred to her that it might have been a personal call for Joyce, but when she heard her assistant say something about 'The McAllister'—and say it in a hushed voice that implied secrecy—Stephanie cleared her throat to make her presence known.

Joyce looked around sharply. At the sight of her boss, she bit her lip, and her cheeks turned bright pink. Averting her gaze, she listened to the person on the other end of the line for a few seconds more, before saying, 'Will do, Marjorie. Talk to you later then.'

When she put down the phone, she threw Stephanie a smile, but the smile seemed forced.

Not for the world would Stephanie have admitted to the curiosity she was feeling; if Joyce and Marjorie wanted to discuss The McAllister, that was their business, not hers.

'Well, we can leave now,' she said in a brisk tone. 'I can't wait to get out of here—'

'Oh, let's have a cup of coffee, since we're ahead of schedule. There's just enough left in my thermos, I think. It would be a pity to let it go to waste.' Joyce peeked at her watch, and Stephanie could have sworn she saw a look of anxiety cross her face, but it was gone so quickly she thought she must have imagined it. 'If you take off now,' Joyce went on, 'you're going to have to wait about twenty minutes for the next bus, and it's darned cold out.'

Slightly bemused, but deciding Joyce was just loath to end their day, since it would, after all, be their last together, Stephanie said, 'Oh, sure. Let's do that.'

They returned to the back room and Stephanie leaned against the countertop as Joyce poured the coffee into two foam cups and handed her one.

'Thanks, Joyce.' Stephanie took a sip from her cup before saying in a deliberately idle tone, 'How's your friend Marjorie these days?' Mentally she rolled her eyes; so much for keeping the lid on her curiosity!

'Marjorie? Oh, I'm afraid she's down. Really down.'

'What's wrong? No problem with Gina's pregnancy, I hope?'

'No, Gina's doing well. It's The McAllister.' Joyce's sigh sounded as if it had been dredged up from her toes. 'Marjorie's thinking of giving up her job. The man's impossible to work with.'

'But I thought——'

'That she enjoyed working for him? Yes, I remember telling you that. But that was...before.'

'Before...what?'

'Before he fell in love.'

'In love?' Her voice sounded rusty. 'The McAllister? No, you're wrong there, Joyce. That man would never...allow himself to fall in love!'

'Whatever you say, dear, but Marjorie's a bit of an expert on these matters—she has six brothers and over the years she swears she's learned to spot the signs—and all I know is what she tells me. The McAllister has turned into a bear. An absolute bear. Grouchy, rude, unpredictable, and sometimes even downright nasty.' Joyce shook her head sadly. 'Poor Marjorie.

It'll be hard for her to find another job at her age, and—'

'I'm sure it's only temporary.' Stephanie wished she'd never enquired about Joyce's friend—whoever said 'curiosity killed the cat' had been spot on. 'You should tell Marjorie not to make any rash decisions...and she should try to make allowances. Everybody's entitled to the odd mood, from time to time—why should The McAllister be any different!'

She turned away so Joyce wouldn't see the bleak look in her eyes. She knew only too well that she was the woman Joyce and Marjorie believed The McAllister had fallen in love with. Well, she had news for them both: What the man felt for her was not love, but raging lust.

And that raging lust, unslaked and destined to remain forever unslaked, was at the root of his rotten moods.

Sexual frustration did not engender a sunny temper.

Of that, she was herself only too well aware!

Marjorie Sutton whisked off the sheet covering the sign propped against her office wall. She grinned as she recalled how she and Joyce had driven down to the Warmest Fuzzies at midnight last night, and by flashlight, hunted in the back shop for the box containing the Christmas display.

'This is illegal.' Joyce had chuckled.

'I know,' she had responded, with a snicker. 'Who'd ever have guessed that stealing would be such fun!'

It had taken about fifteen minutes to carry the box over to the M.A.G. offices, lug it up in the elevator, set it against the wall in Marjorie's office and drape it with the old sheet Marjorie had brought for that purpose.

'Won't The McAllister wonder what's under there?' Joyce had asked.

'Uh-uh. He pays no attention to anything in my office. But how about Miss Redford...won't she miss the sign, when the movers come in?'

'Stephanie's so unhappy, she wouldn't notice if her gray velvet elephants ran amok and thundered out of the store!' Joyce had replied.

And she'd been right.

They'd both been right: The McAllister had noticed nothing amiss, and Smoover Moovers had come and gone without incident.

And now...

Marjorie felt her heartbeat quicken. From the adjoining office she could hear her boss pace back and forth, back and forth, as he fought the battle raging within himself.

A glance at her watch told her it was time to make her move.

Reaching under her chair, she retrieved the ghetto blaster she'd borrowed last night from Joyce. Setting it beside her computer, she slipped in the tape they'd chosen for the occasion, and then she clicked the player on. Immediately soft music drifted faintly to her ears.

Pulses pounding, she turned the volume knob to High.

Then feeling as if she was going to explode with excitement, she sat up straight and gazed in breathless—and somewhat fearful—anticipation at the adjoining door.

'Well, I really ought to get along now.' Stephanie tucked her empty foam cup into the garbage bag. 'Are you ready to go?' she called after Joyce, who had wandered—somewhat restlessly, Stephanie thought—through to the front shop, her footsteps echoing hollowly in the now-empty area.

'Stephanie,' Joyce's voice held a lilt of excitement, 'guess what? It's snowing! Isn't it odd, after the wonderful spring weather we've been having?'

'Very odd indeed,' Stephanie called back. She wandered through to join Joyce. As she did, she heard music. 'Where's that coming from?' she asked casually. 'I thought you took your ghetto blaster home yesterday.'

Joyce paid her no heed. She was standing at the front door, which she'd flung open. Large snowflakes, as ragged as paper scraps, were drifting down in the street outside—and it was from outside that the music was coming. Feeling a sense of confusion, Stephanie moved forward. Now she could hear quite clearly...and what she heard was Christmas music.

'Joy to the World.'

She was hardly aware of brushing past Joyce and stepping out into the wide doorway. The sidewalks were busy, as they always were in the lunch hour...but the four lanes of traffic had slowed, almost to a stop. Stephanie soon saw why. A long canary yellow Oldsmobile was coming slowly up the street, every window open, and from its stereo speakers the Christmas carol was blasting out full force.

As she took in the scene, Stephanie was suddenly struck by the weirdest sensation. Like déjà vu...only in reverse! A vivid image flashed before her eyes, an image of her next Rockfield family Christmas...and the vision made her blood run cold: she was with all her relatives, in the old family home, but instead of being blissfully happy as she would have expected, she was gut-wrenchingly miserable. There was no joy in her heart, and the reason for that was—

Something...a movement, maybe...caught her attention and made her look up at the second story of the building directly across the street.

Her eyes flew wide open, and blood rushed so wildly through her veins that she thought they might burst. In the huge window...McAllister's window...was a sign, with blinking red and green neon lights.

It was her sign. There was no mistaking it. She would have recognized it anywhere...and its message.

Merry Xmas To U And Yours

'That's Marjorie's car,' Joyce said proudly. 'And that's Marjorie driving. Isn't she something?'

Stephanie's eyes were glued to the sign. 'What's going on, Joyce?'

'I think,' Joyce said, with a soft chuckle, 'that The McAllister is trying to tell you something.'

'What?' she asked, her voice a mere whisper.

'Why don't you go across and ask?'

It wasn't going to work.

McAllister paced his office, hardly hearing the Christmas music blasting down below in the street. All he wanted was to make her happy, to see her eyes light up the way they used to...but no matter what Marjorie Sutton had said, it wasn't going to work.

And who'd have thought the scrupulously principled Mrs. Sutton could have been so sneaky? He'd almost choked when he'd strode into her office to order her to turn off that damned Christmas music and he'd been confronted with the huge sign propped against the wall. The sign from the Warmest Fuzzies. He'd have known it anywhere.

Merry Xmas To U And Yours.

That cursed sign, there was apparently no escaping it! He'd fled from it in December; now here it was again, probing relentlessly—and painfully—at the very core of him. In April, yet!

He'd stared at it for an endless moment, with despair and yearning and need all jumbling chaotically inside him, till it was a wonder tears hadn't spurted like hot geysers from his eyes. But though he'd managed by a thread to keep control of himself, at least on the surface, his emotions, so intense they were almost unbearable, must have communicated themselves to the woman sitting watching him.

'You're going to lose her, if you don't do something,' Marjorie had said quietly. 'And you're going to regret it for the rest of your life.'

'What can I do?' he'd asked helplessly.

And she'd told him.

She's right, he'd decided. This is what I have to do.

But it wasn't going to work. If she came to him...and Marjorie had assured him she would... she'd see in a minute, by the look in his eyes, that he was just going through the motions. He'd never known a real Christmas; he didn't even know what Christmas meant. Oh, he knew about the gifts, and the tree, and the food, and the parties. But, deep in his gut, he sensed that there must be more. A whole lot more. And he didn't have a clue in the world what that whole lot more entailed. No, she would come over, and she would see the emptiness of his gesture, and that would be it.

Finito.

Forever.

He moved over to the window, and looked out. The snow was still falling, though it was starting to taper off; Marjorie's canary yellow Olds had reached the intersection; the strains of 'Joy to the World' were steadily becoming fainter; and the door of the Warmest Fuzzies was closed.

'McAllister.'

He closed his eyes as he heard her voice. Oh God— his prayer was silent and soul-deep—make this come out right.

Slowly he turned, and feeling as if his life had been put on hold, he searched her face, desperately hoping she'd been fooled by his uncharacteristically senti- mental gesture.

She was standing in the doorway, her cheeks slightly flushed, and snowflakes in her hair. She was wearing jeans and a cherry red sweatshirt, and no jacket. Her eyes were shimmering, so he couldn't read their expression. There might have been stars there…but he couldn't be sure.

'I thought I was dreaming,' she said, 'when I saw your sign.'

'Your sign,' he corrected her, hardly able to breathe.

'And I thought—'

'You thought I had changed.' His heart lay heavily behind his ribs. 'I have to be honest.' He must be out of his mind, to be saying what he was, and throwing away all his chance to win her. 'I haven't changed, Stephanie. I'm sorry. You see, I was going to tell you I'd celebrate Christmas with you, every year till the end of our lives, and I would have, but it would have been a sham. It was just that I couldn't bear to see you so unhappy, and I thought…if only I could put the stars back in your eyes…'

Stephanie's heart was pounding harder than it ever had in her life. He'd never looked so good, and she ached to throw herself into his arms. He was wearing a soft gray flannel shirt, open at the neck, and a pair of pleated navy pants, the navy leather belt fastened with a pewter buckle of a plain design. His dark hair looked as if he'd been running distraught fingers through it, and his eyes—those beautiful steel blue eyes—were strained and shadowed. Yes, she ached to throw herself into his arms, ached to kiss away the taut lines around his mouth, but that would come later. Instead she said lightly, 'I've come over to take you up on your offer.'

It was obviously the last thing he'd expected. He blinked. Frowned. Blinked again. 'Offer?'

'Your offer to find me a new location for my store. If it still stands, that is…?'

'Well, sure…it still stands, but—'

'I've decided I'm going to stay. After all, I love Boston…and you were right—I sure as heck can cut it in the big city! Besides…' She managed to keep her voice steady. 'I have some unfinished business here.'

'You have?' His eyes had the blank look of someone who has completely lost the gist of the conversation.

'You need educating, McAllister.' Stephanie shook her head at him, in mock-chastisement. 'You don't put up red and green lights in April, for pity's sake! You're an impatient man…and besides, you're far too ambitious…'

'Ambitious?' If anything, he looked even more dazed.

'A person who's never "done" Christmas,' she explained with exaggerated patience, 'can't just leap in and celebrate the occasion without any preparation. You have to walk before you can run, McA! And fortunately, December is at the end of the year, a long way down the road, so by the time it comes around, you should be ready for it.' She saw his Adam's apple jump convulsively, and compassion welled inside her; the mere mention of Christmas distressed him, because his memories of that time were so very bad. But bad memories would surely fade and die, if new memories...good memories...joyful memories...were piled on top of them.

He wasn't ready to hear that yet, though, so she kept her tone casual as she continued. 'Normally I'd start you at New Year, work you through Valentine's Day, then St. Patrick's Day, and Easter weekend...but in your case, I'm willing to bend the rules and start you off with Mother's Day. The fourteenth of May this year. We'll set off at the crack of dawn, drive up to Rockfield and spend the day with my folks. That is—' her gaze challenged him but inside she felt as wobbly as half-set Jell-O '—if you feel up to it?'

She hadn't realized the depth of her love for him till she'd been visited by that mind-shattering image of her next Rockfield Christmas. She'd known when she'd seen it that without McAllister she'd never again be happy...and it had been like stepping from firm land onto quicksand. From the known...to the unknown. Oh, she loved her family, loved them dearly, but wherever McAllister was, that was where she wanted—no, that was where she needed!—to be. It was time to step from the security of all that had been familiar since childhood, to uncharted territory. It was a move that was not without risk, but it was a risk she was ready to take. There would be sacrifices, she knew, but they were sacrifices she'd gladly make. She was willing—at last—to accept him on his terms. And if those terms had limitations, she could happily live with them.

She was prepared to settle for less.

But she had asked for more.

Not for her own sake. For his.

He had to let go of the past, before he could become the man he was capable of being, a man able to celebrate life to the fullest. She had asked him if he was up to it; she wasn't certain that he was. But she prayed it would be so.

She braced herself for his response.

He started toward her, and in his eyes she saw a purposeful glint. 'I'm not sure,' he said softly, 'if I do feel up to spending Mother's Day with your folks.' He reached her, and looped his arms around her. Her heartbeat picked up speed. 'They sound intimidatingly perfect, the Redford family...'

He pulled her hard against him. 'It's not easy,' he murmured, 'being around people who are perfect.'

'Oh, they're not so perfect.' Stephanie was finding it difficult to breathe, with her body pressed right against his, and his lips brushing the crown of her head, and his hands running up and down her back. 'My aunt Prue drinks a little too much and tends to flirt at parties, my uncle Herb's more boring than a woodworm, my dad has no sense of time so he's always late, my mom spoils the grandkids rotten, and my two grans have been feuding since the year dot over some supposed slight they can't even remember—'

'As I said.' McAllister's lips hovered close to hers. 'A perfect family.' His mouth brushed hers tantalizingly, till every cell in her body was screaming for a proper kiss. But just as she parted her lips to beg for just that, he obliged. Only it was rather an *im*proper kiss, she decided blissfully after a few mindless minutes; she'd never known that a tongue was designed for such a slyly arousing purpose. With a tiny sound in her throat, she gave herself up to his clever seduction.

When he at last allowed her to come up for air, she whispered, 'Oh, McAllister...'

He grinned down at her, his eyes teasing. 'Don't you think it's time you started calling me by my given name?'

She threaded her fingers through his hair, glorying in its rich texture, and returned his gaze dreamily. 'Damian. It's a nice name. A good name. What does it mean?'

'It means "One who tames." Though in your case,' he planted a kiss on the tip of her nose as she wrinkled it, 'I haven't had much success, have I!'

'Do you want to tame me?'

He kissed her again, to show her he liked her exactly the way she was.

Afterward, as she snuggled close, her palms pressed to his chest, she murmured, 'You were wrong about something, you know.'

'And what was that?' Lazily he kissed the last unmelted snowflake from her hair.

'You said sharing secrets doesn't make a difference, but when you told me about...your childhood...it helped me understand why you are the way you are—'

He stiffened, just a little. 'And what way is that?' he asked, his tone careful.

'You...grew up without love. Perhaps your mother loved you—she probably did—but she died when you were so young you'd have retained no memory of it. Your father,' her voice became grim, 'showed you only hate. As a child, you must have ached for love...not only to receive it, but to give it. And I'm sure you tried to give it, at least in the beginning, but your father would have thrown it back in your face. So you grew up with all that love locked inside you.' She hesitated, then went on in a rush, 'So now, I think, you're afraid to offer love, in case your offer's rejected.'

He closed his eyes briefly, as if he'd felt a slash of pain, and then opened them again. 'And if I were to offer you my love?' There was a whiteness around his nostrils that hadn't been there before. 'What then?'

'If you were to offer me your love—' she traced a shaky fingertip over his upper lip '—then I would give you my answer. You can't have the answer, before you ask the question...that would be a cop-out, wouldn't it! So...are you?' She swallowed hard, over the lump that had swelled in her throat. 'Going to offer me your love?'

She could barely guess at how very difficult this must be for him. Giving love, taking love, had for her been the easiest thing in the world. She had grown up with it, she'd always been surrounded by it. It came as naturally to her as breathing. But for McAllister...this simple exchange was beyond the scope of his experience. She felt tension coil inside her as she waited for his response. After a moment that had seemed endless, he closed a hand around one of hers.

'Come over here.' He led her across to the high stool in front of his drawing board. He lifted her up onto the stool, and stepped back. As she cupped her hands around the seat, for balance, he got down on one knee.

'Stephanie Redford.' His eyes fixed hers with a look so intense it made her want to weep. 'I love you with all my heart. Will you marry me, and live with me forever?'

Tears welled up in her eyes, and she felt one spill over and run down her cheek. She smiled down at him, unable to speak for the constriction in her throat.

He stood, and as she started to lower herself from the stool, he caught her under the arms. Holding her close, he slid her, with excruciating slowness, to the floor, letting her body brush against his, every delicious inch of the way.

'Stephanie.' His voice was husky, his eyes glistening. 'You've got to say yes, I'll die if you don't!'

She framed his face with her hands, and through her tears, smiled. 'Yes, I'll marry you, my darling Damian!'

He exhaled a shuddering breath, as if his nerves had been strung almost to breaking point, and her words had come just in time to save them from snapping.

She stood on her tiptoes and kissed him on the lips. 'When?'

Hungrily he returned her kiss, then pulled his head back. 'Demanding little madam!' he growled. 'When would—'

'June! If there's one thing I've dreamed about since I was a little girl, it's a June wedding! Oh, please, Damian, can it be June?'

'Mmm.' He frowned. 'Actually, August can be a really nice month—'

She chuckled, and gave him a little shake. 'Oh, you…!'

He kissed her again, so passionately it made her toes curl. 'If a June wedding is what you want, my sweet, then a June wedding you shall have.'

'We can make all the plans when we go to Rockfield in May! Golly, it doesn't give us much time, but since Uncle Pete's the Rockfield minister, there should be no problem there, and since Aunt Prue owns the Bridal Store, I'll get a good price on my dress. Jason plays the drums for the Greased Lightning Rock Band so we can get them to play at the wedding dance, and as for the catering, why—'

'Your feudin' grandmas run Rockfield's classiest catering establishment!'

Stephanie did a double-take. 'How on earth did you know about Kate and Konnie's Katerin' Korner?'

Damian threw back his head and his delighted laughter rolled out through the office, echoing back from every corner. *'Kate and Konnie's Katerin' Korner?* Good Lord, only in Rockfield, Vermont! Who on earth came up with a name like that!'

'And what is wrong with that name?'

He wiped a hand over his eyes, and let one last chuckle escape. 'It's so schmaltzy—' He broke off as he saw the look of outrage on her face, stared for a moment, and then guffawed. 'Oh, Lord, I've put my foot in it, have I?'

'I was only nine when I came up with that name, I'll have you know—I won a damned contest!' Despite herself, she giggled. 'You're right.' She grimaced. 'Schmaltzy.'

'And I suppose—' he somehow managed to keep

his face straight '—one of your relatives has a perfect little place where we can go for our honeymoon?'

'As a matter of fact, yes! Uncle Herb has a cute little fishing cabin in the woods, by a lake, where—'

'Where your whole family will feel free to pop in and visit us, any time of the day or night! No, my love, you can have your own way over everything except the honeymoon hotel. I'll choose that…and I can assure you, it'll be at least a thousand miles from Rockfield!'

'I don't mind.' Honeymoon. Stephanie felt her cheeks grow warm. 'I'll be happy to go wherever you want—'

'You're blushing! Surely you're not embarrassed at the thought of—' His eyes narrowed and he stared at her for a long moment. 'Good Lord,' he said at last, 'don't tell me you're still a—'

'Would that bother you?' she asked, her voice quavering just a little.

'Of course not!'

And she knew he was telling the truth; knew by his expression of dawning wonder, and by the gentleness of his touch, as he placed a cool palm against her heated cheek.

'You're something else, Stephanie Redford,' he said quietly. 'Did I tell you just how much I love you?'

'Yes, you did.' The stars in her eyes almost blinded him with their brilliance as she smiled up at him through her tears. 'But you can tell me again if you like!'

So he did.

HARLEQUIN PRESENTS

HARLEQUIN PRESENTS
men you won't be able to resist
falling in love with...

HARLEQUIN PRESENTS
women who have feelings
just like your own...

HARLEQUIN PRESENTS
powerful passion in
exotic international settings...

HARLEQUIN PRESENTS
intense, dramatic stories that will keep you
turning to the very last page...

HARLEQUIN PRESENTS
The world's bestselling romance series!

Harlequin® Historical

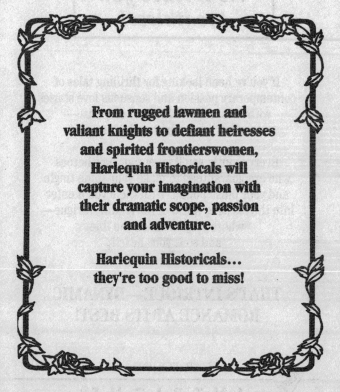

From rugged lawmen and
valiant knights to defiant heiresses
and spirited frontierswomen,
Harlequin Historicals will
capture your imagination with
their dramatic scope, passion
and adventure.

Harlequin Historicals...
they're too good to miss!

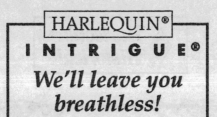

HARLEQUIN®

I N T R I G U E ®

We'll leave you breathless!

If you've been looking for thrilling tales of
contemporary passion and sensuous love stories
with taut, edge-of-the-seat suspense—
then you'll *love* **Harlequin Intrigue!**

Every month, you'll meet four new heroes
who are guaranteed to make your spine tingle
and your pulse pound. With them you'll enter
into the exciting world of Harlequin Intrigue—
where your life is on the line
and so is your heart!

THAT'S INTRIGUE—DYNAMIC
ROMANCE AT ITS BEST!

HARLEQUIN®

I N T R I G U E ®

INT-GENR

"Tell me what's wrong so I can fix it."

She blinked. Had she actually wished upon a star? One with magical wish-granting powers? "You can't fix this."

"Yes, I can," he growled. "I need you to be there, Jeannie." He took another step up, another step closer to her. "I need..."

"Robert." Without thinking, she put her hand on his chest because she couldn't let him get any closer.

She felt his muscles tense under her palm. It was a mistake, touching him. That phantom contact a week ago in the bar? The little sparks she'd felt then were nothing compared to the electricity that arced between them now.

He looked down to where she was touching him and she followed his gaze.

Then his fingertips were against her cheek and she gasped, a shiver racing down her back. "Jeannie," he whispered, lifting her chin until she had no choice but to look him in the eye. His eyes, normally so icy, were warm and dark, and they promised wonderful things.

His head began to dip. "I need...you."

* * *

Seduction on His Terms is part of Harlequin Desire's bestselling series, Billionaires and Babies: Powerful men...wrapped around their babies' little fingers.

Dear Reader,

Dr. Robert Wyatt is a billionaire and a renowned pediatric surgeon—plus he's gorgeous and has been named one of the top five billionaire bachelors in Chicago. He's got it all! Robert keeps his secrets close to his heart—so close, in fact, that the only person he's comfortable talking to is his bartender, Jeannie Kaufman. But when Jeannie becomes the sole guardian of her niece, Melissa, she can't come to work.

Robert needs to see Jeannie. What's the point of being a billionaire if he can't use his money to get what he wants? If she needs a nanny and a maid and a lawyer, easy. But Jeannie doesn't want to be in Robert's debt. He may be her favorite customer... but she can't let him just take over. Can she accept Robert's help without falling for the haughty billionaire?

Seduction on His Terms is a sensual story about fighting for your dreams and falling in love. I hope you enjoy reading this book as much as I enjoyed writing it! Be sure to stop by sarahmanderson.com and sign up for my newsletter at eepurl.com/nv39b for all the latest updates!

Sarah

SARAH M. ANDERSON

———

SEDUCTION ON HIS TERMS

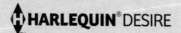

Recycling programs
for this product may
not exist in your area.

ISBN-13: 978-1-335-60344-9

Seduction on His Terms

Copyright © 2019 by Sarah M. Anderson

www.Harlequin.com

Printed in U.S.A.

Sarah M. Anderson is happiest when writing. Her book *A Man of Privilege* won the 2012 RT Reviewers' Choice Best Book Award. *The Nanny Plan* won the 2016 RITA® Award for Contemporary Romance: Short.

Find out more about Sarah's conversations with imaginary cowboys and billionaires at sarahmanderson.com, and sign up for the new-release newsletter at eepurl.com/nv39b.

Books by Sarah M. Anderson

Harlequin Desire

Seduction on His Terms

The Beaumont Heirs

Not the Boss's Baby
Tempted by a Cowboy
A Beaumont Christmas
His Son, Her Secret
Falling for Her Fake Fiancé
His Illegitimate Heir
Rich Rancher for Christmas

First Family of Rodeo

His Best Friend's Sister
His Enemy's Daughter

Visit her Author Profile page at Harlequin.com, or sarahmanderson.com, for more titles.

To the Quincy Public Library and the lovely librarians and staff, especially Katie, Farrah and Jeraca, who feed my book addiction!
Thank you for helping make my son a reader and for making literature a part of so many lives!

One

"Good evening, Dr. Wyatt," Jeannie Kaufman said as the man slid into his usual seat at the end of the bar. It was a busy Friday night, and he sat as far away as he could get from the other patrons at Trenton's.

"Jeannie," he said in his usual brusque tone.

But this time she heard something tight in his voice.

Dr. Robert Wyatt was an unusual man, to say the least. His family owned Wyatt Medical Industries, and Dr. Wyatt had been named to the "Top Five Chicago Billionaire Bachelors" list last year, which probably had just as much to do with his family fortune as it did with the fact that he was a solid six feet tall, broad chested and sporting a luxurious mane of inky black hair that made the ice-cold blue of his eyes more striking.

And as if being richer than sin and even better looking wasn't tempting enough, the man had to be a pediatric surgeon, as well. He performed delicate heart surgeries on babies and kids. He single-handedly saved lives—and she'd read that for some families who couldn't afford the astronomical costs, he'd quietly covered their bills.

Really, the man was too good to be true.

She kept waiting for a sign that, underneath all that perfection, he was a villain. She'd had plenty of rich, handsome and talented customers who were complete assholes.

Dr. Wyatt…wasn't.

Yes, he was distant, precise and, as far as she could tell, completely fearless. All qualities that made him a great surgeon. But if he had an ego, she'd never seen it. He came into the bar five nights a week at precisely eight, sat in the same spot, ordered the same drink and left her the same tip—a hundred dollars on a twenty-dollar tab. In cash. He never made a pass at anyone, staff or guest, and bluntly rebuffed any flirtation from women or men.

He was her favorite customer.

Before he'd had the chance to straighten his cuffs— something he did almost obsessively—Jeannie set his Manhattan down in front of him.

She'd been making his drink for almost three years now. His Manhattan contained the second-most expensive rye bourbon on the market, because Dr. Wyatt preferred the taste over the most expensive one; a vermouth that she ordered from Italy exclusively for him; and bitters that cost over a hundred bucks a bottle. It was all precisely blended and aged in an American white oak cask for sixty days and served in a chilled martini glass with a lemon twist. It'd taken almost eight months of experimenting with brands and blends and aging to get the drink right.

But it'd been worth it.

Every time he lifted the glass to his lips, like he was doing now, Jeannie held her breath. Watching this man drink was practically an orgasmic experience. As he swallowed, she watched in fascination as the muscles in his throat moved. He didn't show emotion, didn't pretend to be nice. But when he lowered the glass back to the bar?

He *smiled*.

It barely qualified as one, and a casual observer would've missed it entirely. His mouth hardly even moved. But she knew him well enough to know that the slight curve of his lips and the warming of his icy gaze was the same as anyone else shouting for joy.

He held her gaze and murmured, "Perfect."

It was the only compliment she'd ever heard him give.

Her body tightened as desire licked down her back and spread throughout her midsection. As a rule, Jeannie did not serve up sex along with drinks. But if she were ever going to break that rule, it'd be for him.

Sadly, he was only here for the drink.

Jeannie loved a good romance novel and for three years, she'd imagined Robert as some duke thrust into the role that didn't fit him, nobility that hated the crush of ballrooms and cut directs and doing the pretty around the ton and all those dukely things when all he really wanted to do was practice medicine and tend to his estates and generally be left alone. In those stories, there was always a housekeeper or pickpocket or even a tavern wench who thawed his heart and taught him to love.

Jeannie shook off her fantasies. She topped off the scotch for the salesman at the other end of the bar and poured the wine for table eleven, but her attention was focused on Wyatt. She had to break the bad news to him—she'd be gone next week to help her sister, Nicole, with the baby girl that was due any minute.

This baby was the key to Jeannie and her sister being a family again. Any family Jeannie had ever had, she'd lost. She'd never met her father—he'd left before she'd been born. Mom had died when Jeannie had been ten and Nicole…

It didn't matter what had gone wrong between the sisters in the past. What mattered was that they were going to grab this chance to be a family again now. Melissa—that was what they were going to call the baby—would be the tie that bound them together. Jeannie would do her part by being there for her sister, just like Nicole had been there for Jeannie when Mom had died and left the sisters all alone in the world.

In an attempt to demonstrate her commitment, Jeannie had even offered to move back into their childhood home with Nicole. It would've been a disaster but Jeannie had still offered because that was what family did—they made sacrifices and stuck together through the rough times. Only now that she was twenty-six was Jeannie aware how much Nicole had sacrificed for her. The least Jeannie could do was return the favor.

Nicole had told Jeannie that, while a thoughtful offer, it was absolutely *not* necessary for them to share a house again. Thank God, because living together probably would've destroyed their still-fragile peace. Instead, Jeannie would keep working nights at Trenton's—and taking care of Dr. Wyatt—and then she'd get to the house around ten every morning to help Nicole with the cooking or cleaning or playing with the baby.

Jeannie might not be the best sister in the world but by God, she was going to be the best aunt.

That was the plan, anyway.

The only hiccup was sitting in front of her.

Wyatt didn't do well with change, as she'd learned maybe six months into their *partnership*, as Jeannie thought of it. She'd gotten a cold and stayed home. He'd been more than a little upset that someone else had made him a subpar Manhattan that night. Julian, the owner of Trenton's, said Tony, the bartender who'd subbed for her that night, had gotten a job elsewhere right after that. Jeannie knew that wasn't a coincidence.

Maybe half the time Dr. Wyatt sat at her bar, he didn't say anything. Which was fine. But when he did talk? It wasn't inane chitchat or stale pickup lines. When he spoke, every single word either made her fall further in love with him or broke her heart.

"So," he started and Jeannie knew he was about to break her heart again.

She waited patiently, rearranging the stemware that hung below the bar in front of him. He'd talk when he wanted and not a moment before.

Had he lost a patient? That she knew of, he'd only

had two or three kids die and those times had been… awful. All he'd ever said was that he'd failed. That was it. But the way he'd sipped his drink…

The last time it'd happened, she'd sobbed in the ladies' room after he'd left. Below his icy surface, a sea of emotion churned. And when he lost a patient, that sea raged.

After three years of listening to Dr. Wyatt pour out his heart in cold, clipped tones, Jeannie knew all too well how things could go wrong with babies. That was what made Jeannie nervous about Nicole and Melissa.

"I heard something today," he went on after long moments that had her on pins and needles.

She studied him as she finished the lemons and moved on to the limes. He straightened his cuffs and then took a drink.

She fought the urge to check her phone again. Nicole would text if anything happened and there'd been no buzzing at her hip. But tonight was the night. Jeannie could feel it.

Wyatt cleared his throat. "I was informed that my father is considering a run for governor."

Jeannie froze, the knife buried inside a lime. Had she ever heard Dr. Wyatt talk about his parents? She might've assumed that they'd died and left the bulk of the Wyatt Medical fortune to their son.

And who the heck had *informed* him of this? What an odd way to phrase it. "Is that so?"

"Yes," Dr. Wyatt replied quickly. That, coupled with the unmistakable bitterness in his voice, meant only one thing.

This was extremely *bad* news.

Jeannie had been working in a bar since the day she'd turned eighteen, three whole years before she was legally allowed to serve alcohol. She'd been desperate to get away from Nicole, who hadn't wanted Jeannie to get a job and certainly not as a bartender. She'd wanted Jeannie to go to college, become a teacher, like Nicole. Wanting to own her own bar was out of the question. Nicole wouldn't allow it.

After *that* fight, Jeannie had moved out, lied about her age and learned on the job. While pouring wine, countless men and women poured their hearts out to her. In the years she'd been at this high-priced chophouse, she'd learned a hell of a lot about how the one percent lived.

But she'd never had a customer like Robert Wyatt before.

Wyatt finished his drink in two long swallows. "The thing is," he said, setting his glass down with enough force that Jeannie was surprised the delicate stem didn't shatter, "if he runs, he'll expect us to stand next to him as if we're one big happy family."

Wiping her hands, she gave up the pretense of working and leaned against the bar. "Sounds like that's a problem."

"You have no idea," he muttered, which was even more disturbing because when did precise, careful Dr. Robert Wyatt *mutter*?

His charcoal-gray three-piece suit fit him perfectly, as did the shirt with cuff links that tonight looked like sapphires—he favored blues when he dressed. The blue-and-orange-striped tie matched the square artfully arranged in his pocket. It was September and Chicago still clung to the last of the summer's heat, but the way Dr. Robert Wyatt dressed announced that he'd never stoop to *sweating*.

She could see where the tie had been loosened slightly as if he'd yanked on it in frustration. His hair wasn't carefully brushed back, but rumpled. He made it look good because everything looked good on him, but still. His shoulders drooped and instead of his usual ramrod-straight posture, his head hung forward, just a bit. When he glanced up at her, she saw the worry lines cut deep across his forehead. He looked like the weight of the world was about to crush him flat.

It hurt to see him like this.

If it were any other man, any other customer, she'd honestly offer him a hug because Lord, he looked like he needed one. But she'd seen how Wyatt flinched when someone touched him.

"So don't do it," she said, keeping her voice low and calm.

"I have to." Unsurprisingly, he straightened his cuffs. "I won't have a choice."

At that, she gave him a look. "Why not?" He glared but she kept going. "For God's sake, you have nothing *but* choices. If you wanted to buy half of Chicago to raise wildebeests, you could. If you opened your own hospital and told everyone they had to wear blue wigs to enter the building, there'd be a run on clown hair. You can go anywhere, do anything, be *anyone* you want because you're Dr. Robert *freaking* Wyatt."

All because he had looks, money and power.

All things Jeannie would never have.

His mouth opened but unexpectedly, he slammed it shut. Then he was pushing away from the bar, glaring at her as he threw some bills down and turned to go.

"Dr. Wyatt? Wait!" When he kept going, she yelled, "Robert!"

That got his attention.

When he spun, she flinched because he was *furious*. It wasn't buried under layers of icy calm—it was right there on the surface, plain as day.

Was he mad she'd used his given name? Or that she'd questioned his judgment? It didn't matter. She wasn't going to buckle in the face of his fury.

She squared her shoulders and said, "I have a family thing next week and I'm taking some vacation time."

Confusion replaced his anger and he was back at the bar in seconds, staring down at her with something that looked like worry clouding his eyes. "How long?"

She swallowed. She was taller than average, but looking up into his eyes, only a few inches away… He made her feel small at the same time she felt like the only person in his universe.

He'd always leave her unsettled, wouldn't he?

"Just the week. I'll be back Monday after next. Promise."

The look on his face—like he wouldn't be able to function if she wasn't there to serve the perfect Manhattan to the perfect man—was the kind of look that made her fall a little bit more in love with him while it broke her heart at the same time.

"Will you be okay?" she asked.

Something warm brushed over the top of her hand, sending a jolt of electricity up her arm. Had he *touched* her? By the time she looked down, Robert was straightening his cuffs. "Of course," he said dismissively, as if it was impossible for him to be anything *but* perfectly fine. "I'm a Wyatt."

Then he was gone.

Jeannie stared after him. This was bad. Before she could decide how worried about him she was going to be, her phone buzzed.

It's time! read Nicole's message.

"It's time!" Jeannie shouted. The waiters cheered.

Dr. Wyatt would have to wait. Jeannie's new niece came first.

Two

Jeannie was back tonight.

Robert hadn't gone to Trenton's, knowing she wouldn't be there, and he felt the loss of their routine deeply. Instead, he'd spent a lot more time in the office, reviewing cases and getting caught up on paperwork and not thinking about Landon Wyatt or political campaigns.

But finally, it was Monday and Jeannie would be waiting for him. On some level he found his desire to see her again worrisome. She was just a bartender who'd perfected a Manhattan. Anyone could mix a drink.

But that was a lie and he knew it.

He never should have touched her. But she'd stood there staring at him with her huge brown eyes, asking if he was going to be okay, like she cared. Not because he was the billionaire Dr. Robert Wyatt, but because he was Robert.

That was what he'd missed this week. Just being… Robert.

Lost in thought, he didn't look at the screen of his phone before he answered it. "This is Wyatt."

"Bobby?"

Robert froze, his hand on the elevator buttons. It couldn't be…

But no one else called him Bobby. *"Mom?"*

"Hi, honey." Cybil Wyatt's voice sounded weak. It hit him like a punch to the solar plexus. "How have you been?"

Almost three years had passed since he'd talked to his mother.

He quickly retreated to his office. "Can you talk? Are you on speakerphone?"

"Honey," she went on, an extra waver in her voice. "You heard from Alexander, right?"

That was a *no*, she couldn't talk freely.

Alexander was Landon's assistant, always happy to do the older man's bidding. "Yes. He said Landon wanted to run for governor." A terrible idea on both a state level and a personal level.

Robert knew the only reason Landon Wyatt wanted to be governor was because he'd discovered a way to personally enrich himself. He wasn't content having politicians and lobbyists in his pocket. He always wanted more.

"Your father wants you by his side." The way she cleared her throat made Robert want to throw something. "*We* want you by *our* sides," she corrected because the fiction that they were all one big happy family was a lie that had to be maintained at all costs, no matter what.

"Are you on speaker?"

She laughed lightly, a fake sound. "Of course not. All is forgiven, honey. We both know you didn't mean it."

Hmm. If she wasn't on speaker, she was probably sitting in Landon's opulent office, where he was watching her through those cold, slitted eyes of his—the same eyes Robert saw in the mirror every damn morning—making sure Mom stuck to the script. "Let me help you, Mom. I can get you away from him."

"We're having a gala to launch his campaign in two weeks." Her voice cracked but she didn't stop. "It's at the Winston art gallery, right off the Magnificent Mile."

"I know it."

"It'd mean a lot to your father and me to see you there."

Robert didn't doubt that his mother wanted to see him. But to Landon, this was nothing more than another way to exert control over Robert and he'd vowed never to give Landon that much power again—even if it cost him his relationship with his mother.

"Tell me what I can do to help you, Mom."

There was a brief pause. "We've missed you, too."

Dammit. He didn't want to pretend to be a happy family, not in private and most certainly not in public. But he knew Landon well enough to know that if he didn't show, Mom would pay the price.

Just like she always did.

Robert couldn't let that happen. Of all the things

Landon Wyatt had done and would continue to do, dangling Cybil as bait to ensure Robert cooperated was one of the meanest.

He had to fix this. "Think about what I said, okay? We'll talk at the gallery."

She exhaled. "That's wonderful, dear. It starts at seven but we'd like you to get there earlier. Your father wants to make sure we're all on the same page."

Robert almost growled. *Getting on the same page* meant threats. Lots of them. "I'll try. I have to make my rounds. But if I can get you away, will you come with me?" Because after what had happened last time...

"Thank you, Bobby," she said and he hoped like hell that was a *yes*. "I—*we* can't wait to see you again."

"Me, too, Mom. Love you."

She didn't say it back. The line went dead.

Robert stared at nothing for a long time.

This was exactly what he'd been afraid of. Landon was going to force Robert to do this—be this...this *lie*. He was going to make Robert stand next to him before crowds and cameras. He was going to expect Robert to give speeches of his own, no doubt full of bold-faced lies about Landon's character and compassion. And if Robert didn't...

Would he ever see his mother again?

Landon would do whatever he wanted, if Robert didn't stop him. There had to be a way.

You can do anything you want because you're Dr. Robert freaking *Wyatt*, he heard Jeannie say.

Maybe she was right.

Now more than ever, he needed a drink.

* * *

"Well?" he said in that silky voice of his.

Once, Cybil had thought Landon Wyatt's voice was the most seductive voice she'd ever heard.

That had been a long time ago. So long ago that all she could remember was the pain of realizing she'd been seduced, all right. She could barely remember the time when she'd been a naive coed right out of college, swept away by the charming billionaire fifteen years her senior.

She'd been paying for that mistake ever since. "He's coming."

Landon notched an eyebrow—a warning.

Cybil smiled graciously. "He'll try to get there early, but he has rounds," she went on, hoping Landon would dismiss her. Hearing Bobby's voice again, the anger when he'd promised he could get her away from her husband of thirty-five years…

God, she'd missed her son. Maybe this time would be different. Bobby had grown into a fine man, a brilliant surgeon. Landon hated that both because Bobby worked for a living and, Cybil suspected, because Landon knew Bobby was far smarter.

If anyone could outthink Landon Wyatt, it'd be his own son.

Something warm and light bloomed in her chest. With a start, she realized it was hope.

What if there really was a way?

But Landon would never let her go.

A fact he reinforced when he stood and stroked a hand over her hair. Years of practice kept her from flinching at his touch. "I know you've missed him," he murmured as if he hadn't been the one keeping her from her son. His hand settled on the back of her neck and he began to squeeze. "So I know you'll make sure he does what's expected. Otherwise…"

"Of course," Cybil agreed, struggling as his grip tightened.

Like she did every day, she thanked God Bobby had gotten away. If he were still trapped in this hell with her, she didn't know how she'd bear it. But the knowledge that he was out there, saving children and living far from *this*—that kept her going. As long as her son was safe, she could endure.

She looked up at the man she'd married and smiled because he expected her to act as if she enjoyed being with him. Maybe… Maybe she wouldn't have to endure much longer.

"Mr. Wyatt?" The sound of Alexander's reedy voice cut through the office. "My apologies, but the campaign chairman is on line one."

"Now what?" he growled, abruptly letting her go.

Cybil did not exhale in relief because he'd already forgotten she was here. She merely escaped while she could.

She didn't want Bobby to be drawn back into his father's world, and the fact that Landon was using her to get their son to fall into line sickened her. But Bobby's anger, his willingness to stand up to his father…

No, maybe she wouldn't have to endure this marriage much longer at all.

She needed to be ready.

*　*　*

Would Robert convince his mother to leave Landon? The last time, it'd gone...poorly.

He needed a better plan this time.

More than just hiding Cybil Wyatt, Robert needed to make sure Landon wouldn't ever be in a position to track her down.

His heart beat at a highly irregular pace. Last time he'd merely tried to hide his mother, in his own home, no less. He hadn't had a contingency plan in place and without that plan, the whole rescue had been doomed to fail.

This time would be different.

Wyatts didn't fail. They succeeded.

He entered Trenton's at five past eight. Thank God Jeannie was back tonight. She might not be able to offer assistance but she could at least tell him if New Zealand was a good idea or not. She might be the only person he knew who'd tell him the truth. Now all he had to do was find a way to ask.

A soft, feminine voice purred, "Good evening, Dr. Wyatt. What can I get you?"

His head snapped up at the unfamiliar voice, the hair on the back of his neck standing up. The bar at Trenton's was dimly lit, so it took a few moments for Robert to identify the speaker.

The woman behind the bar was *not* Jeannie. This woman was shorter, with long light-colored hair piled on top of her head. Jeannie was almost tall enough that she could look Robert in the eye, with dark hair cropped close.

"Where's Jeannie?" he growled.

It was Monday. She was supposed to be *here*.

The woman behind the bar batted her eyes. "I'm Miranda. Jeannie's on vacation. I'm more than happy to take care of you while she's gone…"

Robert glared at her. Dammit, Jeannie had said one week. She'd *promised*. And now he needed her and she wasn't here.

The pressure in his head was almost blinding. If he didn't see Jeannie tonight—right *now*—he might do something they'd all regret.

"Dr. Wyatt?"

The world began to lose color at the edges, a numb gray washing everything flat.

He needed to leave before he lost control.

But he couldn't because his mother had called him and there had to be a way to save her and he *needed* to see Jeannie.

She was the only one who could bring color back to his world.

"She's not on vacation. Tell me where she is." He leaned forward, struggling to keep his voice level. *"Or else."*

Miranda's teasing pout fell away as she straightened and stepped back. "She's not here," she said, the purr gone from her voice.

He wasn't going to lash out. A Wyatt never lost control.

So instead of giving in to the gray numbness and doing what Landon would do, Robert forced himself to adjust the cuffs on his bespoke suit, which gave him enough time to breathe and attempt to speak calmly.

He studied Miranda. She held his gaze, but he could see her pulse beating at her throat. She was probably telling the truth.

"I'd like to speak with the owner. Please."

The buzzing in his head became two discordant sounds. He could hear Landon snarling, *Wyatts don't ask*, at the same time as he heard Jeannie say, in that husky voice of hers, *There, was that so hard?*

When was the first time Jeannie had said that to him? He didn't remember. All he remembered was that she was the first person who'd ever dared tease him.

When he was sure he had himself back under control, he looked up. Miranda the substitute bartender wasn't moving.

"Now," Robert snarled.

With a jolt, she turned and fled.

It felt wrong to sit in his seat if Jeannie wasn't on the other side of the bar. Like this place wasn't home anymore.

Which was ridiculous because this was a bar where he spent maybe half an hour every night. It wasn't his sprawling Gold Coast townhouse with million-dollar views of Lake Michigan. It wasn't even the monstrosity of a mansion where he'd been raised by a succession of nannies. This was not home. This was just where Jeannie had been when he'd walked into this restaurant two years and ten months ago and sat down at this bar because he'd felt…lost.

It had been thirty-four months since Jeannie had

stood in front of him, listening while he struggled to get his thoughts in order because his mother had refused to stay with him and Landon had come for her. Everything in Robert's carefully constructed world had gone gray, which had been good because then Robert didn't have to feel anything. Anything but the overpowering need for the perfect drink.

Sometimes, when Robert allowed himself to look back at that moment, he wondered if maybe Jeannie had been waiting patiently for him.

Where the hell *was* she?

Then it hit him. She'd said she had a family thing. She wasn't here now.

Something had gone wrong.

The realization gave him an odd feeling, one he did not like. He liked it even less when Miranda the substitute bartender returned with a man that looked vaguely familiar.

"Dr. Wyatt, it's so good to see you, as always," the man said, smiling in a way Robert didn't trust. "I'm sorry there's a problem. How can I correct things?"

Robert was running out of patience. "Who are you?"

"Julian Simmons." He said it in a way that made it clear Robert was supposed to remember who he was. "I own Trenton's. You're one of our most valued customers, so if there's a problem, I'm sure we can—"

Robert cut the man off. "Where's Jeannie?"

Robert couldn't tell in the dim light, but he thought Simmons might have gone a shade whiter. "Jeannie is taking some personal time."

Only a fool would think personal time and vacation

time were the same thing. Robert was many things, but foolish wasn't one of them. "Is she all right?"

Simmons didn't answer for another long beat.

Something *had* happened; Robert knew it. Helplessness collided with an ever-increasing anger. He was not going to stand by while another woman was hurt. Not when he had the power to stop it.

"Jeannie is fine," Simmons finally said. "We're hopeful that she will rejoin us in a few weeks. I know she's your personal favorite, but Miranda is more than happy to serve you."

Both Miranda the substitute bartender and Simmons the restaurant owner recoiled before Robert realized he was snarling at them. "Tell me where she is. Now."

"Dr. Wyatt, I'm sorry but—"

Before he was aware of what he was doing, Robert had reached across the bar and took hold of Simmons's tie.

Robert could hear Landon Wyatt shouting, *No one says* no *to a Wyatt*, in his mind.

Or maybe he hadn't heard the words. Maybe he'd said them out loud because Miranda squeaked in alarm.

"You," he said to the woman, "can *go*."

He didn't have to tell her twice.

"Dr. Wyatt," Simmons said. "This is all a misunderstanding."

Belatedly, he realized he was probably not making the best argument. Abruptly, he released Simmons's tie. Robert realized he had overlooked the path of least resistance. Instead of allowing his temper to get the

better of him, he should've started from a different ne-
gotiating position.

"How much?"

"What?" Simmons winced.

"How much?" Robert repeated. "I have frightened
you and your employees, which wasn't my intent. I like
coming here. I would like to return, once Jeannie is
back in her position. I would like to...to make amends."

Which was as close as possible to apologizing without actually apologizing because Wyatts did *not* apologize.

Ever.

Simmons stared at him, mouth agape.

"Shall we say..." Robert picked a number out of thin
air. "Ten thousand?"

"Dollars?" Simmons gasped.

"Twenty thousand. Dollars," he added for clarity's
sake. Everyone had a price, after all.

Jeannie was in trouble and he had to help her. But to
do that, he had to know where she was. If Simmons refused to take the bribe, Robert had other ways of tracking her down, but those would take more time. Time
was one commodity he couldn't buy.

The buzzing in his head was so loud that it drowned
out the hum of the restaurant. He gritted his teeth and
blocked it out.

Simmons pulled his pocket square out and dabbed
at his forehead. "Do you realize how many laws you're
asking me to break?"

"Do you realize how little I care?" Wyatt shot back.

When it came to things like abuse or murder, Wyatt

knew and respected the law. When it came to things like this? Well, he was a Wyatt. Money talked.

Simmons knew it, too. "Do I have your word that you won't hurt her?"

"I won't even touch her." *Not unless she wants me to.*

The thought crossed his mind before he was aware it was there, but he shook it away.

Simmons seemed to deflate. "There was a family emergency."

The longer this man stood around hemming and hawing, the worse things could be for Jeannie. Belatedly, Robert realized he did not have twenty thousand dollars in cash on him. He placed a credit card on the bar. "Run it for whatever you want."

After only a moment's hesitation, Simmons took the card. "Let me get you the address, Dr. Wyatt."

About damn time.

Three

Jeannie all but collapsed onto the concrete step in front of Nicole's house, too numb to even weep.

No, that was wrong. This was her house now.

Nicole was dead.

And since there were no other living family members, Jeannie had inherited what Nicole had owned. Including their childhood home.

Everything left was hers now. The sensible used family sedan. The huge past-due bills to fertility clinics. The cost of burying her sister.

The baby.

It was too much.

Death was bad enough because it had taken Nicole, leaving Jeannie with nothing but wispy memories of a happy family. But who knew dying was so complicated?

And expensive? Who knew unraveling a life would involve so much damned *paperwork*?

That didn't even account for Melissa. That baby girl was days old. It wasn't right that she would never know her mother. It wasn't right that the family Nicole had wanted for so long...

Jeannie scrubbed at her face. It wasn't Melissa's fault that delivery had been complicated or that Nicole had developed a blood clot that had gone undiagnosed until it was too late. Dimly, Jeannie knew she needed to sue the hospital. This wasn't the 1800s. Women weren't supposed to die giving birth. But Jeannie couldn't face the prospect of more paperwork, of more responsibilities. She could barely face the next ten minutes.

She looked up at the sky, hoping to find a star to guide her. One little twinkling bit of hope. But this was Chicago. The city's light pollution was brighter than any star, and all that was left was a blank sky with a reddish haze coloring everything. Including her world.

She was supposed to be at work. She was supposed to be fixing the perfect Manhattan for the perfect Dr. Robert Wyatt, the man whose tipping habits had made her feel financially secure for the first time in her life. A hundred bucks a night, five nights a week, for almost three years—Dr. Robert Wyatt had single-handedly given Jeannie the room to breathe. To dream of her own place, her own rules...

Of course, now that she had an infant to care for and a mortgage and bills to settle, she couldn't breathe. She'd be lucky if her job at Trenton's was still there when she was able to go back. *If* she would be able to go back. Julian might hold her job for another week or so, but Jeannie knew he wouldn't hold it for two months. Because after an initial search of newborn childcare in Chicago, she knew that was what she'd need. Jeannie had found only day care that accepted six-week-old babies, but the price was so far out of reach that all she'd been able to do was laugh and close the browser. If she wanted childcare before Melissa was two months old, she needed a *lot* of money. And that was something she simply didn't have. Even if she sued the hospital, put the house on the market, sold the family sedan—it still wouldn't be enough fast enough.

Even though there were no stars to see, she stared hard at that red sky. This time she caught a flicker of light high overhead. It was probably just an airplane, but she couldn't risk it. She closed her eyes and whispered to herself, "Star light, star bright, grant me the wish I wish tonight."

She couldn't wish Nicole back. She couldn't undo any of the loss or the pain that had marked Jeannie's life so far. Looking back was a trap, one she couldn't get stuck in. She had no choice but to keep moving forward.

"I need help," she whispered.

Financial assistance, baby help, emotional support—you name it, she needed it.

There was a moment of blissful silence—no horns honking in the distance, no neighbors shouting, not even the roar of an airplane overhead.

But if Jeannie was hoping for an answer to her prayers, she didn't get it because that was when the small sound of Melissa starting to cry broke the quiet.

Sucking in a ragged breath, Jeannie dropped her head into her hands. She needed just a few more seconds to think but…

The baby didn't sleep.

Was that because Jeannie wasn't Nicole? Or was Melissa sick? Could Jeannie risk the cost of taking Melissa to the emergency room? Or…there was a pediatrician who'd stopped at the hospital before Melissa was discharged. But it was almost ten at night. If anyone answered the phone, they'd probably tell her to head to the ER.

The only person she knew who knew anything at all about small children was Dr. Wyatt, but it wasn't like she could ask him for advice about a fussy newborn. He was a surgeon, not a baby whisperer.

Jeannie had helped organize a shower for Nicole with some of Nicole's teacher friends and she had picked out some cute onesies. That was the sum total of Jeannie's knowledge about newborns. She wasn't sure she was even doing diapers right.

"Please," she whispered as Melissa's cries grew more agitated, although she knew there would be no salvation. All she could do was what she had always done— one foot in front of the other.

Jeannie couldn't fail that baby girl or her sister. But more than that, she couldn't give up on this family. She and Nicole had just started again. It felt particularly cruel to have that stolen so soon.

A car door slammed close enough that Jeannie glanced up. And looked again. A long black limo was blocking traffic in the middle of the street directly in front of the house. A short man wearing a uniform, complete with a matching hat, was opening the back door. He stood to the side and a man emerged from the back seat.

Not just any man.

Oh, God, Dr. Robert Wyatt was here. Her best, favorite customer. All she could do was gape as his long legs closed the distance between them.

"Are you all right?" he demanded, coming to a halt in front of her.

She had to lean so far back to stare at him that she almost lost her balance. He blocked out the night sky and her whole world narrowed to just him.

Yeah, she was a little unbalanced right now. "What are you doing here?"

Because he couldn't be here. She looked like hell warmed over twice, and the shirt she was wearing had stains that she didn't want to think about and she was a wreck.

He *couldn't* be here.

He was.

He stared at her with an intensity that had taken her months to get used to. "Are you *all right*?"

It wasn't a question. It was an order.

Jeannie scrambled to her feet. Even looking him in the eye, it still felt like he loomed over her. "I'm fine," she lied because what was she supposed to say?

She liked him as a customer. He was a gorgeous man, a great tipper—and he had never made her feel uncomfortable or objectified. Aside from that phantom touch of his hand brushing against hers—which could've been entirely accidental—they'd never done anything together beyond devise the perfect Manhattan. That was *it*.

And now he'd followed her to Nicole's house.

The man standing in front of her looked like he would take on the world if she asked him to.

His brow furrowed. "If everything's fine, why aren't you at work?"

"Is that why you're here?"

"You promised you'd be back today and you weren't. Tell me what's wrong so I can fix it."

She blinked. Had she actually wished upon a star? One with magical wish-granting powers?

"You can't fix this." It didn't matter how brilliant a surgeon he was, he couldn't help Nicole. No one could.

"Yes, I can," he growled.

He growled! At her! Then he climbed the first step. "I need you to be there, Jeannie." He took another step up, another step closer to her. "I need…"

"Robert." Without thinking, she put her hand on his chest because she couldn't let him get any closer.

She felt his muscles tense under her palm. It was a mistake, touching him. That phantom contact a week ago in the bar? The little sparks she'd felt then were nothing compared to the electricity that arced between them now. He was hot to the touch and everything had gone to hell, but he was here.

He'd come for her.

He looked down to where she was touching him and she followed his gaze. He wasn't wearing a tie, which was odd. He always wore one. She stared at the little triangle of skin revealed by his unbuttoned collar.

Then his fingertips were against her cheek and she gasped, a shiver racing down her back. "Jeannie," he whispered, lifting her chin until she had no choice but to look him in the eye. His eyes, normally so icy, were warm and promised wonderful things. His head began to dip. "I need…"

He was going to kiss her. He was going to press his perfect mouth against hers and she was going to let him because she could get lost in this man.

Just as she felt his warmth against her lips, Melissa's cries intruded into the silence that surrounded them.

"Oh! The baby!" Jeannie hurried into the house.

"The *baby*?" he called after her.

How much time had passed since Robert had emerged from the back of that sleek limo? Could have been seconds but it could've just as easily been minutes. Minutes where she'd left Melissa alone.

By the time she got back to the baby's room, Melissa was red in the face, her little body rigid, her arms waving. Was that normal? Or was Melissa in pain? Or…

"I'm sorry, I'm sorry," Jeannie said as she nervously picked the baby up, trying to support her head like the nurse had shown her. She was pretty sure she wasn't doing it right because Melissa cried harder. "Oh, honey, I'm so sorry." Sorry Nicole wasn't here, sorry Jeannie couldn't figure out the problem, much less how to fix it. "What's wrong, sweetie?" As if the baby could tell her.

Melissa howled and Jeannie couldn't stop her own tears. She couldn't bear the thought of losing this last part of her family.

"Here," a deep voice said as the baby was plucked out of Jeannie's arms. "Let me."

She blinked a few times, but in her current state of exhaustion what she saw didn't make a lot of sense.

Dr. Robert Wyatt, one of the Top Five Billionaire Bachelors of Chicago, a man so remote and icy it'd taken Jeannie years to get comfortable with his intense silences—*that* man was laying Melissa out on the changing pad, saying, "What seems to be the problem?" as if the baby could tell him.

"What…" Jeannie blinked again but the image didn't change. "What are you doing?"

Instead of answering, Robert pulled out his cell. "Reginald? Bring my kit in."

"Your kit?"

He didn't explain. "How old is this infant? Eight days?"

She wasn't even surprised he hadn't answered her question, much less come within a day of guessing Melissa's age. "Nine. Nicole, my sister, went into labor right after I last saw you." She tried to say the rest of it but suddenly she couldn't breathe.

Robert made a gentle humming noise. The baby blinked up at him in confusion, a momentary break in her crying. "What was her Apgar score?"

"Her *what*?"

Who the hell was this man? The Dr. Wyatt she knew didn't make gentle humming noises that calmed babies. There was nothing gentle about him!

Robert had Melissa down to her diaper. The poor baby began to wail again. He made a *tsking* noise. "Where is the mother?"

Jeannie choked on a sob. "She's…" No, that wasn't

right. Present tense no longer applied to Nicole. "She developed blood clots and…"

Robert's back stiffened. "The father?"

"Sperm donor."

He made that humming noise again. Just then the doorbell rang and Melissa howled all the louder and Jeannie wanted to burrow into Robert's arms and pretend the last week had been a horrible dream. But she didn't get the chance because he said, "My kit—can you bring it to me, please?"

"Sure?" When Jeannie opened the door, the man from the car was there. "Reginald?"

"Miss." He tipped his hat with one hand. With the other, he hefted an absolutely enormous duffel bag. "Shall I bring this to Dr. Wyatt?"

"I'll take it. Thank you."

"Babies cry, miss," he said gently as he handed over the bag. "The good doctor will make sure nothing's wrong. Don't worry—it gets easier."

The kind words from an older man who looked like he might have dealt with crying babies a few times in his life felt like a balm on her soul.

"Thank you," Jeannie said and she meant it.

Reginald tipped his hat.

It took both hands, but she managed to lug the kit back to the baby's room. Melissa was still screaming. Probably because Robert was pinching the skin on her arms. "What are you doing?" Jeannie demanded.

"She's got good skin elasticity and her lungs are in great shape." He sounded calm and reasonable. "Ah, the kit. Come," he said, motioning right next to him. "Tell me everything."

Jeannie did as she was told, putting her hand on Melissa's little belly as Robert dug into the duffel. "She hasn't stopped crying since I brought her home two days ago. Nicole never even left the hospital. I don't know anything about babies."

"Clearly." She couldn't even be insulted by that. "Which hospital? Who were the doctors?" He came up with a stethoscope and one of those tiny little lights.

Oh. His kit must be an emergency medical bag. "Uh, Covenant. Her OB was some old guy named Preston, I think? I don't remember who the pediatrician is." She realized that, at some point, Robert had shed his suit jacket and had rolled up his sleeves. He still had on his vest but there was something so undone about him right now...

He'd almost kissed her. And she'd almost let him. The man who didn't like to be touched, didn't show emotion—she'd touched him and he'd come within a breath of kissing her.

Even stranger, he was now touching—gently—Melissa.

This just didn't make sense. Robert didn't like touching people. Simple as that.

What exactly had she wished upon? No ordinary star had this kind of power behind it.

Robert listened to Melissa's chest and then peered into her mouth and ears before pressing on her stomach.

With a heartbreaking scream, the baby tooted.

"Oh, my gosh. I'm so sorry," Jeannie blurted out.

"As I expected," Robert said, seemingly unbothered

by the small mess left in the diaper that was thankfully still under Melissa's bottom. He listened to her stomach. "Hmm."

"What does that mean?" Dimly, Jeannie was aware that this was the longest conversation she'd ever had with him.

"When was the last time you fed her?"

"Uh, about forty-five minutes ago. She drank about two ounces." That, at least, she could measure. She'd watched a few YouTube videos on how to feed a baby. Thank God for the internet.

Wait—when had she started thinking of him as Robert? Except for that one time, she hadn't allowed herself to use his given name at Trenton's because that implied a level of familiarity they didn't have.

Or at least, a level they hadn't had before he'd shown up on her doorstep to make an accidental house call. Or before she'd touched his chest and he'd caressed her cheek and who could forget that near-kiss?

Robert it was, apparently.

"What are you feeding her?"

"The hospital sent home some formula…" She couldn't even remember the brand right now.

"Get it."

She hurried to the kitchen and grabbed the can and the bottle she hadn't had the chance to empty and clean yet. By the time she got back to the baby's room, Robert had apparently diapered and dressed the baby and was wrapping her in a blanket so that only her head was visible.

"This is called swaddling," he explained as, almost

by magic, Melissa stopped screaming. "Newborns are used to being in the womb—not a lot of room to move, it's warm and they can hear their mother's heartbeat."

Embarrassment swamped her. "I thought... I didn't want her to get too hot."

"You can swaddle her in just a diaper—but keep her wrapped up. She'll be happier." He scooped the baby burrito into his arms and turned to Jeannie, casting a critical eye over her.

"Where did you learn how to do that?"

"Do what?"

She waved in his general direction. "Change a diaper. Swaddle a baby. Where did you learn how to take care of a baby?"

He notched an eyebrow at her and, in response, her cheeks got hot. "It's not complicated. Now, some babies have what we call a fourth trimester—they need another three months of that closeness and warmth before they're comfortable. Hold her on your chest as much as you can right now. She doesn't need to cry it out." His lips curved into that barely there smile. "No matter what the internet says."

She blushed. Hard.

He tucked Melissa against his chest as if it was the easiest thing in the world. He didn't seem the least bit concerned about how to support her head or that he might accidentally drop her or any of the worries that haunted Jeannie. Nor did he seem worried in the slightest about holding a baby in the vicinity of a suit that probably cost a few thousand dollars. He made the whole thing look effortless. Because it wasn't that complicated, apparently.

She wanted to be insulted—and she was—but the sight of Dr. Robert Wyatt *cuddling* a newborn, for lack of a better word, hit Jeannie in the chest so hard she almost stumbled.

"Here," she managed to say, holding the formula out for him.

With a critical eye, he glanced at the brand. Then, without taking it, he pulled out his cell again. "Reginald? Find the closest grocery store and pick up the following items…"

He rattled off a list of baby products that left Jeannie dizzy. When he ended the call, he nodded to the formula. "That brand has soy in it. Her symptoms are in line with a soy sensitivity."

"Crying is a symptom?"

He gave her a look that was almost kind. But not quite. "Her stomach is upset and she's not supposed to be that red. Both are signs she's not tolerating something well. Reginald will bring us several alternatives."

"So…there's nothing wrong with her?"

"No. Of course it could be colic and something more serious…"

All the blood drained from Jeannie's face so fast that she felt ill. *More* serious?

Robert cleared his throat. "I'm reasonably confident it's the formula."

"Oh. Okay. That's…" She managed to make it to the rocker that Nicole's fellow teachers had all pooled their money to buy. The baby just had a sensitive stomach. It wasn't anything Jeannie was doing wrong—the hospital had given her the formula, after all. "That's good." Her voice cracked on the words.

Robert stared at her. "Are you all right?"

Only *this* man would ask that question. She began to giggle and then she was laughing so hard she was sobbing and the words poured out of her. "Of *course* I'm not okay. I buried my sister and there was so much we didn't say and I'm responsible for a newborn but I have no idea what I'm doing and I don't have the money to do any of it and you're here, which is good, but *why* are you here, Robert?"

He stared at her. It would've been intimidating if he hadn't been rubbing tiny circles on the back of a tiny baby, who was making noises that were definitely quieter than all-out wailing. "You weren't at the bar."

"This," she said, waving her hand to encompass everything, "qualifies as an emergency."

"Yes," he agreed, still staring at her with those icy eyes. "When will you be back?"

If it were anyone else in the world, she'd have thrown him out.

Jeannie had made sure Miranda at work knew exactly how Robert liked his drink. Because Jeannie aged it in a cask, Miranda didn't even have to mix it. She just had to pour and serve. Even someone with standards as impossibly high as Robert's could be content with that for a few damn nights while Jeannie tried to keep her life from completely crumbling.

But for all that, she couldn't toss him onto the curb. He'd examined Melissa and calmed the baby down. He had a good, nonterrifying reason for why she kept crying and he had sent Reginald to get different formula. For the first time in a week, Jeannie felt like the situation was almost—*almost*—under control.

But not quite.

"Why do I need to go back to work?" she asked carefully because this was Dr. Robert Wyatt, after all—a man of few words and suspiciously deep emotions.

He looked confused by her question. "Because."

A hell of a lousy answer. "Because *why*?"

His mouth opened, then shut, then opened again. "Because I... I had a bad day." He seemed completely befuddled by this.

"I'm sorry to hear that. I'm currently having a bad life." He didn't smile at her joke. "Look, I don't know what to tell you. I have to put the baby first—you know, the baby you're currently holding? She's the most important thing in my life now and I'm all she's got. So I can't go back to work until I figure out how to take care of an infant, pay for childcare, possibly sue a hospital for negligence, settle my sister's outstanding debts and get a grip on my life. You'll have to find someone else to serve you a Manhattan!"

If he was insulted by her shouting, he didn't show it. "All right."

"All right?" That was almost too easy. "Good. Miranda at the bar knows how to pour... What are you doing?"

He had his cell again. "I don't like Miranda." Before Jeannie could reply to that out-of-the-blue statement, he went on, "Len? Wyatt. I've got a case for you—malpractice. Postpartum mortality. I want your best people on it. Yes. I'll forward the information to you as I get it."

"Robert?" Admittedly, she was having an awful day. But…had he just hired a lawyer for her?

"One moment." He punched up another number, all while still holding Melissa, which was more than Jeannie had been able to accomplish in the past two days. "Kelly? I'm going to need a full-time nanny to care for a newborn. Yes. Have a list for me by eleven tomorrow morning. I'll want to conduct interviews after I'm out of surgery."

Jeannie stared at him. "Wait—what are you doing?"

"My lawyer will handle your lawsuit. It won't get that far—the hospital *will* want to settle, but he'll make sure you get enough to take care of the child."

She heard the threat, loud and clear. His tone was the same as one time when he'd threatened a woman who'd groped him once. This was Robert Wyatt, a powerful, important man. He might be Jeannie's best customer and she might be infatuated with him but he also had the power to bend lawyers and whole hospitals to his will.

This was what she couldn't forget.

If he really wanted to, he'd bend *her* to his will.

She had to keep this from spinning out of control. "Melissa."

"What?"

"Her name is Melissa."

"Fine." But even as he dismissed that observation, he leaned his chin against the top of the baby's head and—there was no mistaking what she was seeing.

Dr. Robert Wyatt *nuzzled* Melissa's downy little head.

Then it only got worse because he did something she absolutely wasn't ready for.

He smiled.

Not a big smile. No, this was his normal smile, the one so subtle that most everyone else wouldn't even notice it. But she did. And it simply devastated her.

She had to be dreaming this whole thing. In no way, shape or form should Dr. Robert Wyatt be standing in what was, essentially, Jeannie's childhood bedroom, soothing a baby and somehow making everything better. Or at least bearable.

"Now," he went on, "I'll have a nanny over here by two tomorrow." He made as if he wanted to adjust his cuffs, then appeared to realize that he'd not only rolled his sleeves up to his elbows but was also still holding an infant who wasn't crying at all. He settled for looking at his watch. "You should be back at work on Wednesday."

Her mouth flopped open. *"What?"*

"You don't know how to care for an infant. I need you to be back at work. I'm hiring a nanny to help you." He glanced around the room. "And a maid."

He was already reaching for his phone when she snapped, "I don't know whether to be offended or grateful."

"Grateful."

Oh, she'd show him grateful, all right. "I'm not going back to work on Wednesday."

He paused with the phone already at his ear. Something hard passed over his eyes, but he said, "I'll also need a maid. Three days a week. Thanks." Then he ended the call. "What do you mean, you won't go back?"

She pushed herself to her feet. Thankfully, her knees held. "Dr. Wyatt—"

He made a noise deep in his throat.

"Robert," she said, trying to keep her voice calm and level because if she didn't at least try, she might start throwing things. "I'm sorry you're having a bad day and I appreciate that you're willing to throw a bunch of money at my problems, but I'm not going back to work this week. Maybe not next week."

"Why not?" His voice was so cold she shivered. "What else could you possibly need?"

She'd been wrong all these years because it turned out that Dr. Robert Wyatt really didn't have a heart. "To grieve for my sister!"

Four

Jeannie was yelling at him. Well. That was…interesting.

As was Robert's response. Very few people shouted at him and from an empirical standpoint, it was curious to note that his body tensed, his spine straightened and his face went completely blank because betraying any response was a provocation.

Rationally, he knew Jeannie was upset because of the circumstances. And he also understood that she wasn't about to attack him.

But damn, his response was hardwired.

He forced himself to relax, to exhale the air he was holding in. There was no need to let his fight-or-flight instincts rule him.

Jeannie was not his father. This was not a dangerous situation.

He would make this better.

In his office, when there was bad news, he had a basic script he followed. He offered general condolences, promised to do his best to make things better and focused on quantitative outcomes—heart valves, ccs of blood pumped, reasonable expectations postsurgery. And on those rare occasions when he lost a patient, either on the table or, more frequently, to a post-op infection, he kept things brief. *I'm sorry for your loss.* No one wanted to talk to him when he'd failed them, anyway.

Then there was the baby—*Melissa*, as Jeannie had insisted. Robert didn't often think of his patients in terms of their names because children were entirely too easy to love, and he couldn't risk loving someone who might not survive the day or the week or even the year.

But Melissa wasn't a patient, was she? Her heart and lung sounds had been clear and strong, with no telltale murmur or stutter to the beat. This was a perfectly healthy infant who simply needed different formula.

Robert couldn't remember the last time he'd held a healthy baby. By the time patients were referred to him at the hospital, they'd already undergone a barrage of tests and examinations by other doctors. The closest he got was seeing patients for their annual postoperation checkup. Most of them did well but there was always an undercurrent of fear to those visits, parents praying that everything was still within the bounds of medically normal.

Aside from general condolences, though, none of his scripts applied here. He'd already done everything obvious to fix the situation and somehow that had upset Jeannie. If he wasn't so concerned about her reaction, he'd be interested in understanding where the disconnect had happened.

But he was concerned. Jeannie wasn't the parent of a patient. She was... Well, he couldn't say she was a friend, either. She existed outside of work or personal relationships. She was simply...

The woman he'd almost kissed.

Because when the car had pulled up in front of her house, it had felt as if she'd been sitting out there, waiting for him.

Thankfully, he hadn't kissed her. Because she didn't look like she'd appreciate any overtures right now. She was a mess, her short hair sticking up in all directions, dark circles under her eyes, her stained, threadbare T-shirt hanging off one shoulder, revealing a blue bra strap.

He tore his gaze away from that bra strap. He normally didn't respond to the exposure of skin but knowing what color her bra was made him...uncomfortable.

Which was not the correct reaction, not when she was sitting there, quietly crying. It hurt him to see her like this, to know that she was in pain and there was a hard limit on what he could do to fix the situation. And, more than anything, he felt like a bastard of the highest order because he wasn't really doing anything for *her*. The lawyers, the nanny, the maid—that was all for his benefit. The sooner he took care of Jeannie, the sooner she could be there for him.

She swiped her hand across her cheeks and looked

up at him. The pain in her eyes almost knocked him back a step.

"I'm sorry," she mumbled.

"Excuse me?"

She sniffed and it hurt Robert worse than a punch to the kidneys. How odd. "I didn't mean to yell at you. It's not your fault everything's gone to hell in a hand-basket and you're just trying to help." She blinked up at him. "Aren't you?"

Wasn't he?

Say something. Something kind and thoughtful and appropriate. Something that would make things right. Or at least better.

The doorbell rang.

"That'll be Reginald." Although it certainly wasn't the brave thing to do, Robert hurried to the door.

"They had everything but that one brand—Enfamil," his driver said, straining under the weight of the bags.

"Make a note—have some sent over tomorrow." Robert stepped to the side as Reginald nodded and carried the bags into the house. The smell of something delicious hit Robert's nose. Chicken, maybe? "What did you get?"

"I thought the young lady might enjoy dinner," Reginald said, nodding at Jeannie, who was standing in the hallway, a look of utter confusion on her face. "It's hard to cook with a newborn."

"I… That's very kind of you. I'm not sure I've eaten today," she said, her voice shaky.

Robert experienced a flash of irrational jealousy because Reginald was the kind of man who didn't need a script to recite the appropriate platitudes at the appropriate times. He had a wife of almost forty years, four children and had recently become a grandfather. If anyone could help Robert find the right way to express condolences, it'd be Reginald.

But then Landon's voice slithered into Robert's mind, making him cringe. *Wyatts never ask for help.*

Right. Reginald was an employee. Robert paid him well to fill in the gaps, which was all he was doing here. It simply hadn't occurred to Robert that Jeannie might not have eaten recently.

Reginald smiled gently at Jeannie. "Where would you like the groceries?"

"Oh. The kitchen's right through there." She stepped past Robert and Melissa, her gaze averted. "Thank you so much for this."

Robert glanced down. The baby had fallen asleep, which was a good sign. Robert went to the nursery and laid the child on her back in the crib. She startled and then relaxed back into sleep.

He frowned. A blanket and two stuffed animals littered the mattress, both suffocation risks. He pulled them out. Jeannie really didn't know what she was doing, did she?

If he didn't want the chance to personally interview prospective nannies, he'd have one over here tonight. Maybe he should stay instead...

But he shut down that line of thinking. He had surgery tomorrow, which meant he needed to be at the hospital at four in the morning. He'd never needed a lot of sleep but he always made sure to get at least four hours before surgery days. He never took risks when lives were on the line.

He studied Melissa. The sound of murmuring from the kitchen filled the room with a gentle noise and the baby sighed in her sleep. Robert had handled so many babies and children over the course of his career but this infant girl was…different. He wasn't sure why.

"Sleep for her," he whispered to the baby.

By the time he made it back to the living room—really, this house was little more than a shoebox—Reginald was at the front door as Jeannie said, "Thank you so much again. How much do I owe you?"

Reginald shot Robert a slightly alarmed look over Jeannie's shoulder.

"That's all, Reginald."

"Miss, it's been a pleasure." With a tip of his hat, Reginald was out the door before Jeannie could protest.

A moment of tense silence settled over the house. No babies crying, no helpful drivers filling the gaps of conversation. Just Robert and Jeannie and the terrible feeling that instead of making everything better for her, he'd made things worse.

"Robert," Jeannie began and for some reason, she sounded…sad? Or just tired?

He couldn't tell and that bothered him. This was *Jeannie*. He was able to read her better than he could read anyone. "I'd recommend starting the baby—I mean, Melissa—on this formula," he said, picking the organic one. "No soy."

In response, she dropped her head into her hands.

"It'll take a day or two before the other formula is

completely out of her system," he went on in a rush, "but if she gets worse at any time, call me."

Her head was still in her hands. "Robert."

"The nanny should be here by two tomorrow at the absolute latest," he went on, because he was afraid of what she might say—or what she might not say. "She'll teach you everything you need to know. Don't put blankets or stuffed animals in the crib."

She raised her head and stared at him as if she'd never seen him before. *"Robert."*

Inexplicably, his heart began to race. And was he sweating? He was. How strange. "Do you need any other financial assistance? Until Len is able to negotiate a settlement with the hospital, that is? Just let me know. I can—"

"Stop." She didn't so much as raise her voice—it certainly wasn't a shout—but he felt her power all the same.

He swallowed. Unfortunately, he was fairly certain it was a nervous swallow. Which was ridiculous because he was not nervous. He was a Wyatt, dammit. Nerves weren't allowed. Ever.

Still, he stopped talking. Which left them standing in another awkward silence.

Jeannie ran her hands through her hair, making it stand straight up as if she'd touched a live wire. She looked at him, then turned on her heel and walked the three steps into the kitchen.

What was happening here? He took a step after her but before his foot hit the ground she was back, hands on her hips. He stumbled as she strode to him.

"Robert," she said softly.

"I put Melissa in her crib," he said as she advanced on him. "She was asleep."

Relief fluttered across Jeannie's face but she didn't slow down. Unbelievably, Robert backed up. He'd learned the hard way that Wyatts didn't retreat and never, ever cowered.

But before her, he retreated. Just a step. Then all his training kicked in and he held his ground. But he felt himself swallow again and damn it all, he knew it was nervously.

Her mouth opened but then it closed and he saw her chest rise with a deep breath. "Why are you doing this, Robert?"

Doing what? But he bit down on those words because they were a useless distraction from the issue.

He knew what *this* was. So did she.

How could he put it into words? He wasn't entirely sure what those words were, other than he needed her. She was having problems that prevented her from being where he needed her to be so he was solving the problems.

But none of that was what came out. Instead, he heard himself say, "You need the help."

Her eyes fluttered closed and she did that long exhale again. "So that's it? You're not going to tell me why you tracked down my address, performed a medical examination on my niece, ordered your staff to hop to it and are now standing in my living room, condescendingly refusing to answer a simple question?"

"I'm not condescending," he shot back before he could think better of it.

"Of course you're not." Was that…sarcasm? "If you can't tell me why, then I have to ask you to leave." Her throat worked. "And not to come back."

A raw kind of panic gripped him. "I need you. At the bar."

She leaned away from him. "Miranda is perfectly capable of making your drink. I showed her how and there's enough blend in the cask to last a few months. Worst case, I can always go mix up more."

"But she's not you."

Jeannie's brow furrowed. "And that's a problem?"

She was too close. He could smell the sour tang of old formula on her shirt and see how very bloodshot her eyes were. But, in this light, he could also see things that he'd missed in the dim bar at Trenton's. Her dark hair had red undertones to it and her eyes were brown but with flecks of both green and gold. If anyone else had him in this position, Robert would either get around them or force the issue. It was always better to go on the offensive than be left in a weakened position.

But that's where he was now. Weakened.

"I…" To admit weakness was to admit failure and failure was not an option. "I can't talk to her. Not like I can to you."

"Robert, we barely talk," she said, her exasperation obvious. He was doing a terrible job of this. "I mean, I get the feeling you just don't talk to anyone. That's how you are."

"But you're different."

She stilled under his touch, which was when he realized he was, in fact, touching her. His hand had somehow come to rest on her cheek, just like it had earlier. Her skin was warm and soft and just felt…right.

"I can't afford to pay you back," she whispered, her hand covering his. But instead of flinging his fingers away from her face, she pressed harder so that his palm cradled her cheek.

Finally, he found the damned words. "That—that right there is why you're different. Anyone else, they'd look at me and you know what they'd say?" She shook her head, but carefully, like she was afraid she might break that singular point of contact. "They'd be calculating how much they could get out of me, what they'd have to do to get it. Your Miranda—"

"She flirts with everyone, Robert," Jeannie said softly. "Bigger compliments mean bigger tips. That's how things work. Everyone does it."

The thought of Jeannie acting like Miranda for money wasn't right. "You don't. Not with me."

She leaned into his touch. "What happened?"

What *hadn't* happened? Without conscious effort, he wrapped his arm around her waist and pulled her into his chest. "I might have made some threats. There may have been bribes exchanged."

She gasped but didn't pull away. She should have. For years now, he'd kept that part of himself on lockdown, refusing to let Landon win. But tonight he'd been a Wyatt through and through. Thank God she hadn't been there to see it.

"Oh, Robert," she said, his name a sigh on her lips. "Just because I wasn't there?"

No. The denial broke free but somehow, he kept it in because it was a damned lie and he'd come this far. Lying to her would be worse than what he'd done at the bar. "Yes."

"Hmm." Her body came flush with his, soft and warm. She felt right in his arms, her breasts pressed against his chest.

How long had he been waiting for this moment?

"You're touching me," she murmured, tucking her chin against his neck.

"That is correct." He felt her lips move against his skin. Was she smiling? He hoped she was smiling.

"You don't like to be touched."

Of course she knew. That was why he'd needed to see her tonight, needed to do whatever it took to get her back behind the bar. Because she understood him. "No."

Of course, if she were back behind the bar, he wouldn't have this moment with her. She sighed into him, her arms around his waist, her chest flush with his and it should've been too much, too close, too dangerous but…

It wasn't.

He gathered her closer in what he belatedly realized was a hug. How strange.

"I'm sorry for your loss." The words felt right so he kept going. "You must've loved her very much."

"I didn't love her nearly enough. It's…it's complicated. We had a pretty messed up family and we'd gone almost five years without speaking. We were just…"

She sniffed. "We were just figuring out how to be a family again," she went on, her voice tight. "And now we'll never get that back. It's gone forever."

An odd sensation built in his chest. "I'm sorry to hear that."

Was it possible to start a family over like that? Obviously, Landon Wyatt would never be a part of a do-over. But if Robert could get his mother away… Could they figure out how to be a family again?

"So I can't come back to work right now. You understand? I have to protect Melissa and make things right and…and honor my sister, imperfect as she was and as I am. I have to honor our family."

Moisture dampened his skin. He leaned back and tilted her chin up. Tears tracked down her cheeks. He wiped those away with his thumbs. "Anything I can do to help, I'll do."

Her smile was shaky at best. "You mean, besides the lawyer, nanny, maid and your chauffeur making grocery runs for me?"

"Yes."

"Can you tell me why you're here?" It wasn't an ultimatum this time, merely a question.

He opened his mouth to tell her because talking to her was the whole reason he was here, wasn't it?

But she'd had the worst day of her life. And although things were not particularly wonderful for him right now, he simply couldn't bear to add his burden to hers. "No. I won't make things harder for you."

Was that disappointment in her eyes? Or just relief? "You understand that I might not be able to go back to work, right? Julian will hold my job for a few weeks but—"

"Your job will be there," Robert interrupted. "If I have to buy the restaurant from him at triple what it's worth, you'll have a job there."

Her eyes got very wide but she didn't pull away. "You would do that for me?"

"If that's what you need, I'll make it happen." His gaze dropped to her lips, which were parted in surprise or shock or, hell, *horror*, at his autocratic ways for all he knew.

"Why?"

"I told you," he said, his voice gruff. He dragged his gaze away from her mouth and saw what had to be confusion on her face. She was closer than she'd been outside on the front steps, closer than she'd been during that hug.

"Tell me again," she said, her voice barely a breath on his lips.

Close enough to kiss.

"Because I need you," he whispered against her and then he took her mouth with his.

Five

Fact: Robert was kissing her.

Fact: He didn't like to be touched. But seeing as his mouth slanted over hers, his hands cupped her face and angled her head so he could deepen the kiss, it seemed he was okay with this type of touching. But that just led her back to…

Fact: Dr. Robert Wyatt, heir to the Wyatt Medicals fortune, one of the Top Five Billionaire Bachelors in Chicago, was providing her with a lawyer, a nanny, a maid and was also apparently willing to buy a restaurant just so she could serve him a Manhattan.

And, unavoidably, it came back to this fact: *He was kissing her.*

Heat cascaded from where he touched her, shivering

sparks of white-hot need that burned through her with a pain that was the sweetest pleasure she'd ever felt.

When was the last time she'd showered?

That thought pushed her into breaking the kiss, which was really a shame because for all his overbearing, condescending, threatening behaviors, he was a hell of a kisser.

Right man, wrong time.

That was the thought that ran through her mind as she stared at him, her chest heaving. She crossed her arms in front of her to fight off a shiver. Why now?

"That was…" He seemed to shake back to himself. He started to straighten his cuffs and then realized they were still rolled to his elbows so instead he fixed his sleeves. "That was not what I intended."

"Oh, for Pete's sake, Robert." Okay, so she'd kissed *the* Robert Wyatt. Her favorite customer. The man who had fueled more than a few years' worth of hot dreams and needy fantasies. But even if that kiss would keep her going for a few more years, it didn't change anything.

This was still Robert. Small talk was beyond him.

His brow furrowed as he got one cuff fixed. "What?"

"That's not what you say after you kiss a woman."

He paused and then, amazingly, straightened the sleeve he'd just fixed. "It's not?"

"No." She took a deep breath, but that was a bad idea because without the bar to separate them and the tang of wine and whiskey in the air to overpower her senses, she inhaled his scent, a rich cologne that was spicy and warm and still subtle.

So. There was one aspect of him that wasn't designed to dominate. One and counting.

She headed toward the kitchen where the scent of chicken was stronger. Her stomach growled and she knew she needed to eat. The chauffeur hadn't been wrong. She wasn't sure she'd eaten today and if Melissa would just sleep for another few minutes, Jeannie might be able to get both a meal and a shower out of the deal.

That was a huge *if*. That baby hadn't gotten more than thirty minutes of sleep at a time since... Well, in her whole life. Frankly, Jeannie was probably lucky she'd made it through one of the most perfect kisses she'd ever had without interruption.

"What am I supposed to say?"

She almost smiled because the man had *no* clue. "Something that doesn't make it sound like you wish you hadn't just kissed me." She waved this away. "It's not important."

A rumbling noise caught her attention and she spun to realize that not only was Robert growling, he was moving fast, too. With both cuffs fastened. "You're important," he said and if anyone else had said that in that tone of voice, it would've been a threat but for him? His voice was possessive and demanding and needy all at the same time and it wasn't a threat.

It was a promise.

Oh, how she wanted him to keep that promise.

"The kiss was important," he went on, his ice-blue eyes fierce and surprisingly warm. "But I don't want to make you feel like you *owe* me a kiss or your body. That's not what this is. I'm *not* like that."

"Then what is it?" She managed to swallow. "What are you like?"

His mouth opened and then snapped shut and he stepped back. Damned if he didn't adjust his cuffs again.

"Will you be all right tonight? I can have a nanny here for the night."

Part of her was so, *so* thankful that he wasn't going to suggest he should stay because…she might take him up on that.

So yeah, the other part of her was disappointed that Robert had suddenly become Dr. Wyatt again. Super disappointed. Because if that kiss was any indication, *man*. All that precision and control combined with the heat she felt every single time their bodies touched?

He would be *amazing*.

"We'll be okay." She rested her hand on his arm. Even through the fine cotton of his shirt, she could feel the rock-hard muscles in his arm.

Focus, Jeannie.

"Are you sure?"

Frankly, Robert Wyatt was kind of adorable when he was concerned. Perhaps because the look did not come naturally to him. "Positive. I had this kind man teach me about swaddling, get me different formulas and generally be amazing." She squeezed his arm.

He lifted her hand away from his arm and her heart dropped a ridiculous amount because he was back to being Dr. Wyatt and she shouldn't be touching him. But again, he surprised her because he didn't drop her hand. Instead, he brought it to his lips and, with that hint of a smile tugging at the corners of his mouth, kissed her knuckles.

It was an old-fashioned move right out of a romance novel but damn if it didn't work all the same.

He would be *so* amazing.

She had always managed to keep her lustful thoughts about this man safely contained, but nothing was contained right now, not with his lips warming her body.

His eyes shifted to the side. "Ah," he said, finally releasing her and moving to where Nicole had a message board hung up by the coat hooks. He picked up the marker. "This is my personal number. Call or text anytime. I have surgery in the morning so this," he added, writing a second number, "is my assistant."

She started to protest that she could handle things for another twenty-four hours, but that was when Robert added, "I'll stop by tomorrow night, see how the nanny is settling in."

Oh. He was coming back. The thought sent a little thrill through her, even though she knew it shouldn't. She would definitely make sure she'd showered by then. "That's not necessary."

"I disagree."

Of course he did.

"It should be fine."

"I'll expect the pleasure of your company, then."

The air rushed out of her lungs because that was not only a good line, but coming out of Robert's mouth?

A pleasure, indeed.

"Will you tell me what's bothering you, then?"

A shadow crossed over his eyes. She could feel him

retreating—emotionally and physically, because he opened the door and walked out of Nicole's house. "No."

"Why not?" she asked his back.

He was halfway down the steps when he turned, with that confused look on his face. "Because."

She rolled her eyes. "That continues to be a terrible answer, you know."

"Because I won't put you in danger," he said.

Then he walked off to where Reginald was waiting, with the car door open.

The chauffeur tipped his cap at Jeannie and then they were gone.

What the ever-loving *hell*?

Melissa was crying when the doorbell rang because of course she was.

"One second!" Jeannie yelled.

No matter how many times she watched the video tutorial, she couldn't get the baby swaddled. At least, not anything like Robert had done. And while Melissa had definitely slept more after drinking the soy-free formula Robert had recommended, Jeannie was still unshowered and exhausted. Getting ninety minutes of sleep at a time was an improvement over forty-five minutes at a time, but not much of one.

Screw it. She picked Melissa up and settled for tucking the blanket around her little body.

The doorbell rang again at almost the exact same moment her phone buzzed. Jeannie grabbed her phone and looked at the text. Of course it was from Robert.

Maja Kowalczyk
Text me immediately if you don't like her.

This was accompanied by a photo of an older woman, her hair in a bun and her face lined with deep laugh lines.

"Miss Kaufman? Are you able to get the door?" an accented voice yelled—politely—over the sounds of Melissa wailing.

That man was lucky she'd been able to check her phone. That was just like him to expect her to drop everything to respond to him when, in reality, texting back was a pipe dream, one that ranked well below showering.

Jeannie shoved the phone in her pocket and gave up on the blanket. Instead, she wrapped her arms around Melissa and held her tight against her chest, like Robert had been doing last night. It helped, a little.

The doorbell rang and this time, it was accompanied by knocking. Her phone buzzed again but she ignored it and managed to make it to the front door.

"I'm here," she snapped, which was not the most polite start to any conversation but seriously, could everyone just give her a second?

"Ah, good." The woman on the stoop matched the woman in the photo. But Jeannie was surprised to see a rolling suitcase next to her. The older woman smiled warmly and said, "It's all right—she's here. Yes, everything is fine. Thank you, Dr. Wyatt."

Which was the point that Jeannie realized that Maja wasn't talking to her but on her cell phone. To Robert.

And to think, Jeannie had once concluded that Nicole was the biggest control freak in the world.

The nanny ended the call and clasped her hands in front of her generous bosom. She was wearing a floral dress, hideous tan shoes and a cardigan, for Pete's sake. It was at least eighty degrees today! "Hello, Miss Kaufman, I'm Maja Kowalczyk."

"Hi. I'm Jeannie."

Maja's eyes crinkled as she went on, "Dr. Wyatt said you needed…" Her voice trailed off as she took a good look at Melissa and Jeannie. Melissa chose that moment to let out a pitiful little wail. "Oh, you poor dears," she clucked. "May I come in?"

"I guess?" Jeannie didn't have much choice. She needed help and, if Robert was still planning on stopping by at some point in the near future, she needed a shower.

Frankly, she wasn't sure she hadn't hallucinated last night. She'd wished upon something that probably wasn't a star and then Robert had shown up, kissed her, thrown a whole bunch of money at her problems and…driven off into the night.

It was the stuff of dreams. And also possibly nightmares. She wasn't sure which.

Because there was definitely something unreal about watching Maja wheel her little suitcase into the house. Jeannie peeked out the front door, but no long black car blocked traffic and no gorgeous billionaire climbed her stairs, hell-bent on upending her world.

Maja gasped at the mess and Jeannie figured if it was a dream, the house would be a whole lot cleaner.

It wasn't like she hadn't tried because she *had*. But Melissa was still super fussy and a splotchy red color. Jeannie had not somehow acquired the power to swaddle anything, much less an agitated infant, and housekeeping had never been a priority for her in the first place, which had always driven Nicole nuts.

So yeah, everything was still a disaster.

"Sorry about this," Jeannie began, but Maja just shook her head.

"That nice Dr. Wyatt, he told me what to expect. I am so sorry about your sister."

And that was when Jeannie found herself folded into a hug against Maja's impressive bosom. Tears pricked her eyes but she didn't know this woman and could only hope that Robert knew what he was doing in hiring her.

"There now," Maja said, taking a step back and looking completely unruffled. "I think I will take this *babisui* and get her dressed and you, my dear, will take a shower and lie down, yes?"

If Jeannie stood here much longer, she was going to start crying because a shower and a nap sounded like the best things ever. "Yeah, okay." Maja reached out for Melissa but Jeannie interrupted. "Um, just so we're clear, what are your qualifications?"

Any qualifications were better than what Jeannie had. But if she was going to hand Melissa off to a complete stranger and then fall asleep with said stranger in the house, she wanted reassurances.

Jeannie had full faith that Robert wouldn't just hire some random woman but she needed to be a part of this decision. Robert might be paying the bills because...

Well, she was still really unclear on his reasons at this point.

"Ah, yes." Maja nodded firmly as if she approved of Jeannie's caution. "My husband died and there wasn't much left for me in Poland, so I came here twenty-seven years ago, when my son married a nice American girl. I was a nurse in a hospital nursery in Poland and here I cared for my grandchildren when they were small. When they went to school, my daughter-in-law had a friend who was starting the nanny business and she took me on. I speak fluent Polish, English and Russian, as well as some German and French. Not much French, actually," she said with a rueful smile.

"I, uh, speak English. And some bad Spanish," Jeannie blurted out, feeling woefully outclassed by this woman. Five languages plus she'd been a nurse? No wonder Robert had hired her.

Maja nodded. "I have cared for small babies my entire life. I have copies of my medical certifications and background checks for you. Dr. Wyatt also has copies. He has instructed me to stay for a week, including overnights, with your approval until you feel more confidence. Then I am to come every day from noon until midnight, unless you have a different schedule in mind?"

Yeah, noon to midnight was Robert gaming the system so she could be back at Trenton's, serving his drink.

Maja was a former nurse. Someone who'd spent a lifetime with babies. Someone who would know if something was really wrong and would teach Jeannie how to handle the basics and…and…

Relief hit her so hard her legs began to shake. This was going to work out. Things were going to get better. They *had* to.

She almost smiled to herself. Robert simply wouldn't allow them to get worse, would he?

Melissa fussed and that was when the blanket and diaper fell off. "Uh, sorry about this," Jeannie muttered as Maja gave her a sympathetic smile. "You're hired and I would *love* a shower."

"And a nap, dear." She took the naked, fussing baby from Jeannie's arms. "Go on. The *babisui* and I will get to know each other, won't we?" she cooed at Melissa, who responded by straightening her legs and arms and farting loudly.

Without a diaper.

"Ah, good," Maja said, not horrified in the least even as Jeannie's face shot hot with mortification. If only Melissa could stop doing *that* when someone walked into the house! "The bad milk is working its way out. Better, my little angel? Let's get you cleaned up. Oh, yes, it's very hard to be a *babisui*, isn't it?" Murmuring softly, she carried Melissa back to the nursery as if she'd spent more than ten minutes in this house.

"Nicole," Jeannie whispered, looking up at the ceiling, "I'm doing the best I can. I hope this is okay."

Her phone buzzed. It was, unsurprisingly, Robert. What was surprising was that he was actually calling her. "Yes?"

"Does Maja meet with your approval?"

"And hello to you, too."

He made that noise that was almost a growl again

and although Jeannie was exhausted in ways she'd never even imagined possible, a thrill of desire raced through her. "Is she acceptable or do I need to find a replacement?"

"She's lovely, Robert," Jeannie sighed. "Thank you for sending her over."

"Good. I'll be by later." Before she could get any details about that—like a specific time—he ended the call.

That man.

He was only coming to make sure Maja would be able to get Jeannie back to work as soon as possible. His visit likely had nothing to do with the way he'd held her last night and less than nothing to do with the kiss.

She glanced at the clock. It was two-thirty. If she knew Robert...

That man would walk into this house at exactly eight tonight.

She all but ran to the shower. The clock was ticking.

Six

Last night he'd held Jeannie in his arms. She was right; he didn't like to be touched but with her…

"Sir?"

When he'd felt the light movement against the skin of his neck—she'd been smiling, he was just sure of it. Smiling in his arms and it hadn't been wrong. He hadn't had his guard up like normal. But that'd been the problem, hadn't it? If he'd been operating with his usual amount of caution, he wouldn't have kissed her.

Or ruined it by apologizing. Would she have kissed him again if he'd kept his mouth shut?

"Dr. Wyatt?"

Robert dragged his thoughts away from Jeannie and looked at Thomas Kelly, his assistant.

"Will there be anything else, sir?"

"You have the maid lined up?" Jeannie's house was such a disaster it was veering close to being a health hazard for the child.

Melissa, he corrected.

"Yes, sir," the young man said eagerly.

Everything Kelly did was eager. Only twenty-three, he'd been working for Robert since he'd graduated from Loyola, on the recommendation of a professor whose grandson had come through open-heart surgery with flying colors. Thomas Kelly was someone who existed outside the spheres of influence of Landon Wyatt, which made him valuable.

Kelly checked his tablet. "Rona will arrive at the house tomorrow at ten a.m. She's Darna's sister and the background check was clean."

"Ah." Darna was Robert's maid and had, over the past few years, proven to be trustworthy. He would've preferred Darna handling Jeannie's house herself but Darna's sister was the next best option.

If Landon Wyatt knew that Robert had developed a soft spot for a bartender…

Dammit. What was he supposed to do? He couldn't abandon Jeannie to the winds of fate. Nor could he turn a blind eye to that baby girl. Yes, her allergic reaction had been mild and not life-threatening and yes, Robert could turn the case over to a pediatrician but…

Jeannie had kept him going after what had happened the last time he'd seen his parents. God willing, she'd never know how much he owed her, but he wasn't about to let her twist in the wind. Jeannie needed that infant to be well. Robert needed Jeannie.

What was the point of being one of the most powerful men in the country if he didn't use that power to get what he needed?

"Rona signed the nondisclosure agreement?"

"Yes. Copies are on file."

"Good."

Everyone who worked for Robert signed NDAs. Unlike Landon, who used NDAs to hide his monstrous behavior, Robert used them to keep his employees from talking. To the press, to Landon, to the board of Wyatt Medicals.

Not that NDAs stopped the talk completely. Robert had still been named to that ridiculous list of billionaire bachelors, which had the same effect as painting a big target on his back. And he didn't make his patients sign NDAs, although after the last time a family had gone to the newspapers to tell everyone how Robert had quietly covered their hospital bills, he'd considered it. Sadly, the hospital lawyers had informed him that making patients sign NDAs was not allowed.

Funny how it'd never even occurred to him to have Jeannie sign one. But then again, she existed on a different level. Besides, she wouldn't tell anyone anything. He trusted her.

He eyed Kelly. "You enjoy working for me, don't you?"

"Yes, sir." The young man didn't even hesitate.

"You feel you're adequately compensated for your work?" Kelly was on call twenty-four hours a day.

Kelly smirked. "If I say yes, have I talked myself out of a raise?"

Robert would give anything to discuss this plan with Jeannie. She'd see things from a different angle, spot any holes in his plan. But she had so much to worry about right now that Robert couldn't add to her burdens.

Kelly was his assistant, not his friend. As much as he liked the young man, Robert couldn't risk weakening his position by confiding uncertainty to an employee.

Which meant Robert was on his own here. "I need a plane."

"I can have your jet ready to take off inside of forty-five minutes," Kelly said, already tapping on his tablet.

"No." Robert must've said it more forcefully than he intended because Kelly's head snapped up. "I need a hired plane and an independent flight crew on standby. They're not to know who's paying them and they can't ask questions."

A look crossed Kelly's face. Confusion? Or concern? It didn't matter. "When?"

"Saturday after next." He straightened his cuffs as Reginald turned onto Jeannie's street.

"That's the night of…" Kelly trailed off and Robert realized he was glaring at the man.

"Yes." This idea felt risky, with a high probability of failure. If he got Mom away, Landon would do everything in his prodigious power to punish his wife and Robert.

If Mom didn't agree… Could Robert really leave her to Landon? Could he abandon his own mother a second time?

It wasn't even a question.

"The destination will be Los Angeles," he went on.

"From there, I'll need two first-class tickets to Auckland."

"New Zealand?" Kelly's voice jumped an octave.

"Yes. And it goes without saying that, if you mention these arrangements to anyone, I will be *upset*."

"Completely understood, sir." Kelly cleared his throat. "I'll need names for the commercial tickets."

"Cybil Wyatt."

Kelly inhaled sharply. How much did he know about Robert's family? Kelly had to interact with Landon's assistant, Alexander, from time to time. Surely, he at least suspected...

"I cannot guarantee we'll be able to use her passport, so make arrangements for travel documents."

Kelly nodded. "And the second ticket?"

Robert considered adding his name to that second ticket but someone had to stay in Chicago and throw Landon off the trail.

The possible outcomes played out in his mind. If Robert did this right, not only would he get his mother to safety, but he'd also expose Landon's behavior during the aftermath of Mom's disappearance and single-handedly knock Landon out of politics. Hopefully, for good.

The car stopped in front of Jeannie's house. Robert's heart did an odd little skip at the sight of the small box of a house. It was squat, with a distinctive air of disrepair. He should hire contractors to fix the siding. That roof looked like it was on its last legs. Plus, the yard was a mess...

Jeannie needed help and he couldn't help her from a different hemisphere, could he?

Plus, you can't kiss her from Auckland, a voice whispered in his mind.

Right. Well. It had been a perfect kiss. But it'd be best for all parties if he didn't kiss her again.

"Make sure there's a nurse on board—that's the second ticket," he said. He wanted to be there for his mother because he missed her in ways that it hurt to think about but if she wasn't around Landon, he could talk to her whenever he wanted. "All expenses paid, with generous bonuses. Be sure to run every check on whoever you hire. This situation requires complete secrecy and discretion. They may be required to prevent Cybil from contacting Landon or returning to Chicago before…" *Before it was safe.* "Before it's appropriate."

Because if he got his mother to Los Angeles but she gave in to fear and tried to back out of the plan like she had three years ago, Robert knew Landon wouldn't stop at just cutting off all contact like he had before. No, the man would salt the earth behind him.

Robert dealt in life and death every day. This was another situation where he couldn't risk a loss.

"Arrange housing in New Zealand," he directed Kelly. "Someplace secluded and safe, with an openended lease. Make sure it's staffed appropriately. And hire a guard for this house," he added, motioning to Jeannie's house. It didn't even have a fence to slow someone from approaching the front door. Jeannie had been just sitting on the stoop last night, with the door open behind her. "I don't want anyone to realize the house is under surveillance." Just in case Landon started digging and came across Jeannie.

No, Robert couldn't risk losing anything.

It might not be enough to just get his mother away. If Robert left Landon with the means of tracking her down, the bastard would.

Which meant only one thing.

His stomach turned.

"Yes, sir. Anything else?"

"Schedule a meeting tomorrow morning at six a.m. with Len at my office in the hospital. Who do we know in the prosecutor's office? And a private investigator—someone we trust. Oh, I'll expect you to be there, as well."

Robert had to go on rounds at seven and then see patients. But he could get a lot of strategic planning laid out before that. Kelly could make a great many things happen, but if Robert wanted to take on Landon, he'd need more than just an escape plan.

He'd need to be the one to salt the earth behind him.

Kelly didn't even blink at the early hour. "Of course."

Reginald opened Robert's car door at precisely 7:58 p.m. "That will be all for now."

"Yes, sir," Kelly said as Robert climbed out of the car. He called out, "Have a good evening, sir."

Robert didn't bother to respond as Reginald snapped the car door behind him. "See Mr. Kelly home," he told Reginald. "I won't need you for at least an hour."

It would take that long to get a report from Maja and check Melissa over and make sure that everything he'd ordered had been delivered and…

And see Jeannie.

But just to find out how she was doing. Not because

he needed her or anything. He was Robert Wyatt. He didn't need anyone, most especially not a bartender. Last night had just been…

One of those things.

"Very good, Dr. Wyatt."

He strode up the stairs to Jeannie's house but before he could knock, the door opened and suddenly all the air rushed out of his lungs because there she was.

"Robert," she said, her voice soft. "You're on time. As usual."

She'd been waiting for him. Again, he had that sense that she'd always been waiting for him.

"Jeannie." She looked better, he realized. She had on a pair of loose-fitting denim shorts and an old-looking Cubs T-shirt and her feet were bare.

She looked good. She'd showered and the dark circles under her eyes were less prominent and she was smiling.

It hit him like a kick to the chest.

He must have been staring because she asked, "Is there something on my shirt?" as color washed her cheeks. "I just put it on…" She held it out from her chest, which made the deep vee of the neck gape even lower.

Her bra was white today. And moments ago she hadn't been wearing that shirt.

He was here to check the baby and make sure Jeannie had the support she needed for the optimum outcome. He was here to confirm that the people he'd hired were doing a satisfactory job. Jeannie was his bartender and he wanted everything to get back to normal. Because the longer he stepped outside of his routine and the more attention he drew to Jeannie, the more dangerous things were for all of them.

None of that careful logic prevented what happened next.

Knowing he was putting her at risk didn't stop him from stepping into her. Understanding that she'd suffered a painful loss didn't prevent him from pulling her hands away from the shirt and settling them around his neck.

"Oh," she breathed, her eyes wide as she stared up at him.

And God help him, he captured her small noise with his lips and then drank deep.

Today she smelled of…oranges, bright and tart and incredibly sweet.

So he was kissing her. Which was not what he'd planned. But it just felt right, her body flush against his, her arms tightening around his neck, her whispering, "Oh, Robert, *yes*," against his mouth.

He went hard at that. How he wanted her hands on him. His name on her lips, her body moving over his…

"Jeannie," he all but groaned.

"Yes," she whispered back. His hands went to her waist and then he was walking her backward and kicking the door shut and—

Bang.

The sound of the door slamming jolted them apart. And not a moment too soon because the nanny emerged from the baby's room, a perfectly swaddled Melissa in her arms. "Ah, Dr. Wyatt," Maja said, smiling broadly. "We are doing well."

Robert straightened his cuffs to give himself a moment to get his body back under control but then he made the mistake of glancing over at Jeannie. She was bright red and staring at her toes but he thought he saw a smile tugging at the corners of her lips.

Lips swollen with his kiss.

That made him feel oddly proud of himself, as if he'd done something noteworthy instead of making a messy situation even messier.

Damn it all, he'd lost control and that wasn't allowed.

When he was sure he had his responses locked down, he said, "Yes, Mrs. Kowalczyk. What is your report?"

"The organic formula is helping and lovely little Melissa is already less fussy. Miss Jeannie is an excellent student and has already learned how to properly swaddle a *babisui* and change a diaper." She cast a maternal look at Jeannie. "I think, however, it would be good for Miss Jeannie to get out of the house. She has been under a great deal of stress and we all need a break, don't we?"

"Excellent idea."

He already had his phone out to call Reginald back as soon as he'd dropped Kelly off at home when Jeannie made a noise of surprise. "Not tonight, Robert! For Pete's sake!"

"What?" That was how she'd sounded last night after he'd ruined the kiss. Like there was an expected code of conduct in situations like this and he wasn't following it.

"I'm not going anywhere tonight," she said, her tone gentler. "Just because I had a nap and a shower doesn't mean I'm operating on all cylinders today." Her gaze dropped to his lips and, as he watched, the tip of her tongue darted out and swiped over her lower lip.

Hmm. That was interesting. Did that mean she was having second thoughts about that second kiss? All he knew was that he could still catch the scent of oranges in the air.

Cautiously, Robert looked at Maja. She nodded in agreement. "Perhaps for lunch tomorrow?" she suggested.

"Lunch." He didn't eat lunch on a regular basis. He was always at the hospital, making rounds or seeing patients.

"It's a meal? Most people eat it around the noon hour?" Jeannie was definitely smiling now. Something in his chest loosened.

She was teasing him, he realized. No one else would dare, but she did. "Yes, I'm familiar with the concept." Her smile got even bigger. "I have appointments tomorrow but we could do lunch on Saturday." He already knew Maja would be here. He was paying her an exorbitant rate to live in the first week, but it was worth it to see Jeannie without that haunted look in her eyes.

Maja was doing her job. Robert had made it clear that the nanny was responsible for making sure both people in this house were cared for.

Maja gave him that approving nod again as Jeannie said, "Okay, but nothing too fancy. And not Trenton's."

"Of course not." He wasn't entirely sure that he was welcome back. Better to wait until Jeannie could return.

Jeannie eyed him warily. "You do eat, don't you? You never order anything but the Manhattan at the bar."

"Of course I eat." Darna made sure there were fresh-cooked meals for him at home. She cooked to his specifications and that was all he needed. He didn't need to try the latest food craze or go out to be seen. He liked his corner at Jeannie's bar and then he liked his peace and quiet.

For a second, he considered just bringing Jeannie to his town house and serving her the cuisine Darna left for him. If he called Darna right now, she'd probably have time to put together something special. Her roast pork was amazing and those little rice cakes wrapped in banana leaves—Jeannie would like them. He could show her his home and...

And...

That was a terrible idea. Yes, he'd kissed Jeannie twice now—but taking her to his home felt dangerous.

So Kelly would find a restaurant. Someplace quiet, but not romantic. Someplace where Jeannie could relax. Someplace where gossip would not reach Landon Wyatt.

Someplace where she could smile at Robert but a table would keep them from touching.

It was safer that way.

"I know the perfect place," he hedged. He would know it by noon tomorrow, anyway. Kelly did good work. "Now," he went on, because Reginald would be back soon enough and Robert had a role to fulfill. He held out his hands and Maja placed the baby in his arms without hesitation. Melissa squirmed at the change in elevation but when he cradled her, she blinked up at him with her bright baby-blue eyes. "Let's see how we're doing."

* * *

Forty minutes later Jeannie had demonstrated everything she'd learned today—how to properly change a diaper, how to swaddle an infant securely, even how to hold the bottle so Melissa didn't have to work as hard to drink.

The whole time Robert had watched her with those icy eyes, doing little more than nodding when she apparently passed inspection. Because that was what it felt like. An inspection. One she'd definitely failed yesterday. Today?

He'd kissed her.

He'd walked right up to her and kissed her and she'd kissed him back and everything felt so much better and that much worse at the same time because he was here and that was great but nothing made sense.

Because he'd kissed her.

And now he was standing there, judging her as she burped a baby.

A baby who thankfully fell asleep.

"Maja," Robert said after Jeannie had laid Melissa down in the completely empty crib and they'd all returned to the living room, "you've done well today."

Jeannie glared at him. Maja was a good teacher who obviously knew what she was doing but *come on, Robert.* Jeannie was the one learning everything from scratch on a few hours of sleep. But the man wasn't even looking at her!

"Thank you, Dr. Wyatt," Maja said, her eyes twinkling. "Jeannie is a most capable student."

"Hmm," he murmured as if he wasn't sure he agreed with that assessment. Which made Jeannie glare harder.

But before she could tell him where to shove his humming noises, he said to the nanny, "Take an hour and get dinner."

Wait. Jeannie cut a glance at Maja, who looked mildly surprised at this…well, this *order*. Which was pretty much how Jeannie felt, as well, considering they'd eaten dinner around six. But Maja was obviously used to taking odd orders from her clients, because all she said was, "Of course, Dr. Wyatt. I need to pick up more formula."

"What…" Jeannie started to say as Maja grabbed her purse and was out the door in seconds. She moved awfully quick for a woman easily in her sixties.

"Reginald?" Robert said before the front door had closed behind Maja. Because of course Robert was on the phone. Probably ordering a butler or something. "An hour from now. Yes."

She stared at him as he ended the call. What was Robert even doing here? Besides continuing to completely take over her life.

"I'm not going to work tomorrow," she said. Unfortunately, it came out sounding petulant and immature. "I don't want to and I'm not ready."

"Of course you're not," he said, sounding almost agreeable about it.

"O…kay. So if you're not going to convince me to get back to work, why are you here?"

He adjusted his cuffs. He still had on his jacket today, although she noted he had foregone a vest. Probably because it'd been close to ninety danged degrees today. To the average person, it might not look like he was stalling but she knew this was how Robert played for time.

He cleared his throat. Yeah, totally stalling. "Are you better?"

"I am." God, this felt six kinds of awkward. She wanted…to go back to where they'd been when he'd walked up her front steps like a man on a mission.

Where he'd come because he wanted to see her.

"Will you sit with me?" she asked, holding out her hand.

He looked at her hand like he didn't trust it. Or maybe he didn't trust himself?

"Are you sure?" he asked and she heard the strain in his voice.

He didn't trust himself. At least, not around her. The realization set her back on her heels.

"Yes," she said because she knew he could be terrifying but he'd never once made her feel unsafe. "Are you?"

He hesitated.

"I only want to sit with you," she said. "Come here." It was as close to an order as she'd ever given him.

An emotion rippled across his face, one she couldn't quite identify. She had to wonder—had anyone ever tried to tell him what to do before? Surely, at medical school?

"*Please*, Robert."

Why didn't he trust himself around her?

She didn't think he was going to bridge the divide between them but then he laced his fingers with hers. They moved to the couch, and he sat. Stiffly at first, but when Jeannie sat next to him and tucked her head

against his shoulder, she felt a tremor pass through his
body and then, bit by bit, he relaxed.

She didn't let go of his hand. Instead, she covered
it with her other hand and stroked along the side of his
thumb with her own. His hands were strong, with long
fingers and impeccably groomed nails.

"Maja was what I needed," she told him, but what she
really wanted to say was that *he* was what she needed.
"Thank you."

"Good," was all he said, because of course.

Her mind raced even as her body calmed. Like last
night when she'd needed a hug, tonight she needed to lay
her head on his shoulder and let his warmth seep into
her body. If Robert was here, then things were okay. He
wouldn't allow it to be otherwise.

She thought of the nanny, the maid that would probably show up in the next few days, the lawyers, the insis-
tence that she go back to work as soon as was humanly
possible, hell, even lunch on Saturday—it all pointed
back to something big in his life.

To the bad day he'd mentioned when he first showed up.

"Robert?"

"Yes?"

"Are you okay?"

She had the distinct feeling that, if she hadn't been
holding on to his hand with both of hers, he would've
straightened his damned cuffs. "I won't let any harm
come to you. Or Melissa."

She tensed. "Are we in danger?"

"No," he answered too quickly and then, "No," again,
but softer.

"You're touching me." He smelled faintly antiseptic today. *Surgery*, she remembered.

"I...don't mind." He swallowed. Was he nervous? Because they were discussing feelings or because they were touching? "Because it's you."

The man might not spout romantic poetry or random compliments but... "That was probably the nicest thing you've ever said to me."

"What a low bar to meet." Was that humor in his voice? He cleared his throat again. "You did well today. I'm impressed at how quickly you picked things up." Her breath caught in her throat and she tilted her head back to find his face less than four inches from hers. "There," he said, sounding almost cocky about it. "How was that?"

"Better," she told him breathlessly. "Much better."

He smiled. Just the corners of his mouth moving upward but it took everything warm and comfortable about him and kicked it right on over to pure, simmering heat.

"Good," he said again.

That did it. Before she could talk herself out of it, she slid into his lap, straddling his powerful legs and bringing her pelvis flush against his. He inhaled sharply and she felt him tense underneath her.

"What are you doing?" he asked in a strangled voice. His arms stretched along the back of the couch, as far from touching her as he could get.

"Listen to me, you silly man," she said, motioning in the narrow space between them. "I'm not afraid of you, Robert. I trust you."

"You shouldn't," he ground out, digging his fingers into the couch cushions.

"Well, it's too late because I do." She cupped his face in her hands and made him look at her. "I've known you for years and *I trust you* so get used to it. I don't understand you, but for the love of everything holy, stop acting like you're a villain in this story."

"Do you have any idea what I'm capable of?" he demanded, glaring.

Now she was getting somewhere. He couldn't hide behind his shirt cuffs or the bar or the Manhattan. He couldn't hide from *her* anymore.

"Yes," she said, touching her forehead to his. "You're capable of single-handedly saving incredibly sick children, you're rescuing me and Melissa and you're the most obnoxious perfectionist I've ever met. By, like, *a lot*."

His chest heaved. "You don't know." As he spoke, his hands came to rest on the curve of her waist. "You just don't understand."

"No, I don't." She wrapped her arms around his neck and buried her face in his shoulder and hugged the man for all he was worth. "But I will because you'll tell me when you're ready," she murmured against his skin.

After a heart-dropping pause, his arms curled around her. "Jeannie."

She knew what he was going to say and she cut him off with a growl. He really was the most infuriating man. "This is not an obligation, dammit."

"But—"

She leaned back. "Robert—did you ever think that I *wanted* to kiss you? That I'd want to do it again?"

Seven

She was sitting in his lap.

His *lap.*

Worse, she wanted to kiss him. *Just* kiss? Perhaps not, what with the way she straddled him, her breasts flush against his chest.

It should be wrong, the way her weight pressed him against the couch cushions. She shouldn't be like this, definitely shouldn't trust him. Not if she knew what was good for her.

"You want to kiss me."

"I do." She sighed, her warm breath stroking over his neck. "I've wanted to kiss you for years. *Years.* You never realized it, did you?"

He opened his mouth to point out the flaw in her

logic, realized he had no idea what that flaw might be and snapped it shut again.

"I'll take that for a *no*," she said. Smugly.

People didn't touch him. Yes, he'd shake hands with worried parents and examine their children, but outside of the office? *Never.*

Except for her, apparently. Because not only had he kissed her, but he also...*liked* her touch.

Jeannie molded herself to him. Her body was warm and light against his and it reached inside him, drawing an answering pulse from his blood. Her thighs felt strong and sure as they bracketed his legs and although he most certainly did not want an erection right now, all that pounding blood began to pound in his dick, as well.

Oh, yes—he liked it.

The heat of her core settled against his groin and he almost groaned at the delicious tension because she was sitting *in his lap* and he couldn't remember wanting to be this close to a woman.

Much to his surprise, he realized he was stroking her back and he'd turned his face into her hair so he could inhale her scent.

It was good.

Because it was her.

She was a temptation he couldn't resist.

She really had no idea what he was capable of, did she?

A tremor raced through his body. It wasn't fear. Because Wyatts weren't afraid of anything. He was merely holding himself back.

For her sake. Not his.

She wanted him…but not for his money or his power?

She was right. He didn't understand a damn thing.

"Stop thinking, Robert," she murmured against his neck. "Just *be*. We've both had crappy weeks and this is nice." She sighed into him. "You're a good hugger."

He highly doubted that. When was the last time he'd been hugged?

Suddenly, he was talking without being entirely sure what was coming out of his mouth. "I'm *not* taking you out to lunch. You're coming to my home. We'll have a quiet meal on the terrace and…" He swallowed, trying not to sound desperate because desperation wasn't allowed. "I… I can just *be* there. With you."

What if she said no or demanded a fancy meal at a trendy spot, like he'd promised? The sort of thing that Dr. Robert Wyatt, a Top Five Billionaire Bachelor, should do?

The thought was almost physically painful. Because, he realized with alarm, that wasn't who he was with her.

Say yes, he thought and dammit, there was desperation in those unspoken words.

Say yes to me.

Her lips moved against his skin. His body responded accordingly. He'd made her smile. It felt like a victory.

"Of course," she agreed. She pushed back to look at him, her weight bearing down on him. God, she was perfect. "No obligations, no expectations. Just two people who can *be* together."

All those colors in her eyes played with the light, making her look soft and otherworldly, like a princess who'd disguised herself as a commoner to test the prince.

He might have failed his mother but by God, he wasn't going to fail Jeannie. She didn't know what he was capable of. He prayed she never would.

"I'll pick you up at twelve," he told her, stroking his thumb over her cheek.

She leaned into his touch. "I'll be waiting."

"Are you sure this is okay?" Jeannie asked for the fourth time. Or maybe it was the fortieth.

Her sleeveless sundress was bright yellow, with a happy print of little pink and blue flowers all over it. Rona, the maid who'd arrived promptly at ten this morning, had even ironed the dang thing.

Jeannie had bought the dress for a date some years ago and then repurposed it with a shawl to attend Easter services with Nicole, who'd been a church regular. It'd been part of their reconciliation.

It was the fanciest dress Jeannie owned. Hopefully, paired with the shawl and her platform brown sandals, it would be nice enough for a private meal with Robert. He always cut such a dashing figure in his custom three-piece suits and gemstone cuff links and she had…a cotton sundress she'd gotten on clearance four years ago.

But what else did one wear to a private meal with the billionaire bachelor next door? Cutoffs seemed like the wrong answer.

This was ridiculous.

She couldn't go to lunch with him. She shouldn't be alone with him. If she was smart, she'd change into her jean shorts, curl up on the couch and let Maja boss her around in a highly educational way.

"Yes, yes," Maja said again, patting Melissa's back. "You look lovely. Very sweet. Rona, doesn't she look lovely?"

"Oh, yes," the tiny Filipino woman called from the kitchen, where the smells of something delicious wafted throughout the house. "Very pretty."

Upon arrival, Rona had promptly taken over everything Maja hadn't. Dishes had been washed, laundry laundered, the bathroom was already immaculate and who could forget the cooking? It was a little bit like living in a hotel.

Jeannie had no idea who would appear next but she had a feeling Robert wasn't done hiring a staff of potentially dozens to take care of her. She was going to draw the line at a butler, though.

The baby let out a tiny little belch—without crying. Seriously, Maja was magic. Jeannie didn't know how much Robert was paying her, but it was worth it.

"Caregivers need breaks," Maja went on, shifting from side to side. Jeannie was sure the older woman didn't even know she was doing it. Would Jeannie ever get that level of comfort handling Melissa? "The *babisui* and I will be fine together—she will sleep, I will help Rona and you will enjoy a break with your handsome doctor."

Jeannie's cheeks heated so she quickly turned back to her room to rifle through her meager jewelry collection. "He's not *my* doctor." No disputing the handsome part, though.

"Mmm," Maja replied. Or maybe she was just talking to the baby.

Trenton's didn't let employees wear more than simple stud earrings, and most of Jeannie's jewelry was like her sundress—cheaply made, purchased on clearance and several years old. And most of it felt…juvenile. From a period of her life that had passed.

She wasn't the same girl who could ironically wear neon-pink plastic hoops, not anymore. She was something very like a mother now. Besides, the neon hoops definitely didn't match this dress. So in the end, she went with her basic fake diamond studs that she wore at the bar every night.

"He's *not* my doctor," Jeannie reminded her reflection.

This was just lunch. With her favorite customer. While wearing her best dress.

And the cutest pair of matching panties and bralette she owned. The set she'd ordered online in a pink that was more dusty than neon and was very lacy.

Very lacy.

She'd tossed and turned all night long, drifting in and out of lust-fueled dreams that left her hot and bothered. She hadn't stopped with just straddling Robert or holding him. She hadn't stopped at all.

The doorbell rang. "He's here," Maja sang.

Although it wasn't ladylike, Jeannie sprinted out of the bedroom, yelling, "I'll get it!"

Which turned out to be pointless because Maja had already opened the door. Jeannie stumbled over her sandals and nearly took a header at the sight of the man waiting for her.

He wasn't wearing a suit.

Had she thought Robert looked undone days ago when he hadn't been wearing a tie? Because the man standing before her was so far from a suit and tie that she barely recognized him.

Except for his eyes. She would never forget the burning intensity of Robert's eyes for as long as she lived.

Especially when they darkened. "You look lovely," he said. A shiver raced down her back at the sound of his voice, deep and raw and—this wasn't about lunch, was it?

"So do you." Instead of that suit, he was wearing a dark blue button-up shirt that had short sleeves and maybe some little pattern on it, all paired with light khaki shorts.

Shorts. That revealed his well-muscled legs. Her pulse began to stutter as she stared at those defined legs. When had calves gotten so damn sexy? Lord.

"I didn't think you owned anything but suits."

"I didn't know you wore anything other than vests before this week," he returned with a smile that melted her.

"Dr. Wyatt," Maja interrupted. Jeannie startled. She'd forgotten the older woman was in the room. "Would you like a report?"

"The thirty-second version," he replied, not taking his eyes off Jeannie. Dear God, she could practically smell the sexual desire coming off him in waves.

"Little Melissa continues to improve, Rona has made an excellent start and Jeannie—"

"Is late for lunch," he said, coming forward to take her by the arm.

When he touched her, electricity raced over her skin, taking everything that had started to melt and tightening it to the point of delicious pain. She fought to keep from gasping as his hand slid down until his fingers laced with hers.

She threw a glance back at Maja, whose expression clearly stated, *your handsome doctor.*

"We'll be back later," Robert announced in that way of his.

"Enjoy yourselves," Maja said with a conspiratorial wink, shooing them out. "We'll be fine here."

Oh, Jeannie would. If she got the chance, she was going to enjoy this with every fiber of her being.

Reginald was waiting at the car for them. "Miss," he said, tipping his hat to her as she approached.

"Hello again." Reginald's expression was remarkably similar to Maja's, like there was a conspiracy to make her and Robert...

Well, not fall in love or anything because that simply wasn't possible. He was a billionaire surgeon whose family owned a huge medical company and his father was maybe going to be the next governor. She was a bartender who'd never finished college and whose grand dream to own her own bar had been completely derailed by becoming the legal guardian to an infant. Their paths could only ever cross at a place like Trenton's.

She would never fit into his world and he would never understand hers.

Jeannie didn't know what to do with her legs. The hem of the sundress was well above her knees and Robert sat across from her. His gaze roamed over her. Was that hunger in his eyes? Or was he noting the shabby dress, the worn leather straps on her sandals, the hundred other little things that marked her as a different class?

She tucked the hem of her dress around her thighs and stared right back. Of course he looked completely at ease sitting there. In shorts. Shorts! She still couldn't get over it, or the way the sight of the dark hair on his legs stirred something deep inside her.

The man was sin in a suit but there was something so casually masculine about him right now that her clothes felt too tight.

He, at least, had no problem crossing his legs. "So," she began because several quiet moments had passed and Robert showed no sign of breaking the silence. "What's for lunch?"

"Darna—that's Rona's sister—is preparing a traditional Filipino meal of chicken satay, tinola soup and suman for dessert."

She stared. "Did you hire Darna just for today?"

"No, she's worked for me for almost six years. I trust her," he added as an afterthought.

For some reason that made Jeannie happy. He needed people he could trust. She just wished he counted himself on that list.

He didn't say anything else. They were driving toward downtown and, for once, traffic was light. "What else are we doing today?"

She heard him inhale sharply and felt an answering tug in her chest. "Nothing."

She met his gaze. "Pity."

The tension between them sharpened. "Jeannie…"

"Robert," she replied. If he didn't want to sleep with

her, that was fine. But she wanted him to say it. She didn't want any misunderstandings. "Aren't we on a date?"

His mouth opened and snapped shut and Jeannie got to appreciate that rare, wonderful thing where Dr. Robert Wyatt was flummoxed.

"Because this seems like a date," she went on. "I'm wearing a dress, you picked me up in a limo and we're going to eat a meal. Pretty standard date stuff, really."

He was doing that fish thing, his mouth opening and closing and opening again. "I don't date."

"You mean, you're not currently seeing anyone? That's good. I'm not involved, either. Which," she added, "is good for the status of our date. I'm not into being anyone's side piece."

"Side... Never mind." He shook his head. "No. I mean, I don't date. Ever."

"Ever?" Because that sounded ominous. She knew he wasn't married—kind of went with the territory when he was named a top bachelor—but...

He had kissed her. Twice now. And he had definitely started it the second time.

"No," he said sharply. Ominously, even.

"Just going out on a limb here, but you're not going to tell me why?"

That got her a hard look.

"Right." She looked out the window again. They were making great time. "So sex is off the table, then?"

He made a choking noise. "Do you have a filter?"

"Yes. In case you've never noticed, I use it all the time—at work. But we're not at Trenton's. I don't know what's going on with you or what's going on between us but..." His face was completely unreadable, so she went on with a sigh. "This is who I am, Robert. I'm a bartender who hasn't completed a college degree and barely passed high school. My big dream is to open my own bar. I left home when I was eighteen and didn't talk to my sister for almost six years. I can be mean and bitter and a huge pain in the ass when I put my mind to it and I am *not* a shy, retiring virgin. I like sex and I'd like to have sex with you." It was hard to tell in the darkened interior of the limo, but she would've bet large sums of his money that he was blushing. "But I'm not going to push you into anything that makes you uncomfortable."

"Well, there's that," he said under his breath. She detected sarcasm.

"But," she went on, "beyond that, I'm a hot mess. I am singularly unqualified to raise a child, not to mention I have no way to pay for what a baby needs." Robert opened his mouth, no doubt to find another way to spend his money on her. "No, I'm not going to take more of your money. She's not your daughter and we're not your responsibility. I'm in this car with you because I like you. I know what I want from you, you confounding, infuriating man. Not your money, not your name—I want you, Robert. I have for a long time. And I know I may not get it and that's okay, too." She leaned forward and put her hand on his knee. "But the question is, do you know what you want from me?"

He stared at her hand, resting on his knee. She could feel him practically vibrating with nervous energy.

But he didn't say anything.

The car came to a stop.

Eight

If there was one thing Robert had learned growing up in Landon Wyatt's house, it was how to control his physical reactions, because showing joy or sorrow or, worst of all, fear, was the quickest way to pain.

Over the years Robert had gotten so good at controlling those giveaways—the increased heart rate, the stomach-wrenching nausea, the shallow, fast breathing—that, for the most part, he'd simply stopped feeling distress. Even when a surgery went wrong, he was able to keep his emotional reactions on lockdown and he'd lost count of the number of times his cool head had prevented disaster or, worse, death.

Which was good. Great, even. No one wanted to go through life afraid. He certainly didn't.

So why did he feel like he was going to vomit as he led Jeannie up the stairs to his house?

He didn't know. Jeannie was many things—including, apparently, a self-described "hot mess"—but one thing she wasn't was a threat.

At least, not the kind Robert was used to.

"This is...*wow*," she marveled as the front door swung open.

"Welcome home, Dr. Wyatt. Miss Kaufman." Darna beamed at Jeannie. She had a crisp white apron over her uniform and a welcoming smile.

Odd. Darna was efficient and did exceptional work for him. But had he ever seen her smile?

"Darna, is it? I was just getting to know Rona. She's your sister, right?" Jeannie took Darna's hand in hers and half shook it, half just held it. "It's such a pleasure to meet you. I hope you didn't go to too much trouble for this."

Darna's eyes danced with what was probably amusement. "No, no—no trouble at all. I hope you enjoy the meal." She retrieved her hand and turned to Robert. "Everything is set up on the terrace, sir. Will there be anything else?"

"No." Jeannie slanted him a hard look. "No...thank you?"

Jeannie beamed at him. For her part, Darna looked as if Robert had just declared his undying love. "My," she all but giggled. "My, my. Yes." She patted Jeannie on the arm and giggled. "Yes," she repeated.

Robert could feel his pulse beginning to speed up,

beating wildly out of time. Which was ridiculous because this was not a risky situation.

This was, as Jeannie had pointed out, lunch. Between two people who...liked each other?

All right, fine. He *liked* Jeannie. He needed to see her on a near-daily basis to function, it seemed. And he was doing everything in his power to help her through a difficult time. True, he'd done that for some of his patients, the ones where the bills would've bankrupted the families.

But he hadn't ever wanted to see those people again. And he certainly hadn't ever wanted to kiss any of them. Like he'd kissed Jeannie. Twice.

Kissed her and held her close—so, so close.

His pulse jumped to a new level of erratic.

With a nod, Darna disappeared into the house and Robert was left standing in the foyer with Jeannie. He needed to move but he wasn't sure he could. Every system he'd spent years mastering was in open revolt right now and that was when Jeannie turned to him, a knowing smile on her lips. "I take it you don't bring a lot of people home?"

"No," he replied. There. At least his voice was still under his control. He sounded exactly normal, even if he felt anything but.

A few nights ago she'd straddled him. Today—mere moments ago—she'd boldly announced that she not only liked sex, but she'd also like to have sex with him.

He would not lose control. He would not hurt her and he would not risk destroying this...liking.

She took a few steps away from him, staring at the ornate ceilings. "This place is huge."

"Yes."

She looked back over her shoulder at him. "Is it just you?"

He began to shake. "Yes. I value my privacy."

"I must say," she went on, running her fingers lightly over the hand-painted wall coverings, "this is more... floral than I would've guessed."

"Oh?" His voice cracked a little as she moved into the parlor. Had she always had that sway to her hips?

"I pictured you in a modern, stark condo—all harsh lines, lots of stainless steel and black. This?" She made a little turn in the parlor. "This is *extravagant*. Obnoxiously so."

No one else would tell him his house was obnoxious, but it was true. And Jeannie saw it. The dress swung around her legs, exposing more of the bare skin of her thighs, and Robert had to brace himself against the door frame. "It came like this."

She stopped twirling, the dress falling back around her legs. "You...bought the house like this and didn't change anything?"

He shook his head because he wasn't sure he could speak, not with her making her way back toward him, that sway in her hips, that smile on her face. Like she'd been waiting for him.

It wasn't alarm knotting up his tongue and making him feel light-headed and dizzy. It wasn't panic sending his pulse screaming in his veins. It wasn't fear that had given him a rock-hard erection, the one he'd been fighting to contain ever since this woman had slid onto his lap. No, that wasn't right. He'd been fighting this ever since she'd opened the front door and announced she'd been waiting for him. Since she'd been waiting on her stoop.

This was desire. Raw, pure, dangerous desire.

Oh, hell.

Somewhere below, he heard the faint sound of the alarm system being engaged and then a door shut. The noise echoed through the house—the sound of Darna leaving. They were well and truly alone, and Jeannie wanted to have sex with him and he was starting to think it'd be a good idea but how could he let her strip him bare without his control snapping?

"Hey," she said softly, coming toward him. He almost flinched when she put her hand on his cheek. "Just *be*, Robert. Nothing has to happen." She notched an eyebrow and instead of sympathy or worse, pity, he saw nothing but a challenge. "Although I reserve the right to make fun of this wallpaper because who wallpapers a ceiling?"

Odd. He was sure he was glaring at her, which normally sent people running for the closest exit. But instead, this woman smiled and absorbed it. Understood it.

Understood him.

"I don't want to hurt you," he got out and dammit, his voice shook with the force of emotions that tumbled through him. Desire. Fear. Need. Pain. Want.

An emotion shimmered in her eyes and was gone before he could identify it. "Oh, I don't know about that. Those floral drapes are borderline painful," she said with a mischievous grin and oddly, he was able to draw in a breath. "Why haven't you changed them?"

"It was done by someone famous back in the thirties, and my mother…"

Against his will, his eyes shut. But that was a mistake because he could see his mother delicately arranged on the cushioned chair by the fireplace, a blanket tucked around her legs to help hold the ice packs in place. She'd gazed at the obnoxious wallpaper and frenetic drapes and the gold leaf and said, *I love this room. The riot of colors…it's wild but free.* Then she'd smiled at him, her eyes unfocused from the pain or the meds or both, and had said, *Silly, isn't it?*

He wanted Cybil Wyatt to enjoy riotous colors and silliness and freedom. He had to get her away from Landon. The alternatives were unthinkable.

He heard himself say, "My mother liked it."

"Ah," Jeannie said, her tone softening with what he hoped was understanding and not pity. "So you keep it this way for her?"

He nodded. Darna dusted this room—all the rooms done in this overblown style—twice a week. They were kept in a permanent state of readiness, just in case.

But three years ago it hadn't been enough to keep his mother here. *He* hadn't been enough to keep her here.

"Does she visit often?"

Twice. His mother had been in his home exactly twice. The second time he'd had to carry her in because she couldn't climb the steps. She'd stayed only long enough to be able to walk back down on her own power. Robert had stood in the window, watching her get into Landon's black limousine.

Cybil Wyatt hadn't looked back.

Robert had found himself at Trenton's that night. "No," he said shortly, remembering to answer the question.

"I see."

He was afraid she did.

Suddenly, her touch was gone and Robert stumbled forward, his eyes popping open to find Jeannie moving through the room, her happy yellow dress both clashing with the greens and reds and blues of the formal parlor and, somehow, blending in perfectly.

"So if this is for your mom," she said, running a hand over the hand-carved marble fireplace mantel, "where *do* you live?"

This was a mistake. He didn't bring people here for a good reason. He kept to himself because it was better that way—safer, easier. He preferred being alone.

But Jeannie…

He held out his hand to her and she didn't even hesitate. Her fingers wrapped around his and, on impulse, he lifted her hand and let his lips trail over her knuckles. The contact pushed him that much closer to the edge.

She inhaled sharply. Did she feel the same connection he did? Or was she just looking to get lucky?

Did the answer even matter?

It did. God help him, it did.

"Come with me."

Jeannie did the math as Robert led her up one garish flight of stairs—really, this wallpaper was *something*— to another.

She'd spent about an hour with him five nights a

week, approximately fifty-one weeks out of the year, for almost three years. That meant…uh…somewhere around eight thousand hours with this man.

She'd never imagined him living like this. High-rent, yes. Opulent? Sure. But…

It was like she'd entered Opposites Land, where up was down, quiet was loud and Robert was surrounded by hideous decorating. The man was so incredibly particular about everything—the precise formulation of his Manhattan, the cuffs on his sleeves, hell, even where his bartender was. How did he live *here*?

Even accounting for the fact that his mother liked it…it just didn't make sense. If she woke up to these walls and marble and what was probably real gold leaf, she'd have a headache every day of the week and two on Sunday. Jeannie had never pegged Robert for being a momma's boy.

Except he'd sounded so raw when he'd said his mother liked it. Like he had the first time he'd ever walked through Trenton's doors.

Was Mrs. Wyatt a good person or not? Jeannie had a feeling that, if she knew where the woman fell on the spectrum between Sainted Angel and Worst Mother in The World, she'd understand Robert's choices better.

But she also understood that he wasn't going to tell her. In that eight thousand some-odd hours she'd spent with him, she'd barely heard mention of his parents until a few weeks ago. The man knew how to hold his cards close.

When they reached the landing on the third floor, things changed. The landing opened up onto a short, wide hallway and at the end, she could see two French doors thrown open. On either side of that hallway was a door.

That wasn't what caught her attention. Instead of gaudy wallpaper, the walls changed to a soft peach color. She wouldn't have chosen this color for Robert but at least it didn't make her eyeballs bleed. Compared to the explosion of pattern downstairs, this was downright calming—and that was including the fact that Robert had art hung on these walls. It looked old and expensive.

She tore her gaze away from the priceless paintings. Robert unlocked the door on the right side of the stairs and stood at the threshold. Jeannie studied the tension in his shoulders, the way he practically vibrated with nervous energy. She was just about to suggest they go straight to the terrace, where their meal had been set up, because it was clear that Robert wasn't exactly jumping at the chance to show her around.

But the moment she opened her mouth, he turned and held his hand out. She couldn't pass up this opportunity to understand a little bit more about what made the man tick.

Not to mention the way he'd kissed the back of her hand earlier.

So she put her trust in him and let him lead her into a...

"This is my study," he said, softly shutting the door behind him.

Jeannie gasped. *Books.* Shelves and shelves of books and not the kind that had been tastefully arranged to look good. Oh, no. These were paperbacks with broken spines that had been crammed into every square inch of available space—which went all the way up to ceilings that had to be at least twelve feet high. The walls were lined with shelves, and the long room appeared to run the entire width of the house. She turned to the closest one and saw at least twenty Tom Clancy books wedged together. The next shelf had John Grisham and after that, Janet Evanovich. And it just went on and on. Was that an entire bookcase of Nora Roberts?

Thousands and thousands of books in this room. So many he even had one of those little ladders to get to the top shelves.

The rest of the room had an almost cozy feel. Skylights kept the room bathed in a warm glow. The exterior wall housed a fireplace, which, unlike the one down in the formal room, looked like it had actually seen a fire in the past year. It was also only one of two places that didn't have shelves. But even that mantel was crowded with books underneath what was probably another priceless work of art. Before that was a leather chair with matching footstool, next to a side table with a lamp and paper, pens—book clutter, basically—next to it. Behind that was a long desk, piled high with even more books and a computer holding on to a corner of the desk.

She spun, breathing in the smell of paper and leather and trying to grasp the sheer number of books here. "You read," was the brilliant observation she came up with.

"Yes." He sounded embarrassed by this admission. "I don't watch much television."

"This is your room?"

"My study, yes. Darna only comes in here once a quarter to dust."

In other words, this was his private sanctuary. And he'd invited Jeannie inside.

Oh, Robert.

Light streamed in from the French doors that led outside. Robert unlocked them and then wrapped his strong fingers around hers and led her outside to the terrace.

Jeannie gasped, "Oh, my *God.*" She was sure the space itself was impressive. She was dimly aware of the sweet smell of flowers, of green and orange and space. A lot of space. But beyond that, she couldn't have described the terrace at all.

Because somehow, despite the fact that they were three blocks away from the shore and surrounded by high-rise condos, she had an uninterrupted view of Lake Michigan. The afternoon sun glinted off the water, marking the only difference between the water and the sky. A breeze blew off the lake, bathing them in cool, fresh air.

"You have a view of the lake." She turned to him. "*How* do you have a view of the lake?"

He wasn't looking at the water. He was staring at her with the kind of intensity she should be used to. But that was in the dim interior of Trenton's, with a bar between them. Here, under the bright sunlight, his gaze felt entirely different.

Entirely possessive and demanding and maybe just a little bit needy.

"I bought the buildings blocking my view and had them razed," he said in the same way he might've said

I got whole milk instead of skim. "They're parks now. I had playground equipment installed. One has a community garden. The kids plant things, I'm told."

Jeannie's mouth dropped open. "You did *what*?"

He shrugged. "I wanted this house, but with a view."

Jeannie looked back out at the water. The buildings surrounding the view were four or five stories tall, prime Gold Coast real estate that had probably housed condos and apartments that sold for a few million dollars. *Each.*

It made her nightly hundred-dollar tip look like a handful of pennies, didn't it? She knew he was rich. Billionaire bachelor and all that crap. But...

In this real estate market, Robert had single-handedly erased maybe a hundred million dollars of potential profits. So he could sit on his terrace and see the lake.

Sweet Jesus.

Really, why was she here? This man could have any woman he wanted. He could have a wife and mistresses and private jets and his own art museum and nannies and chefs and limos and...anything. He could have it all with just a snap of his fingers.

She was just a bartender. Working-class at best, nowhere near owning her own place. She could never exist in his world. She shouldn't have accepted his help, shouldn't have come to lunch and most definitely shouldn't have told this man she would like to have sex with him.

But she had.

She couldn't have him. Not forever. But she could hold him for just a little bit and then let him go. It was definitely a mistake and just might break her heart, but it was better to have loved and lost...or something like that.

He might just be the best mistake she was ever going to make.

"Do you like it?" he asked, his voice deep and riveting. She felt it all the way down to her toes, that voice.

She nodded. Out on the lake, a sailboat drifted by. It was so perfect it was almost unreal. Much like Robert.

She asked, "Can you see the stars from here?" Because Chicago's light pollution blotted out everything for her. But for him?

Only Robert Wyatt could make the stars shine.

His lips moved in that small way that meant he was smiling and her heart began to pound. "On clear nights, if you look right there..." He stepped in behind her and pointed toward a distant section of the horizon.

His body was warm and solid against her back and the lake breeze teased at the hem of her dress. Jeannie didn't know if this was a seduction or not, because this was Robert and who the heck could tell, but she had to admit, she was being seduced. Perfect, rich, gorgeous Dr. Robert Wyatt, who had his own personal section of the night sky.

"I'd love to see that," she said quietly.

One of his hands came to rest on her waist. Then the other followed suit. "I can show them to you," he said right against her ear.

Oh, thank God. Her nipples went hard as his lips brushed ever so lightly over her earlobe. That lightest of touches sent little bursts of electricity racing over her skin. She had to clench her legs together to keep her knees from buckling, but even that small movement spiked the pressure on her sex to almost unbearable levels of need.

Moving slowly, she lifted his hands off her waist and wrapped them around her stomach so she could lean back into him.

All she felt and heard was Robert.

How he'd turned his head and his breath cascaded over her ear as if he'd buried his face in her hair. Of the rise and fall of his chest as he inhaled her scent. Of the way his arms tightened around her, so slowly as to be almost imperceptible, until he had her locked in his grip. Of how he slowly lowered his chin until it came to rest on her shoulder.

Of the way his entire body seemed to surround her as if he was afraid of startling her or worse, driving her away.

Of how she felt safe in his arms because this was a man who would never let anything hurt her. Hadn't he spent the past few days showing her just that, over and over again?

"You're touching me," she said softly as she ran her hands over his exposed forearms. The hair there was dark and soft and intensely male. Her blood pounded harder, demanding satisfaction as it coursed through her body.

She felt him swallow, then felt his lips move against her neck. "I am."

She turned her head toward him, her mouth only centimeters away from his cheek. She could press her lips against his skin if she wanted, but she waited. More than anyone she'd ever been with, she needed to make sure he wanted her to move, to touch, to *take*.

"Do you like touching me?"

He shifted his arms, grabbing her hands and holding them flat against her stomach so she couldn't pet him. "Yes," he growled.

She shivered, wanting to pull him down into her, wanting to unbutton his shirt and strip off his shorts and leave him well and truly bare to her. Just her and no one else. "Then touch me," she breathed against his skin.

"I don't want to hurt you." He sounded like a man begging for salvation.

She rested her head against his shoulder and he automatically supported her weight. "You won't. But if something's not right, I'll say—" she cast about for a word "—*sailboat*," she said as another boat came into view. "If I say that, you'll stop."

He didn't reply for the longest of seconds—so long, in fact, that she began to think he wasn't going to agree, either to the safe word or the sex. *"Sailboat?"* he finally asked, shifting his grip so that he held both her wrists in one hand. The other hand he set low against her stomach.

She arched her back, pushing her torso into his arms. "It's not a word I shout during sex a lot," she said with a smile.

He jolted as if she'd jabbed him with a needle, his grip tightening. She couldn't touch him, couldn't turn into him. All she could do was stand there, watching Lake Michigan shimmer in the summer heat.

"Jeannie." Her name on his lips was like a call to arms because this wasn't going to be some soft-focus, romantic intimacy marked by sweet words and tender touches. Oh, no.

Sex with Robert was going to be a battle.

She'd always loved a good fight.

Then he kissed her like it was a challenge and for the life of her, she couldn't figure out if he was throwing down the gauntlet for her or for himself. Either way, she met him as an equal on the field, kissing him back just as fiercely as he was kissing her. Their mouths met with a savageness that made her legs shake with need.

She nipped at his lower lip and felt the responding tension ripple through his body. Something hard and long and so, *so* hot began to push against her hip.

She began to pant as the tension spiraled in her body. He didn't loosen his grip on her, didn't give her anywhere else to go. And damn him, he didn't touch her anywhere else. He was holding himself back too carefully, so she bit him again. This time he growled and pulled away, burying his face against her neck. She felt his teeth skim over her skin so she angled her head to give him more.

"Yes," she whispered, hoping encouragement would help him get over this whole *don't want to hurt you* hang-up.

He bit her—gently—right at the spot where her shoulder met her neck. *"Yes,"* she hissed again. When was the last time she'd been this turned on? Every part of her body practically begged for his touch. "Oh, yes. Just like that."

"Don't," he growled against her neck. "Don't talk."

Even through the haze of desire, she laughed at the sheer ridiculousness of that order. "Seriously? Come on, Robert. Have you *met* me?"

"Please," he said. "I...need it to be different."

Different from what? She pulled away from him and he let her go. "But I thought you said you didn't..." He didn't have girlfriends or dates or people he brought back here. But he'd made it clear—he wasn't a virgin. He was breathing hard, panting almost, looking like he was being torn in two.

Oh, God—he really was going to break her heart, wasn't he?

"Okay," she told him. "Those are your rules? No touching, no talking?"

"I... Yes. Those are my rules."

Talking was almost half the fun and touching was definitely the other half. But she was getting a clearer picture of Robert all the time and she was beginning to think he hadn't had a normal, happy childhood. Neither had she, but she had to wonder—how much of what was happening here was Robert letting his scars finally show?

"Fine. My rule is that either one of us says *sailboat*, the other person stops immediately."

"That's it?"

"That's it." She nodded toward the other set of glass doors. This pair was behind a table and chairs set for two. "Is that your bedroom?"

"Yes." But he didn't move.

This man. Honestly, what was she going to do with him? "Can we use your bed?"

"Oh. Yes. Of course." This time he didn't hold out his hand and she didn't reach for him.

He unlocked the glass doors and led her into a masculine bedroom. The walls were a deep navy blue paper with a subtle blue-on-blue pattern. A fireplace with another marble mantel stood in the same spot where the one in the study had been, another impressive piece of art hanging over it.

But what really drew her eye was the massive four-poster bed. Truly, it was huge. She'd heard of California king beds but she'd never seen one in person and the bed probably took up more space than Melissa's whole room back home. Which would've been overwhelming enough but that didn't take into consideration the drapes. Around each of the four posts, airy white drapes were overlaid with pale blue damask that made it look almost like a fairy bed.

"I hope this is all right," Robert said, jamming his hands into his pockets.

"It's amazing and you're cute when you're nervous."

"I'm not nervous," he shot back in a way that was 100 percent nervous.

"That's good, because you're not cute, either." She took a step toward him. He didn't move back, but he inhaled sharply. Not nervous, her fanny. Besides the fireplace, she saw one of those wooden butler things men used to set out their suits. Over the shoulder of a royal blue jacket was a red silk tie. "Here," she said, stepping around him. She snatched up the tie, trying not to wince at the label—Armani, of course. She was about to permanently mangle a tie that probably cost a few hundred dollars.

But then again, this was Robert, who'd knocked down some of the most expensive real estate in the world so he could have a lake view. To hell with the tie.

She looped a quick slipknot around one wrist and turned back to him, her arms outstretched. "How about this? You can tie my wrists to make sure I don't grab you."

His mouth dropped open as color rushed to his cheeks and Jeannie took a perverse sort of pleasure in shocking him. He was barely hanging on to his control and after so many thousands of hours of watching him lock down every emotion, practically every response and expression, she was demolishing those walls.

"You— I—" He snapped his mouth shut and tried to straighten cuffs he wasn't wearing. *"No."*

"No?" She loosely wrapped the other end around her wrist and then lifted the tie to her mouth, letting the silk play over her lips. "Not even to keep me quiet?"

He had to grab one of the bedposts to keep upright. She smiled but didn't get any closer to him. Instead, she circled around him, kicking off her sandals. "Unless you wanted me to leave the shoes on?"

He managed to shake his head.

The bed was so damn big there was a little step stool at the foot of it. She climbed up onto the bed and walked to the center of it.

Robert's eyes never left hers. At this angle, he probably had a decent view of her legs and, if she twirled, maybe even her panties. She knelt on the bed and held out her hands. "*Robert.* Come to me."

"No," he said again, more forcefully. "I could hurt—"

"I don't believe that for a second," she interrupted. "You're not a damned monster, Robert, so stop acting like one. You're a man. And not even a cute one. You're the most gorgeous, complicated, outright *kind* man I've ever met and you're learning how to be a good hugger and you take care of babies and kids and I've spent literal actual years dreaming about you, about this moment. Besides, I'm not that breakable. I trust you."

"I don't trust myself," he ground out, clinging to the bedpost. "Don't you see? I…" He set his jaw. "You shouldn't trust me, either."

Oh, Robert. She let the tie drop away from her wrist and undid the slipknot as she pushed back to her feet.

"Fine," she told him. "Give me your hands."

He shot her a look of disbelief. "What?"

"Your hands. Don't talk. Just do it." For a second she didn't think he was going to do it. "You don't trust yourself? *Fine.* I'll tie you to the bedpost and then you won't be able to do anything."

Nine

Robert sucked in air as Jeannie got closer to him. "I'll tie you down and ride you hard. I won't talk and I won't touch you and you won't be able to do anything about it."

"Wyatts don't submit," he got out, sounding like she'd rabbit-punched him.

That sounded like…like something that had been said to him, but she couldn't think about what it meant right now. The look he gave her would've turned a lesser mortal to stone but she knew him far too well to let a well-placed glare put her off.

"Don't make me wait," she pleaded. Because if he said no…

"Would you really wait for me?" His voice was ragged.

She wasn't supposed to touch him—that was the

rule. But she couldn't *not* touch him, not when he looked so desperately devastated. She touched the tips of her fingers to his forehead and, when he didn't pull away, she skimmed them down the sides of his face.

"Always," she whispered against his forehead. "I'll always wait for you. But trust me. Trust yourself."

He made a choked noise and pushed her away. She stumbled a little because this bed was so danged plush and yeah, she'd broken the rules and that was that. But when she got her balance back, she saw he'd held out his hands.

He didn't look at her. He kept his eyes down, shoulders back and yep, this was war. But she knew now—he wasn't fighting her.

He was fighting himself.

Oh, Robert.

She looped the silk tie around his wrists and then around the bedpost. Nothing was tight—if he wanted, he could twist his way free. But this wasn't about restraining him for safety, no matter how he tried to frame it like that.

This was about proving he could trust himself. Because he needed that. She was afraid to ask why.

The knot secured—sort of—she scooted off the edge of the bed so she could stand next to him. "Just to help you on the bed," she said softly as she put her hands on his shoulders.

The man was shaking as she turned him around and undid his belt and the fly of his shorts. For all his defensiveness, there was no mistaking that erection. Dear God, even contained behind his boxer briefs, Robert swelled upward, long and rock-hard. There was so much she wanted to say—that he was as impressive as hell, all the ways she'd dreamed of having him, asking him what he liked, telling him how to touch her—if only to break the oppressive silence of the room.

But she didn't because those were the rules. Instead, she focused on the harsh panting sound of his breathing, the way he tensed when her hand brushed along that impressive ridge. But she didn't palm him, didn't slip her hand inside his briefs. Hell, she didn't even push his briefs down. She could do that when she was on the bed.

She could explore quite a bit before he could get free. She could rip open his shirt and finally take what she wanted from him.

She didn't. He'd given her so much—his money, his time, peace of mind when it came to Melissa. But this? Robert was giving her the most precious gift of all.

His trust.

No way in hell was she going to abuse it.

So she guided him down onto the bed and then swung his legs up. "Scoot down," she said, keeping her voice low and calm. "Just—yeah, like that."

She was trembling, too, she realized. This man was broken in ways she was afraid to understand and definitely couldn't fix, but that wasn't the sum total of who he was. He was still Robert—thoughtful in his demands, overbearing in his caring, seductive in his intensity.

She arranged him so his legs pointed to the center of the bed—which left her plenty of room to work with.

"Okay?" she asked, watching him closely as she slid her panties off.

He nodded.

Okay, she thought, climbing back onto the bed and standing over him.

Even tied to the post, his pants undone and his color high, there was something so ethereal, almost other-worldly, about the way his pale eyes stared at her.

"Dress on or off?" she asked, lifting the hem.

His gaze snapped to where she'd exposed her sex and he inhaled sharply. "On."

Yeah, that didn't surprise her. She stepped over him, still holding on to the hem, letting him get a brief glimpse of her body. Heat flooded her sex as he stared at her hungrily, his hands trapped over his head. He made no move to get free.

She had one of the most formidable men in the city, maybe even the whole country, at her mercy. The power was intoxicating.

She let her hem drop. Robert made a noise of need, in the back of his throat, but she didn't let him look again. Instead, she lowered herself to her knees, sitting on his thighs. "Okay?"

"Yes." His voice was deeper now as he stared at her breasts, and underneath his briefs, his erection jumped.

She pulled his briefs down, gasping as he sprung free. His length was proud, long and ruddy and curving slightly to the right. She wanted to wrap her hand around it and feel the hot skin sliding over his hardness, wanted to suck him deep into her mouth and let her tongue drive him wild until he broke.

But she'd promised, damn it all. So instead of exploring, she just said, "Condoms?"

He jerked his chin to the bedside table. "The drawer." Somehow, his voice was even deeper now. She felt it rumble throughout her body.

Oh, he was going to be so good.

She slid off him and, half sprawled across the massive mattress, got the box of condoms out of the drawer. The box was unopened, but the expiration date was several years off. Had he bought these just for her?

She got one out and opened the packet, then made her way back to Robert. As efficiently as she could, she rolled the condom on—although he kept twitching, which made it a bit of a challenge, she thought with a smile.

Then she scooted forward so his erection was right beneath her. She could feel him pulsing, sending little sparks of desire throughout her sex. She wanted to touch him so badly but because she couldn't, all her attention was focused on where their bodies met.

"Okay?"

He didn't hesitate. "Yes." If anything, he sounded a little surprised by that.

"Good." She began to rock her hips, letting his erection drag over her sensitive flesh without taking him inside. Her whole world narrowed to the way she moved, how she had to be careful with her balance. To the ragged sound of his breathing mingling with hers. To the splash of red around his wrists that stood out in the sea of blue. To the way he couldn't take his eyes off her.

This was the most erotic moment of her life.

She cupped her breasts through her dress, lifting them and tugging on the nipples. The sensation was dulled by the fabric and her bralette, but she didn't care. She tugged harder, her legs clenching around his hips, her weight bearing down on his erection. Robert groaned as she teased herself, his hips thrusting faster, his movements wilder.

Unexpectedly, an orgasm broke over her, showering her with stars. Moaning, her head dropped back. She would've toppled right off him if he hadn't shifted, bringing his knees up and catching her.

The sound of their panting filled the room. He pulsed against her swollen sex, hot and needy and unable to do a damn thing about it. When she could sit up again, she stared down at him with a dreamy smile on her face. "That was wonderful," she said. What she wouldn't give to lower herself to his chest and kiss him because orgasms like that didn't exactly grow on trees.

He growled. Because of course he did.

She *tsked* him as she lifted herself up and felt his erection rise to meet her. Slowly, she took him inside.

There was nothing else in the world but this. The slash of red above his head. The intense pale blue of his eyes. The cords of his neck straining as he filled her, inch by agonizingly wonderful inch. She bit back a cry of need because *oh, God* she'd never felt anything as wonderful as Robert inside her.

She sucked two of her fingers into her mouth and then lifted the hem of her dress just enough so she could press her slick digits against herself. Robert groaned again, trying to roll his hips, trying to thrust up into her, but she used all her weight to pin him to the mattress.

"Wait," she said, letting her fingers move in slow circles, brushing against where he was joined with her, adjusting to the fullness of him. "Just *be*, Robert. Be with me."

He nodded, a small movement. Maybe it was all he was capable of.

She kept her word. She didn't touch him, except where he was buried deep inside, except where her hips rested on his. She didn't moan or scream his name, didn't tell him what she wanted. She waited until his breathing had started to even out, just a little—until she was sure he had himself back under control and could focus on this intimacy between them.

She tightened her inner muscles around him, pleasure spiking hard and fast as he inhaled sharply. Even that small movement from him—she felt it travel up his length, felt her own body responding. She rubbed herself as she began to shift her hips, rising and falling on him at a languorous pace.

With her free hand, she went back to her breast. She pulled the neckline of the dress down, shoved the pink lace of the bralette aside and, after licking her thumb, began to tease her own nipple.

Robert's eyes were almost black now and he shifted underneath her, using his feet so he could thrust. But that wasn't it. As Jeannie stared down at him, she saw that he reached for the tie.

She froze, just managing to keep her balance. But instead of jerking at the knots, Robert gripped the loose ends of the tie and held on tighter. "Don't…stop, Jeannie." He swallowed. "Please."

Relief broke over her almost as potent as another climax. "There," she said, tugging at her nipple, pulling the hard tip until the most pleasurable pain rocketed through her. "Was that so hard?"

She felt him jolt deep inside her. Then, miracle of miracles, he smiled. Just that small movement of his lips, so tiny no one else would notice it. Just for her.

He was just for her.

This time, when he thrust up into her, she met him as his equal, taking his thrusts and setting her own slow rhythm. She kept rubbing herself, pulling at her nipple, feeling him straining for his release, refusing to make it easy for him. If she wanted to, she knew she could get him off in a matter of minutes. Seconds.

She had no idea if she'd ever get to have him like this again and she wasn't going to waste a single moment of their time together. This moment might have to last her the rest of her life.

She moved over him, fighting for control when all she wanted to do was fall upon him. The noises of sex filled their room, the slap of her flesh against his, their mingled breathing, the squeaking of the mattress.

The red of the tie, the dark desire of his eyes, the pressure on her sex, the way he moved inside her— perfect and strong and right. So, so right.

Oh, God. She gave first, pitching forward. She managed not to plant her hands on his chest, but it was a close thing. Instead, she braced her hands on the mattress and drove her hips down onto him faster and faster.

"Robert," she got out, her climax spiraling but not breaking—building, pushing her faster, slamming onto him harder and harder. "Oh, God."

"Jeannie."

She came apart at the need in his voice and then she kissed him as her orgasm robbed her of thought, of the ability to hold herself apart from him. She kissed him in victory and in defeat, for love and for loss.

She kissed *him*.

He groaned into her mouth, a noise of satisfaction, of completion. He groaned and pistoned his hips up into her before holding and straining and she took him in, all of him. Everything he had, she took—and it all pushed her orgasm even higher. She couldn't help it when she tore herself away from him, throwing back her head as she peaked.

Then she collapsed onto his chest, struggling to get enough air. She barely had the energy to pull herself free of him. "Oh, Robert," she sighed, snuggling down into his chest.

She felt the sharp intake of his breath, felt his hands on her arms as he moved her off his body. He didn't follow her, didn't cover her with his weight.

All she saw was Robert's back as the door slammed shut.

He was gone.

Ten

Robert stood at the top of the stairs. He needed to go to Jeannie. Maybe apologize. Maybe wrap his arms around her and kiss her again.

Probably both.

He couldn't move.

He saw a shadow cross the terrace. Ah. She'd gone outside. Pulled by the lake, no doubt. He was glad she liked his view. He hoped she approved of him buying the land and donating the cleared spaces to the city.

Would she be here long enough to see the stars?

He slipped into his room and grabbed new clothes. Aside from the faint scent of oranges, there was no trace of her in the room. The tie had been returned to its starting place. The bed sheets had been straightened; the condom wrapper gone. Even her shoes had been removed.

Strangely, he found himself longing for her to leave her mark.

Silently, he got cleaned up and changed and then stood, watching her through the open doors.

She'd opened the wine. Hadn't needed his help at all. Of course she didn't—she was a bartender. And she'd found the kitchenette, where Darna had undoubtedly had all the food arranged in containers that kept it warm.

Robert wasn't sure how long he stood there, watching Jeannie through the doorway. She looked…the same. Beautiful, but the same.

He envied her that.

It wasn't until she went to refill her wineglass that he moved. He stepped out onto the terrace. "Here," he said, his voice gruff but unable to do anything about it.

She didn't seem surprised when he appeared, nor when he pulled the bottle out of her hand. "I know how to pour wine," she scolded, but at least there was no acid in her voice. He dared to hope she sounded amused.

"You've served me for years," he replied, pleased to see that his hands weren't shaking. Surgeon's hands should always be steady. "It's my turn to serve you."

He saw her smile, but she didn't look at him. Instead, she kept her gaze fixed on the lake.

Robert topped up her glass and then poured a healthy glass for himself because he could use a drink, he realized. Then he put a little chicken on a dish. He wasn't hungry. He rarely ate lunch. But moving around the terrace gave him something to do.

Normally, Robert was fine with silence. He worked in silence. He read at night with nothing but the faint sounds of the city wafting through his terrace doors. He was old friends with quiet.

But at this exact moment, the fact that Jeannie wasn't talking bothered him.

He pushed his food around his plate. She ate silently. They both drank their wine.

"You can talk now," he finally blurted out, feeling ridiculous.

"No," she said slowly, "I've already said my piece. It's your turn."

He forced himself to breathe slowly, to keep his pulse from running away. He was just…overwhelmed by the new sensations, that was all. He'd never dined with company on the terrace. Never shared his view with anyone. Never brought someone to his bed. Never let his arms be tied.

It was a lot to take in. That was all.

Then he was talking. Words flowed out of his mouth as easily as wine flowed from the bottle. "Something changed when I was fourteen," he was horrified to hear himself say. But it was too late. The bottle had been smashed and he couldn't contain the spill. Not around her. Not anymore. "I grew, I guess. *He* called me into his office. It was never good, being called down. Always bad."

Out of the corner of his eye, he saw her grip tighten on her glass. But all she said was, "Oh?" And strangely, that made it easier to keep going because that was what she would've said if they'd been at the bar, shielded by the dim lights.

It was bright out, but the small table stood between them.

"This time there was a woman there. She…" He

swallowed, but kept going. "She wasn't wearing much. She was pretty."

Shame burned through him as he remembered his confusion. He'd been braced for threats, for pain. But not for a woman in a slip and nothing else.

"He said—" Robert drained his glass "—I was a man now. I needed to know how to treat a woman, how to dominate."

Jeannie inhaled sharply. She didn't say anything, though. And for once, Robert hated the silence.

"He made me touch her. Kiss her. He wanted me to…" He took a breath, trying to find the words without remembering all the terrible details. "And when I couldn't…"

Unexpectedly, Jeannie stood. Before Robert could process what she was doing, she'd plucked his plate and glass from his hand. Wine dripped from his fingertips. He hadn't realized his hands were shaking.

She sat sideways in his lap, burying her face against his neck, and it should've been awful because he didn't like to be touched and *never* talked about why but she was touching him and he was talking.

He couldn't stop.

"He pulled me off the woman and told me to watch. Then he showed me what he wanted me to do."

Jeannie's arms tightened around his neck and he realized he was gathering her closer, holding her like he was afraid she would rip herself away from him.

He didn't allow himself to think of that day. He was very good at controlling his reactions, and those memories weren't allowed.

But now?

He remembered everything. The woman's muffled screams. The way his father had smiled. The familiar guilt that, if he'd only done what Landon had wanted, he might've protected her. The realization that he couldn't protect any woman.

Only the knowledge that he would've been beaten senseless for displaying weakness had kept him from leaving the room.

"Breathe," Jeannie whispered against his skin. "It's okay. I'm here. Just breathe."

He wasn't sure his lungs would ever properly draw in air again. "I told my mother what'd happened. I shouldn't have because it wasn't safe. If you were too happy, too sad, too angry—he didn't like it. But I couldn't keep it inside. I *couldn't*…and she was so mad that she marched into his office, screaming and throwing things and…"

And Landon had exacted his revenge in a thousand small cuts. He'd been exacting that revenge with interest over the past three years, no doubt.

"Did it ever happen again?" Jeannie asked softly.

Out on the lake, a speedboat raced through his view and was gone. "Not right away." His mother's anger had somehow bought Robert a few months of grace.

"Oh, Robert." Something wet and warm ran over his skin as she held him. She didn't push him aside, didn't look at him with disgust. "What did your mom do after the next time?"

"I didn't tell her." Robert hadn't been willing to risk his mother. So he'd buried his disgust and horror and tried to be the man Landon wanted.

He almost laughed. If Landon could've seen him a few short minutes ago, tied to the bed and helpless while Jeannie gave him the gift of her tenderness, her touch—the gift of herself—the old man might just have had a stroke.

Even more so if he heard what Robert was going to say next. "I was overwhelmed when you kissed me. Earlier. I…"

That kiss had been perfect and terrifying. He'd wanted to never let go of her and he hadn't been able to leave fast enough and it had not been his finest moment.

"It's okay," she said softly. "I'm fine. I broke the rule. I'm sorry."

He pulled her in closer because he liked her there. "Me, too."

Oh, how Landon Wyatt would mock him for that apology, even if it barely qualified as such.

He didn't know how long they sat there. The sun glittered off his own personal view of the lake. Finally, he heard himself say, "I haven't seen her in almost three years. My mother, that is."

He had no reason to tell Jeannie any of this. What had happened in his bed earlier…that hadn't come with the obligation that he owed her the truth.

But he couldn't stop himself.

"What happened?" Jeannie asked softly.

The sun began to dip behind the buildings, casting the sky in deeper shades of gold. No matter what happened—who lived, who died or who walked the fine line between the two states—the sun rose and set every day. It kept going. Just like he did.

"She wouldn't stay with me. He'd beaten her badly and I brought her here. But she didn't trust me to keep her safe. She went back to him and…" He swallowed around the rock lodged in his throat.

"When was this?"

"The day I walked into Trenton's."

The day he'd been utterly lost had been the day he'd found Jeannie. It hadn't been an accident. It couldn't have been something as random as a coincidence.

She'd been waiting for him.

She gasped, drawing air across his throat like a caress.

"Will you get to see her again?" Her voice wavered and Robert prayed she wouldn't cry. There was no point to tears. Never had been.

"That's why I have to go to the campaign kickoff. He's using her as bait so I will pretend we're this perfect happy family."

"To lie for him, the asshole." This time she sounded mad. Strangely, her anger made Robert feel better. "What are you going to do?"

"If she'll come, I'll take her away. Send her where he can't get to her."

Jeannie leaned back. He could tell she was staring up at him, but he couldn't look at her, couldn't risk drowning in her brown eyes. He kept staring at the water. "You're not going to bring her *here*, are you? You can't hope that this time she'll walk away just because she has a weak spot for tacky wallpaper."

He almost smiled because he hadn't just spilled his deepest, most shameful secrets. He'd told Jeannie. Somehow, that made things better. "Of course not. I'm sending her to New Zealand." Now he did look down at her. The impact of her watery eyes hit him square in the chest. "That was why I needed to talk to you, the night you weren't there. I had to see you. I needed…" He brushed her short hair away from her eyes. "I needed to know I was doing the right thing."

Because he was technically going to be kidnapping his mother and he didn't doubt that she might hate him, at least a little. Not to mention Landon might punish him and get Cybil back.

The man would try.

But Robert wasn't a kid anymore. Lawyers, accountants, reporters—all were eager to be a part of what had the potential to be the biggest scandal in Chicago since Al Capone had run this town. And Robert was pulling all the strings.

It was time Landon knew what Wyatts were truly capable of.

"You are," Jeannie said simply. "You're absolutely doing the right thing, Robert." She cupped his face in her hands. "What happened before—that was *never* your fault. And you're not like him. He didn't break you, do you understand? You're stronger than he is. You always were. He knows it, too, I think."

Robert's eyes stung, so he closed them. He wanted desperately to believe what Jeannie said. Wanted to feel the truth of it in his bones.

But if he was really that strong, he would've been able to keep Mom safe all these years. And he hadn't.

Jeannie pushed off his lap, pulling him to his feet. Silently, she led him back into his bedroom. For some reason, she stripped him down to his boxers and then pulled her dress over her head. But instead of removing the pretty lingerie she wore, she turned down the sheet and pushed him into bed. He didn't resist. He couldn't. Whatever she was doing, he needed it. He needed her. So he made space for her and she climbed in after him, pulling the sheet over them both.

Then she curled into his side. "I can't stay to see the stars. Not tonight," she murmured, her breath warm against his chest. "I have to get back to Melissa."

His arms tightened around her even as he forced himself to say, "Of course," even though he wanted to argue.

How very odd. He *wanted* her to stay. All the more so when she threw a bare leg over his, tangling their limbs together. It felt…right. Good, even.

"But Robert?"

"Yes?"

Something warm and soft pressed against his chest. A kiss. One of forgiveness, he hoped. "I won't let you face him alone." Before he could process what she could be talking about—because she couldn't *possibly* be suggesting that she would voluntarily place herself anywhere near Landon Wyatt—she leaned up on one elbow and stared down at him with a look he couldn't identify. "I'm coming with you to the kickoff."

Eleven

Jeannie hadn't seen Robert since he'd walked her to her door three nights ago, kissed the back of her hand like an old-fashioned prince and then been driven off by an absolutely beaming Reginald.

She knew he was talking to Maja or Rona or both. Like when Maja said, "Dr. Wyatt wants you to make sure you're getting fresh air, so let me show you how to use this stroller."

Or when Rona said, "Dr. Wyatt asked me to make sure you're enjoying the meals? I can cook other things, as well," as if anyone would turn down real Filipino cooking, which Rona prepared every other day when she came to tidy the already spotless house and do the laundry. Even the next-day leftovers were fabulous. If Jeannie

SARAH M. ANDERSON   141

had been on her own, she would've been living on frozen pizza and beer.

But Robert didn't ask *her* how she enjoyed the meals
or the walks or the time with Melissa. He didn't talk to
her at all and her texts thanking him for a nice time went
unanswered. Which was unnerving. Jeannie knew he
was busy—with his practice or Wyatt Medical or making plans for his mother. She refused to think that he
was avoiding her because she'd tied him up or kissed
him or listened to his secrets. He wasn't a chatty man to
begin with. She could see that he simply wouldn't know
how to strike up a conversation after what they'd shared.

But after another day of silence passed, she began to
wonder if he was trying to keep her from going to the
kickoff. And she had no intention of letting him do that.

So instead of small talk, she went to war over text.
And it turned out, he was downright chatty.

What time on Saturday?

No.

Yes. I'm coming with you.

You are not. It's not safe for you.

It's not safe for you, either.
Why should you face him alone?
You need backup.

Absolutely not. I won't risk you like that.

Jeannie smiled at that one, pausing to rub Melissa's back. They were snuggled up on the couch and the house was silent. Maja wasn't here. Rona would be back tomorrow. It was just Jeannie and a drowsy infant.

A week ago this situation would've inspired sheer panic, but now? Jeannie let the baby's warmth sink into her chest as Melissa dozed. She still had no idea how she would handle raising a child when Robert stopped paying a small army of people to help her but she was at least no longer panicking at the thought of holding her niece. As long as Melissa got the right formula and stayed swaddled while she slept, things were better.

I won't risk you, either.

I'm not taking you.
End of discussion.

Then I'll just crash the party.

No, Jeannie.

She chuckled softly to herself. She could hear his exasperated tone, see him glowering at his phone. He could get anyone to do anything he wanted with a snap of his fingers and money—anyone but her.

Yes, she'd talked to Miranda at Trenton's. Robert had handed over a credit card and rumor had it that Julian had run that sucker for thirty thousand dollars and Robert hadn't disputed the charge.

Robert hadn't been back since. Which was fine by

Miranda. She didn't care how hot and rich Robert was, she wasn't dealing with him ever again, she'd said. Miranda had related the whole thing in breathless, disbelieving tones but Jeannie believed it all. Thirty thousand was nothing to Robert.

"He's freaking *terrifying*," Miranda had said.

Jeannie had just laughed. As far as she could tell, no one at work had any idea that Robert had appointed himself her guardian angel—or that they'd shared a wonderful, messy evening together.

I *will* crash.
I've been sneaking into parties and clubs since I was 14.
I'll show up in my yellow dress and be loud and obnoxious.
Trust me I'm good at it.

No.

You can't keep me away so just accept that you're taking me.
If you take me, you can keep an eye on me.
Who knows what kind of trouble I'll get into otherwise?
Might step on a candidate's toes or splash red wine on his face.

Jesus.

Whoopsie.

Robert didn't answer that salvo right away but Jeannie let the space build between them. Melissa grunted in her sleep, warm and perfect and okay. She was seventeen days old today. It'd been ten days since Nicole had died, nine days since Jeannie had brought this baby home and eight days since Robert had turned out to be the star she'd wished upon. Today was the first day Maja wasn't living in the house full-time.

The next time Jeannie was at Robert's house—assuming he invited her back—she wasn't leaving until she'd seen the night horizon over the lake.

She could almost see Nicole walking into the small living room, trying her best not to roll her eyes or let fly with a cutting comment about how this was exactly what Jeannie always did—rushing into something *way* over her head without thinking.

"You're trouble," Nicole had always said. "And like follows like."

When Jeannie had been a little girl, Nicole had hissed it at Jeannie with pure venom, usually seconds before she got Jeannie in trouble. Maybe there'd been a time when Nicole had set Jeannie up—shoving a ruined sweater under Jeannie's bed and then blaming it on Jeannie.

All Jeannie could really remember was deciding that if she was going to get into trouble, she was going to *earn* it.

After their mom had died and it was just Nicole, still only seventeen, and Jeannie, barely ten, Nicole had kept on saying it. But the hatred had changed, deepened. Now Jeannie could look back and see the pure fear Nicole must have been living with, an unwelcome guest who refused to leave. The same fear Jeannie had been stuck in when she'd wished upon a star.

Jeannie had kept right on getting into trouble. Parties, boys, alcohol—driving her sister to the breaking point. They'd both been relieved when Jeannie had packed a bag and left.

Then, when the two of them had finally reconciled, after Nicole had decided she was having a family come hell or high water, Nicole had still said that. Jeannie was still trouble. But now Nicole had said it with almost fondness, and instead of hearing it as an attack, Jeannie heard what Nicole was really saying.

I'm sorry. I'm glad you're here. I love you.

That was how Jeannie chose to remember Nicole. Someone who was complicated, who did the best she could with what she had—a missing dad, a dead mom, a hellion for a sister.

I'm sorry, Jeannie thought. Hopefully, wherever Nicole was, she would know the truth. *I'm glad you were here. I'm doing the best I can. I love you.*

Jeannie's phone chimed again.

I can't allow this.

Oh, wasn't that just like the man? If he were in front of her, she'd be hard-pressed to pick between strangling and hugging him. Hell, maybe she'd just tie him to the bed again and work through some of the frustration he inspired.

He was a very inspiring man.

It'd been three days since their lunch date. Three days since the unreachable, untouchable Dr. Robert Wyatt had let himself be touched. Since he'd held out his hands for her and she'd ridden him in silence. Since he'd shared his darkest secret.

He'd done so much for her and Melissa and all Jeannie had ever done for him was serve him the perfect Manhattan. She might not be able to provide material comfort for the man but by God, she could help him face his demons.

Specifically, one demon.

Like followed like, after all. But this time she promised herself it would be good trouble. The plan was simple. Back up Robert. Help his mom. Hell, protect the good people of Illinois from a damn monster.

Really, it was going to be one hell of a party.

She shifted Melissa so she could text faster.

Robert. I am not your employee.
You don't ALLOW me to do anything.
Let me be there for you.
It's not weakness to accept help.

I can't ask this of you.

You're not asking.

This is not an obligation.

I'm coming. Let me come with you.

Melissa stirred, pushing against her blanket. The little noises she made—Maja had said those were hungry noises. Jeannie glanced at the clock—right on schedule. Who knew babies had schedules? But this baby did, thanks to a stand-in grandmother and by God, Jeannie wasn't going to screw that up. Which meant she couldn't lie around texting much longer.

Robert. Let me come with you. Please.

You can't wear the yellow dress.
This is a formal event.

I don't have anything more formal.
Unless you want me to wear my vest and bow tie?

Lord.
I will send some things over.
If we're going to do this, we're going to do it right.
He can't know who you really are.

I can blend. Promise.

The typing bubble showed for a long time but Jeannie knew she'd won. She absolutely could blend. She'd been serving the upper crust drinks for years now. She knew the mannerisms, the topics the one percent discussed. She could be just as obnoxious and ostentatious as Robert's wallpapered ceilings or as cold and aloof as Robert himself. She could absolutely fake it until she made it, whatever form *it* took.

It couldn't be a small lie because those were obvious and easy to disprove. To pull one over on someone like Landon Wyatt, it'd have to be a grand lie, so bold and ostentatious that no one would dare question her or her place on Robert's arm. She'd have to not just belong there—she'd also have to own the room.

She glanced at the book on her coffee table. *To Dare a Duke.* Hmm.

Of course, it all depended on what she'd be wearing. Heaven only knew what Robert would be sending this time.

Finally, the typing bubble disappeared but instead of a long paragraph of text, all that popped up were two little words that made her grin wildly.

Thank you.

There. Was that so hard?

Saturday at six.

I'll be waiting.

He didn't reply, but then, he didn't need to. He'd said *thank you.* For Robert, that was the equivalent of a regular dude standing outside her bedroom window with a boom box blaring '80s love songs.

Melissa fussed more insistently and Jeannie struggled to her feet. She had to feed the baby and check her diaper and then?

Then she had to get ready for Saturday night.

She had a date with the hottest bachelor in Chicago and she had a feeling that, before it was all over, she was going to see stars.

Twelve

Robert was not nervous because he was a Wyatt and Wyatts didn't get nervous. Anxiety was a symptom of uncertainty, and Wyatts were confident and sure at all times.

So the sense of unease, the sweaty palms, the unsettled stomach—absolutely not nerves. He wasn't concerned about how tonight would go. He had no worries about the traps he'd laid and how it'd all unfold in the public eye. He was confident he could get his mother away and handle Landon.

Robert was positive he could handle himself. Which was why he wasn't nervous at all.

He was excited to see what the stylists had done with Jeannie, that was all. Kelly had sent over a team of three people—hair, makeup and clothes. He anticipated seeing her dressed for his world.

God, he *missed* her.

It'd been a week since he'd brought her into his home. Seven days since he'd allowed her to touch him. Allowed himself to take comfort in another person. All he'd focused on in that time was laying the groundwork to remove the threat that was Landon Wyatt.

Missing her was more familiar now, a sensation he recognized. It was the same feeling that had thrown him off the night she hadn't appeared at the bar. The same longing that had gripped him after he'd brought her home after their date.

Date. Ha. As if that word got anywhere close to accurately describing their afternoon together. Something as simple as lunch didn't leave him a changed man.

And she had changed him, damn her.

The strange thing was…well, he'd missed her. Not just the way she talked to—or texted—him, although he did miss that because no one else dared argue with him. But then, no one else listened like she did, either.

Because of what she'd done—what he'd *let* her do—he had achieved something he'd always assumed to be beyond him.

Sex with Jeannie had been different. So very different, in fact, that he'd been able to keep it separate from his previous experiences. He'd stayed in the moment. Did she have any idea how unusual that was? Of course not. But he'd been lost to the way the silk had bitten into his skin, the way she'd ground down onto him, her weight warm and slick and silent. Perhaps too silent but after all those times marked by fake moans and real screams, it'd been a gift.

She'd given him the gift of something new, something real. He'd watched her take her pleasure, her body drawing his in, tightening around him, and she'd been raw and honest and even now, after a week, it still left him wanting more.

Which was bad.

Wasn't tonight proof? She'd left him in a weakened position, one where he allowed her to convince him to bring her to meet his parents, of all the damn things.

He wasn't entirely sure he wasn't losing his grip. Because Robert Wyatt would've never agreed to this. Introducing her to Landon was not just a bad idea—it carried real risks for Jeannie. For them both.

Reginald parked in front of Jeannie's little house and some of what was definitely not nervousness eased. Well. It was too late to turn back now. The plans had been set into motion. The newspaper photographer and guards were already in place. Kelly, Robert's assistant, had a plane on standby.

And Robert had personally interviewed the nurse, a young single woman with impressive grades, exceptional references, a valid passport and a desire to see the world, in addition to numerous outstanding student loans and a sister who had no means of affording higher education. She had been more than willing to relocate to a foreign country for six to twelve months at the salary and signing bonus Robert was offering.

Perhaps tonight would go well. He would get his mother to leave with him and, ideally, they'd show the world who Landon Wyatt really was.

They'd just need a distraction.

Would Jeannie really throw a glass of wine into Landon's face? Oh, who was he kidding? Of course she would. The better question was, what else would she do?

This was madness.

Reginald opened Robert's door and he stood, surveying the scene before him. Good. The yard had been trimmed and he was fairly certain there were new shrubs around the foundation. The housepainters were due to start after the roofers had finished, which was scheduled for next week.

He almost smiled as he strode up the sidewalk. Jeannie's little house was small and cramped and no one would ever accuse it of conveying wealth or power or even taste but…there was something he liked about climbing those three simple steps, about the way her door swung open before he could ring the bell, about seeing her…

Everything came to a sudden halt. His breathing, his heart, his forward movement—all stopped.

"Robert." She smiled, this goddess, blessing him with her benevolent kindness. "I've been waiting for you."

Oh, dear God. He had to catch himself on the railing to keep from stumbling back. *"Jeannie?"*

The goddess's eyebrow notched up as she grinned at him and then it all snapped back into place and he could see Jeannie underneath the dramatic makeup, the big hair and that *dress*.

"Well?" she said with what sounded like a knowing smirk. He couldn't tell for sure because he was too busy staring at *that dress*. She did a little turn. "What do you think?"

Robert lurched forward, grabbing on to the door frame. A wave of lust, pure and intense, nearly brought him to his knees. He'd seen her body dressed in nothing but those lacy pink underthings. Seen the trimmed swath of dark hair that covered her sex, watched in fascination as her fingers had stroked over it while he strained to be deeper inside her, more a part of her.

But he'd never seen her like *this*.

His bartender was nowhere to be seen. Instead, Jeannie had been completely transformed. Her short hair had been blown out so that it crowned her head, a far cry from the sleek style she normally wore. Her eyes were dark and mysterious, lips two shades darker than the red dress. Diamonds dripped off her ears and an enormous diamond teardrop pendant hung nestled between her breasts, which were barely contained by the vee of her dress that went almost to her waist. The rest of the dress clung to her hips and legs in a way that could only be described as *indecent*.

She was bold and scandalous and, most important, completely unrecognizable.

She was perfect.

"Hmm," she mused, her lips forming a little pout. He noticed, which meant he'd apparently stopped staring at her body. "I do believe I've stunned you speechless. It's quite different from your normal silence." She touched the tip of her tongue to her top lip. Robert had to bite back a groan. "Yes," she practically hummed and he realized he barely recognized her voice. She bit off her vowels differently, held herself taller. Although maybe it was the dress? "*Quite* different."

Maja appeared from the baby's room. "See?" she clucked in that grandmotherly way. "I told you it'd work."

Jeannie beamed and there she was again, *his* Jeannie. "I was afraid the dress was too much—to say nothing of the danged diamonds, Robert," she explained, as if Robert had asked a question when all his brain wanted to do was peel that dress off her and get lost in her body again. And again. And again, until nothing else mattered. "The stylists brought a black one but—"

"But with her coloring—" Maja added. Dimly, Robert realized she was holding the baby "—red was the obvious color," she concluded, sounding triumphant. "The color of luck."

"Yes," he managed to agree. Somehow.

Jeannie turned back to him and she was different again. He couldn't say how, but she was. "And you," she said, her hips swaying indecently as she moved toward him. "That's quite a tuxedo you're filling out there, Robert." She reached out and straightened his tie.

He nodded, which was probably not the correct reaction but it was all he had. What had she texted him?

She could blend. She'd promised.

By God, this was not blending. And he couldn't care less.

"Go on now," Maja said, scooping something off the coffee table and handing it to Jeannie. A handbag, small and black and sparkling. "Enjoy your night. I'll be here the whole time so…"

Her words trailed off and Robert realized the nanny was giving them both permission not to come home.

Well. He did pay her for going above and beyond, didn't he?

He nodded again, this time managing to find his usual imperiousness. Jeannie smoothed his lapels, sending licks of fire over his chest. But then she notched an eyebrow at him again and he saw the challenge in her eyes.

"Thank you," he added. Maja inclined her head in acknowledgment.

Jeannie beamed up at him and it took every last bit of self-restraint he had not to pull her into his arms and mess up her lipstick. This time he wanted to touch her, to see her body bared completely. By candlelight. He wanted to feel her hands on him. He wanted to taste her, every single part, his lips on her skin, inside her body.

To hell with the perfect Manhattan. He would be forever drunk on her.

"We should go," she said softly in that strange voice of hers, giving his lapels a pat.

"Yes," he said, barely recognizing his own voice.

She turned and walked—swayed—back to Maja. "Be good tonight, sweetie," she said, brushing her fingertips over Melissa's head. "Love you."

Robert had to grip the door frame again because this was something new and real and he didn't know how to make sense of it, this display of maternal affection. There was something so right about Jeannie looking down at the baby with such tenderness.

Then she turned back to him, a sultry smile playing across her lips. "Shall we?"

"Yes," he repeated again.

"Have fun!" Maja called out after them.

Working in silence, Cybil applied the thick foundation liberally, blending it all the way down her neck. Lupe, her maid, spread it over Cybil's back and shoulders, covering the bruises. They hadn't faded yet and if Landon saw any trace of his violence…

It'd be so much easier if she could wear a dress with a jacket, but Landon had chosen a deep blue gown for her to wear tonight and of course it was off the shoulder, with an attached capelet. Elegant and sophisticated— and it left her décolletage and shoulders bare.

Lupe finished with the makeup and began to fix Cybil's hair into an upswept French twist. They worked in silence. In theory, Lupe's English was not very good, which made conversation difficult. In practice, Cybil had learned long ago not to trust a single person on staff.

Tonight she was going to see Bobby again. He was coming, his assistant had assured Landon's assistant, Alexander. He *would* be there. She would see her son with her own eyes, see that he was healthy and whole and, she dared to hope, happy, even. That she'd kept him safe by staying, by keeping Landon away from Bobby.

She dared to hope that Bobby had forgiven her for leaving. That he understood she'd done so to protect him.

She dared to hope…

But she did not allow any of this hope to show. No excitement danced in her eyes as she watched Lupe work in the mirror. She was resigned to her role as hostess for the gala, a role she could perform effortlessly. She was prepared to act the politician's wife, smiling widely as her husband lied through his teeth about how he cared for this state, this city, the millions of people whose lives he could improve—or ruin. She'd had years of practice, after all.

And if Bobby offered her shelter again...

She couldn't go to his home. She couldn't risk him like that again. But surely, he knew that. Surely, he wouldn't make the same mistake again.

Dear Lord, Cybil prayed, *please don't let me make the same mistake again, either.*

There had to be a way.

"Are you breathing?" Jeannie asked as the car crawled through downtown traffic.

She stroked her thumb over Robert's knuckles. He had a hell of a grip on her hand. She'd explained the persona she was adopting tonight and she could tell he wasn't 100 percent on board. Not that she could blame him.

This was, hands down, the craziest thing she'd ever done.

"Yes," he said after a long moment in which she was pretty sure he hadn't breathed. "I'm fine."

"I doubt it." She saw a quick flash of teeth. "Is there a plan? Because I can wing it but this sort of feels like one of those situations where a plan would be a good idea." After another few seconds, she added, "Sharing it would be an even better idea."

His grip tightened on her hand and she had to work hard not to gasp. "Reginald will be parked by the service entrance in the basement, engine running. There's a service elevator in the back, next to the restrooms. It's down a short hallway." He cleared his throat, sounding painfully nervous. "If I can get her to come with me, we'll leave without a look back."

She thought on that for a moment as she fiddled with the heavy diamond pendant. The rock alone was probably worth more than she made in a year, not to mention the earrings or the dress. A Valentino dress, for God's sake! She was easily wearing thirty, forty thousand dollars' worth of fabric and diamonds. Which was not a huge deal to Robert but, if she let herself think about it too much, it would easily freak her the heck out.

But tonight she wouldn't fret about cost or Robert's world. Tonight she was going to waltz into that gala party on his arm like she owned the damn room and if it took three stylists, diamonds and a Valentino to do it, so be it. "So I'm to…what, distract your father while you two make a run for the airport?"

"God, no—you stick with me." He pulled his hand free and—shockingly—adjusted his cuffs. "You are not to be alone with him under any circumstances. Ever."

She almost rolled her eyes at his tone. "I can handle myself, Robert. I've been fending off drunks and avoiding wandering hands since I was a teenager. Don't worry."

His head swung around and even in the dark interior

of the car, she shivered at his intensity. "You are *not* to be alone with him, Jeannie." His voice was dangerously quiet, all the more menacing for it. *"Ever."*

"O…kay. So how do we know he won't follow us?"

"He won't want to make a scene. The whole point of tonight is to put on a public performance."

She mulled over the options. "What if—and I'm just throwing this out there—what if I can get your mom alone? Like, we go to the ladies' room together. You can stay behind to keep an eye on your father and I can get her to the car." Assuming Mrs. Wyatt would go with Jeannie. A complete stranger.

But it would be easy to get her alone. She needed a drink. One that stained would be best.

Robert's expression reflected doubt. "Reginald knows where to go. Everything else is ready. Take her and leave." He leaned over, his fingertips barely brushing over her cheek. "Just be safe. I…I can't bear the thought of anything happening to you."

Oh, Robert. "Listen to me, you stubborn man. I will be fine. It's you I'm worried about." He was already a mess. The average person wouldn't be able to tell, but she knew. His voice was rough and he was straightening his cuffs *again*. Worst of all, his leg had begun to jump. "If you can get an opening, promise me you'll take it. Send me two texts in a row—so I know you're gone and I'll get away. Trust me, Robert. Don't worry."

"I'm a Wyatt," he said sternly as the car pulled up in front of a building right off the Magnificent Mile, as if that was the cure for the world's ills. "We never worry." But then the hard lines of his face softened and the very corners of his lips curved up in a faint smile. "Ready to crash a party?"

She grinned. "Hell, yes."

Reginald opened the door for them, his normally jovial face a blank mask. Robert handed her out of the car and then tucked her fingers into the crook of his arm. Then he murmured, "Be ready," as they passed and Reginald nodded smartly before closing the door behind them.

A crush of people waited to get through security. The crowd was a sea of black—black tuxedos, black gowns—Jeannie was suddenly glad she'd gone with the red. Her role was to be a distraction and in this dress, she stood out like a siren. Seriously, her boobs in this dress were practically works of art. For how much this dress cost, they damn well better be.

Jeannie squared her shoulders, lifted her chin and tried to look bored as Robert cut through the crowd. A weaselly-looking man with thinning hair stood at the front of the line.

Robert leaned down to whisper in her ear, "Alexander, Landon's loyal assistant."

She nodded, sticking close to Robert's side. Loyal? In other words, this was not a person to be trusted. It was easy to look all icy and disapproving when that was exactly how she felt.

When the weasel caught sight of Robert, he waved them past security, calling, "Dr. Wyatt? This way." Someone in line started to protest, but Robert swung around, daring anyone to complain with a cold glare. Jeannie tried to match his look.

The crowd fell oddly silent in the face of Robert's displeasure. Somewhere nearby, a camera flashed.

Which was good because Jeannie needed to remember that she wasn't here with Robert, a complicated and conflicted man who cared for sick children and infants and who had literally been the answer to her prayers. No, she was here with Dr. Robert Wyatt, of the Chicago Wyatts, a billionaire bachelor and one of the most powerful, dangerous men in the state.

Time to own this room.

She let her gaze slide over the people she passed as if she couldn't be bothered to see them. Alexander led them through the crowd, up a spiral staircase. She was barely able to keep up with Robert's long strides in the strappy black sandals the stylist had put her in to go with this dress.

But even if she didn't acknowledge the other party-goers, she could feel their reactions as she and Robert moved effortlessly through their ranks. People stopped and stared as they passed, but the moment they'd gone by, the loud whispers started.

Hadn't there been rumors of a falling-out between the elder Wyatt and the younger?

How gauche that Wyatt dirtied his hands practicing medicine.

And who was *she*?

Dear God, was Jeannie really doing this? This was more than just crashing a gala. This was pulling a fast one over on the person who could put the fear of God into Robert.

She stiffened her spine. Go big or go home.

"This way," Alexander said. He glanced at Jeannie and she stared down her nose at him, daring him to make a comment about Robert bringing a date.

He didn't. Instead, he led them to where a handsome man, almost as tall and almost as broad as Robert, was holding court. Landon Wyatt, billionaire gubernatorial candidate and total asshole. Not that anyone else would know it. All the tuxedoed men and glamorous women around him laughed heartily at his jokes, champagne flutes in hand, gems glittering at their necks and wrists and ears.

They sounded like jackals. Maybe they were. Thank God she didn't recognize any of them as customers from Trenton's.

Next to Landon stood an elegant older woman, smiling brightly and occasionally touching her husband on the arm or shoulder as he talked, as if she had to let him know where she was at all times. As Alexander wormed his way through to the inner circle, Robert's mother caught sight of them.

Although the crowd was too loud to hear Cybil Wyatt, Jeannie physically *felt* the woman's sharp inhalation, saw the overwhelming longing in her eyes.

Alexander tugged on Landon Wyatt's sleeve and motioned to Robert with his chin. By the time Landon turned to his wife, her face was carefully blank.

Wyatt's face was how Jeannie might've imagined kings of old looking when a foreign dignitary dared grace his throne room. "Ah, here he is. Robert, my boy, how have you been?"

Jeannie felt the tension in Robert's arm. *Say something*, she mentally ordered him.

"Father," he managed. Then he looked to Cybil. "Mother." He cleared his throat and his arm moved and Jeannie knew that if she hadn't had a hold of him, he would've been straightening his cuffs.

This was exactly why she'd insisted on coming tonight. Robert could be intense and scary—boy, could he—but when faced with his father in front of a crowd, he froze up.

Landon's gaze flicked over her. "What do we have here? I didn't realize you were bringing a date, *son*."

She gave Robert a whole two seconds to respond but when he didn't she stepped into the gap. "How do you do," she said in her snootiest British accent. She released Robert's arm and extended her hand to Landon, palm down. "Lady Daphne FitzRoy. Charmed."

"*Lady* FitzRoy?" Landon said, his lip curling as if he instinctively knew she was an imposter.

"Of the London FitzRoys?" She sighed heavily and let her gaze narrow dismissively. She hadn't been reading historical romances for the last fifteen years or so for nothing. All those ballroom scenes, with cuts direct and dukes and duchesses—an informal education in the British aristocracy was about to pay off *big time*. "But of course. I forget how you Americans are. Perhaps you've heard of my brother? The Duke of Grafton?"

Because nothing caught the attention of a bully like a good old-fashioned reminder of where he really stood in the food chain.

And it worked like a freaking charm. Landon Wyatt

inhaled, his nostrils flaring as his pupils darkened and for a fleeting second, Jeannie understood exactly why Robert was terrified of this man. She felt like a little rabbit who'd just realized the wolf was pouncing.

But she was no meek bunny. She cleared her throat and shot a disdainful look at her extended hand.

Wyatt got the hint. He pressed cold lips to the back of her hand. Jeannie refused to allow her skin to prickle. "I'm not familiar with the FitzRoys of London," he admitted, putting humor into his voice. "But welcome! Any sister of nobility is a friend of mine. And, apparently," he added, cutting a glance to Robert, "a friend of my son's. Well done, Robert."

Had she thought a wolf? That was wrong. He was a snake, one with hypnotizing eyes.

She wouldn't let him charm her. She tugged her hand free and turned to Robert's mother. "You must be Cybil. Delighted, I'm sure." Jeannie kept her voice bored, determined not to give away her interest in Robert's mother.

"I didn't realize Bobby—Robert—was bringing a guest," Cybil said, her gaze darting between her son and Jeannie. "How...nice to make your acquaintance."

Years of observing customers kicked in and Jeannie noticed Cybil Wyatt wore her makeup too thick and that it went all the way down her neck and across her chest. Hiding bruises, maybe? She held her left shoulder higher than her right and her smile only used half her mouth, as if her jaw on the right side pained her.

Jeannie caught sight of a waiter and impatiently snapped her fingers, mentally apologizing to the dude.

People who snapped for attention at the bar got either too much ice in their glasses or a small pour.

He hurried over, looking not the least bit bothered by her rudeness. Jeannie took two glasses from his tray and handed one to Robert. "Is this champagne or that American knockoff you all seem so proud of?" she asked in a voice too loud to be a whisper.

She physically felt people pull back. Good. She'd shocked them—which meant they wouldn't be able to stop looking at her.

With a light laugh, Cybil said, "The champagne is French, I assure you. Sparkling white wine just isn't the same, is it?" Her gaze darted to her husband and then she stepped around him. "It's so good to see you," she said, gripping Robert by the biceps. Jeannie could hear the truth of it in her voice. "I'm so glad you came."

"So am I," he said, staring down at his mother, his concern obvious. Then he seemed to snap out of it. "Daphne was curious how politics work in America."

Right. This was her role. She waved this comment away, slugging back half her glass. She'd need to look drunk in relatively short order. "He exaggerates, of course. Politics and politicians are a complete and utter bore."

The hangers-on actually gasped out loud at this brazen insult but Jeannie refused to cower. She would not cede a bit of her pretend high ground. She was counting on keeping Wyatt's attention by pretending to be beyond his spheres of influence. Instead, she rolled her shoulder in a not-apology.

After a beat too long, Wyatt burst out laughing and

quickly, everyone around them joined in. "Ah, that dry British humor," he said out loud, his hand closing around her wrist like a manacle and drawing her by his side. Which was not a safe place to be, but it had the advantage of pushing Cybil and Robert a little farther away. "Tell me about yourself, *Duchess*." This last was said in an openly mocking tone.

"Oh, I'm not a duchess. That's my sister-in-law. You may address me as Lady FitzRoy." She said it pointedly because a true lady would demand respect.

"My lady," Wyatt said, his mouth moving in what might have been a grin. Oh, he was playing along but Jeannie knew he hadn't decided if she was legit or not. "Do tell."

"What is there to say?" She finished her champagne and snapped at the waiter, who hurried to exchange her glass for a full one. "Grafton—my brother—does his part in the House of Lords but he's dreadfully dull, as I said. So responsible." She let her lip curl in distaste but at the same time, she brushed an invisible piece of lint off Wyatt's shoulder and let her fingers linger. "Tell me, why would anyone want to run for office? Especially someone of your *considerable* stature? Public service is just so public. I'd think it'd be beneath a man of your obvious…talents." She cut a dismissive glance at Robert. "Like working. In a hospital, for God's sake," she added in a stage whisper that everyone heard.

Oh, that did the trick. Wyatt threw back his head with a brutal laugh—real humor at the expense of his son. A shiver of terror went down her back, but she smiled and notched an eyebrow at him, playing along.

She saw the answer in Wyatt's eyes when he looked at her—he was drunk on power and like any addict, he needed more.

But like a good politician, he said, "As you know, we Wyatts are quite well-off."

She rolled her shoulder in that dismissive shrug again as if being billionaires was just so much dross.

His pupils dilated. He was enjoying himself. Good. "I don't seek the office of the governor for myself, you understand. I have everything I could ever want." Wyatt's gaze dipped to her breasts. She repressed a shudder. "It's time to give back to the good people of Illinois. They deserve more and, having managed my company for so long, I alone have the skills to set things right and steer this great state into the future!"

The fawning jackals broke out in applause. Flashbulbs flashed.

Jeannie snapped for the poor waiter again because Lady Daphne FitzRoy was a bitch—and an alcoholic at that. She exchanged her half-empty glass for a full one and drank deeply. She needed to look sloppy drunk.

She could feel Robert's gaze on her.

She refused to look.

Thirteen

"Come with me."

Robert kept his voice low, using the laughter of the crowd to hide his words. He didn't look at Cybil Wyatt as he spoke. Instead, his gaze was locked on to Jeannie—or, rather, Lady FitzRoy. He couldn't believe people were buying this line of BS, but even Landon seemed smitten with her. Or at least smitten with her breasts.

"…in a hospital, for God's sake," she said, wobbling toward Landon as she said it. How much had she drunk? Aside from the wine at lunch last weekend, he'd never actually seen her drink before.

Everyone laughed at his expense, Landon loudest of all.

"I can keep you safe," he added as Landon's predatory gaze zeroed in on Jeannie. Jeannie had sworn she could handle herself. And he had to admit, she was one hell of a distraction.

His mother's grip on his arm tightened before she removed her hand entirely. "It's not safe," she said, smiling that smile he hated because it was a mask, a lie. "He'll come after you. He'll find me."

Like last time. She didn't say it, but she didn't need to.

Mom looked awful. The way she held her body—didn't anyone else here see the lines of pain around her eyes? The way her shoulders weren't even? Had that bastard broken her ribs again?

Landon Wyatt was going to pay for everything he'd done.

The world went a little red at the edges, narrowing to Landon and Jeannie. She had another champagne flute in her hand and was waving it around. Champagne sloshed everywhere and people stepped back to make sure they didn't get hit. Then she took another long drink and all but dropped the flute. A beleaguered waiter caught it before it hit the ground and then Jeannie had a fresh glass.

Landon slid a taunting glance his way and then slid his arm around Jeannie's waist, pulling her closer so he could whisper in her ear.

Robert's stomach rolled. Hard. Because he was supposed to be protecting the women he cared about. He wasn't a kid anymore, forced to stand by and watch helplessly as Landon hurt women in the name of a teachable moment.

This wasn't happening. Jeannie wasn't a paid escort. And she knew who she was dealing with.

Trust me, she'd said.

Did he have a choice?

She looked at Robert, a mean smile on her lips. But then her glance bounced to his mother and back to him, her eyes widening just a little, and Robert got the distinct feeling she was telling him something.

"He won't find you," Robert told his mother, hiding his mouth behind his glass as he spoke. His plan had been set into motion tonight and he couldn't stop it if he wanted to—and he didn't want to. He just needed to be sure Cybil was nowhere near Landon when the chips began to fall. Robert couldn't bear to think of that bastard blaming Mom when things all fell apart. "He can't win. But I need you to come with me."

For what felt like a century, she didn't answer, didn't look at him. She laughed politely at something rude Jeannie had said—about Robert, probably. He wasn't paying attention.

"When?"

Relief hit him so hard he almost cried. "My car is waiting. Jeannie or I will take you there."

That got her attention. She turned to fully face him, which was a rare mistake. It was never a good idea to give Landon Wyatt your back. "Who?"

"My date."

Color deepened on Mom's cheeks as if she was embarrassed that someone else knew their private shame. But all she said was, "Ah," and turned back to face Landon just as Jeannie pulled away from his grip.

She took another deep drink of her champagne and then held the glass at such an angle that nearly half the contents poured directly onto the floor. "But I'm ignoring our hostess!" she cried in what was truly a terrible British accent.

Robert couldn't *believe* people were buying this act. How was he even looking at the same person who blended behind the bar at Trenton's, ready with the perfect Manhattan and a sympathetic ear? How was this the same woman who'd wrapped a silk tie around his wrists and then wrapped her nearly nude body around his?

She was so much more than just the sum of those moments.

And she was heading straight for him and his mother, pausing only long enough to get another glass of champagne. Landon's friends—men who had power and wealth, although never as much of either as Landon had—sniggered at the sight of this supposed *lady* making a complete ass of herself.

"Do you know," Jeannie began, her words now noticeably slurred, "that I do think this is very good champ—*whoopsie*!"

She stumbled forward, splashing Mom right in the chest and somehow managing to get a good part of the champagne onto Robert's sleeve and face, as well.

He nearly burst out laughing. *Whoopsie.* She'd had this planned from the moment she'd informed him she was coming with him, hadn't she? By God, he'd never known a woman like Jeannie before.

She wobbled dangerously on her heels, her dress nearly falling off her shoulders and exposing her breasts as she stumbled into Mom. "Oh, dear," Jeannie said, a hysterical laugh in her voice that made her accent even more awful. "Oh, I've made a mess of your lovely dress. Oh, what a pity, it was so pretty. Grafton will be *so* displeased. Oh," she said, clutching Mom by the arm and looking properly terrified, "you won't tell him, will you?"

Mom looked around wildly, wine dripping off her chin and running down her chest. Her makeup gave up its hold on her skin as flesh-colored rivulets ran onto the bodice of her dress.

An uneasy hush had fallen over the crowd. People weren't sure if they should laugh or offer assistance or what. Another round of flashbulbs went off, reminding everyone that this series of unfortunate events was on the record.

Landon Wyatt shot Robert a look that promised pure pain. Robert didn't allow himself to shy away. He met Landon's stare head-on and then wiped alcohol from his chin. Really, Jeannie had done an excellent job making as big a mess as humanly possible.

"No, no," Mom said, finding her voice and grabbing Jeannie's hand before she could start smearing the body makeup. "But why don't you and I go to the ladies' room? I bet you'll feel better after we both freshen up." She looked to her husband—for permission. The pause made Robert's teeth grind.

This, he vowed, would be the very last time Cybil Wyatt asked her husband for permission to do anything.

Landon nodded. "Perhaps we should cut the duchess off." He turned back to the crowd. "I suppose the Brits can't hold their liquor."

"I'd like to hold *her*," someone muttered. Robert didn't see who'd spoken but he refused to allow himself to react.

Leaning heavily on Mom, Jeannie allowed herself to be led toward the ladies' room, babbling about how Grafton would be *most* upset...

She'd missed her calling as an actress; that much was clear. Robert felt an odd sort of pride at her performance. But that was immediately followed by an even odder sort of fear as he caught Landon looking after the women. Robert recognized that look. It seemed benign, that level gaze, that slight quirk to the lips. Friendly, almost.

A shiver raced down Robert's back and he had to dig his nails into his palm to keep from letting it out. Because the times he'd seen Landon Wyatt look like that—especially if he made it to a full smile—those were some of the worst moments of Robert's life.

Like a nightmare come to life, Landon's smile widened.

It didn't matter that Jeannie hadn't looked or acted like herself. She was in danger for embarrassing Landon in front of his friends and donors and cameras. Jeannie might as well have painted a big red target on her back, and Robert? He would be in just as much trouble for bringing the notorious Lady FitzRoy to the party in the first place.

That was bad enough. When Landon discovered Jeannie had actually absconded with his wife...

Robert's lungs wouldn't move, wouldn't inflate. It

only got worse when Landon turned back to the crowd. His gaze snagged on Robert and the man smirked.

Smirked.

This was Robert's doing, all of it. He'd agreed to let her come, agreed to let her act the part of a noble drunk. It was Robert's job to keep Jeannie safe. A deadening hole opened up in his stomach as he realized what that meant.

He had to stay as far away from her as possible. No more lunch dates, no more evening drinks at Trenton's. It didn't matter if she went back to work or not; Robert couldn't risk her by ever darkening the restaurant's doors again.

Well, that was being a little melodramatic. But as long as Landon Wyatt had power and a means to wield it, he was a threat. Robert had always known that. That was why he was sending his mother halfway around the world. Landon was a threat to Robert, to Mom and now to Jeannie.

Tonight would be it, then.

Robert fought the urge to look at his phone. God willing, in less than two minutes, Reginald would be on his way to the private airfield north of the city, where the plane and flight crew were on standby.

Landon's smile shifted subtly into a more genial look as Robert felt another trickle of champagne drip off his chin. "She got you, too, eh, son?" he said to chuckles, as if he was a sympathetic father.

"I shouldn't have let her drink," Robert replied, because that was a sentiment Landon would approve. "I'm sorry for the mess."

How many seconds had passed? Had it been a minute? Were they in the elevator yet?

Landon stared at him, his eyes flinty, before his whole face changed into one of good humor. "Go get cleaned up—but I expect to see you back here. I'm giving my big speech in a few minutes and the cameras will be rolling."

"I wouldn't miss it," Robert said, managing to paste some sort of smile on his face. It must have been appropriate because people made noises of sympathy.

He hadn't taken three steps before his phone buzzed. Jeannie. *Thank God.*

In car

Go

Waiting for you

Go, dammit

Thirty seconds

Jesus, that woman.
Robert broke into a run.

"Buckle up," the woman in red said, sounding not particularly drunk nor particularly British.

"Who are you?" Cybil asked, impressed that she could speak at all.

This was really happening. She was really in a private car with a complete stranger who had dragged her into an elevator and then shoved her into a car.

And she was going along with it because the alternative to what was potentially a kidnapping was to stay with Landon.

"A friend of your son's," was the reply she got, which was almost comforting. Then the woman in red had her head through the dividing window and was talking to the driver. "Thirty seconds!" the not-lady all but shouted. "Just a few more seconds!"

The driver replied, but Cybil couldn't make out his words over the pounding of her pulse in her ears.

Landon would be so mad if he knew about this. Bobby was putting himself directly into harm's way— the very place Cybil had worked so hard to keep him from—and for what? For her?

"I should get back," she said, fumbling with the seat belt.

"Sorry, Mrs. Wyatt, but that's not happening." The woman in red slid into the seat next to her and put a firm hand on the buckle. "And I apologize for ruining your dress. It was pretty." This strange creature turned her head to the side, appraising Cybil with unnervingly frank eyes.

"He'll come after Bobby," Cybil said, her voice breaking on the end. She scrabbled at the woman's hands, trying to pry them loose of the seat belt. Panic tasted metallic in her mouth. "He'll hurt my son! I have to protect him!"

"He's a grown man," the stranger said, taking hold of Cybil's hands. Her grip was firm but not cruel. "Bobby is capable of protecting himself. And you, if you'll trust him. Just trust him."

The car started to move. "Five more seconds!" the woman yelled at the driver.

"He said to go now!" the driver yelled back.

"What's happening?" Cybil said, hating how the weakness bled into her voice. Hating that this was what she'd been reduced to. Begging a complete stranger for information.

To her surprise, the woman carefully wrapped an arm around Cybil's shoulders. "You're going somewhere safe. Believe me, your husband will never be able to find you."

The car began to roll again just as the passenger door wrenched open and Cybil screamed as the woman in red shielded her because for a second she thought it was Landon there, eyes blazing, chest heaving, and she knew this time, a few broken bones would be child's play. But then it was Bobby, her Bobby, climbing into the car and slamming the door shut behind him. Bobby yelling at the driver to *go, dammit*. Bobby helping the woman into the seat across from Cybil.

Bobby sitting next to her, wrapping his arms around her.

"My son," she said, promptly ruining his tuxedo jacket with her tears and smeared makeup and spilled champagne.

"I've got you, Mom," he said, his voice breaking as he held her—but gently, like he could tell where she was hurting. "You're safe now."

"You're not," she wept because Landon would destroy him. Landon would destroy them all. "*Why*, Bobby? Why would you risk yourself for *me*?"

"He's stronger than you think," the woman said, her voice kind. "Because that's how you raised him to be."

Cybil got herself under control. Years of practice made it practically second nature. "Who are you?" she asked because clearly this was someone her son trusted.

The woman smiled. It looked real and soft, and unfamiliar hope fluttered in Cybil's chest. Had Bobby found someone?

But then the woman spoke and dashed her hopes. "I'm his bartender."

Fourteen

"Are you sure about this?" Mom asked as Robert guided her up the narrow stairs into the plane.

"I'm sure. We'll talk anytime you want and in a few months, I'll fly down and visit you." Robert settled her into her seat. "He won't keep us apart."

Mom was crying softly. "Don't let him hurt you," she said, her voice surprisingly level despite her tears. "I couldn't live with myself if…"

Robert pressed a kiss to her good cheek. "I'm not a little kid anymore, Mom. I promise you, I've got the situation under control. You focus on getting well." He motioned the nurse forward. "Bridget here will be with you the whole time."

Mom nodded, looking panicked. Then she glanced out the window and seemed to calm. Robert followed her gaze and saw Jeannie standing near the limo, wind billowing her skirt. "I hope you know what you're doing," she whispered.

"I do."

Landon Wyatt wouldn't have any idea what'd hit him. The disappearance of his wife was merely the first domino to fall.

Mom turned back to him. She took a deep breath and nodded. "All right. But promise me this, Bobby— if you get the chance at real happiness, grab it. Hold on to it." She gripped his hand with surprising strength. But then, she'd always been so much stronger than she let on. "Be happy, Bobby." She looked at Jeannie again. "Be well and be happy. It's all I've ever wanted for you."

Robert had to swallow a few times before his throat worked right. He'd gotten a little bit of happiness for a short time. It would have to do. "That's what I want for you, too." Mom gave him a scolding look, tinged with a smile, so Robert promised. "I will. I swear."

He kissed her goodbye and checked in with Bridget one last time. Then he was climbing down the stairs and Jeannie was waiting for him. After tonight he wouldn't get the comfort of going to her when he needed her.

How was he supposed to go on without her?

But he didn't have the luxury of loving Jeannie, not until Landon was either behind bars or six feet under and not until Robert could be sure the bastard hadn't left behind instructions that would endanger Jeannie or his mother.

Jeannie slipped her hand in his and a brief moment of hope flared in his chest as the plane door shut and locked. She'd said she'd wait for him, hadn't she? If Robert knew that she'd be there with the perfect Manhattan and that take-no-crap smile—maybe even with a silk tie tangled in her fingers—after this thing with Landon was settled, he'd be content to wait.

But that wasn't fair to her. She had a life—a baby to care for, a job she enjoyed. He was a customer, a benefactor—and a lover, perhaps—but that didn't make her his.

Robert knew what Landon would say. He'd say Jeannie belonged to Robert. He was a Wyatt and Wyatts took what they wanted. Landon would spout off about how Robert had to demand respect when he meant fear, as if fear was somehow more magical than love or trust.

Yes, that was what Landon Wyatt would do.

Which was exactly why Robert would let Jeannie go.

As the plane began to move, Robert caught a glimpse of his mother's face, tear-streaked and shocked. She lifted a hand and Robert returned the small wave.

Jeannie leaned against him, shoulder to shoulder, almost the same height he was in her heels. They stood together in silence as the plane taxied down the runway and took off.

It was done. Mom was on her way. Everything else was falling into place.

So why couldn't he move?

Because moving would bring him closer to the end of tonight. To the end of his time with Jeannie.

He wasn't sure he was strong enough to do what had to be done.

"Sir?" Kelly came forward. "Do you want the updates?"

Mechanically, Robert nodded. But he turned to Jeannie. "Wait for me?" Because he wasn't strong enough. Not…yet, anyway.

Her fingers tightened around his hand. She was less than a breath away—closer than that when she lifted her other hand and brushed her thumb over his cheek. "Of course."

Then she kissed the spot she'd just stroked, her lips lingering. He could smell champagne on her breath mingling with the orange scent she always wore.

He had to let her go. He *had* to. And if she wouldn't listen—because this was Jeannie, after all—then he'd have to keep her away.

He wrapped his arm around her waist and held her tight, inhaling her scent deeply. Each moment was another memory he tucked away, another glimpse of happiness that he'd hold on to for later.

He'd promised, after all.

"I'll wait in the car," she whispered in his ear.

But he didn't let her go. Not just yet. Another moment, that was all he needed. He couldn't take her home because Landon might show up at any moment, full of rage and hate, and follow them. And Maja was at Jeannie's house, to say nothing of the baby.

"After this," he murmured against her temple, "I'll take you to see the stars."

He felt the tremor of excitement move through her. "From your terrace?" Her body pressed against his, a promise of more than just another moment. She reached up between them and tugged the ends of his bow tie loose and just like that, he went rock-hard for her. "I'd like that. But I couldn't wish for anything more."

He shook his head. "You deserve more than one star. You deserve them all." That would be his parting gift to her. The night sky and all those stars to wish upon.

She pulled the tie from around his neck as she put distance between them. Black silk dangling from her fingertips, her knowing smile in the dim lighting made him want to forget about Landon and revenge and corporate takeovers and everything but Jeannie and him and this wanting that existed between them.

She turned on her heel and, with a come-hither look over her shoulder, strode to the car, where Reginald was waiting to open the door for her. Robert couldn't move as she climbed in, revealing the curve of her leg as she pulled her foot inside. He wasn't even sure he was breathing until the car door closed.

Then Reginald had the nerve to wink. At Robert! Really, this was too much.

But that cheekiness broke the spell Robert was under. He turned to find Kelly pointedly looking at everything but Robert or the limo and, one presumed, Jeannie.

"Is everything on track?" Robert asked, straightening his cuffs. He felt undressed without his tie. Which was most likely the point.

Well, one of them.

"Yes. The photographer reports that Landon is still at the gallery, although he's delaying the start of his speech and growing more agitated by the second." Kelly held out his phone. "Would you like to see the shots?"

"No." The less space Landon took up in Robert's brain from here on out, the better. "The lawyers have been notified?"

One for the divorce, a few from the District Attorney's office and several for the former employees who'd been subjected to Landon's sexual assaults. In just a few short days they'd found four former maids and six former employees of Wyatt Medical willing to come forward. A few claims were past the statute of limitations, so Robert was funding the civil suits. The others had been turned over to the authorities. The actual number of victims was probably quadruple the ten they'd confirmed, easily.

"Yes. The judge should be approving the emergency search warrant as we speak."

"Excellent. The guards are on standby?" One posted at Jeannie's house, just in case Robert had left a loose thread out there for Landon to pull. The others, including two off-duty police officers—one of whom was extremely grateful that his eldest son had just celebrated his sixth birthday after a successful heart valve repair—were watching his house.

"Yes. The forensic accountant has already found some very large…discrepancies between the Wyatt Medical financials and Landon's campaign fund." Kelly closed his portfolio. "You're sure about this?"

This was completely and methodically destroying his father, piece by piece.

Robert almost smiled. He was a Wyatt, after all, and Wyatts demanded respect. They didn't hesitate or have second thoughts. When someone slighted a Wyatt, they responded by dominating. By destroying, if that was what it took.

It wasn't enough to have Landon publicly humiliated.

He had to be ended. Simple as that.

And Robert was the only person who could do it. Because he was a Wyatt and this was what Landon had made him into. Someone cruel and hard and utterly without mercy.

So he nodded once. Landon Wyatt would get no mercy. Not from his only child.

Kelly let out a breath he apparently had been holding and said, "Then we're doing this."

Kelly was a good kid, not the kind of man who'd been raised to engage in this level of back-channel manipulation. Robert appreciated that his assistant wasn't entirely comfortable with the situation but he also appreciated an employee who did as he was asked.

"I may be...offline for a few hours," Robert told Kelly, fighting the urge to touch his shirt collar, "but keep me informed."

He thought Kelly's cheeks might have darkened but it was hard to tell. "Yes, sir."

Robert nodded again and turned back to the car but then an image of Jeannie notching an eyebrow at him in challenge floated before his mind's eye. He turned back before he could think better of it. "Kelly?"

"Sir?" The young man snapped to attention.

"Thank you. I know this is far outside your normal purview but..." Bordering on criminal, in fact. "But I appreciate everything you've done for me and my mother. So thank you."

There, was that so hard? Jeannie's laugh echoed in his mind.

No, it wasn't. In fact, it was getting easier all the time.

"Oh. Well. Uh, you're welcome?" Kelly sounded just as confused by receiving this compliment as Robert had felt giving it.

"Where to, sir?" Reginald asked and dammit, the man had a twinkle in his eye.

"The beach," Robert said decisively because he was a Wyatt and the time for second-guessing was over. "Take us to see the stars. Please."

Reginald nodded smartly as he opened the door for Robert. It wasn't until the door had closed behind him, leaving him completely alone with Jeannie, that Robert was able to breathe.

Champagne and oranges and Jeannie. The scent surrounded him and he felt his shoulders relax. "Well?" she asked as he settled into his seat. Instantly, she was at his side, curling into him.

Without consciously choosing to do so, his arm went around her shoulder, gathering her tight. He could hold her like this now without hesitation, without flinching. She'd given him that.

"Everything is fine," he said and, at least for the next hour or so, it truly was.

"Good," she replied, her hand sliding under his tux jacket. She undid his vest and then rested her hand on his stomach. That simple touch, muted through the layers of his shirt and undershirt, still pushed his pulse faster. It took so little for her to affect him now.

She pushed herself onto her knees without letting go of him, her breasts brushing against his chest as she shifted. Her scent, warm and inviting, filled his nose. He could get drunk on her, he realized. Maybe he already was. "What are the rules?"

Here in the dark interior of his car, nothing else existed. Just him and her. A woman who had stood by his side through one of the hardest moments of his life and yet still wanted *him*. Not his fortune or his name or any of it. Just him.

It was a hell of a thing.

He wished he could give her so much more. But tonight was all he had. So he said, "Same as last time."

But this time it wasn't because he was worried he would hurt her. He wouldn't. No, this time he needed the restraint to remind himself that she was not his to have and to hold.

Would that she was. But it wasn't safe. Not now. Maybe…

If her lips twisted to the side in disappointment, he couldn't say. "Hold out your hands."

It felt right, letting her do this again. It'd worked the last time. He'd lost himself in her, but he hadn't lost control. Hadn't become the man Landon had demanded he be.

Tonight Robert had come closer to being that man, that *Wyatt*, than he ever had before and it was necessary and important but it was also…unsettling that he had it in him.

He could do bad things, even if for good reasons.

But not to her. Never to her.

He trusted Jeannie, tonight more than ever. He needed her this one last time and then he'd let her go.

Jeannie lifted his arms into the air and then slid onto his lap. Instantly, the warmth of her core rocketed through his body. She wasn't wearing panties, he realized with a jolt. "Jeannie," he groaned as she pulled his arms down so his knotted wrists were looped around her neck. Because this counted as touching and God help him, he needed it. Needed to feel her over him, around him, under him.

One last time, he repeated silently to himself. That was all this was.

"Hush." She shifted back, her weight perfect on his lap as her hands moved to his trousers. She undid his belt and zipper in silence.

He opened his mouth to tell her where the condoms were—inside pocket of his jacket—but that was when she reached over and snagged that tiny purse Maja had handed her. When she opened it, a strip of condoms popped out like a jack-in-the-box without the terrifying clown.

"You're prepared," he said, his breath coming faster as she snapped off one and tore it open.

"Luck favors the prepared. Now quiet." She had to grab at his jacket as they took a corner. In that moment he felt the strength of her thighs' grip on his legs. She was so strong. God, he loved it.

Then she grinned at him as she smoothed out his lapel and added, "Or else."

Desire pounded through him at that challenge. She'd already tied him up. How far would she go?

She rolled on the condom and Robert realized he was holding his breath as her fingers stroked over his length, hard with wanting her.

"Or else what?" he heard himself ask through gritted teeth.

Her grip on him tightened. "Or else," she whispered, leaning forward to let her lips brush over his earlobe, trapping his aching erection between them, "I'll touch you. Slowly."

As if to demonstrate, her fisted hand slid up over his shaft, the lubrication of the condom smoothing the way. His breath caught in his throat as he strained against her. It was too much—far, far too much—and yet not enough.

"Yes, like that," she whispered, her voice nothing but breath that caressed over his skin. "And harder." Her grip tightened as her hand moved back down, inch by agonizing inch.

A groan ripped free because she was touching him and he was letting her and it was something new, and he'd never been so turned on in his entire life.

"Then," she said, shifting so his length was pressed against her sex, trapped in her embrace, "then I'd touch you here, too."

Her hand slipped down, cupping his balls and pressing up ever so gently as her hips moved, dragging his tip over her.

"Jeannie," he moaned, helpless to stop her, helpless for her.

"And then?" She pushed back, his arms still around her neck, his hands in tight fists as he let go of everything but the way her hand squeezed him, tormented him—made him whole again.

She smiled, wickedness brought to life. "Then I'd stop."

She pulled her hand away.

For all that he'd trained himself to control his emotions, control his reactions, Robert couldn't help it—he whimpered.

Her smile was pure victory. "Will you be quiet?"

He nodded. It was all he could do.

"Thank God," she said, raising herself onto her knees and positioning him at her entrance.

Then she sank down on him, taking him in completely until Robert was on the verge of losing control.

"Just be," she said, her breathing faster now. "Just be with me, Robert."

Although it was a risk, he had to let her know. "Always."

She would always be this perfect memory, this utterly wonderful moment in time when he was the man she needed and she was his everything.

One last time.

The car came to a somewhat sudden stop and she scrabbled to grab hold of his jacket to keep from falling right off him. He used his bound hands to pull her back to him, her breasts flush with his chest and in that moment, he wished he hadn't insisted on the clothing because he wanted to see her in her nude glory, feel her body against his.

He didn't just want part of her. He wanted all of her.

One last time. Dammit.

Giggling, she leaned back, but he didn't let her pull away. He kept her against his chest, feeling her nipples harden through the thin fabric of her dress as she rose and fell on him.

He needed to touch her. He'd never needed anything so badly in his life.

Somehow, he got his wrists shifted so he could cup the back of her head and tangle his fingers in her short hair.

"Robert," she sighed softly as he angled her head toward his. "What…"

"Kiss me." He wasn't begging because Wyatts didn't beg, but it wasn't an order, either. "I need you to kiss me while I'm inside you."

He felt the shudder move through her body and then her lips were on his, their tongues touching and retreating and touching again, all while she rode him and he held her, and this was the moment he would never forget. No matter what happened in an hour or tomorrow or next month, no one would ever take this moment from him.

She moved faster and faster, chasing her climax and all he could do was grit it out and hold on until she'd found her release.

When she threw back her head, the lines of her neck taut, he did the only thing he could—he leaned forward and buried his face between her breasts. The diamond pendant hit him in the nose but he didn't care as he kissed her there, thrusting up into her as he let go.

He let go.

How could he ever let her go?

Fifteen

Jeannie could feel the goodbye in the air as Reginald opened the car door after what felt like an unnaturally long pause. Probably giving them time to set their clothing to rights.

Thoughtful man, that Reginald. She hoped Robert gave him a raise.

But he needn't have worried because after the most amazing orgasm of her entire life—which was saying something because the one last week had been pretty damn spectacular—Robert had gently lifted her off him and then buttoned up. In complete silence.

Yep. The goodbye was definitely in the air.

Robert helped her out of the limo and then, with an unbelievable, "Thank you, Reginald," he swept Jeannie right off her feet. Literally.

"Robert!" she shrieked as he tossed her into the air a little, adjusting his hold.

"Your shoes aren't made for sand," he said as if that was all the explanation necessary.

"Honestly," she laughed, but she linked her arms around his neck and let her head rest on his shoulder.

He hummed. He sounded happy. *Please*, she thought, *let him be happy*.

Without another word, he carried her down the beach. She didn't know where they were, but far north of Chicago proper, she guessed. She could see the orange glow of the city to the south but out over the lake, all she could see were…

"Stars," she breathed. Hundreds of them. Millions, maybe.

"Yes," he agreed in that Robert way as if he had personally decreed there would be stars and lo, the universe had made it happen.

He walked on, his pace slow as he ruined his shiny tuxedo shoes in the sand. "Where are we going?"

"Away from the light," he replied, as cryptic as ever.

The night sky stretched out vast and endless before her. The moon was nowhere to be seen, so the only way to differentiate between the water and the sky was the twinkling of light.

"It's beautiful," she sighed. So many stars—if only she had that many wishes.

But she'd already gotten what she'd asked for, hadn't she? More than that. She had a nanny and a maid and a reasonably good grip on how to care for Melissa. She had a lawyer who was working on a settlement from the hospital to make sure Melissa would always be cared for.

And she'd had the most amazing, complicated, messy, perfect man in Chicago at her mercy.

No, she wouldn't wish on another star. If there was one thing she'd learned over the years, it was not to push her luck.

After long, quiet minutes, Robert set her down on her feet. She slid her hand into his and leaned against his shoulder. A breeze flowed off the lake and despite the warm summer temperature, she shivered. It was always cooler by the lake.

"Here," he said gruffly, removing his jacket and draping it over her shoulders.

"Thank you." The superfine wool smelled like him, dark and spicy with just a hint of champagne and orange on top. The smell of them together. He wrapped his arm around her shoulders, holding her tight.

Her knees began to shake. "Robert?" She wanted to ask before she lost her nerve.

"Hmm?"

"Have you ever been in love?"

"No." He didn't even hesitate. The word was out like a gunshot and it made her heart ache for him.

Then he leaned down and pressed his cheek against her hair. "At least...not yet."

Dammit. He was going to make this painful, wasn't he?

"What about you?" he asked when she failed to come up with anything to say.

Oh, how their situations had reversed. "A few times."

"What happened?"

She shrugged. "I was young and foolish. Sometimes…" She had to swallow to get around the rock that had suddenly appeared in her throat. "Sometimes you fall in love with the wrong person at the right time and you don't realize it until times change. And sometimes…"

She blinked against her stinging eyes and focused on the stars. Their light, hopeful and bright against the darkest of times, wavered. Must be the breeze.

"And sometimes," he finished for her, his voice thoughtful, "you fall in love with the right person at the wrong time."

She had to blink some more. Damned wind.

"I don't want this to be the wrong time," she said. *Demanded.* "This isn't the wrong time. And you're *not* the wrong person."

"No," he finally said.

But she knew him too well, didn't she? She heard the pain and confusion and loss and love in his voice, all blurred together in that one syllable. Two measly letters were all it took to break her heart, apparently.

"Robert, listen," she began, desperate to hold on to him. They'd only just gotten started! There was so much more between them. So much more than a perfect Manhattan and a fake lady. "I'll—"

"No." Another two measly letters. She was really beginning to hate that syllable. He looked down at her, cupping her cheek in his strong hand. "I won't ask it of you."

"Please," she whispered. "We can—"

He just shook his head and then he leaned down and kissed her.

He kissed her goodbye.

"Ask me," she murmured against his ear. "Please, Robert. Just ask."

He stared down at her, his forehead resting against hers. "I have to keep you safe, Jeannie. I won't let any harm come to you or Melissa."

"You won't. I know you won't."

When he didn't reply to that, she snapped. To hell with his rules. She dug her fingers into his hair and dragged her lips across his, biting and sucking and showing him how much more there could be between them, if only he'd trust her.

If only he'd trust himself.

He was breathing hard when he broke the kiss. He pulled her hands away from his head and then swept her back into his arms. The walk back was silent and awful and far, far too short because he'd made up his mind and who was she to try and change it? She was nobody.

She was just his bartender. A pretend lady, a willing accomplice, a sympathetic ear and a shoulder to lean on. Nothing more.

She would not cry. Wind be darned.

Eventually, they made it back to where Reginald and the limo were waiting. This time Robert opened her door for her and handed her inside. But instead of climbing in after her, he shut the door.

"Robert," she almost shouted, feeling frantic. Was he not even going to give her a proper goodbye?

Of course not, because talking was not Dr. Robert

Wyatt's strong suit. Instead, he heard the muffled sound of Reginald getting behind the wheel and, even more distant, Robert saying, "Take her home."

"Yes, sir."

The car started and she rolled down the window. "Robert!" she yelled. "I'll wait." The car started to move. "I'll be waiting!" she shouted out the window.

The car turned and the breeze blew so she couldn't be sure but she thought she heard him say, *"Sailboat."*

Damn him.

But then, what had she expected?

"You're back early. How was your evening?" Maja said from the recliner where Melissa was asleep on her chest. The whole place smelled like lemons and every surface shone like the top of the Chrysler Building.

That was because of Robert.

The right man at the wrong time.

"Fine," Jeannie said dully. Because, really, it was the wrong time. He was about to go to war with his father, and Jeannie had to figure out how to be a mother for the rest of her life and she couldn't expect Robert to foot the bill for polished woodwork and overnight nannies forever.

Maja's grandmotherly face wrinkled in concern. "Is everything all right, dear?"

"Fine," Jeannie repeated. She stared down at her sandals and the Valentino dress that had cost God only knew how much, at the heavy diamond pendant that had definitely cost too much.

Robert was the right man and she was hopelessly in love with him.

But Dr. Robert Wyatt, billionaire bachelor and noted surgeon—he was the wrong man. For someone like her. Because she could pretend to fit into his world, but they both knew she didn't belong there.

God, she hated goodbyes.

"Dear?"

Jeannie looked up with a start to see Maja standing in front of her. "I've decided to go back to work. In two weeks. I don't know how long you're going to be able to watch Melissa for me but—" she swallowed "—if you could at least help me line up alternative childcare before you go. Something I could afford."

Because she couldn't afford Maja or Rona or Reginald or any of them.

Maja looked tired in the dim light. "I'm paid for three months, which leaves us quite a bit of time to make plans." She sighed again, disappointment on her face. "I'm sorry things didn't work out with your handsome doctor."

But he'd never been hers, had he? They had been like…this outfit. Like Lady Daphne FitzRoy. An illusion.

"So am I," she said, the tears starting to fall. "So am I."

Sixteen

Robert called for a ride, which was a novel experience. By the time the driver picked him up, Robert had himself under control. He'd done the right thing. Jeannie might be upset now but he was confident that a woman as worldly and intelligent as she was would see how this was for the best by the light of day.

She still had his jacket, but his vest smelled faintly of oranges.

God, he was tired. Tired of dealing with Landon, worrying about his mother, tired of holding himself back, tired of being Robert Wyatt.

Just be with me, Jeannie had said. Of all the things she'd given him, that might've been her greatest gift.

But it didn't matter how tired he was—his night was just beginning.

Kelly texted just as the car hit Lake Shore Drive.

He's at your house.

Status?

Speech was a disaster.
Social media is asking if he was high.
Visibly upset.
Banging on your door.
Hasn't broken anything.

Don't interfere yet.

Yes, sir.

Robert focused on breathing. Slow. Steady. Orange-scented. Everything was going according to plan. Landon had discovered that his wife, son and a random woman who might or might not have been nobility had all disappeared from his grand kickoff campaign gala. As Robert had hoped, Landon had not taken the news well.

Robert was counting on the next part. He didn't have long to wait.

He just put a planter through your front door.
Alarm is blaring.

Wait until he gets in
then have him arrested.

* * *

Because that was the fail-safe of his plan. He could fund civil lawsuits and give federal investigators access to financial reports but Landon was a slippery bastard and money talked.

Breaking and entering, however, was harder to disprove. Especially when there were security tapes, off-duty officers as witnesses and a son who refused to drop charges.

The driver turned onto Robert's street. "Here is fine," Robert said, fishing a hundred out of his wallet. He didn't know what the tipping protocol was but rare was the person who'd turn down cash.

"Hey—anytime, man! You're going to get a great rating out of this!"

Robert had no idea what the man was talking about but he didn't care. As he got out of the car, he could hear his alarm screaming into the night and, underneath that, sirens in the distance.

"Get your hands off me! Do you know who I am?" Landon Wyatt's screech of rage cut through the noise.

"What's going on here?" Robert said, aiming for concerned innocence. "Father? What are you doing here?"

"Where is she?" Landon screamed, lurching at Robert.

"Easy, buddy," the officer said, hauling Landon back. Robert recognized Officer Hernandez; he'd covered the Hernandezes' outstanding balance for a recent procedure.

Landon's arms were handcuffed behind his back. The sight made Robert almost smile because it was something he could definitely get used to seeing. "Where is who?"

"You know damned well, you useless bastard. Where is *she*?"

Robert made a big show of looking up at his dark house. "No one's home. I just got here." Kelly sidled up the sidewalk and Robert spotted the reporters, cameras flashing and video recording. "My date got sick and I took her home. I don't think we'll be seeing each other anymore," he explained for the audience.

Landon snarled and lunged again. This time the other officer had to use so much force to hold him back that Landon wound up on his knees in the middle of the sidewalk.

"You'll pay for this," he said, his eyes bugging out. "By the time I get done with you, you all will wish you'd never been born!"

The officers made as if to haul him up but Robert waved them off. Instead, he crouched down in front of Landon, who was struggling to get to his feet. Robert put a hand on the older man's shoulder and forced him back down because that was what a Wyatt would do. Dominate. Control.

Robert demanded respect, but right now, from this man, he'd settle for fear.

The older man's eyes widened with surprise as his muscles tensed under Robert's hands. "What do you think you're doing?"

Robert leaned close. He didn't want anyone to hear this. "You'll never see her again."

"I'll find her," Landon barked with a truly maniacal laugh. No wonder everyone at the gallery had been asking if he was high. Robert's plan was working perfectly. "You can't keep her safe. You never could. She's mine! And after I find her, I'll find that duchess of yours, whoever she was. And I'll make her pay." He licked his lips and tried to surge to his feet again. "I can't wait. Will she scream your name in the end, do you think?"

Robert didn't allow any emotion to cross his face. But he tightened his grip on the old man's shoulder, feeling the muscles clench and grind under his hand and he made *damn* sure Landon stayed down on his knees.

"Do you have any idea how easy it would be to get you out onto a boat and drop you in the middle of the lake?" It was a struggle to keep his voice level, but given the way Landon went rigid with what Robert hoped was fear, he thought he'd done a good job. "But I'm not going to do that because you deserve so much more than a quick, easy death." He tightened his grip on the old man's shoulder and by God, he bowed under the pressure. "No matter how hard you look, you'll never find either of them."

Robert had lived his entire life in fear of this man but in the end, it wasn't that hard to take control. He was a Wyatt and that was what they did.

"Try me," Landon said but the menace had bled out of his voice and instead, he sounded like a man who was starting to realize he'd made a grave tactical error.

Because he had.

"You're going to be divorced, sued, arrested and tried and, if I have anything to say about it, found guilty on charges of sexual assault, embezzlement, campaign finance fraud, breaking and entering, and God only knows what else my people are uncovering as we speak." Robert forced himself to stare into Landon's eyes because Robert was in charge now. It was Landon's turn to cower because he'd come up against a force he couldn't dominate. "And we haven't even rolled Alexander yet. But we will."

"Sir?" Kelly cleared his throat. Robert was running out of time to say his piece. "Sorry to interrupt but I've just received word that Alexander Trudeau has been picked up on charges of money laundering."

It was hard to tell under the yellow light from the streetlamps, but Robert thought Landon had suddenly gone pale. "See?" he said with a smile. Because now he could smile in front of Landon, just to watch the old man squirm. "Not that hard to roll, after all."

"You son of a bitch," Landon said, starting to struggle again. "I'll get you for this."

"Oh, you'll try, but you'll be busy with the lawsuits and trials. And I do think this marks the end of your career in politics, doesn't it? Everything you ever had or wanted, gone." Robert snapped his fingers. "Just like that. And do you know why, *Dad*?"

Landon glared at him but Robert didn't feel the usual panic churning up his stomach.

He smiled again, this time for real. "Because this is what you raised me to do." He let go of the old man's shoulder and, as he broke that singular point of contact, a sense of finality washed over him. "I hope you're happy with what you created."

This wasn't over, not by a long shot. But they were done.

Freed of Robert's grip, Landon surged up. "I'll kill you!" he screamed, flecks of spittle flying off his lips. "I'll kill that bitch and that whore in front of you and then *I'll end you*!"

Robert got ready to throw a punch but then Officer Hernandez and his partner were there. One drew his gun but Robert said, "No need for that, Officer." Landon straightened and smiled in victory, but then Robert added, "If you have to subdue him, use the Taser."

Landon screamed in rage but Robert just smiled. God, it felt good to smile.

It felt good to *win*.

The cops led a struggling, furious Landon to the police car. As they closed the door on what had, just a few hours ago, been the most powerful man in Chicago, Robert straightened his cuffs and stood tall.

Landon Wyatt's era was over and there would be no redemption tour.

There was a lot of talking after that—Robert gave a statement to the cops and confirmed that, yes, he would like to press charges and yes, his father had a temper but no, he'd never made death threats before and yes, perhaps a restraining order would be a good thing.

He obtained security footage and talked with lawyers and judges and began circulating rumors that Cybil Wyatt had been on the verge of leaving Landon but had been convinced to stay for the campaign but after this...

And even when dawn broke over Lake Michigan and the last star blinked out of sight, Robert didn't stop because there was so much to do. He had to contact members of the board of Wyatt Medical and make sure that his mother had landed safely in LA and taken off again and he had to do rounds at the hospital.

He couldn't stop.

Because if he did, he'd think of Jeannie. And if he thought of her, he might not be able to stay away and it wasn't safe yet. Not yet, damn it all.

Sailboat.

Seventeen

"He's not going to come back just because you're back, is he?" Miranda asked as Jeannie grabbed the crate of clean wineglasses. "If he is, I'm not dealing with him."

"He won't," Jeannie replied. "Can you move? This is heavy." Honestly, could Miranda just give her a little space?

It'd be nice if everyone at Trenton's could give her a little space on her first night back. Sure, there'd been a cake and a few baby presents but did anyone actually ask about Melissa? Nope. It was all Robert, all the time. Had he contacted her after he'd left the bar? Did she know anything about the all-out war being waged in the press and in the courts between the elder Wyatt and his son? Or, worst of all, what did she make of that mysterious "duchess" who'd appeared on Robert's arm at the ill-fated campaign kickoff but had disappeared right before everything had gone to hell and didn't she look familiar?

Maybe Robert had left a bigger mark on her than she'd realized because she had apparently perfected his icy glare. At least she could blame her mood on the baby. Poor Melissa, taking the fall.

But it was fine. Things were always rough after a breakup and this was kind of one.

She was just about to back through the swinging door that separated the kitchen from the bar when it burst open, knocking into her. She had to juggle the crate of glasses but she managed not to drop the danged thing. "What the—"

"He's here!" Julian said in a panic, moving so fast he ran into her again.

Jeannie managed to get the crate of glass onto a countertop because suddenly, her hands had started to shake.

Miranda asked, "Who?" in a terrified whisper, the blood draining from her face.

"Him! Wyatt!"

"Breathe," Jeannie said. What was he doing here? He'd made it clear they were done and he was protecting her or something by staying away and she wasn't to wait for him. Done, done, *done*.

Or not.

"Should we call the police?" Julian asked, hands clutched in front of his chest.

Jeannie rolled her eyes. "For the love of everything holy, no. I'll handle this."

She took a second to compose herself. Which wasn't easy because not only did she have to deal with Miranda and Julian quaking in fear but also the whole kitchen staff had gone quiet, and even the normal sounds of the restaurant and bar were almost nonexistent.

She pushed through the swinging door to find herself squarely in the sights of Dr. Robert Wyatt, in his normal spot. When he saw her, his eyes narrowed and—big surprise—he adjusted his cuffs.

He'd come for her. And to think, there hadn't been a single star in the sky last night. Not even an airplane she could pretend was a star. But she'd hoped against hope that one day Robert might slide into his seat and order his Manhattan and give her that almost invisible smile and tell her everything was perfect again.

That they could be perfect together, because the time was right.

But Jeannie saw more than that. She saw how he was moving as if his leg was bouncing against the rung of the bar stool. And how, when he wasn't adjusting his cuffs, he was tapping his fingers on the bar.

How about that. Not only had Robert put in a surprise appearance, but the man was nervous about it, too. None of that mattered, though, because he'd come for *her*.

Unless something else had gone wrong? That thought led to a sickening drop in her stomach because what if he wasn't here for her? What if he…just needed a sympathetic ear and a drink?

"Well?" asked Julian from behind the door. "Cops?"

"*No*, for Pete's sake. Just leave us—him—alone." She let the door swing back and heard a muffled yelp. That was what Julian got for peeking. She made her way down the bar. Robert's intense gaze never once left hers.

"Robert." She winced. "Dr. Wyatt. The usual?"

"Jeannie."

For as long as she'd known this man—years now—every word he spoke could either make her fall further in love with him or break her heart.

Dear God, please don't let the sound of her name on his lips be another heartbreak. She couldn't take much more.

Then he smiled. That small movement of his lips curving up just at the corners, where no one else would think to look for it. But she saw it. She saw him. Maybe she always had.

Her hands hadn't stopped trembling but she ignored them as she filled a glass with his Manhattan and added the twist. She had to use both hands to steady it as she placed the drink on the bar.

"Here for your drink?" she managed to get out, proud of the way her voice stayed level. Not a verbal tremble in sight.

"No." He didn't even look at his drink. "I'm here for you."

Her breath caught in her throat. "Me?" she squeaked. Dammit.

"Us," he corrected. Before she could process those two little letters—that one measly syllable—he dropped his gaze to a tablet she hadn't noticed on the bar next to him. "Here's the thing."

"Oh?" Her heart began to pound wildly out of control but she didn't say anything else. He'd get to it in his own sweet time.

He tapped the screen and called up a picture of a... mansion?

"Robert?" If he'd bought her a huge house out of guilt or something, she was going to have to draw the line. She and Melissa did *not* need a mansion.

"I bought it through a shell company, so there aren't any names on the paperwork, just to be sure," he began, tapping more to bring up additional pictures of a gorgeous house with amazing decorating—clean lines, warm colors and not a single shred of tacky wallpaper. "It overlooks the lake and there's a path down to a small private beach." More pictures whizzed by—was that an indoor pool? "It's got a clear view of the night sky—the light pollution doesn't drown out the stars." A victorious smile spread across his face. "I made sure of that."

"Robert," she said, barely able to get the words out. "What is this?"

He straightened in his chair before straightening his cuffs. "My mother sends her thanks for your help. I put my home in her name so that, when she's able to come back, she can enjoy the wallpapered ceilings to the fullest extent."

Oh, God. "Did you...give up your house?"

He nodded once, a quick and efficient movement. But she could tell that his leg was still jiggling and, when he started to straighten his cuffs for the third time in as many minutes, she reached over the bar and took his hands in hers. Behind her, someone gasped. Probably Miranda.

"Robert," she said again, softly. "Tell me what's happened."

A look of need flashed over his face and was gone, replaced by imperial iciness. "I don't want you to wait for me," he said in a gruff voice.

None of this made sense. There was something going on here, something that would tie the houses and his jumping leg and his very straight cuffs together and she was missing it.

"I will," she told him. "As long as it takes, I will."

He shook his head firmly and said, "No, I mean… wait." He took a deep breath and then, miracle of miracles, laced his fingers with hers. "I was supposed to stay away from you because Landon still has a lot of power and if he knew who you were, you'd be in danger and you…" Jeannie's heart kicked into overdrive. "You're very important to me."

"Oh?" He wasn't the only one who could wield single syllables in a conversation, dammit.

He stared down at their hands. "I've never been in love so I don't know for certain that this is that. But I need you. I need to see you every day so I can talk to you and you can make me laugh and touch me and make me feel…right. I don't feel right without you anymore and I tried. *I tried*," he repeated, sounding mad about that.

No, she couldn't imagine that Dr. Robert Wyatt tried and failed at too many things. Her eyes began to burn and this time there was no lake breeze to blame it on.

"But then I realized that by staying away from you

to keep you safe, I was still letting him win because he still dictated what I did and how I did it and you know what?"

"What?" she said breathlessly. Why was there a stupid bar between them? Why wasn't he in her arms for this—this—this declaration of love? Because that was what it was.

He loved her.

Oh, thank God.

"To hell with him. He can't win," Robert said fiercely and she knew this was a man who would lay down his life to protect her. "I won't allow it. If I want to be with you, I'm going to be with you because you are the right person for me, Jeannie Kaufman, and I will *make* it the right time."

Of course he would. He was a Wyatt. "So you bought a mansion?"

"For you. You and me and Melissa and…us." He looked up at her and she saw love and worry and hope in his eyes. Finally, hope. "For our family, whether it grows or not."

She almost fell over. *"Robert."*

"Marry me," he said and damn if it didn't sound like an order. But before she could call him on it, he quickly added, "Wait. No, let me do that again." He lifted her hands to his lips and kissed her knuckles like he really was a duke of the realm and she was the tavern wench who'd won his heart. "You've shown me what love is, Jeannie. And I want to spend the rest of my life sharing it with you. We can get married or not. I'm not your boss and you're not my employee or even my bartender.

You're the woman I need and I hope I can be the man you want."

"Oh, Robert," she said, tears flowing.

"You're crying," he said, alarmed.

"I love you, too, you complicated, messy, wonderful man." But then the past few weeks flashed before her eyes—his reaction after the first time they'd made love, the way his father had treated him and his mother, the fact that the legal mess was going to be the headline for weeks and months to come. "And I do want to marry you—on one condition."

"Name it," he said with a devastatingly gorgeous smile. "Anything. I can buy a different house or…"

"I've never wanted you for your money." Something deepened in his eyes. An answering shiver of desire raced down her back. "But I want you to see a counselor to help you work through your…*issues* because marriage isn't a magical cure-all. You have to work on some things yourself."

He didn't even hesitate, bless the man. "Yes. Of course. I'll work on talking and hugging and…" His cheeks darkened and she had to wonder—was he *blushing*? "What else?"

She began to laugh and cry at the same time and that was when Robert let go of her hands and then vaulted over the bar. *Vaulted!* Then he had her crushed to his chest, his mouth on hers and those were definitely gasps because not only was he kissing her, he was also doing so in public. "Anything else, Jeannie?" he said against her lips. "*Anything* for you. If you want to work a bar, I'll buy you one. I'll buy you this one, if you want."

Behind them, she heard a squeak of alarm and rolled her eyes.

"We can make plans later but—will you adopt Melissa?"

He scoffed at that. "Of course."

"Will you just *be* with me, Robert? Through good times and the not-great times?"

His hands flattened against her back. She couldn't get close enough. "There is nowhere else I'd ever want to be if it's not by your side."

"Then the answer is yes because you're the right man, Robert."

He grinned wolfishly and dear Lord, he was just the most handsome man in the world and he was choosing her. "You're the right woman for me and when it's right, there is no wrong time. Not if I have anything to say about it. After all, I'm a Wyatt." He leaned down but instead of kissing her, he whispered in her ear, "And soon you'll be one, too."

And just like that, she fell more in love with him.

"Perfect," she told him.

Because it was.

Epilogue

"Package for you, Cybil," Bridget said as the physical therapist, Anne, moved Cybil into the last stretch. "It's on your chair. I'll get your water."

"Thank you." Cybil smiled, despite the burning exhaustion that went with a tough PT appointment.

She liked being *just* Cybil. She liked being Bridget's equal. She liked the quiet villa in Kauri Cliffs, at the far north end of New Zealand. She even liked being disconnected from the rest of the world. By and large, she didn't want to know what was happening back home. She had no interest in keeping up-to-date on what her soon-to-be ex-husband was doing. She wasn't available for comment on news stories.

She could focus on herself. It was selfish and something she was still getting used to—but with the help of a psychologist and a physical therapist, she was re-discovering who she'd been before Landon Wyatt and, more important, who she wanted to be after him.

But most of all, she was getting used to talking with her son again. Not every day, because he was still a busy man, but at least every other day. At one in the afternoon her time, Bobby would call at what was eight his time. They talked of her progress and his work. They'd avoided discussions of Landon, but after a while, Bobby had begun to mention Jeannie more and more.

She wished she could've been there for the wedding, but someone named Darna had streamed the whole civil ceremony, all fourteen minutes of it, for Cybil to see.

For the first time in decades, she could breathe again.

"There," Anne said, helping Cybil to stand. She wobbled a little—today had been tough. "Make sure to drink plenty of fluids, okay? I'll see you in two days."

Cybil patted the young woman's shoulder and gratefully sank into her chair, the package in her hands.

She'd received mail from Bobby before, legal notices of her divorce proceedings, usually—her son had hired an absolute shark of a lawyer. But this felt different.

Her hands began to shake and it wasn't just from the physical exertion.

Ah, her divorce papers. It was done. She was no longer legally bound to Landon Wyatt and it appeared half of his earnings from throughout their awful marriage were now hers. She was an independently wealthy woman. No longer would she have to beg for money or wear what Landon bought for her. She could do as she saw fit.

The next thing in the envelope was the front page of the *Chicago Tribune*, with a handwritten note that said, "Any deposition can be handled safely and your income will be protected—R." Landon Wyatt was being charged for criminal sexual assault—several maids and employees had come forward to press charges. Represented, she knew, by a lawyer Bobby had chosen. Oh, but this was new—Wyatt Medical had voted him out as CEO and Landon was also being investigated by the SEC for insider trading and campaign fraud? Apparently, Alexander, Landon's assistant, had turned on him. All his friends had abandoned him and his political aspirations were dead in the water. His disgrace was complete and if Bobby had anything to say about it, Landon would spend a good chunk of the rest of his life in jail.

How fitting. She wanted to savor this moment, this permanent freedom.

But then a cream envelope fluttered out of the package and Cybil's breath caught in her throat. She knew she was crying as she read the engraved print, but she simply didn't care.

"Dr. Robert Wyatt and Jeannie Kaufman are pleased to announce their marriage in a private ceremony on October 12. They are also proud to welcome Melissa Nicole Wyatt to the family."

The next thing was a slim hardbound book. Oh, he'd sent her a wedding album! When she opened the cover, a handwritten note slid out. "I took a chance on happiness," the note read in Bobby's scrawled handwriting. "That's because of you."

"Oh, Bobby," she sighed. He'd always been such

a thoughtful boy. Thank God Landon had never succeeded in destroying that.

She flipped through the album, greedily taking in the signs of happiness.

The first picture showed Bobby and Jeannie standing side by side. Bobby was smiling down at his bride. Smiling! Dear God, it did her heart good to see her son looking at peace—the same peace she was beginning to feel.

Cybil barely recognized Jeannie as the same woman who had gotten her away from Landon with a well-placed glass of champagne. In real life, Jeannie smiled wider, had kinder eyes and looked downright sweet in her tea-length lace gown in a soft shade of rose pink that was gorgeous on her.

Cybil fondly traced a finger over the picture. Bobby would need someone bold and daring, someone strong enough to withstand his personality—and someone who would understand why he was the way he was but would never pity him. If that was his bartender, then that was the perfect woman for him.

The second picture showed Bobby and his new wife with a small infant. Only a few months old, the little girl was wrapped in a soft blanket, grinning a toothless grin up at Bobby from Jeannie's arms. Bobby's hand cupped the baby's cheek with such tenderness that Cybil's eyes watered again.

A note was paper-clipped to the page. "We'll bring her out soon—R."

"Everything all right?" Bridget said, concern in her voice as she sat the tea tray down. "You're crying!"

"I'm a grandmother," Cybil got out as she showed Bridget the album. "Look at my family!"

"Oh, wow," Bridget said, sounding wistful. "They look so happy!"

Happy. It was a long-cherished dream, one that had gotten Cybil through so many dark times. "You know," Cybil said, dabbing at her tears, "I do believe they are."

* * * * *

Get 4 FREE REWARDS!

We'll send you 2 FREE Books plus 2 FREE Mystery Gifts.

Harlequin® Desire books feature heroes who have it all: wealth, status, incredible good looks... everything but the right woman.

FREE Value Over **$20**

*I have a new boss—and he's hot but irresponsible, a
youngest son. If he thinks he can march into this office
and act like he owns the place, he needs to think again…
If only I didn't want him as much as I hate him…*

Read on for a sneak peek of
Boss
by New York Times *bestselling author Katy Evans!*

My motto as a woman has always been simple: own
every room you enter. This morning, when I walk into
the offices of Cupid's Arrow, coffee in one hand and
portfolio in the other, the click of my scarlet heels on
the linoleum floor is sure to turn more than a few sleepy
heads. My employees look up from their desks with
nervous smiles. They know that on days like this I'm
raring to go.

Though it sounds bigheaded, I know my ideas are
always the best. There's a reason Cupid's Arrow swept
me up at age twenty. There's a reason I'm the head of
the department. I carry the design team entirely on my
own back, and I deserve recognition for it.

The office doors swing open to reveal Alastair
Walker—the CEO, and the one person I answer to
around here.

"How's the morning slug going, my dear Alexandra?" he asks in that British accent he hasn't quite been able to shake off, even after living in Chicago for a decade. He's adjusting his sharp suit as he saunters into the room. For his age, he's a particularly handsome man, his gray hair and the soft creases of his face doing little to steal the limelight from his tanned skin and toned body.

At the sight of him, my coworkers quickly ease back.

"The slug is moving sluggishly, you might say," I admit, smiling in greeting.

When Alastair walks in, everyone in the room stands up straighter. I'm glad my team knows how to behave themselves when the boss of the boss is around. But my own smile falters when I notice the tall, dark-haired man falling into step beside Alastair.

A young man.

A very hot man.

He's in a crisp charcoal suit, haphazardly knotted red tie and gorgeous designer shoes, with recklessly disheveled hair and scruff along his jaw.

Our gazes meet. My mouth dries up.

And it's like the whole room shifts on its axis.

I head to my private office in the back and exhale, wondering why that sexy, coddled playboy is pushing buttons I was never really aware of before. Until now.

Don't miss what happens when Kit becomes the boss!
Boss
by Katy Evans.

Available March 2019 wherever
Harlequin® Desire books and ebooks are sold.

www.Harlequin.com

Want to give in to temptation with
steamy tales of irresistible desire?

Check out **Harlequin® Presents®,**
Harlequin® Desire and
Harlequin® Kimani™ Romance books!

New books available every month!

CONNECT WITH US AT:

Facebook.com/groups/HarlequinConnection

 Facebook.com/HarlequinBooks

 Twitter.com/HarlequinBooks

 Instagram.com/HarlequinBooks

 Pinterest.com/HarlequinBooks

ReaderService.com

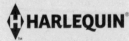 **HARLEQUIN®**

ROMANCE WHEN
YOU NEED IT

PGENRE2018